But Tell It Slant

But Tell It Slant

Fierce Fictions

Matt Pavelich

Bar R Books

But Tell It Slant

By Matt Pavelich

Published by Bar R Books,
Helena, Montana
© 2025 by Matt Pavelich

Cover: *Artist on Tightrope,* by James Gilbert Todd, Jr. © 1973

Design: Wyatt Design, Helena, Montana

10 9 8 7 6 5 4 3 2 1

Bar R Books celebrate the art and literature of Montana and the West. The press's name derives from the brand owned by Louis Kaufman and Louis Stadler, Helena, Montana, butchers who became prominent cattlemen during the open-range days of the Montana frontier. Louis Kaufman was the rancher to whom Charlie Russell sent his famed watercolor, *Waiting for a Chinook,* during the disastrous winter of 1886–87.

Helena, MT & San Francisco

Also by Matt Pavelich

Beasts of the Forest Beasts of the Field

Our Savage

The Other Shoe

Himself Adrift

Survivors Said

The Harrows

The story *What I Owe* first appeared in *The Montana Quarterly*

For

Nick & Riley

It doesn't take long for Mr. Pavelich to launch a world. Two or three sentences and you are there in the milieu he has in mind. For this collection he refers to his writing as "fierce fictions." That would seem to imply violence or hostility, which is fairly rare in his stories. There is much more humor and a great deal of wit. The story *Viola, a Long Earner* begins: "She had already lived two full generations past her regular expiration date before I was born, but because her DNA tested very high for memory and probable longevity my great grandmother had been continued as a profit generator." Pavelich sets things up quickly, but you never know where they'll go. You just read on with a smile on your face. Although at the conclusion of the first story in the book, *Mouth Organs*, you will probably think—that was fierce.

Then it's just a hop, skip, jump, and Quantum leap from Montana and environs to Samoa where Pavelich transports us in his novella *But Tell it Slant* with the story of Mike Vinich who has accepted a job as a Public Defender in the South Pacific. The pay is not great, and Vinich doesn't speak the local language, which presents some difficulties, but he's presented with translators and—there it is! The endlessly beautiful Pacific Ocean. There is also stifling heat and pummeling rain. Then he is assigned a case that will change everything.

A man has been killed in the jungle. A young prosecutor (also a stateside hire) has a suspect whom he intends to charge with murder in the 1st degree. It looks quite grim for the man Vinich has been assigned to defend. But what is the truth? As Emily Dickinson has it, "The Truth must dazzle gradually," to avoid blinding us.

Pavelich's prose accomplishes this—dazzlingly.

Bill Borneman, book seller

Matt Pavelich's stories wait quietly for a reader to discover them, and once they do—drawn in no doubt through a mesmerizing opening line or through seeing newly captured even the most mundane and familiar elements in our lives—they will keep turning pages, unaware of anything else around them until the reverie is broken by impending darkness, and they have to stand up to turn on a lamp so as to keep reading. From the moment he first appeared on the literary horizon with his Montana Book Award—winning story collection, *Beasts of the Forest, Beasts of the Field* in 1989, Pavelich has distinguished himself as a master of the form, penning story after story (and a few novels along the way) to remind discriminating readers what honest, organic wordsmithing looks like. Absent any of the lingering electronic glow of the writing factories, Pavelich's stories gleam like embers in a woodstove; the odors of larchsmoke and oranges cling to them the way that true insight comes from hiking alone over the continental divide, or sewing a quilt, or chopping cordwood. If you want to remember what well crafted writing used to mean, get a copy of *But Tell It Slant*. Actually, get two copies and pass one along to any reader with taste; you'll have a friend for life.

Aaron Parrett
Author, *Montana Then and Now*

With vivid prose and a compassionate heart, Matt Pavelich's stories in *But Tell it Slant* help us experience the worlds of a wide cast of characters ranging from jazz musicians returning to a class reunion to an attorney defending a trans murderer in American Samoa. Whether depicting small town cafes or on claustrophobic road trips, Pavelich has a gift for exploring the intimacies of relationships between those who are powerful and powerless and everyone else in between.

Caroline Patterson
Author, *The Stone Sister*

CONTENTS

Mouth Organs

Behind the music store, a fairly tolerant location, he had built a cardboard pup tent over his cardboard pallet so that he might sleep past sunrise, and he was doing that when a truck backed up to the loading dock and nearly ran over him. Two doors slammed; he heard people rushing around, someone worrying, "We'll never make it." Freestyle heard the back of the delivery truck being opened, more rushing around, amateur cursing, then the back of the truck banged down, the doors of its cab slammed again, a motor gunned, and a moment later something heavy hit the concrete, a thick collision of two flat surfaces.

Reveille. Freestyle had slept in for once, so it was already too late in the day to do a good reconnaissance of the area. He lay under cover for a while, gathering his wits, rubbing his hip where this summer's crop of shrapnel was working its way out of him; he lay under cover waiting for that truck to be well gone before he went to see what had fallen from it. His door and roof the same, he lifted his house off him to reveal an overcast sky—this city had only its weather to recommend it, and even that was going sour—and he smelled a new, tarry, asphalt odor on himself; he would have to make the long walk to the river today.

The dimensions of the cardboard box suggested it might contain a bulky, old-time television—but no. That couldn't be. That wouldn't be. How quickly Freestyle had lost touch with the economy, he was already several generations of consumer goods behind the times. He surveilled the immediate area, saw he was alone in it and likely to remain alone, so he skittered to where the box had fallen just under the loading dock, tested its weight, and when it wasn't too heavy, he picked it up, made a quick scan of his perimeter, and effected his egress. He knew the key to successful appropriations was to be casual about it, to act like whatever you were stealing belonged to you, but Freestyle also knew he lacked the look of ownership, that so much of anything would look funny in his arms; it was impossible for Freestyle to ever really run but especially so while lugging this thing—he was blind behind it—he proceeded in a herky-jerk quick march, down an alley, across a quiet street, down another alley, and he arrived winded at his command center, the shopping cart he had stashed behind a metal grease pit that served two restaurants, one of which would be serving chicken soup today. Already the cruel, savory odors.

He arranged the box on his shopping cart so that it would ride and wheeled it away toward the park, his head on a swivel. He hadn't yet looked in the box, wanting some privacy for that ceremony, wanting to consider everything such a box might contain before he could be disappointed. He should be grateful if all he got from his windfall was so much fresh, high- quality cardboard, but the whole business of an unopened box recalled for him ancient Christmas mornings, the wonderfully pure greed of childhood.

There was a ravine at the park, small and narrow but thickly overgrown with the local foliage, dry, rusty, and rattly in early summer. The place was sometimes infested with hostiles, so Freestyle crept down to patrol the ravine, which he approached in part in a low crawl. See without being seen. No one to see here this morning. Someone's soggy clothes lying around, a half dozen emptied cans of Old Dubuque. What people left of themselves was so ugly. This was why it was important to police your area. Freestyle imagined this as a pristine little grove, how nice it might have been before civilization. He returned for the shopping cart, and because there was no track for it down into the ravine, he had to carry the box and the shopping cart separately down into the bottom.

P.T. Feels *good.*

Freestyle breathed very hard, taking in draughts of his morning's exertions, the bitter salts of himself. Pain, he had once been told, is only weakness leaving the body; he had reason once again to question this proposition. In a recent season there had been a flash flood here, and much more recently hostiles had occupied the space, crazy and unpredictable. For now, though, it was all his, safe, quiet, and cool, and he sat on a plastic bucket, the kind he had seen street drummers use for their tom-tom.

He addressed the box. He kept a pocketknife in the hip pocket of his good hip, the better to dispose of it quickly if it looked like he was about to be rousted for vagrancy. The knife was only just keen enough to get a box open.

The box contained smaller boxes stacked inside, these were about as wide and long as a shoebox but not so deep. Each of the smaller boxes bore the word Hahn in a blue, medieval script. Freestyle opened one of these and found that each of the lesser boxes contained about twenty still smaller boxes and each of these also bore the trademark. Not until he opened one of the smallest boxes did Freestyle finally understand that Hahn made harmonicas. He could not begin to guess how many of them there must be in the big box, but it would have to be enough to stock music stores in several states. Hahn, since 1859. Harmonicas. His better days sometimes saw Freestyle thinking of himself romantically as a hobo, and here was proper hobo equipment. A harmonica was the just the machine he needed to attack those lonely hours. Why hadn't he thought of it before? No harmonica. Now he had enough to supply the Western United States, or all the generations to follow in his line if he'd ever been a father.

Freestyle assessed the morning's intelligence. If he left these here in the ravine they would be stolen, or worse, somehow profaned by hostiles, and he wasn't certain of being able to protect them even if he stayed here with them—the hostiles often traveled in packs. As a boy he had heard sermons aimed at convincing him that earthly possessions were only a burden in the life of the spirit; Freestyle had finally taken that lesson to heart in the streets, in the necessity of having to carry everything he owned. One of the harmonicas joined his knife in his hip pocket. He closed the big box back up, then carried his shopping cart out of the ravine, then the box, and he wheeled it all away looking for a place of proper conceal-ment. At this hour the park was empty of both hostiles and friendlies and was therefore serene, and usually Freestyle would have lingered to take advantage, but there was no place in the park to stash the box. Freestyle preferred to travel without the shopping cart unless he was effecting a major movement of materiel—that right rear wheel always wanting to wobble away. But the box. Freestyle had his mission and would have to develop an operational plan on the march, so out onto the street again, the morning clouds burnt away above him, out onto streets now flowing with morning drivers, people glancing askance at him on their way to work, and maybe the sight of him would be the one thing that could make them happy about going to work.

Diggety-diggety-diggety. The cart was hypnotic, then clumsy at every curb. Freestyle didn't know precisely what he was looking for, and he usually wouldn't use this cart to make a cross-town, mid-day kind of trip; his route took him through the back lot of a supermarket that was usually good for stale bread and wilted lettuce, but he felt he shouldn't forage dumpsters or do anything about provisions before he had found a secure keep for the box. Freestyle was still enjoying that morning's sun, but a brutal sun was coming, and he wanted to solve his problems before noon.

All he needed was a few cubic feet of this town that he, and only he, could call his own where he could hide the box—which shouldn't be a lot to ask. It was hard not to be impatient when his only desire was to travel light. The cart, clinkety-klink, and the box—what next? A dinette set? Two car garage, plastic crap piled to the rafters? Calm down, Freestyle. The box was his destiny, and he must accept it. He wheeled it toward a more industrial neighborhood where he recalled rusting equipment and chain link fence, vigorous stands of weed.

He came to two vast lots, one containing spools of cable, the other scrap metal, and somehow between these there remained a narrow sliver of a lot with what would have been someone's starter home eighty years ago, its porch sagging away from its face, its windows broken out. Freestyle knew the house's condition didn't necessarily mean it was empty. He pulled his cart backward to negotiate the broken and heaved sidewalk, and he regretted the noise he made approaching the place. He stopped. He listened. Patience. He waited and listened until he was satisfied that he was alone on the premises, then pulled his cart back behind the little house, away from the street, and there he was struck once again by the day's surprising bounty; settled right up against the back wall of the house was the hulk of a Rocket 88, its trunk sprung—what a magnificent vault for his harmonicas. To stash the box was the work of a moment, and he was glad to be rid of it. He stashed the cart separately in another lot, and he was glad to be rid of that.

After so much activity, Freestyle knew he should find some rations now, if only to refuel, but he smelled so wrong that he would need to get desperately hungry before he was hungry at all, and he decided to go straight to the river. When he needed to move through town, he preferred to do it in the manner of a raccoon or any other covert operator, at night. He knew the old trick for keeping his night vision sharp—avoid the light. By day, along any traveled street, he was a little spectacle, disturbing the civilians with their dear-God-there-but-for-the-grace-of-God looks, and worse, scaring them if they happened to catch the right side of his face with its eye patch and Phantom of the Opera rebuild. His molded hand, at least, usually went unnoticed. Freestyle, always the reserved sort, found it impossible to make a good first impression, didn't like to leave any impression at all, no but slide through the night. It was only reasonable. He had always been quite reserved.

But today he needed the river so much that he was going to violate protocol and make the trek by day. Though he was near the river's bank almost anywhere in town, he had to make a long hike of it to reach that place downstream where concealment and flowing water were both available. Freestyle got a tee shirt from his rucksack and made headcover with it, and this made a more piratical look than he wanted, but, really, what difference did it make? He traveled by absolute instinct along less-traveled streets, making a march of some miles in his route, and with every step he was more ready to be clean again, clean for once, clean for a while. He would wash himself and all he owned in the river. Washed in the river? Hymn? Anyway, he had his tooth set for cleanliness, cleanliness for its own sake and to celebrate his good fortune.

Freestyle regretted that the Hahn harmonica box, white as it was, might not stay white in his pocket for long. The harmonica itself was a gleaming wonder no bigger than a candy bar, and it should, in the right hands, the right mouth, make music. Music. Sometimes the big absences really struck him; such music as Freestyle heard anymore was nearly always fragmentary, vague or thumping things that drifted out of people's windows, or the frantic stylings of street people playing way out of tune. At some point his heart had got set hard against marches. But music. He loved it. Didn't he? Hadn't he?

Hahn stamped on a face plate with filigree and numbered portals, holes one through ten, left to right. There was a system about it. Freestyle blew into the middle of the instrument and made a young child's wilting whine. Discouraging, but then he thought that surely the Hahn company hadn't been making these more than a hundred years to no better purpose than this. There was a system about it, and he would have to discover that, patiently learn to use it, and then he would have music again. His own music. There was more to it, he knew, than the system. Once, when there had been music all around him, music that he might sit and listen to, and enjoy—back then he couldn't be bothered to pay attention, and now it seemed such music was one of the big absences, one of those aches that came from time to time in living rough.

Freestyle went into a convenience store on the outskirts of town that advertised the presence of a money machine; he took twenty dollars from the machine, accepting as always the three-dollar service charge, and he selected two bars of Spring Zing soap, a liter of bottled water, and a small bag of granola that would soon prove moldy. When the young woman clerking that morning scanned these items, he lay the twenty on the counter and said, "Keep the change." Freestyle spoke so infrequently that his vocal cords seemed at times to have rusted.

"But, sir—that would be way more than. . ."

"Thank you, now," said Freestyle. The young woman had never winced or curled her nose or lip at him, and he wanted her to have a nice tip, and he preferred not to carry more cash than the ten he kept stashed reeking in his shoe for emergencies. She was the only person he had ever seen in red eyeliner—it was very red and suggested a difficult life, as if she wanted to be somewhat menacing behind the counter but couldn't pull it off even in such vivid makeup. The door dinged again as Freestyle left the store, and by way of parting he said, "*Hava Nagila.*" He did not know what this meant, or where it had come from. Some of his mental faculties, the ones to do with human discourse, had also rusted with disuse.

The clerk's hair was yet another shade of red, another red never found in so-called nature, and shiny red beads were aligned along the incurve of one of her ears. Freestyle saw her smile at him as he was leaving, but when he'd left, he saw through the plate glass that the young woman's smile was the thing of a moment and that she was deploying some kind of chemical agent in her area, using the hell out of a large, lavender spray can.

To the river, then.

As a boy, as a civilian, he tended to know the names of things he bought or wanted to buy, and that was about all; the things that mattered to him now had a different kind of nomenclature, not brand names. Willow, cottonwood, sandbar, catfish, carp. There was a place where the river formed a backwash, a little pool where he could bathe unseen, and Freestyle remembered the moment he'd discovered it. It might be the reason he had remained in this town. Bird's nests high in the cottonwoods. He'd seen a crane here, and any fool knows the name of a crane. This was what people were thinking, Freestyle thought, when they used the term 'nature' so favorably. He stripped and waded in, and the pool was a pocket of warmly circulating water, and Freestyle, nearly weightless, let it caress him, smooth stones underfoot.

Again and again, he went underwater and sat completely submerged, a repeated and practical baptism, a good rinsing. Freestyle took one of the bars of Spring Zing and one of his tee shirts from his ruck sack and used these to lather and scrub. He rinsed again. Lather and scrub. The soap reminded him of locker rooms, those improbable smells men put on themselves between exertions. The soap made him itch from head to foot. So, into the pool again, under the pool again, and rinsing and rinsing, and it did occur to Freestyle that he had only to step out into the flow of the river, out from behind this curved sand bar, and he might be rinsed away altogether. This seemed better as a sacred image than as a plan.

Freestyle rinsed and rinsed himself in the pool, he rinsed everything he owned susceptible to being cleaned by water, then he arrayed these items and himself in the rocks to dry. The sun was hot, pleasantly so. Freestyle lay on a flat rock in his bum's stringy and starkly two-tone body, drying, and he no longer smelled of soap or of pavement, and his thoughts turned forcefully now to food, and it was good to be hungry but not to be hungry for very long, and Freestyle smiled at himself, thinking he was about to wade into his pool again when into that pool came a man in a bucket hat, a vest, and a drift boat. The man, once out of the river's current, shipped his oars and regarded Freestyle on his rock. "Sorry," he said, "didn't mean to intrude."

The man and his drift boat turned away from him but remained floating in the pool. Freestyle pulled on his pants. He thought he should announce this, but didn't know what to say. The man had a tackle box on the deck between his feet; eventually he glanced back over his shoulder, and, seeing Freestyle decent again he dipped an oar and turned the drift boat. "Sorry," he said again.

Freestyle made a gesture with his hands, opening them as if they were the pages of the book of inevitability.

"You mind if I do some casting in here?" said the fisherman

"Sure," said Freestyle. "I mean, no. Or. I don't mind." He was clean. His shirt was clean as he pulled it over his head. How long had it been since his permission had been asked? Since he had permission to give?

The fisherman leaned out of his boat with a net like a distended tennis racket and he scooped something out of the water. Freestyle's eye patch. Freestyle was alarmed to think he'd got so dangerously relaxed that he hadn't even noticed it missing. He touched his marble eye to be sure that hadn't slipped out; Freestyle, on determining the marble was still there kept his hand over it, the ugliness of all that injury there, and he raised his other hand toward the fisherman; this was formed as if to take the boy scout oath or as a symbol of benediction, or of affirmation, or of 'yes, that is my eye patch.'

The fisherman rowed as near as he could to Freestyle's rock, slipped an oar out of its oar lock and put the eye patch on its blade which he extended toward Freestyle. The thing was just within his reach. Freestyle had long quit most of his vanity, but he did need that eye patch, and perhaps the fisherman sensed his gratitude when he asked, "I'm sorry, and it's none of my business if you don't want to—if it's none of my business. But what happened to you?"

"Homemade claymore." Freestyle knew this only second hand, long afterward.

"A—?"

"IED," said Freestyle. "A bomb. Mesopotamia, man."

"So—" said the fisherman. "A war? You were in a war?"

"A little," said Freestyle. Thirty-six hours in a war zone, and he'd never heard a shot fired in anger, never even heard the explosion that made such quick work of his tour of duty and killed the man in front of him.

The fisherman floated thoughtfully. "You must be eligible for a lot of benefits."

Freestyle's disability income flowed directly into an account he rarely accessed. Someone from the Veteran's Hospital kept bouncing mail off his last known address regarding the new and improved hand that had been built just for him.

"If you were wounded, you wouldn't have to—you shouldn't have to live like this. There must be benefits. You really shouldn't have to live this way."

"You might be surprised, sir," said Freestyle. "Thanks for everything." He packed his laundry back into his ruck sack, slipped the Spring Zing bar back in its wrapper and packed that, too. His gratitude toward the fisherman was insupportable, inexpressible, so, to try and escape it, Freestyle scrambled up the bank as best he could.

"Sorry," called the fisherman. "Didn't mean to—but this is such a great hole."

Freestyle passed right by the convenience store where he had stopped before, not wishing to startle the red-eyed clerk with his return or take a chance on buying any more corrupted food. There were packages on those shelves that may have been there since before the clerk's birth. He wondered if the poor girl took a lot of complaints. To distract himself from his hunger, Freestyle got the harmonica out and made a series of noises that began to sound something like 'Taps.'

Bad planning. Bad coordination. Freestyle found himself headed back into the busy part of town in the hot and busy part of the day. And hungry. He thought it was Wednesday, but perhaps it was only because he wanted it to be Wednesday when produce trucks pulled up behind

Monumart all day long, leaving delicious spillage sometimes, or things that got culled from the delivery. Eat your vegetables. The shortest route to Monumart took him through a parking lot near a Mexican restaurant where deep-fried tortillas among other aromatic projects brought him near to tears. Mexican food. Music. He was clean, clean for once. Debit card in his pocket. No reason at all why he couldn't go in and eat chips and salsa and try their lunch special like a normal human being, and—no—he would not be going in. This was boiling up into one of those moments when Freestyle would be so angry with himself about the things he could no longer bring himself to do.

Two people came out of the restaurant with Styrofoam containers, and they hadn't got very far into the parking lot before one of them, a young woman with a ponytail erupting from the crown of her head and earrings elaborate as chandeliers, opened her tray and shrieked. Her companion, a nicely made and nicely dressed young man whose girlfriend may have been his only hardship, looked concerned. Freestyle, as it happened, was very near this scene. The young woman caught him looking at her. She would be accustomed to people looking at her, but. . .The young woman was wearing high heeled shoes in the parking lot of a Mexican restaurant, and black pants molded to long legs, and on these she began to move toward him, a predatory dancer. Freestyle was frozen, and he wondered why the young man was pleading, "Babe. Baaabe. Come on."

The young woman was coming at him, outraged. Freestyle was not accustomed to give such specific offense. Hers was a terrifying certainty, the kind of beauty that is rarely denied anything, but something was amiss for her, too, and she seemed to think it was Freestyle, and she strutted toward him. That face of hers so set, as if its perfection should never be marred by much expression.

"Sir," she said, and she could only be speaking to him. "Are you all right with onions?"

"For eating?" said Freestyle. He knew when he was fumbling but couldn't prevent himself from it. The girl thrust the Styrofoam tray at him, and said, "Onions." She called back to her young companion, "I didn't stutter. No. No onions, I said. Is that so hard?"

Freestyle wasn't sure what response she wanted. The young woman's ponytail seemed to gesture as she moved her head. "Sir?" she said again, and she held the tray toward him. A dream come true, and she was so sure he wouldn't refuse it, and she was right.

"Romi," called the boyfriend. "Come on. I mean, can you even make fajitas without onions? Maybe you wanted something impossible."

Romi said, "Here," and she took Freestyle's hand, and winced just a little when she noticed what she had taken hold of, that coolness, that weird texture, and she turned it palm up and placed the tray in it so that it couldn't be refused. Having come to like herself in that moment even more than usual, the young woman slipped Freestyle a sly smile that began to recede even as she turned back to her boyfriend. "That," she said, "is absolutely the last time for Los Crapos."

Freestyle watched her walk away, watched the pair of them drive away, and only then did he look around to determine that he was entirely anonymous again and unworthy of notice, so he ate what he'd got exactly where he'd got it, and he ate fast despite the limitations of a small plastic fork. He knew that a wise man would slow himself down and do everything he could to extend this pleasure, but there was a certain kind of pleasure in wolfing it down, too, and when he'd eaten he felt for a moment accomplished and full, and then with the wad of paper napkins in the lid of the Styrofoam box, he wiped the grease from his fingers and lips, and only then did he begin to yearn for cover again, for shade. He knew a network of alleys by which he could safely get back to the park.

◊ ◊ ◊

The ravine was still unoccupied, still cool when he returned to it. A full belly, a stand of grass that grew on a slope shaped much like a recliner. Freestyle drowsed in his satisfaction. Drowsed in the day. In truth, he drowsed in the night, too. Did he sleep anymore? Deep sleep? A man with no barriers against whatever might be coming out of the night—sleep? No. But Freestyle did know to drowse at length and very satisfactorily, and in this restful state the most wonderful ideas might unscroll, and he imagined himself a sort of Johnny Appleseed, but with harmonicas, a man dedicated to sowing harmonicas among the poor children of the world. It would be the beginning of a movement, and he would be the source of a good thing. Later Freestyle slid from drowsing into lounging, merely taking his ease, and he was at length assaulted by sober thoughts that recognized he'd made himself a problem where none had existed before, a large box of stolen harmonicas, an item or items that he wouldn't begin to know where or how to sell, or even to give away—Johnny Awful-seed—it was so easy to imagine children, children running, running away having taken nothing from his hand. By the light of day now, with plenty of time to reflect, Freestyle considered the best possible use that might be made of those harmonicas, and he could not avoid the conclusion that it would have been much better if he had never taken them in the first place, if they were still available to people who wanted to buy them.

He took the harmonica from his pocket, from its box, but he wouldn't try and play it here, and Freestyle realized that his use of the thing would be limited to those rare times when he didn't want to maintain concealment. Freestyle was proud of himself as a scavenger, and honor demanded he must be a scavenger without being a thief, so how had he slid across that line? Was it just the first temptation that came his way that brought him to it? No. He moved at night. There were always opportunities, more opportunities than civilians knew.

A big box of harmonicas stashed in a Rocket 88. What now? Had he, Freestyle, made garbage of these innocent items, these promising things? Instruments by which people might extract their souls. Freestyle was not a thief. Freestyle had never meant to take so much positive energy out of circulation. Freestyle feared that in this he'd been thief and a fool. That was not part of the bargain, whatever the bargain was. He would not think of himself as a thief, especially a thief who stole to no better purpose than to deprive someone else of their small pleasure. What now?

He waited until full dark before making his way back to the industrial park and the little house with the Rocket 88 behind it. He retrieved the box, he retrieved his shopping cart. Freestyle wheeled his shame back toward the music store. The hour and his route took him within earshot of revelers reveling. It was that hour when midweek drunks became expressive, so Freestyle thought it was between one and one-thirty a.m. Freestyle knew all the back routes, he would be meeting only with rats and cats on his way back to the music store.

How fine it was to do the right thing, even though he'd had to do the wrong thing to make the right thing necessary—but Freestyle welcomed any chance at restoring, recalling, commemorating his irrelevant honor. He didn't mind the wobbling cart too much for once. The night was mild, and here nights were usually mild, and maybe he'd been taking this luxury for granted; not a bad town; practically littered with kind people, or so it had seemed that day. His eye patch on an oar, people calling him, 'sir.' Not a single unpleasantness, not one evasive action today to avoid contact with hostiles. Not a bad day, not a bad night, not a bad town.

Freestyle rolled into the alley behind the music store. The box had got wedged in his shopping cart and he needed to shake it some to get the thing dislodged. Freestyle set it up on the loading dock where it couldn't be missed. In a spasm of extreme, complete honesty, he thought of returning even the harmonica he'd kept in his pocket, of placing it on top of the large box, but, no, that was silly, who would want it now that it had been used? He was done here. Mission accomplished. He took what he now considered his harmonica out of his pocket and was about to try his rendition of 'Taps' when an engine gunned and headlights were suddenly coming for him, and there was nowhere to run. The headlights drew to a sudden halt, dust roiling up in them, then another, stronger light hit him.

"Show your hands." An amplified voice.

Freestyle complied. This would look bad. Like he was trying to steal all these harmonicas, and this business about having stolen them and then bringing them back, that probably wasn't going to cut him too much slack.

"Drop it," said the voice.

When Freestyle had raised his hands, his harmonica had got lodged in the grip of his government issue limb, a thing none too responsive in the best of circumstances. He understood the misunderstanding. He could not get his hand to release that harmonica, though. "Wait," he said.

"Drop the weapon," amplified and quivering.

"Wait," said Freestyle. "I can't. I—"

Westward the Ill Adjusted

Sands had been allotted so little space that his breath fogged the window whenever he turned to it, and to his other side his suitcase rode atop a pile of his sister's sweaters where it constantly threatened to slide into his head. New to poverty, he had already come to understand it as a very limited range of choices. He could live in discomfort now, or he could die. He could continue riding in the back seat of this car, or he could get out and try to make his way wherever he landed with his last hundred dollars. Early on in a thousand-mile trip and already his sister Ginny and her husband Clint had argued about the map, first its whereabouts and then what was on it, and then they had revived some drama about the coffee fund in the faculty lounge at the high school where they were no longer teaching, and then by means of a long, long dispute over the capacity and proper uses of a cup holder they had finally driven Sands' soul entirely out of his body.

"Could you possibly turn the heat down," he said.

"You know me," Ginny said. "I'm so cold blooded."

"Cold blooded," said Clint, the Voynoviches first point of agreement in many miles.

"I'm sweating back here," Sands said. "Like steaming."

He took the silence that followed to be their stoic anticipation of his eventual body odor. This would make yet another imposition that they in their vast decency would endure for him. They were headed to Umatilla where Clint had graduated high school and where he was now returning in triumph to be the school's superintendent. The job paid well, and they'd bought an inexpensive house recently hauled out of a flood plain so that Ginny would no longer have to work and the Voynoviches could get serious again about starting a family; they were going to do whatever it took now to start that family and seemed, at intervals, to be quite thrilled about it, but if this was how they behaved when they were feeling happy and optimistic Sands could not be too pleased at the prospect of their reproducing. And what if Sands should begin to stink? He was too polite or too beholden to point out that Clint had doused himself in a scent powerfully reminiscent of urinal cakes, that Clint was exactly the kind of guy who intentionally smells of some off brand disinfectant, and that they'd be smelling him now all the way to Oregon.

"Flying Z," said Clint. The winged letter stood raised on a tall steel pole near the freeway. "You get your best food at truck stops."

"No," said Ginny, "you don't. Not even close."

"They'll have a salad bar," Clint said.

"I don't think you're hearing me," said Ginny.

"It's well over a hundred miles away," Clint said. "What do you think, Geno? Big, juicy bacon cheeseburger? Chicken fried steak?"

"Whatever you guys decide." Sands said, as his affairs were now being directed in this way all day long.

Wherever they ate, it would be a meal one of the others would buy for him, and a meal, therefore, that Sands couldn't complain of if he didn't like it, and if he should love it, he couldn't even crow about that without sounding craven. Under a monk's robe of constant gratitude, he felt his actual personality perishing for lack of sunlight. These are the moments a real high roller dares not consider in advance, else who would ever make the big play? Who would go all in? Only the fearless.

"Did I tell you they have a union?" Ginny said.

"You mentioned that," said Sands. "What was it? Brotherhood of Correctional Officers?"

"Union jobs," said Ginny, "are usually *good* jobs. With

benefits. Some job protection."

One third of Umatilla's population was prisoners; Ginny had been looking for ways to lean her poor brother back onto his feet, and corrections seemed to her an obvious choice. Sands had been pretending to entertain the idea. "Maybe they'd have some counseling positions. Maybe I could do some financial literacy, something like that."

Clint smiled his brittle little brother-in-law smile. The joke was financial literacy, or Sands' version of it; Sands' fate had been engineered with a series of choices that in retrospect had clearly guaranteed his ruin. A warehouse full of high-speed blenders, uninsured; a fire; a wife who found him inadequate the moment his money was gone, a wife who'd been the most foreseeable disaster of all. He'd bought blenders by the ton from Taiwan, a product riding just then on an advertising blitz someone else had paid for, and it had been so sweet, so opportune, and Sands having known that momentary thrill of being in the right place at the right time thought that he'd do it all again. But it could be a while, maybe a long while before he had such moves to consider, for he was broke. Every penny? An investment that went against everything in his education and experience. Nothing in reserve. Ha ha. No guts, no glory.

"I think there's always something available out at the chemical depot," Clint said.

"Is there anything like shipping or anything?" Sands said.

"No. Not really. River cruises now, but they don't dock at Umatilla. They couldn't. Do you have any mechanical skills?"

"I managed to keep my lawnmower going," said Sands. He'd ridden that mower so very recently across a graceful green slope and around their gazebo. He'd worn ear protection, taken a nice tan. Sands did not look or feel like anyone's idea of a worker.

"I think the Indians get all the salmon now," Clint said. "The Indians and the dams."

"As they should," said Ginny.

They knew better than to voice the slightest hesitancy concerning her proclamations. Her passion and certainty in these things always drove them into submission anyway, and they were accustomed to minefield periods when anything they might say would be held suspicious or improper; Ginny, the thought police in the passenger's seat, and everyone obliged to keep their thoughts to themselves. Ginny should at least see some justice in her brother's current circumstance, but Mrs. Voynevich was far too prim to show it. Sands had always been generous with his money, generous and superior. The sin of pride. Their mother was a lapsed Catholic, so they too had their early encounters with the various categorized sins. What was it? Cardinal? Ordinal? Original? Something like that. But—pride.

"Is there a brokerage in town?" Sands said. "Anybody doing investing?"

"I wouldn't know," said Clint. "They say the old timers put their money under a mattress, thought it was safer there. Not that it did them any good." Clint never forgot, nor did he let anyone around him long forget that he'd come of humble origins, his father a ranch hand, his mother a cook at a country school. And look at him now—he'd plodded to the pinnacle of his imagination. Not so long ago, Sands had been pleased for Clint and for his sister, and he certainly didn't wish to loathe them now, but Sands was seeing how his practical and spiritual generosity came of the same reservoir. Broke, it seemed, he'd be a complete shit.

Clint said, "You should think about getting your boiler license."

"My—-" said Sands, "boiler license?"

"That can open a lot of doors," said Clint. "And there are home study courses. Every big building needs a boiler guy."

"Boiler *person*," said Ginny.

"Hm," said Sands. "You know, I hate to admit it, but I've never been sure what a boiler even is. What it does. Boils something, I suppose. It's something to do with—heating? Sure. I should look into that. Do you know if there's electricity involved?"

"Maybe as your heat source," said Clint, already trying on his new authority, "but mostly steam, I think. Pressure. Gauges. Have to know what you're doing. They do blow up."

"Sounds exciting," said Sands.

"Not usually," said Clint. "In fact, it really *shouldn't* be. You don't want problems. Even just a ruptured tank that's. . ."

"Bad," Sands concluded, even as he concluded he must shirk this potential responsibility.

"Yeah," said Clint. "Steam. You're mostly concerned with steam. Or—have you ever had anything to do with livestock?"

He'd never had so much as a boyhood dog or goldfish, and for Sands the animal kingdom was only food that arrived on his plate fully processed and bearing no resemblance to its breathing past. "You had that cat," he reminded his sister. "What was that? Boots?"

"That was Mom's name for him," said Ginny. "I hated that name."

"Yeah," said Sands, "but you were trying to call him—what was it?—Zoom-oh?"

"*Zip*-oh," said Ginny. "Because he responded to that. Poor kitty. I almost didn't blame him when he ran away. I'm sure he was confused."

"So cats," said Sands, ". . . you mean he had an identity crisis?"

"Didn't we all?" said Ginny.

Sands had in fact been quite content with himself; but that was money, and that was gone. Now as a lesser person, he was already beginning to guess what an ass he must have been and hoped someday to be again.

Their adult lives had been something like a game in that they'd each been started with an equal portion of a small inheritance. Ginny had made her way through college and toward her teaching certificate; Geno, meanwhile, invested his, not wisely but well, and he used the proceeds of his early successes to buy his own education and to keep making money. His knack for this afforded him a great deal of swagger in the only circles that mattered to him. He'd maintained a swimming pool and an extravagant woman while he was still young enough to enjoy them, and until now he'd been the clear winner in the Sands kids' sweepstakes. Ginny would be almost inhuman to find no pleasure in their present roles. "Too bad," she said, "you couldn't get something at the school. Something in maintenance. But—nepotism."

"There are people in these small towns," said Clint, "who don't know one other thing about the operation of their school, but they'll know in a heartbeat if you hire your third cousin or whatever to paint the bleachers."

"Yeah," Sands said.

Why would anyone intentionally enter into this? Umatilla, as he understood it, was on a great river, but also in the dessert and had for some reason been chosen as a destination for unwanted substances and people. Wastes.

"Walmart," Clint said. "There's always Walmart."

Sands could not bring himself to agree with this, though it was true.

◊ ◊ ◊

The next Flying Z, hoisted on its tall, tall pole, became evident from a long way off, and so the argument had been in progress for some time before they reached it. It was Clint's position that it was snooty of his wife not to want to eat there, and he wanted a steak, but such places were in Ginny's opinion, "Horrible."

"You need to just try," Clint said. "Don't you think we need to eat what the people eat? Where they eat?"

"Which people?" said Ginny.

"*The* people," said Clint. "The *real* people." This proved his prevailing argument. Clint turned onto acres of asphalt, over-the-road haulers parked in ranks there, idling.

"They're just sitting there, burning fuel," Ginny said. "That is just, that is . . ."

"The most fuel-efficient way," said Clint. "To leave those big diesels running instead of restarting them. Why do you think they do it?"

"Ridiculous," said Ginny.

"Oh, no," said Clint. "Very advanced technology. Your modern eighteen-wheeler is a, well, you know. Quite a thing."

"I hope this isn't awful," said Ginny. "I can't believe I was cold just this morning. This can't be healthy."

Sands, ever the big thinker, saw this expanse of asphalt as a passive solar collector, presently absorbing and discharging gigathings of energy to no better purpose than to roast the unwary traveler. Why was no one harvesting all this damned sun?

"Gaawd," said Ginny as they crossed the lot afoot.

"Pretty warm," Clint conceded.

The truck stop café, The Hungry Traveler, had at its entrance the profile of a tramp, bindle stick over his shoulder—in stained glass. Though some amount of grease must necessarily be in its atmosphere at all times, that atmosphere smelled fundamentally of lemon and turpentine. The Traveler's tables, it seemed, were bussed at once; many of them were set among planters containing frequently washed rubber greenery. The booths were also self-contained, allowing for privacy. What would truckers need with so much privacy? Wouldn't they get their fill of that on the road?

"Okay," said Ginny. "I guess it's, it's pretty nice. You can tell they really try." When they settled at last on a certain booth, and settled into it, she looked around appreciatively and said, "The food industry."

"Mhm," said Sands.

"It's always around," Ginny said. "It's always there."

Sands attempted to look as though he found this certainty reassuring.

Clint, a little roguish now that his steak was near, said, "And sewage. Waste disposal. That's always there, too."

"Oh, Clint," said Ginny, never wishing to squish that little bit of fun in her man. Then, suddenly, they were in love again, the Voynoviches, and Sands could not recall being more dejected in his life, and he was grateful for the crisp arrival of their waitress with their menus, three glasses of water, and the specials of the day, which were elaborate but clearly enunciated. Their waitress, a mid-life woman with tightly curled hair, was impenetrably pleasant. "Grilled cheese," she said, "with or without mayo, our famous tomato soup, and salad bar, which can be a meal in itself, believe me." She'd be a pillar of strength, this waitress, in some undistinguished family, and she didn't mess around. Clint fell right into her efficient rhythm.

"Well, I already know what I want. Steak. T-bone. Medium rare. That twelve-ounce. Fries. Garlic toast."

Sensing he was on a roll, the waitress, Billie by her tag, prompted, "Salad bar? Complete salad bar, deserts and everything else—only four dollars extra with your dinner."

"Ahh—No," Clint said. "But my steak, can they sear that on both sides? I really prefer it seared."

"Jim," she said, "our line cook today, that's one of his specialties. He loves to do that."

"Better bring a side of defibrillator and a stretcher," Ginny said.

"Oh, pooh," said Clint. "What about Geno now. Big slab of hand seared meat, buddy?"

"I'm fine with a plain cheeseburger," said Sands. "And, uh—water is fine. But fries. Fries please."

"Almond chicken?" Ginny exclaimed, surprised, condescending. "Oh. Okay. I'll try that. If there's no MSG."

"Oh, no, ma'am. We never use it."

The waitress, for her brief stay with them, became a notable absence when she whisked away. They were facing each other in the booth, a close quarters arrangement causing them to squirm inwardly and fidget outwardly, and to silently, individually acknowledge once again that they were ill adjusted people. Clint unwrapped knife fork and spoon from their paper napkin and arranged these utensils beside his plate, the napkin in his lap. Ginny consulted her cell phone and was a little offended by some news from it. Clint began looking around in a funny, mannered way as if acting a part in a bad play; he was suddenly, visibly struck by an idea. "I'm going to have a look in that shop. They'll have a ton of CB stuff."

"CB?" said Ginny. "Do you need CB?"

"It's radio," said Clint.

"I *know*," said Ginny. "But—do you need it?"

"It's just an interesting technology," Clint said. "I'm going to use the can, and. . . Ok*ay*?"

"With cell phones," Ginny wondered, "why would you need a? Why would anyone need anything but their cell phone?"

"It's just fun," said Clint, completely redefining the word as Sands understood it.

Clint left, and Ginny dived right back into her screen as if to demonstrate just how unnecessary her husband was. Sands had his own expensive phone, but no data. He looked around, uncomfortable at confronting how dependent he too had become on the streaming. This other reality could not simply be shifted as it became boring. And it did become boring. Even before these devices intruded, he'd probably never had much of a conversation with his sister. Sands had the time and leisure to consider this kind of thing now, but he considered it a poor use of both time and leisure.

Their food came. Ginny disliked hers. Sands, currently attuned to life's small pleasures, ate a burger done to medium rare perfection; his fries were golden brown. Meanwhile, Clint had not returned from wherever he'd gone off to, and his meat sat steaming on its hot plate.

Sands wiped his lips, having consumed his pleasure in under five minutes. "Well, I better go see what's become of Clint."

Ginny's meal was obviously abandoned. She regarded her husband's steak, steaming lightly now. "He knows where we are," she said.

"Yeah," said Sands. "But. He was pretty excited about that. . . So, maybe I'll just. . ."

Ginny was absorbed again in her phone. Sands envied her data.

◊ ◊ ◊

The men's room served both the café and the store; it featured a long line of urinals along one wall, a mirror along the other. Presently empty, or so it seemed. Thinking it indiscrete to call out, 'Clint?' in here, Sands found that by crouching low he could look under the stalls for feet. Crouching low, he caught himself in the mirror. Crouching for Clint. There were no feet. No one in the men's room. Sands went into the store.

The store, though small, contained everything necessary to sustain life and would be the first place you'd want to visit in the event of an apocalypse; there were rows of imperishable foods, those big batons truckers use to bop their tires, pornography, first aid kits, tobacco and vape supplies, barometers, brilliant orange apparel, and, just as foretold, a wide array of CB equipment. Breaker one-nine—no Clint.

Outside, Sands scanned the parking lot, a population of ghosts shimmering over sheet metal, and he happened to be looking out at the freight trucks, looking particularly at a bright one that advertised itself as an orange hauler 'From the Sunshine State!' Sands had to wonder at the wisdom of leaving such a cargo parked under a scorching sun, refrigeration or no, and he was sure to take note of the company's name so that he'd know never to buy their orange juice or their stock when from out of that truck's sleeper cab came Clint at last. He'd been shoved or kicked out, then a shoe came flying after, and then from his supine position he made a reaching, grief-stricken gesture. One shoe off, one shoe on, his shirt unbuttoned to the navel. The door of the sleeper cab closed, concluding that conversation.

Sands was drawn across the hot asphalt toward the man, curious, responsible. What wounds would he find?

"Clint?" said Sands, requiring further confirmation of what he unavoidably knew.

Clint turned away to tuck in his shirt tails, his tell-tales; Clint never let these fly, for he was a style icon from an era preceding his birth, it was a point of pride with him. Neat. He kept turned away, as if pulling himself together required his entire attention, as if he hadn't heard his name, and many loaded moments passed before he was able to turn back to Sands and say, feigning mild surprise, "Oh, hey, Geno. These things are *air* conditioned. I mean, you can't believe it. Very comfortable. You just, just can't believe you'd find so many comforts in a truck. It's like a tiny home in there. Cozy. Cool. You wouldn't believe it."

"No," said Sands. "I probably wouldn't. Your steak might be kind of stiff."

"My?" said Clint. "Oh. I. . . You know, it's funny, but I lost my appetite." He had almost contrived to keep the horror from his face, but his twitching right eye was not cooperative in the performance.

"Are you all right?" said Sands.

"Me?" said Clint, as if the question had come out of nowhere. "Fine," he said.

"It should be good cold," said Sands. "And they did get it nice and black for you."

Clint seized on this. "Sure. And we could, you know, take it with us." Then, meekly veering, "Think Ginny will be mad?"

Sands shrugged, for they both knew it was only a question of how angry she would be, and of how many and what kind of reasons she would have to feel that way.

Clint, suddenly charged with an optimism for which there was no obvious basis, said "Yeah, I think we'll just grab it on the fly. One of those Styrofoam things, maybe a refill on our soft drinks. And—off we go. I mean, we do have a long, long way left to go, so—."

"That might be an understatement," said Sands.

◊ ◊ ◊

In Clint's pursuit of authenticity, they had proceeded west on secondary roads; Real America as Clint understood it was rarely to be glimpsed from the freeway. It had been an eerie two hours since they'd left the truck stop. Not a single word from Ginny, and following that cue both men were also entirely quiet. Something, however, was being communicated. They were passing through an emerald corridor, tall corn growing right to the edge of both sides of the road, when Ginny finally said, "A *truck* stop, Clint? A *truck* stop? We were supposed to be through with all that. Your promises are no good."

"I," said Clint. "Well, I. . ."

"Stop this car," said Ginny, a boiler beginning to rupture.

"Honey," said Clint. "Honey, now."

"Stop!" she said.

"If you want to—If you need to stretch your legs or something."

"Stop!" she said, louder still.

Clint stopped. Ginny opened her door, stepped out, seized that door in both hands and slammed it hard enough to rock the car. She marched off toward Umatilla or maybe the nearest lawyer's office. Clint shifted to his lowest gear so that he might follow along behind. "Geeze," he said, "I hope we don't overheat. This idling, you know, is. . ."

"Overheat?" said Sands. "*Man*. What else, huh?"

At intervals of about fifty yards Clint would lean out his window and implore his wife, "Honey—."

"You'd better just let her walk it off," Sands said.

"What if she got dehydrated?"

"Well," said Sands, "Obviously that wouldn't be too good. Look, I haven't said anything. I mean, you've been right there, so you know I haven't said anything, okay?"

"She jumps to conclusions," Clint said. "Sometimes. But, if you did say anything, what would you say, do you think?"

"I haven't even considered it," Sands said, "cause I'm not saying anything. This is strictly between you guys."

"This?" said Clint. "You mean. . ."

"I don't know what I mean," said Sands.

They came to a sign indicating they were twenty miles from Fairhaven. A half mile past that Ginny's pace had slowed considerably, and Clint called to her, his tone drifting from anxiety toward despair, "Honey?"

Slowly then came a tractor toward them pulling a wagon loaded high with what would soon be silage and being driven by a weathered man in a scotch cap entirely inappropriate to the weather and pulling judiciously on a pipe. With the numb wonder he often experienced in his encounters with city folks this man of the soil considered first Ginny then the car that followed. Clint hallowed the man and remarked, "Fine looking part of. . . Fine looking." All they could see from that road was tall corn and the distant red tip of a silo. The farmer, passing so slowly, had plenty of time to form a response, but he never did, and the parties separated just as deliberately as they'd come together, but without the suspense.

Sagging and shining with sweat, Ginny got back in the car then, a greasy forelock plastered to her forehead. She would not look at her traveling companions, and it was easy to believe she might never look at them again. Clint continued poking along through the green corridor as if he feared jostling her, but eventually Ginny said out of an exhaustion that might never be fixed, "I left my phone in here," and Clint, with this information accelerated toward Fairhaven at last, and they rode on in that old strategic silence, needing each other.

Viola, A Long Earner

She had already lived two full generations past her regular expiration date before I was born, but because her DNA tested very high for memory and probable longevity my great grandmother had been continued as a profit generator. Many decades previous she'd been implanted with hair plugs, and that primitive implationist had really overdone it so that a massive mane still grew from her tiny head, engulfed it, and she sometimes applied a glossy product to this that made it even more startling. Living history, she certainly looked the part, and Viola was a steady earner; content providers would come around to buy her memories and use them to develop those popular pieces that illustrate how miserable and confused life must have been before the full development of Market Consciousness. We maintained Viola in the family housing unit as a designated relic, and my first adolescent contract was as her paid helper. My father was calling me Easy Money then, and I was so proud of myself; I too believed at first that our contract was all to my benefit, but just as Market Consciousness tells us, and as the market also demonstrates, every benefit erodes over time and any benefit may become a liability.

There was almost nothing to that job. Viola was past a hundred and forty then but still fanatically tidy within her cubicle and about her person; a service delivered her meals on disposettes through the pneumatube. She had lived through the High Toxicity and had a lot of the usual problems from that period, that extremely eruptive flesh, so I took her every three months to have her fresh moles and skin tags lazed, though she didn't actually need my help with that; Old Viola was quite capable of mounting and dismounting transporters. She was entitled to almost every discount. The Midsanto settlement was still in effect then, so she received her lazings for free from a real artist who very seldom burned any adjacent flesh.

I briefly considered a career in lazing myself, it was such a great business model in those days. Tastes change, though. Now all the money is in grooming and encouraging secondary growths. Tastes change, the market evolves. It isn't always easy to stay current, to keep up, and I can't easily see myself fertilizing fancy skin growths and polishing moles, still, you can believe I will remain viable; you must believe I am absolutely and constantly thrilled to meet the demands of the market.

How often she told me that her name and attitudes had been old fashioned even in her own time. Viola said she was paying me because she needed at least a little company, and for Viola the term 'company' meant talking. And she did—she talked until I felt I was working for my pay after all, enduring so much verbiage, and finally just to preserve my sanity I did develop a passing interest in language and in the strange times she'd lived through, the strange things she still believed. She expected me to talk, too, no matter how often I reminded her that people just didn't do that very much anymore, and that's why I wasn't very good at it. She absolutely refused to wear a thought transmitter. 'Thoughts?' She'd say, "Those things don't work for shit." Her words only made me wonder all the more why anyone would ever prefer that old style dialogue. I got a little better at talking, speaking that is, during my time with Viola, but I certainly never learned to enjoy it. I found that I wasn't long without my transmitter before I slipped right back into making false transmissions with my mouth.

It's only human—you're only human—some version of that idea, that excuse, seemed to come round quite often in the records of her time. Much of that was, of course, just language.

She was an odd candidate for preservation, because Viola hated every improvement, everything you and I consider essential. She hated thought transmitters; she hated Modern Honesty; most of all, she hated Market Consciousness. "You people rattle like dry corn husks." There were certain words and phrases she'd repeat especially often, and the ones she liked best were usually good examples of how words were so often combined to mean nothing at all. Another of her favorites was, 'bankers.' This was her term for all of us there in the family unit, or for everyone I suppose. Though it was just another word, the way she said it made her meaning plain—she thought society and everyone in it had devolved—but I thought the comparison flattering. In her time, as I understand it, it was only much abused bankers who attempted to properly order things, and you can see where the chaos of the ancients would have consumed them completely if not for those few brave bankers daring to generate profits.

She was angry. And why? Because sanity had prevailed.

She insisted I talk, but then if I should happen to mention roast pug or fried Chihuahua Viola would get more specifically angry, and it was in this way that she would eventually acquaint me with so many of the ancients' taboos and superstitions. Dogs, for instance. In Viola's time people happily ate cows and various birds, and on special occasions they ate crustaceans, but dogs, for some reason, were off limits. The ancients wouldn't eat their dogs, not even the bad ones, didn't eat their disabled, and expiration dates hadn't even been established yet for human beings. There would have been so many ugly, useless creatures around, consuming rather than being resources. I asked

Viola about all that negative income flow, and I wondered how that didn't bother the old ones as it should have, and I asked her if there was any particular reason to favor one protein over another, and if they were so squeamish why not subsist on soy as I do? Was it supply and demand? Was it something to do with other sensate creatures, and if so, why be so inconsistent about it? Had they not heard the screaming of the celery stalks they guiltlessly ground in their jaws?

She wanted me to talk, but I'd often make her angry, it was hard to avoid, and she'd generally disrupt any rational conversation with some mention of love. I have the sense that it was all anger and love in her time. How hellish. Viola once told me that she had retained her viability for so long for the sole purpose of somehow making me understand love, and from what she said and from what I learned from some history content I bought I learned that love was something without substance, a word and a particularly useless one in that it was used to describe, by my count, at least nineteen different sensations. In only one of its varieties could love be commodified, priced, and for the rest it was a worm in their thinking that seems to have been responsible for many of the ancients' disasters. The best that can be said of love is that it kept the armaments industry booming all through history; war for profit was once thought to be immoral, so whenever a war was needed some beloved god or country could be called on to serve as cause.

But love. You're only human. Couldn't put a price on it, so everyone who dabbled in it would have been constantly disappointed, and after so much exposure to Viola's stories I see how the old ones wallowed in that disappointment. Most of her stories had to do with loss, not gain. She thought I would learn something important from them.

So, there I was, yet another disappointment; I would have been her final one.

◊ ◊ ◊

One day she was wearing that troubled look she wore when her communicator chip was active. I'd know when a communication ended because calm would return to her face.

"That's ironic," she said.

I would have stared at her. That was all she expected of me when she used certain obscurities, concepts the thought transmitters didn't carry.

I believe she had some pleasure in explaining herself. "No one will buy me but one of the dog ranches. This body is so old, I'm only fit to be ground into dog chow. So, you see?"

I did see, or thought I did. "The negative of long preservation. Your person becomes less valuable. That is most basic, and pretty easily calculated in advance. But you haven't completely saturated your content market, Viola. There's Australasia, the Balkans."

"But, the irony."

I would have stared at her. This was Viola at her most tiresome. I reminded her, "You still have stories you might tell. The past. We feel so well when we hear about the past. Quite a market for your memories."

"I wouldn't eat them," she said. "I would never eat the pooches, but now they'll be eating me. So—you see."

I told her she had been in error then, and she seemed to be in error now. I was upset that she was approaching the end of her viability. I can't think why, except we hadn't got full value for her. "Your stories," I told her.

But Viola was done telling them, and she had no desire to stick around growing scales on herself. At some point she had said everything she had to say; even her transmitter went silent, and toward the end she only expressed herself with an occasional display of her dazzling, high impact dental work.

I inherited her cubicle and live there to this day, comfortably trading flat and round tokens on the Tokyo exchange.

From Fuzzy Dark

After sex they slept spooning, his nose in the sandalwood and apricot swim of her hair. Now he is awake again.

Over her shoulder the time is four forty-three, the hour and the minute separated by a blinking colon. Unaccustomed to sleep on his side this way, he has lain for several hours now on his arm so that it has gone numb under him, except for his thumb which tingles electrically. He thinks of nerve damage, circulatory problems, all the uses he has for that limb. Her hair is still wonderful, sleek on his cheek, the smell of her scalp a savory undertone. A humid zone has developed between them. Within his small agony he is bored and getting hard again. His back is against a wall so that it is impossible to roll away from her, and it seems a boorish move on a first date to try and roll over her. Anyway, there is no clear real estate on the other side of the bed. Her narrow little bed. Once more he is touched, feels chosen—it doesn't seem this woman entertains much. Mona the silversmith, and for a while the whirling wildchild. He knew her last night as a woman who'd decided she just wasn't giving up on romance, he'd seen how she was in bad need of it, just as he now sees in the gray remoteness of four forty-four that he sorely lacks the means to provide that kind of love and that whatever he does next will violate either her trust or her happy slumber or both. He is caught with his need between her need and the wall.

Daylight leaks in little by little, far more somber than the dark of night, and slowly this reveals in the room a child in furred pajamas. He's like a cub, but startling. This would be the boy Mona mentioned last night, the one the babysitter had referred to as 'Raymond' in a carefully neutral tone. Raymond? Yes, Raymond. An odd name for a toddler, a name with criminal connotations. The child is only just inside the door of the room, but at that not far out of arm's reach. Poor people. Tiny rooms. Raymond stares at him. There is little refuge or concealment to be had behind the mother. It seems the child may have been there for some time, staring so intently at them through the gloom, and like any fuzzy little critter Raymond carries within his cuteness a prospect of sudden viciousness.

Maybe they have an understanding. Here for once instinct and good sense insist on the same thing: Say nothing. Raymond, however, does not look away. Shouldn't his presence eventually rouse his mother? What would she say? To either of them? What will any of them say? Say nothing. Raymond's pajamas are footed; he seems very comfortable in them and ready to wait in place until his curiosity is satisfied. What would a little boy want to know? There is a red, Ruberoid heart on the chest of his furry outfit; in the dimness that red is the only color to assert itself.

They stare at each other until it almost ceases to be strange. The child is a purposeful enigma, possessor of a precocious silence. They are both silent because the next development, whatever it might be, is likely to be even weirder.

At last, and against his better judgment—"Mona. Mona?"

"Mmm," she says warmly, invitingly.

He takes note of her willingness, but says, "It's your, uh. Your little. . . Raymond?"

"Oh," she says, semi delighted. "Hi, honey. Can't sleep?"

The little boy doesn't respond at all but seems poised as a cat to pounce. There is no room for him on that bed. Thank God. He is furry and carries a knubbly blanket. He might be expected to squirm. There is no room for him.

Mona the mother says, "Raymond, this is my friend Peter."

"Pete," he corrects her again.

"*Pete*," she says with mock sternness, "this is Raymond. And Raymond is supposed to be in his bigboy bed, aren't you, honey?"

Young Raymond remains motionless and yet extremely articulate.

"Nice to meet you, young man." Phlegm has gathered in Pete's throat so that he sounds like the irascible old timer in an old time Western. What must Mona think of this voice, this shallow fool behind her? Raymond hasn't moved. Raymond has the upper hand. Pete is naked behind the boy's mother and under a sheer sheet, trapped there by propriety, by more modesty than he knew he possessed. Pete of a usual Sunday morning would be in his own pajamas, sleeping in in his own unfurnished bed, his own quietude.

Is he now burned into this poor kid's consciousness forever? Will he be a real bad memory?

"Get yourself a juice box, honey."

Raymond turns to his mission, his blanket trailing him like a toreador's cape, and like a toreador his expression remains fixed at all times. His mother brags, "He never did pee the bed. He's got the opposite problem. He gets thirsty. I had him checked for diabetes, juvenile diabetes and everything, but, whew, he just gets thirsty. Hate to have him take in all that corn syrup, but he loves it, you know. All babies they're like bees. Anything sweet." She thrusts her haunch back at his groin for playful emphasis.

"Should I?" says Pete. "I should probably. . ." But the little boy is already back in the room, offering that box to his mother so that she may drive a tiny straw through a foil membrane and he may drink.

Pete has yet to recover his arm. The hand attached to it

is now entirely atingle. Raymond has resumed his former location and posture, except that between sips he holds the juice box contemplatively as if he were a small connoisseur. And he stares at the pair on the bed.

"I'm wondering if I should. . ." says Pete. "Maybe I should?"

"What?" she says.

"Well, I'm. . . I don't know."

"Go back to bed, honey," she says. "And try not to spill that, okay?"

Raymond shows no intention of moving. His mother doesn't bother to repeat her request.

"Maybe we'd better. . . I should probably. . ."

"What?"

"I don't know. Well. . . I don't know."

Pete Mathias has got by with the most approximate understanding of the elemental energies. He has heard of gravity, electromagnetism, and love, but of these, only the effect of gravity seems very obvious to him. He may not be alone in his confusion, but he is for the most part alone. "Maybe," he says, "could you just scootch forward a bit, so I. . . Oh, thanks. Oooh." His arm and shoulder, though now unencumbered, still ache. He needs to be moving. He is naked. He has wakened into a low-grade nightmare from which it seems there will be no further waking. He would very much like to leave, or at least to have some better covering for his loins. He considers saying something more to Raymond, who seems prepared to hear it, but Pete cannot call to mind the particulars or any general sense of his own childhood, and he can't think of a remark a child might find relevant. "That looks tasty," he finally rasps, and the child turns in that mannered way of his, his blanket flourish, and he goes out of the room. Pete has gained his trousers when the child returns, and as he sits at the foot of the bed putting them on, a second juice box is thrust at him. "Can he have another one?"

"It's for you," says Mona. "He wants you to have it."

"Thank you," says Pete, sounding younger by several decades now, the crust having scaled off his vocal cords. Raymond seems incapable of speech or of bending his outthrust arm.

"Take it," says Mona, proud mother of a generous son.

"Thank you." Pete says again. He has yet to make himself quite decent. He finishes pulling his pants up. He accepts the juice box. Regarding and being regarded by that earnest little face, he plunges the straw into the juice box, draws some juice through it, and says falsely but sincerely, "Delicious." It is sweet unto unpleasantness.

"You got the raspberry," says Mona. "That means he really likes you. Don't you, honey?"

The child seems immune to all his mother's promptings. He looks nothing like her. Pete thinks to commend him, "That's quite nice of you. You're thoughtful."

"He's a very good boy," says Mona, perhaps even accurately. "Aren't you, honey?"

Pete is relieved when the child persists in saying nothing.

"Peter," says Mona. "You're not leaving. Are you?"

"Pete," he insists. "You have a coffee maker or something? I've got kind of a bad habit. In the mornings."

"Phew," says Mona. "I was afraid you might be taking off."

"No," says Pete Mathias, already aware he will never utter a more binding word.

Clean and Smooth

Alan Meyers had felt especially beckoned when he received his invitation, though he knew every living member of his class must have got one, and in the weeks preceding the affair he'd felt as if he'd been encased in a chrysalis, festering with notions of triumph. Standing before a mirrored wall he regarded a dandy in a tailored gray suit and a dove gray homburg with a red feather in its band. He shot his cuff exposing a silver bracelet bearing a stone like a halved robin's egg; his eyes could, he thought, with a minimum of maneuvering seem dreamy, hard, or visionary. He was so much bigger now. Much bigger now, a man's overlay of bulk and definition upon the boy he'd been far too long—that late bloomer, that guy who often smelled of the grease at his workplace. Oh yeah? Well, what about this tailored suit now, these calf skin boots. Meyers gave his face one long last consideration; apart from his abused lips there was nothing much wrong with it anymore. He'd taken a room on the top floor of the hotel, the better to see out, and seeing out had made him wistful, for he did not remember this town for such a beauty. Of course, he'd never seen it from this angle when he lived here; he'd certainly never seen it from above.

Lived here? With beat down Dad and butt hurt Mom and the septic sisters? It had needed all Meyer's energy to avoid seeing the world through their disappointed eyes, and he did not consider he'd lived noticeably until he'd escaped this town and his loving family. It had taken him so long to get out. The then and the now—that was the contrast he'd been lusting after, to arrive here polished with a professional dash of fuck you, you deadend fucking duds.

Meyers strode rolling down the hall toward the

elevator, light footed, hot after the moment and the revelation he was about to be, but then, though the town's tallest building was not very tall, he reverted during the brief trip to the ground floor, and by the time the elevator doors slid open directly across the lobby from the Big River Room Meyers not only remembered but reinhabited that underclassman whose mere existence was reason enough for constant embarrassment; suddenly he was become the bozo again in all his accumulated style. He had willed himself flamboyant, and he had worn it so well and convincingly until he reached home ground, where, he had already discovered, he was prone to feel once more the fool, the dust mote. Meyers waited, however, in a short line for his name tag.

The affair's official greeter was classmate Barbara McCorkle, now Barbara McCorkle-Hale, and she failed to recognize him; Meyers enjoyed supplying his name, but then that too drew a blank with Ms. McCorkle-Hale. "Is it Alan or Meyers?" she said. She fingered the placards with pinkly enameled fingernails. "Oh," she said. "Okay. Here it is. You're registered and everything. So. Sure. It's a no-host bar."

She'd remained succulent, peaches and cream unjustly well preserved; this Barbara had been for him a daily torment through several school years, a person so regal she'd remained unaware of him through all those thousands of times he'd been aware of her. Her voice. That voice was nothing he'd willingly remember—a dental drill, a shrill dismissal.

"Okay?" she said.

Meyers had learned nothing. He knew that given any chance at all he would hasten to forgive this awful woman her awful voice and whatever else he might have to overlook to live in her powdered scent for even a little while.

Because she was pretty. Because she was unavailable. The formula for enchantment had remained so terrible and simple, and he had only tricked himself into thinking he'd grown up. With his placard on his lapel and with a packet of coupons good at local boutiques and pharmacies in his pocket, he went into the Big River Room, an enormous, clam colored room that may have been suitable for industrial trade shows some decades back. Looking little left or right, Meyers went straight for the bar, thinking it best to remain incurious until he reached it, to risk no encounters until he was fortified. Box wine. Ale from the town's most pretentious enterprise, a local brewery. Bottom Rung Ale. These concoctions, Meyers thought, would be sticky or cloudy, so he thought to calm himself with deep breathing. Calm himself? Why should that even be necessary? Breathing. Circular breathing, a trick of his trade, and incidentally a fix for anxiety. Tools. He was equipped. Master of an arcane art. He was a man. Meyers was pleased to see that if he wasn't especially recognizable, he was not the only here one here who had gone obscure with age. Most of them were in some state of disrepair, half remembered faces gone fleshy, hairy, dissolute. He began to condescend and feel better. Breathe. Center. Sure. There must be someone here from the half assed music section; they'd remember him; he'd remember them; they'd know to be impressed with him, and maybe there would even be some talk of music.

Meyer's alma mater was this town's largest employer and had long been reckoned a strange and savage place with students who couldn't do better, dismal graduation rates. But what a band. Three electric guitars when the pep band played for basketball games, and Meyers behind and above it all, riffing. This memory, Meyers thought, should be more satisfying. Wasn't he the rare bird who'd found both his salvation and his business at a community college? Hadn't he riffed from the top of the bandstand?

Meyers had spent the first half of his life in fair proximity to many of the people in this room, and yet he didn't know anyone well enough to initiate a conversation here. What a familiar circumstance. Piped in strings made an audible mush above clutches of pudgies saying goodbye to their youth, some of them trying to misremember it favorably. Here he was at the edge again, just at the edge, just apart. His own memories were all too visceral and accurate; he'd been an eavesdropper then, and Meyers was an eavesdropper again, suddenly back to that grim fascination of old for these people. These people. He knew one member of the group nearest him, because it was Randy Bloch who'd stolen his bicycle when they were boys; Bloch was selling insurance here in town having studied business, and when Bloch glanced his way, he didn't seem to know him, but he probably never had. Meyers had known the names and faces of so many people who did not know his. Looking off, looking away, Meyers listened to one man's long disquisition about a boat and the succession of motors that had powered it; Randy Bloch's wife went on and on in the local monotone, match by match with their hundred-and-nineteen-pound son who'd gone to state that year only to get pinned. Another woman was getting drunk and kept saying so, coyly. Lawn care was discussed. One of the sober women among them objected, too late, to the civic center being torn down.

Even dressed to the nines as he was, Meyers had little trouble to listen inconspicuously to this group, for they formed a literal circle and their interests and attention rarely strayed outside that circle. Mr. and Mrs. Randy Bloch. The inevitable guy named Bob. A woman named Dinnie. There was a big emptiness whistling through them which they seemed to celebrate, and Meyers the man apart, felt just as he had at this periphery so long ago—he was better than this—he just *had* to be. Superior, but envious. Meyers remembered how little they suffered from their lack of curiosity, and he saw how they remained in their sufficiency entirely unaware of him.

He consulted his Bulova. Alan Meyers had places to be. Anywhere, really.

He'd made his point. The then and the now. He had not expected to plunge so suddenly back into the anxious twerp he'd been, but having done so he concluded he didn't need anyone else's acknowledgment to congratulate himself, to be content with himself for having come so far from this. He'd gone to some trouble and expense for this half hour, but he'd made his point, and Meyers was only slightly disappointed that he'd risked no exchange in which he might casually mention how he'd flown in from Vegas to be here, or maybe even work in a few anecdotes from his adventures in the show band, the volcanic life of the diva who employed him, or how he was going on from here to a recording date in Vancouver. See? *This* is my life he'd meant to say just obliquely enough to make it plain. But what was plain was that he'd be of no greater interest to these people than he'd ever been.

Meyers would check out. Immediately. He'd call a cab and wait at the terminal in the airport with his horn, his suitcase, and his Agatha Christie, where, he imagined, he would be at perfect ease with himself, fully sated by his moment at the reunion. Full of understanding, and yes, gratitude. Meyers was imagining himself in the terminal, comfortable as a man with his slippers and pipe, awaiting that mercy flight out, and he was making his way to the exit of the Big River Room and had very nearly reached it when a vested waitress appeared beside him with a tray, free liquor after all, plastic glasses of red wine, and suddenly an overcoifed reunionist shrilled, "O-*kay!*" and reached across the poor waitress to take a glass, pretty obviously another glass, from the tray, and she fell head-long into the waitress who was tipped so that her tray also tipped, and Meyers' suit, both jacket and pants, were well splashed with a funky cabernet.

"Whoops," said the enthusiast, sidling away.

The waitress cradled the underside of her nose in the web of her right hand and was gripping her face as if to keep it from falling apart. "Oooh," she said. "Nooh."

"It's all right," Meyers said. "I was leaving anyway."

"They might fire me," said the waitress from behind her hand, as if holding a mute to the bell of her horn.

"No," Meyers said. "I was leaving. And it wasn't your fault anyway."

"Yeah," she said. "But, as you know, or maybe you don't—that doesn't always matter. Gee, that is such a nice suit." Her hand slid down to her throat, revealing her face, a broad, Slavic thing. "I'm so sorry."

"Thanks," Meyers said.

"Thanks?" she said.

"For noticing," he said. "The suit."

"Yeah, but. . . I just started out here. On the floor. I'm not too good with that tray." The waitress knelt to gather her fallen glasses.

"It's all right," Meyers said, backing away. "I was on my way out. I probably would have changed anyway."

"But the stain," said the waitress with a stricken look. "My mom loves that stuff, so I do at least know how to get those stains out." She stood and nodded significantly toward the bowels of the facility. "Whenever they serve food," she said, "I come in and wash dishes. I do at least know my way around back there. There's a first aid kit."

"First aid?" said Meyers.

"Hydrogen peroxide. That and some dish soap—works great. But you have to get it right away. *Before* it can set."

The waitress led him back to a big but seldom used kitchen where she became authoritative and flipped on a single bank of shuddering fluorescent tubes; Meyers followed her along a row of empty stainless-steel counters through a resonant room; her back made him think 'wood chopper,' a term from out of nowhere to encompass this stout, compact, responsible person whose legs in the black trousers of her uniform were short and serviceable. A woman. A young woman only trying to do her job, and maybe even hold onto it, and Meyers followed her, dutifully brushing away inappropriate thoughts. They came to a tiny office where she located a white plastic case and within that, "This probably'll do it. It's only alcohol, but we better try it. And I'm for sure where I can find some detergent. Got gobs of detergent back here."

She led him then toward a deep sink, explaining, "So, I have to get it wet. You don't mind? If we get it wet? I think the fabric will be okay, if. . . well, I don't know. But we've got to get that out."

Meyers did mind, but it happened this was his favorite suit, and the waitress had convinced him she was its only hope of salvation. He slipped off the jacket, handed it to her, and said, "What was your name?"

"My?" she said. "Name? You mean for the, I mean for the. . ."

"I just would like to know your name," Meyers said.

"Oh," she said, abashed. "Well, uh, it's Betty. So, uh, yeah—Betty. Sorry, I thought you were maybe going to, you know, complain."

"No," he said. Though Meyers knew he wasn't generous, she was letting him feel that way.

"Betty," she said again. "Right?"

"Right?" he said.

"I mean, kind of old fashioned, isn't it? For these days? Always seems old fashioned to me. I like it, but, you know."

"Well, I'm an Alan," said Meyers. "Like from out of Sherwood Forest or something. So, you could say I'm extremely old fashioned. Medieval." Not only old fashioned, he thought, but simply old. He would seem old to her.

"Pleased to meet you," said Betty. "Okay. Here's how we do this. Like I say, I'm not sure if alcohol is exactly right. Who knows, maybe I'll blow us up."

She made a paste of the alcohol and some of the granular detergent used to feed the industrial dishwasher hulking nearby. Betty used a stiff bristled brush to drive this mixture into the stained fabric; Meyers was pleased to see her not apply this treatment to the satin lining inside, though that was also subjected to the paste where wine had leaked through. Meyers noticed her hands, red and violated, they were not new to this kind of work. Staring upon those stains, as if by sheer intention to clean them, Betty said, "So, I take it you graduated from here. From Valley."

"I actually finished out my degree at the conservatory. But they gave me a diploma from here, too."

"Like for stars?" she said.

"Stars?" he said. "Oh. No. For music. That kind of conservatory. I was a musician. I *am* a musician. It's what I do."

"Man," she said. "That must be fun."

From the mouths of babes. Fun was the best and truest thing to be said of his occupation, and he knew fun to be an especially rare commodity in this town. "Yeah," he said, deeply grateful now, "it is. Fun."

Betty pulled down an overhanging high-pressure

nozzle and blasted the jacket until all her cleaning agent had been rinsed away. She held it up, and, though Meyers could see nothing of the original red stain, Betty prepared and applied another batch of her cleaner. "I'm in school myself," she said. "I'm what they call a towny."

"I was, too." Meyers said.

"You probably know a lot of people here," Betty said.

"You would think," he said. "But when I was here, I was always at work or practicing, playing my horn, which is what I do, and I, I had a real bad case of acne, too. Not much of a social life. None, to be more accurate. Except for the band, and then only when we were actually playing."

"Acne?"

"Then," said Meyers, "I discovered the wonders of a plant-based diet. And then, dermabrasion."

"Gee," said Betty. "That worked out pretty good."

"Clean," said Meyers, going so far as to stroke his cheek, "and smooth. Expensive, but it was worth it." Truth be told, he'd made his way to this event to crow and preen a bit, and now here was this poor young woman as if she'd been served up by room service to hear his boasting. Meyers thought to stop before he disgusted himself, and he asked her, "What are you studying?"

"Accounting."

"You like it?"

"Accounting?" she said. "Wanna hear a little secret? No one likes accounting. No. One. And out of all those people who don't like it, I like it about the least. Man, I'd rather, I'd rather do *this*." She blasted the second batch of cleanser from the jacket, which she then inspected in and out and at arm's length to announce, "That wine is *outta* there. See?"

Meyers saw no remnant of the wine but a great wide wet spot. He nodded.

"I think it'll be all right," she said. "You'd have to get it dry cleaned, dry cleaned and pressed, but, and believe me, I've had quite a bit of experience, it should be fine."

"You know," said Meyers, "I never intended to. . . say anything. It was an accident pure and simple, and not even your fault at that."

"Oh, I know," said Betty. "It's just, that suit. Be a shame to—it's a really nice suit."

"Thanks," said Meyers. "Again. And I'm glad you like it, Betty."

"We better do your pants," she said.

"My. . .?"

"Pants," she said. "They got it worse than the jacket."

"That's not. That wouldn't be necessary."

"What do you mean?" she said. "It's a suit. Two parts. They go together."

"Uhm," said Meyers, "how. . .?"

"Well," she said, "you'll have to take 'em off."

"Oh," said Meyers, "I uh. . ."

"You're wearing underwear, aren't you? There's no reason to be shy. I mean, I'm not shy."

"No," said Meyers. "I mean *yes*, I *am* wearing underwear, but, uh. . ."

"Or," Betty suggested, "you could go in the walk-in freezer there, and take 'em off. Hand 'em out to me. If that's more comfortable."

"Is it?" Meyers said. "It's cold in there?"

"Very." she said. "Has to be. They had a thing last week that was supposed to happen but didn't, and there was part of a cow left over. Big part. Wanna keep that thing frozen for sure." Her eyes were hazel and somewhat far apart, her brow heavy but not unattractively so. "But, like I say," she said, "there's no reason to be shy."

Meyers submitted to the freezer plan and soon found

himself stripped to his boxer shorts and the gartered socks that had seemed so stylish before he revealed them. He looked down upon knees clad in stippled chicken flesh and drawn together against the chill. That carcass hung nearby, half a beef hanging from its hindquarters and stretched out in its perpetual sprint and frosted. In this light, Meyers thought, this harsh and frozen light, his were an old man's knees, and there at the end of his preposterous legs his even more preposterous and formerly handsome calfskin boots. Meyers was not long in thinking that he'd somehow been locked in the freezer, and he began bobbing up and down, bobbing on creaky knees to stay warm and wondering why he hadn't thought to wait in the perfectly warm office, and he might at any point have pushed the plunger, the extra obvious means of opening that freezer door from within; Meyers did not wish to seem afraid, though, especially because he was so foolishly afraid, and he didn't want to offend Betty-this Betty had made quite an impression on him. He couldn't have said how opening the door might offend her or why he should worry if it did.

Meyers huddled near the carcass thinking that a thing like this would probably never happen to a man with fully developed social skills. He couldn't bring himself to open the door or to quit wondering about it, and though he remained upright he drew himself up into a nearly fetal position in which he soon began to shiver. When it came, Betty's knock at the door was barely audible through all that metal and insulation, and whatever she was saying out there only a dim humming. Meyers pushed the plunger, the door opened just as he knew and did not know that it would, and he was presented with his pants.

"Thanks," he said, retreating back into the freezer to put them on. A garment with no warmth but another layer of cold in it. Having made of his modesty a completely silly thing, he stepped out of the freezer, still shivering, still obliged to wrap his arms around himself.

"Oh, gee," said Betty. "Are you all right? Maybe that wasn't such a good idea. Sorry I took so long. But they look good, don't you think? The pants?"

"I hadn't noticed," said Meyers. He looked down. "Oh, yeah. Fine."

"Are you all right?"

"I will be when I can get out of these wet things. I need to get up to my room."

"That smell," said Betty. "I'm sure that'll go away after a while. Isopropyl. Smells like you had a lot, a lot of vodka. What's so funny?"

"I was going to make an impression," Meyers said. "You know. I thought I'd make an impression." He'd been thinking fondly of his room, the warmth and clean clothing to be had there, but then he'd thought of making his way to it, and then more specifically of making his way back through the Big River Room, where, he thought, he might finally be worthy of notice, where he'd wear the stigma without the release of lots and lots of vodka and he'd leave droplets from his pants legs on the grim old carpet. "An impression," he said, nodding toward his collected classmates. "Wow."

"Oh," said Betty, full of discernment. "What do they care? Lot of 'em are not in the best shape themselves out there. Some of 'em are kind of weeping in their beer already. Hollering. What do they care?"

"They probably don't," said Meyers. "But I do. Care. Even if I should know better. I don't know why."

"Oh, I get it," Betty said. "Townies, right?"

There had grown between them a sense of conspiracy or an understanding. "Yeah, that has something to do with it, but they're the townies now, some of them, so I should be, I don't know, I. . . It doesn't make any sense. Never has. I just really do not want to go out there. Wet and stinky and everything, maybe kind of suspicious looking. I do not thrive here. It's always been that way."

"I got you," said Betty.

"In fact," said Meyers. "I think the way things have worked out—it was just the perfect reminder, of how. . . But I really don't want to go out there."

"No," said Betty. "I've got you. I do at least know my way around back here. Come on."

There was a store room at the back of the building, and at the back of that a freight elevator housed in a rough wooden cage. Betty said, "I've been working here since before it was even legal. I was too young. Juvenile dishwasher, I was. They used to have me back here a lot, too. Stocking, stacking. Fifteen. Now, this thing they haven't used in quite a while. It doesn't work that great. But it works. What floor you on?"

"Top," said Meyers, still bragging a little.

"I can get you up to three, anyway," she said. "It goes up to the third floor. Then you could go up the stair well. As I happen to know because they left me back here alone, and I was fifteen, sixteen, and you know, you check things out. You can ride this thing."

The elevator's cables were naked within its cage, the car suspended somewhere above them. "It's for freight," Meyers said.

"Yeah," said Betty. "But you can ride it. If you want to. If you wanted to avoid those. . . It's up to you."

She had pressed a large red button and a motor somewhere hummed. The elevator car began, almost imperceptibly, to descend toward them. Meyers had a long time to back out if he wished to, a wait long enough to require some chat, so he said, "You should probably change your major. If that's how you feel about it. It really does help to do something you like doing."

"I guess it would," said Betty. "But I live with my dad. My *mom* and dad. I kind of have to. For them it's down to this or dental hygienist or something. Get a job *right* away."

"But if you hate it," said Meyers.

"Yeah, I probably will change," said Betty. "Eventually. When I figure out what I would like to do. Or how to do nothing, huh? I don't know. With work and everything, I have hard time keeping up, much less making any changes."

"It's a slog," said Meyers. "I remember—work and school. I worked at the Rocket in high school and right on into college. Worked there 'til I left."

"The drive in?" she said.

"Yep. They change the grease in their fryer once a year whether they need to or not. People just loved it."

"My little boy loves it," said Betty. "It's where we go for a special treat. But I did wonder why I always. . . Yeah, I guess I knew it wasn't real healthy."

The elevator car had descended at last to their level and landed heavily there despite its near absence of velocity. Betty wrestled with some planking of the cage, saying, "This thing has got thoroughly screwed up."

"Oh?" said Meyers. "Well, you think it's safe?"

"I think so," said Betty. "Yeeah—it should be." She had pried open an access to the elevator car which was hardly more than a dumbwaiter, and not especially well enclosed. "Hop on."

Meyers stepped onto the platform, and Betty stepped on beside him, explaining, "The thing you open up there to get out of this, you've got to open it from the inside, which means you've got to close it from the inside, and if you don't, if you leave it open, then they've got this idiot security guy—Darryl—anyway, I'll just ride up and close the door behind you."

He felt her breath on his face; it smelled of peppermint.

"You think it can handle all this?"

"Well," she said, "it's a freight elevator. We wouldn't amount to all that much freight, would we? Even the two of us?"

This seemed an existential question to Meyers, who had not yet entirely quit shivering. Betty pressed a green button, and they began their ascent. Weighted, rising, the elevator car traveled even more slowly than it had coming down to them. The motor, wherever it was, whatever it was, sounded as if it might be unequal to the task, and very soon Meyers began to consider the likelihood once again that he was trapped; something in the works just had to be slipping for this little platform to rise so slowly. Betty's hair fell over her shoulder and was that kind of hair that is attractive of its own accord, without a lot of treatments. A nice shade of brown. Her face, with its blunt nose, was frank and within inches of his own, and Meyers, for all Betty's seeming openness, had no idea what she was thinking, or, for that matter what he was thinking. Breathe, he thought. But better not too laboriously. Right there in her face. The motor groaned on. They tried not to examine each other, but within that darkened shaft some inspection was inevitable.

"It's real slow," she said. "I think that's why they quit using it."

Now there was an intimacy, hard to say what kind. Meyers remembered his quaking, chicken-skin knees and ruled out one possibility. Her little boy. She would have had a child when she was herself only a tall child. There was a sweet melting in him and Meyers felt protective of young Betty, but he knew this almost at once for yet another vain and unpromising proposition. The motor groaned on, reluctantly lifting them.

"So," she said. "Do you come back? You ever come back here? Visit your family?"

"They left shortly after I did," Meyers said. "What they were waiting for, I'll never know. Then they went down and found a place just about as bad in Florida."

"So, you don't, you wouldn't have any reason to. . . be around? Ever? This area?"

"This is the first time," Meyers said. "First time I've been back since I left, since I went off to school. Real school. And, as we see once again—I do not thrive here. So."

"Yeah," she said. "I can see that. But you learned how to play that—what was it?"

"Trumpet," he said. "Flugelhorn, and euphonium now. I'm your all-around brass man."

"And they pay you for that, right?"

"Pay me pretty well," Meyers said.

"You are so lucky," she said.

"It wasn't all luck," said Meyers.

"No," she said. "I didn't mean that. You're lucky to be doing something that. . . That wouldn't be rock and roll, would it? With a trumpet?"

"I can play anything your heart desires," said Meyers. "But, usually, no, it wouldn't be rock. In fact, I'm going up to Canada next to lay in some Bach."

"I didn't remember," said Betty. "That it was so dark in here. It is really dark."

Disoriented some by the dark and worried about vertigo, Meyers set his hands high on Betty's hips, as if they were chastely dancing. Her breath smelled of peppermint. His breath was even, he thought, and he happened to recall that card that had invited him here, 'Making NEW Memories.' The car bumped to a stop.

"Oh, oh," said Betty. "Looks like they boarded up the door." She pulled at the boards, and Meyers felt her moving against him. She managed to work one of the boards free, but almost tumbled off the platform when it gave way. Meyers caught her. He was still breathing evenly, but heavily now as if all that exertion had been his. He braced her as she pulled another board free. Betty reached through to the door she'd mentioned and fiddled with something until she'd opened it. "Really dark in here," she said. "You think you can crawl through there? Looks like that's as big as we can make that hole. Be a shame to rip that suit or something after all. . ."

"I think I can do it," Meyers said. He crawled through the small gap she'd made in the boarded closure, trying not to be inflexible. He worked his way through, and came out backward, and onto his back in a long, comparatively brilliant hallway. "He is reborn," he said.

"Good," said Betty.

"Thanks," said Meyers, peering through the gap from which he'd just emerged.

"Yeah," she said. "Good luck in Canada."

"You know," he told her. "There was one other thing I learned when I was here: How to be lonely."

"Oh?" said Betty.

"And. . ."

Betty closed the doors of the elevator shaft and said something that was obscured with the noise of the motor beginning to deliver her back down.

"And," said Meyers, "you don't want to do that. That is the last thing you want to learn."

Dog Bone

Miranda heard it twice in the emergency room: She had been so lucky. Puncture wounds, yes, broken flesh, but how neatly those teeth had avoided hurting tendon and bone. A shot, some stitches, some pain pills if she wanted. No rabies. First a bearded man, then a brisk woman, both of them in their lab coats and so pleased to tell her that with a little rest she was going to be fine. Miranda might have told them that if they'd ever been bitten they would know she was not going to be fine any time soon. That much adrenaline can just about burst a woman's heart. She might have told them that she'd never known rest to solve anything.

◊ ◊ ◊

In high school she had tried to break into at least one social circle by joining the cross-country team, a group that would accept anyone willing to suffer. During her first season on the team Miranda ran the many miles far behind her teammates, panting, awkward, alone again, but the loneliness out on the road was of a better variety, and by year two Miranda had caught up to the pack that ran together in training; by the end of that year she ran well ahead of them, alone again but by choice, complete of herself, and those spooling miles became a source and a symptom of a willfulness that was to serve her well can cost her dearly.

At thirty-five her limbs were corded, her face weathered and defined, and she had yet to enjoy much popularity. She needed her run more than ever.

◊ ◊ ◊

Some years earlier her father, the widowed Edwin, had gone through a soulful period and bought himself a cottage in a remote little town where he meant to retire early and come to some understanding of himself, but Dad didn't come to that understanding before he could move into his retreat. He'd understood instead that he would never voluntarily retire, and never to the podunk town he'd chosen. He was a pediatrician, a cultured bon vivant; what more was there to know or want? People are so smitten with a practicing kiddie doctor, and he had acquired a girlfriend, so Edwin did not retire, and he had given Miranda the little house in the remote little town because his daughter was a single mother who needed all the help she could get.

Though it meant commuting an hour either way to her work, Miranda had lived there ever since with Opal, or as Opal would say, "*I* live here. Mom kind of visits." Opal, who had somehow become quite the young lady and who had a point. All through the winter months her mother left for work in the dark and came home in the dark, and in all seasons she came home diminished, but they were as deeply at home in that house as cave dwellers. Free, but for taxes, it was the only housing they could easily afford, and Opal knew and was known to almost everyone in town. Miranda felt reasonably good about stashing her daughter there.

◊ ◊ ◊

Miranda had sacrificed most of her youth to a rare act of youthful foolishness; she had got pregnant by a boy she knew even then for a puff of smoke—anyone who thought to call themselves Dub—She not only should have known better, she did know better. Dull and distant Dub who, beyond providing a brief thrill and an enduring miracle, had never succeeded in anything except to be forgotten by those few who should have remembered him.

◊ ◊ ◊

As Assistant County Attorney for a county where she did not reside, Miranda was assigned to handle all the shitty little crimes, and fish and game matters, and occasions when the state was fumbling around in some broken family's troubles. Perforce, Miranda had something to say almost every working day about people taking responsibility. She was completely serious in this, for of all the misdeeds she met with in her work, one bothered her the most—hardly anyone in these courts would accept responsibility for anything. Miranda was big on responsibility. People are so apt to inhabit what isn't, and apart from the dangers in this strategy, it was so maddeningly stupid to Miranda, who believed in paying the price.

Oscar Wolf, for instance; the man had come to court, to a sentencing where he knew he would be taken into custody. A florid fifty-year-old in a floral shirt, a head full of orange curls, and the evasive manner of the constant offender, he owed the state at least thirteen months upon his fifth conviction for drunk driving. Miranda stood to argue for more. Those five convictions meant in her mind that Mr. Wolf had probably conducted almost all his activities impaired, usually without being caught. She couldn't mention unproven crimes to the court, but she was free to draw the inference. "Your Honor," she said, "Mr. Wolf is just dangerous. The pre-sentence report mentions his history of messing with ankle monitors and interlock systems, and he's missed a slew of appointments and breath tests. If he spent half the effort getting better that he does to avoid getting caught, we wouldn't be here. We're not talking about one bad choice, Your Honor, it's a life of them."

From the corner of her eye, she happened to see the Defendant grinning, a slyness, a sort of acknowledgment briefly leaking through his fake regret.

Miranda insisted, "Mr. Wolf is dangerous, and the longer he's in jail, the safer we'll all be. Mr. Wolf says he wants to change, but he's never taken the first step in that direction, so it's hard to put much faith in his sincerity. He needs a lot of time to think about this."

At her urging, the judge passed down two years of prison to Oscar Wolf, who as he was being led away stared at Miranda in a way that might signal threat, respect, anything. Leaving the court room, Miranda felt as she often did after such episodes, justified, but also the bitch in the too-tight skirt. This dress imposed a funny, scissoring walk on her as did the high heels she wore only to court. Then, at her right shoulder and just behind, she heard "Hey. Hey, little lady."

Oscar Wolf's wife had a rasping voice suggesting that she too had long liked her drink. "What do you think?" she asked as Miranda turned to her. "You think now he'll be fixed?"

Whatever the Wolfs were drinking gave them very vivid complexions. Inflamed, Mrs. Wolf tilted her head in the manner of a puzzled dog. "Huh, *laaahdy*? All you've done is fuck everything up. *Every*thing. So, I hope you're proud of yourself."

Miranda had been. Proud. Or at least a little accomplished. Only a moment before.

◊ ◊ ◊

In theory her drive home from work, a pretty drive, much of it a long a lake, was her time to unwind. Miranda's responsibilities, however, followed her almost everywhere, and the drive time either way, coming or going, was more prone to stewing than relaxation. She was always driving toward something left undone.

This week's principal mess had to do with Opal being asked to the prom. She was only fourteen. Miranda had wanted to object but saw that she couldn't without implying that she did not trust her daughter. Miranda could not afford to trust the world or certain large portions of it, and she didn't necessarily want to inflict this on her child, but who had ever successfully sunk any faith in boys? Opal was too young. And Opal, that lovely thing, had much to do with Miranda's mistrust of lust. Miranda herself had only finally been asked to a prom as a senior in high school when she was already quite thoroughly over it, so maybe she was only a little jealous. Maybe. Who knew the evil, the vanity that lurks in women's hearts? Jealous? This was how Miranda's thoughts often ran in the car, one consideration butting up against another until she'd convinced herself that whatever she might do, it must be a little wrong. Miranda had consented to the prom but only on the condition that she would chaperone the couple the whole time.

Her daughter, the good, dear Opal said of this plan, "*Now* you want to spend time with me? On a *date*?"

Miranda had been unable to back away from her position even after Opal had argued pretty successfully that it was ridiculous. Opal was in some ways the more mature of them, and she was often in possession of the better argument, though she had never trained for it.

◊ ◊ ◊

Miranda liked to run a dirt road that twisted into the sere hills behind her house, run up onto ground that sometimes grazed cows and nearly always fed mule deer; it was a long, steady prayer, a cleansing going up this road, then a jarring but effortless descent, and along the way she had every kind of country to consider, high prairie, forest, farmland, sharp gray peaks off to the east, and her village near at hand, there at her feet like worn carpet. After work and on weekends, Miranda would run this road to a certain cattleguard, and she had once timed these runs but then thought better of it and left at home the device she'd used to record her time, distance, and heart rate. The whole idea of it, really, was to record these things herself, to abandon herself to her own simple rhythms.

◊ ◊ ◊

There is nothing so pathetic and desolate as twisted crepe paper in a high school gymnasium. A woman with duck's bill lips had been hired for the occasion with a machine that pumped monotonous, industrial music along with a light show, swirling beads of light like flights of fireflies coursing round the room. These lights were enough to make people fall out sick. Then too, that scent that clings to old gymnasiums of sweat and liniment and shellac. Despite herself, Miranda was somewhat pleased that the prom was such a dud this year. At least this way the ruined evening wouldn't be entirely her fault; a thing so dismal as this had required a real group effort. Those lights, perfumes from long stoppered bottles, a bit of nausea for everyone tonight. Miranda tried to tell herself this would have been awful even if she hadn't insisted on coming.

◊ ◊ ◊

She had come against medical advice, against the doctor's strong suggestion that she stay off her feet and keep the wound site clean and elevated as much as possible. Miranda came against her daughter's pleading, pleading that continued right up until they got out of the car at Darren's place. Opal had been saying, "What you do, Mom, you think stubborn is brave. That's a mistake you make. They're not the same thing, Mom."

"But they are," said Miranda. A lot of times they are about the same thing. Or one needs the other. You'll see."

"Oh, no," Opal said. "You're not doing that to me. Because I am not going to see. Okay? Oh, look at you. If you start bleeding, I am going to be really. . . Aw, *Mom*."

Then Darren was at the door wearing a skinny tie and a grave look it seemed he'd selected for use throughout the evening. He bore a corsage. His mother had also come to the door and was rapturous just behind him, still half a head taller than her boy. "Ooohpal," she said. "Girl, you are so gorgeous."

Precociously beautiful, Opal was spectacular. There had been much feminine fussing in their house that week to achieve that end, though in Miranda's opinion none of it was necessary. Opal's friends and a former babysitter had been clucking around, discussing makeup, hairstyles, and shoes. Miranda had almost no part in this. It was not her expertise. Having never had much in the way of breasts herself, she had no idea how best to situate full ones like Opal's in a prom dress.

"Here," said Darren's mother. "Honey, I'd better. . ." She relieved her son of the corsage and pinned it to Opal's dress. The good mother appraised her work and said, "Great. Okaaay. Well, you guys have a magical time." None of prom party attempted a response. Finally, as they were making their way across the lawn to the car, walking three abreast, Opal did find voice to explain, "Mom got bit by a dog. Today. She just had to. . . So she gets bit by a dog. To*day*. That also explains the pants suit, I guess. I mean, lime *green*? So, you got yourself in a dog bite and pants suit deal. Sorry."

Darren hummed a sympathetic 'm', and then nothing more was said between them in the car or in the walk from the car to the gymnasium, a walk during which Miranda could no longer conceal her limp. They went in through the haunted trophy cases.

And now here they were among those whirling lights, Miranda's ankle entertaining two pains at once, the bright pain at the new holes in her, and the hot, dull ache of a swollen leg. They come in as a trio, a discrete little cluster standing at a spot that Darren described as the elbow. He was a basketball player and that was all the information he thought to offer or solicit. No world beater, Darren. Opal seemed to think highly of him, though, and Miranda was just as happy that her daughter had no obvious interest in bad boys.

Maybe embarrassment had made poor Darren mute, or maybe he'd chosen silence because he knew nearly every thought that passed through his head was inappropriate.

They didn't dance. No one except a semicircle of semi attractive girls weaving arrhythmically down by the far foul line did anything like dancing. Miranda recalled her father remarking how her own generation didn't dance. It had been true of her, at least; no dancing. They were approached from time to time by Opal's various friends, but none of them stayed long or had very much to say beyond some initial gushing. If both dancing and talking were out of fashion now, what was the point of a prom? What, after all, could Miranda possibly ruin here?

But poor Darren. After all. And poor, dear Opal who had the good grace to find this bad dance funny. Darren remained so very earnest. Earlier that evening he'd given himself his first shave; there were visible nicks from it. Miranda saw that with each of Opal's kind gestures toward the boy he was more than soothed. Darren couldn't know she was kind to everyone. Darren was in love, just as he should be.

Miranda did not deserve her daughter. This realization rolled around from time to time with varying effect on Miranda's mood and self-esteem. Miranda also realized, and painfully, that her shadow over this thing had wrecked it for these children. She was too old. Having never escaped the uncertainties of childhood herself, she was too old.

◊ ◊ ◊

She was running again before the bandages were off, and the bandages pressed stinging sweat into her wounds, so there was something to be said for the proposition that Miranda was stubborn. She thought she had already made more than enough concessions. She was only running on the flat, and she wasn't running her favorite route because it included the lane where she had been bitten. The dog was there.

She particularly valued a half mile section of that road that ran straight and steadily uphill and which, when run at a certain rate was a perfect dose of oxygen and endorphins—and in that condition the broad view from the top of the lane was especially rewarding. Along that lane there were only two houses, and they were spaced far apart and on opposite sides of the road, and until recently only one of them had been inhabited. Lately Miranda had been noting the empty place showing signs of occupation, a car, a pickup, a mobile hot dog stand, a plastic dome of a doghouse, the black stench of an active burn pit. Miranda had been running by, telling herself it was wrong of her to regret this, that people needed to live somewhere. Until the dog.

She had never encountered people along this stretch, including those who had lived here all along. Even the animals hereabout were distant and indifferent, so the lane of all places was where a woman might feel comfortably alone. Until that dog. Until that Sunday morning.

Early that morning Miranda had been in an argument concerning hairspray, and when listing all the things she disliked about it, she mentioned how it made pretty hair, natural hair, ugly. And Opal had taken this very hard, so Miranda was out pounding up the lane when she first saw it running parallel with her on the other side of a barb-wire fence. Coyote. No, too stout. Dog. Nose down as if to make itself aerodynamic and sprinting by. It rocketed on to the next opening in the fence where it turned with comic urgency, skidding, and onto the road, and then it was coming at her.

Miranda had little time to consider; it had never slacked its pace and was closing fast, a middling dog, middling size, middling coat; splotchy, rusted iron coloring. She tried to read its face for intention, gauged the impossibility of retreat—even if she were to turn downhill again she would never outrun this dog. It came on and sprinted past her, and in that moment Miranda thought it was after something. Else. But then it made another of those crazy turns, whirled in a way that set gravel flying under it, and it came running back at Miranda who told herself that everything was fine, that she'd been selected for an audience by a playful mutt, maybe off its leash, careening around full of joy. Its freedom. There was no snarling or barking, and Miranda kept running along her way, telling herself she would be fine, but glancing back. If she'd read the dog's expression right as it had flashed by her, there was no malice in it but a madcap fixity in its eyes, the kind some comics wear.

So, there was no particular warning, though she couldn't think later that she hadn't been forewarned. Still silent, its lips had rolled up only in the moment it bit, a brief image about to have a long life in Miranda's memory.

◊ ◊ ◊

Right from the bite it had seemed necessary not to overreact, and though the jolt of it had been immense,

Miranda had run halfway home before she stopped to peel down her reddening sock and see about the damage. There was a blood pudding at her ankle and fresh blood still oozing out, there was a spell of wooziness on seeing it, but she had mile and a half left to run to the house, and beyond that a drive twenty-five miles to the nearest emergency room. Nothing for it but to run, to drive. Miranda had collected herself and calmly, or calmly enough gotten herself treated and gone that evening to the prom.

◊ ◊ ◊

Because her Achilles tendon was inflamed she was forced on runs that didn't involve much gain or loss in elevation. No hills. There were more, not fewer dogs on the flat, and Miranda now found that when in passing she set these town dogs to barking she would nearly always flinch, though by rights it should have been quiet dogs she feared. She made some kind of point by healing rapidly without giving her injury much rest, and soon enough she was fit to run any terrain again. She had close access to timbered mountains that were a maze of old logging roads offering all the climbing a runner might ever want but generally not much view. She ran up in the gloomy timber; she ran the streets of her town, flinching as necessary. She bought bear spray at a sporting goods store that she could wear holstered at her hip, and when she strapped it on, it seemed to her that she was hearing a lot less barking when she ran through town, as if her confidence or menace had preceded her. She'd been assured this was devastating bear spray. Still, all healed and holstered, she had not returned to running her lane. Her lane. She had come to think of it as hers now that she'd been warned off it.

Researching, Miranda pulled up images of hundreds of different breeds to see what breed her bad dog might be, but it didn't resemble too closely any of these. Given its size and mottled markings, though, and being in cattle country, it was probably some kind of mongrel working dog. Miranda decided the bite was most likely from the instinctive arsenal of a herding dog, but it might come of an older instinct, the wolf making its first move on dinner. The Achilles heel. The vulnerable part. Miranda wanted to understand, because now, belatedly, Miranda was overreacting, and the longer she stayed away from that lane of hers, the worse she felt; she felt she had a responsibility not to be warned off anything, or at least not a public roadway, and the cure for her anger and reticence would be to run on up there, but for a long time she didn't go.

One day on her way out the door she happened to see herself reflected in the living room window, a sleek person with a broad black band at her waist, another at her thigh—that holster—and she thought, 'What am I afraid of?'

Its teeth, she thought, heading back toward her lane. The pain, certainly, though now the immediacy of that was over. No. The bright white image. The sudden revelation of a well disguised evil. Evil is as evil does, and hadn't those teeth gone deep the moment they were revealed. Such a memory launches and sustains a certain suspicion in a woman, a case of the yips Miranda didn't wish to live with. Public road, she thought again and again, and she ran on to face her fear, and as she ran her ambition ripened into a thirst for revenge: Might be fun to see how it like some bear spray up its nose, see how it liked *its* tender parts attacked.

As Miranda turned up the lane there was a pounding aggression in her stride; she liked this very much. The dog's place was at the lower end of the lane, and she hadn't run very long before she reached it, and at first it seemed there would be no new encounter. Miranda hated fretting about nothing. She was disappointed because she had gone from fearing another toothy event to wanting one. 'Let it come.'

◊ ◊ ◊

Everything that happened seemed to happen so quietly.

◊ ◊ ◊

They were behind a collapsing old shed, right behind it so that Miranda didn't see them until she had run a little way past it. The dog. Her rusty mongrel. Still not a sound out of it even though, as Miranda soon understood, it was being whipped. The dog, haunches up, forepaws and chin down, and this might be taken for a playful posture, but this was not play. The dog was being whipped, making no attempt to run away, and the man was quietly whipping it with an orange extension cord. His hat had fallen off. He did not need to explain himself to the dog, or yell at it. He was workmanlike, steadily swinging that cord, aiming the hard end at its head. The dog did at least duck, but there was no barking or backing away.

All this exceeded Miranda's understanding. She stopped and stood and watched them, and neither dog nor man noticed her there. She, too, was silent. But then she was running again, running at them, running in through the gate, and even in a rush she did not cease to calculate; she may have committed trespass at least, running onto that property, and now the man had seen her coming and stopped, cord dangling from his hand, mouth ajar, oddly pleasant eyes. Still not a thing to say for himself. The dog, still cringing, looked up and askance at her. Still a risk to bite, she thought. Her thoughts came on fast, for she quickly dismissed them as she ran. Trespass, she thought. Assault. Her hand went to her holster. Her weapon. Felony assault. She even thought to check for any discernible breeze and make sure she wouldn't be spraying into it.

What I Owe

I've always got a note coming due. On a limpalong place like the Three Bar you work three hundred and sixty-five days a year or you go under, and chances are pretty good you'll go belly up anyway, no matter how much you work. Every ten years or so, somebody wants to foreclose on you. See, nothing about the economics of it favors a small cow/calf operation—you buy retail, sell wholesale, pay the freight both ways, and I doubt it's ever been a good idea in America to try and be a smalltime cowboy. Price of beef keeps going up at the butcher counter, going down at the sale barn, and that's just one of many things I do not understand. I've lost stock to wolves and weather and scours, seen years where it hardly rained at all, and that's still nothing compared to the toll the market takes on this outfit. They'd run you out of it, if they could. It's better than a real job, I guess. It's kept me out of trouble. Mostly. So far.

The way it's worked out, I've been out here my whole life; I could tell you pretty easy how I got here, be a lot harder to explain how or why I've stayed. This is where they brought us home from the hospital, Dirk and Danita and me. I was a couple years younger than the twins; now they've both been retired for quite some time, cops, and I'm still fixing fence. They get pretty misty sometimes, with their pensions, talking about the good old days on the Three Bar, and good old L.R., and good old Mom and those fresh cookies she supposedly used to bake. Course, they're remembering something that never was, but let 'em. It was all pretty wonderful, but you notice they were both off the place the minute they left high school. They were the sensible ones. Anyway, when I was sixteen we were up on that leased ground one day, me and L.R., up there where it goes right from bog to pure rock, where it's still impossible to keep a fence stood up, and something had run through the wire again, and I'm rolling up barb wire, and I see L.R.'s in a thoughtful mood, which is always dangerous, and when I get back in the Ranchero he has me pull the fifth of Julius P. Kessler out of the jockey box. "Buy me a drink," he says. He chugs some, and this time he tells me I better take a hit, too, it's kind of a ceremony or his idea of one, and he tells me the place is mine if I want it. When he's gone. Well, I was the only one left still around, so that really wasn't much of an announcement. I do still remember it, though. When he was gone—neither one of us had any idea how soon that would be.

Wasn't a month later L.R. rolls the stock truck off Markle Hill, running empty at least, and he gets thrown out and squished in the rocks. He would've been about the same level of drunk he'd always been. So, there I was, and here I still am, king of the Three Bar, lock stock and barrel—and mortgage papers. By now I've lasted a lot longer on the place than L.R. did. Most of those boys from that generation never made it out of their fifties, back then it was old soldiers and cowhands and Kootenais around here, and all those boys tended to live real hard; L.R. never went anywhere under a hundred miles an hour if he could help it, and if they'd had those gizmos that test your breath back then, he would've blown their minds. They liked to live fast and die young way out West, which probably isn't the worst deal.

Now, here I am—old—and I still haven't solved any of the old problems, and I got the new problem of being old, and I've spent too much time out here getting strange, talking to critters who aren't interested, and I've been getting superstitious, too, been noticing how things come at me in threes. I've put three roofs on the old house. Run three strains of beef cattle. Tried three wives out here, had three kids. Three Bar. You spend so much time alone, and you make yourself superstitious. Now it's my third warning from the bank, and this is the third time it's got as far as the third warning, and this time I get the feeling they're serious. It's my sixty irrigated acres down by the reservoir; somebody wants those pretty bad.

Already sold off my four-wheeler and my roping horse, got calves on the ground but there's no market around here for veal, and I'm strapped, got the answering machine turned off, and who shows up but Cornelius Left Hand. And what does he bring but meat, like that's what I need. He's got yet another woman with him, a presentable one this time, and he's on the run—again. He's a good hand, so I've always let him use the place for a hideout. Generally, he'll bring game, and smoking dope, some stories, and he knows how to make himself useful. All his exes are still in the area, they're roaming the rez, and they give him trouble, and to this day he keeps playing hide and seek with his probation officer, and he's got some pissy thing going with the Finleys over on the other side that turns nasty sometimes. Cornelius claims he's a holy man, and he's right for all I know, but he also claims he's a pacifist and then he goes and gets involved in shooting scrapes. I do wish he'd show up sometimes with tomatoes or coffee. I tell him he's getting a little old for this kind of thing, I'm bitching how we appear to have got old without solving the old problems, and, worse, we haven't learned any new tricks in a long, long time—and I'm mentioning all this when Cornelius says we should probably rob the casino. If I feel like trying something new. He was under the impression the casino had swindled his aunty.

The woman he'd brought, Madeline was her name, she'd been to a community college somewhere and had a thingus in her nose, little pearly thing stuck in it, and she thought armed robbery was a fine idea. "It's what outlaws do," she says.

I tell her I wouldn't know. Tell her I'm not an outlaw, and I've got no ambitions that way, and wasn't I just saying how I'm old?

"The time has come," Cornelius says.

We go way back, all the way back to junior high and comic book days, and Cornelius has never quite got over thinking of himself as a superhero. An avenger. He likes things dramatic. "They're crooked," he says. When Cornelius gets in trouble, he's usually looking to justify himself in advance.

"A casino," I say. "Shoot somebody if they don't hand it over? This is your—plan?"

"No. No, no, no," Cornelius says. "It's a tribal operation. No problem. Tribal employees. No resistance."

Madeline says, "The cash drawer alone!"

I can only imagine. "So," I say, "you just wander in and take it? You?" Cornelius is a regular patron. "And smile for the camera?"

"Disguise," he says, one step ahead of me.

"You?" Cornelius is built like a black bear. When he went to prison his grandmother told him he should leave nothing of himself in that place, so he quit cutting his hair in there, and he still hasn't cut it, got a braid runs all the way down his back. But the real trouble with Cornelius is that if he opens his mouth, even behind a mask, anyone would know him. No one on or off the rez sounds quite like Cornelius Left Hand.

"You," he says. "It's where the money is. You say you need money."

"They're ripping the people off," Madeline says.

And I say, "No."

"I've got another idea." Cornelius says. "You'd like this one."

Cornelius hates anybody who's making money off hard drugs, hates 'em worse than any judge and that includes the pharmacies. Now he says he happens to know quite a bit about some people who are bringing heroin in. Who they are. Where they are. He starts with his reasons: "You spend one night in a tribal jail," he says, "or any county lockup, and you know that shit's evil. Those people are evil."

I have to remind him, "Yeah, but they've got some real cooperative victims."

Cornelius says he has a very good idea where they're keeping their money, and obviously it isn't one of these dinky banks. "They'd swoon," he says, and I don't know who he's talking about. "Nobody's that stupid," he says. "I'm hearing it's over by the canal. Or up there a ways above it. It's foreigners. They've got money. Know what I've got? Game cams. We monitor the spot. Remote monitoring. We'd know just when to visit. Now, aren't you glad I talked you into getting on the Internet?"

"They leave it out there under a log somewhere?"

"More or less," says Cornelius. "That's what I've heard."

"Heard, huh? From who?"

"The Great Spirit," says Cornelius. "Among others."

"They take a big wad of money up there, stash it, don't leave anybody around to keep an eye on it. We go in and take it, and no one's the wiser. Gee, that does sound good. Is this real? I mean, I do have to wonder: If this is so easy, why was it plan two?"

"I just need somebody to watch my back going up and down that trail."

It is kind of flattering to be trusted like that.

"You always know," I tell him. "You always seem to know when it's save-the-ranch time and you can drag me into some kind of jackpot."

"Money," he says. "They tell me it's out there, and I do have cousins *every*where, got remote monitoring, and as you say, I got instincts. Far as that goes, I've got a guy on the inside who isn't scared. We'd know exactly where to set the camera up."

"Camera?" I say. This is so far beyond me. "Cornelius," I say, and he knows I'm in. That Madeline is going nuts—'outlaws, outlaws'—I'm starting to get fed up with the thing in her nose, which seemed kind of cute when I first saw it. "She," I say, "she stays here."

◊ ◊ ◊

So that's how we wound up way, way up North Crow, steep country, new country to me, and he was educating me along the way. Showed me some yew, told me the people used it to make weapons and medicine. Kind of a funny little tree, I thought; didn't look that promising to me, but what do I know? I always felt a little dumb around Cornelius; the man was a genius. I was getting the lowdown on all the flora and fauna and coyote tales and about the stuff we were carrying, power sources, and mounts, and camouflage, and linked batteries, and sims cards and whathaveya, but we're going up the trail, and even Cornelius gets gassed after a while; I didn't think much of it when he went quiet.

He never missed a step, never broke stride, just dropped like he'd been shot. And I'm listening for the echo, maybe another round, but nothing, and then I look him over for wounds, and—nothing. Not a mark on him or a hole. He is dead, though. I pump on his chest the way they tell you to do, but I know it's a waste of time. His eyes are rolled up. And he was—dead. Big man, his heart must've exploded on him, which is about right for my friend Cornelius. That would kind of sum him up in a way.

But after everything he'd been through, those goddamn Ursulines, and Vietnam, and Deer Lodge, lot of less official adventures, I think Cornelius would have been real disappointed that his last story sort of fizzled out the way it did. He had every reason to think he'd go out bold. For me, I have to say the man always needed a little too much drama, and he did scare me sometimes, but then he was the only one who ever invited me into his sweat lodge. I'd known him forever, and he'd call me 'the last honest man' which is something none of my wives or kids ever called me, and—I'd known him forever, but that didn't matter much right then.

He was about two thirty, two forty, and I never even thought of trying to carry him out. That would've left two of us dead on the trail. We're a couple miles from the truck. This was something we hadn't planned for, you just don't, but maybe it's a good thing he's such a problem—keeps me from getting too sad about my old pal. I'm sitting there, trying to sort that out when I happen to think at last that if we could put up a camera on this trail, why couldn't they, those heroin people, and then I'm wondering who all might know we're up here, and things were just getting more and more complicated. Then something he said came back to me. Line of sight. Happened Cornelius collapsed there in a clearing, way up on a steep. Line-of-sight—I could see the whole Mission Valley, see the lake, see Baldy all the way back there behind the Three Bar, and I figured somewhere out in that there must be a cell tower, so I fished Cornelius's phone out of his vest and fumbled around with that for a while. Turned out he had an elder on speed dial—elder, we're all elders now—and that's who I happen to call, some *real* old guy, kind of mysterious, I never even got his name, but he got mine, and I told him who I was with and where we were, and what was going on, and he says he'll send somebody. Doesn't say who or when, and that's how we left it. Then I had to wait and wonder. I'd dialed the guy by accident, and I couldn't figure out how to get him back and get a progress report, get some of those details I didn't think of at first. You can kind of see how people get in trouble. You're stupider than you think you are. Then the juice ran out in his phone, and it was just man against wilderness again.

Me and my dead buddy. I wasn't too confident, wasn't too happy, and that was a long old wait up there. Did lot of second guessing, and it would've been a lot easier if I'd had something to do other than sit there and try and ignore that body. Had no backup plan. Did I come to any grand conclusions, waiting? Never really got my thoughts in order at all.

Finally, Matt Finley of all people comes along with one of those game carts; we load Cornelius up and get him out of there. Turns out I was lucky to connect with the right people. Cornelius was a very traditional guy, and if he fell into the hands of the *suyapis* they might want to poke around in him, looking for their reasons, before his body could be properly prepared and waked for his people. So, we wouldn't want that. We're heading back down the trail and Matt Finley is all broke up. Finley's sobbing away, and we're right in the middle of the biggest tragedy that ever happened, and I know for a fact that these are guys who've left scars on each other. So—then—after we get Cornelius down and he's been washed or whatever they do, and they've got him laid out at the hall—then Matt Finley is right back to badmouthing him at the wake.

People. That's another thing I do not understand.

I still owe on that note.

◊ ◊ ◊

You're working your ass off to keep up an illusion. I don't own this place, the bank does, and if there ever did come a time when I didn't owe a penny, say I had no debt at all and cash left over to run on—I still wouldn't own it. Technically. We put the place in Bud's name while they're sorting out the water rights; second son is an enrolled member thanks to some blood from his mama where I'm only a descendant. That's why the place is in his name, and nobody's ever been less interested in it than Bud. He could lose it, and he wouldn't even notice. Water rights. City kids. But say all that was off the table, say there was no money problems, no political problems, no ditch riders, and by magic every paper in the courthouse was saying the place is mine along with any other ground I ever wanted. I still wouldn't own an inch.

Maybe I did learn a few things from hanging around so long. You kind of observe how things are not too permanent. I've seen a lot more than Cornelius Left Hand fizzle out: Seen barns collapse, families fall apart, renegades run ragged. I see people try and cling to the old ways, and a lot of times that's sad. Seen 'em outlive their time, and now I been around long enough to be a joke myself and watch most anything I ever did get undone. I know it sounds like I'm bitching again, but I'm not. I can lay on what's left of my couch, and look out my window, and way across the way there's the Missions where they've always been, and I see 'em many times a day in clear weather, but I never see 'em now without thinking of Cornelius. What Pharoah ever had something like that to remember him by? All over this country there's things like that, places like that that remind me of somebody who's otherwise gone. So, I get reminded a lot—we don't own this place, it owns us. Probably, if that's all I ever get figured out, that'll be enough.

The Risen Roger

When they had been considering parenthood Roger and Mira Max had made a game of lying in bed at the end of their day and bouncing possible names off each other, the names of male and female children. The rules of the game were that one of the Maxes would suggest a name and the other would either accept or reject it—"Naomi"-"No"-"Carmen"-"No"-"Brendan"-"No"-"Luke"-"No." They had by this method never agreed on an acceptable name for a babe of either sex, and in time several math-based discussions led them to the conclusion that they couldn't afford a child anyway, that they lacked the time and the money to think about responsibly bringing a child into the modern world. The bedtime game had morphed into naming or suggesting possible side hustles

"What about dog walking?" Roger, after an especially gruesome day at work, was really spinning.

It was Mira's turn this evening to be the voice of reason and restraint, a role they traded; she said, "Dogs don't necessarily like me. Besides—what a mess."

"Three D printing," said Roger. "You could print dentures. A lot of things."

"Equipment," Mira demurred. "I think that's some pretty expensive equipment you'd have to buy. Then you'd have to know how to find the people who actually wanted dentures."

They were hoping to somehow become self-sufficient with an initial investment of under a thousand dollars, all the capital it seemed they might ever expect to assemble when in lean months they were barely making rent.

"Something to sell on-line," Roger said. "*Something*."

"Sell what? You have to *have* something to sell something. And we don't have anything."

"That's what we have to figure out," Roger said.

"Except each other," Mira, corrected herself. "I mean, we do have each other."

They shared a silence acknowledging that their love was of no use as a commodity and to privately manage their various regrets.

Roger had spent nine hours that day in the warehouse, time interrupted by just two bathroom breaks. Deep in the warehouse, and not a glimpse of the sun. "We could make things," he said. "We *should* make things. Contribute, you know."

"Make what, though?"

"You could teach me how to knit," Roger said. "And we could knit stuff. Real quality. Handmade." Mira had been a knitter in their early courtship. Knitting contributed to a mousy quality in her that had made him feel so safe.

"Think anyone would pay five hundred bucks for hand-knit sweater?" she said. "That's about what you'd have to charge. Those take a long time, and sometimes you have to unravel and start all over if you want it nice."

If they could just lie here, side by side and never leave this bed, then that sense of safety might be enough, it might never be necessary to set bare feet on a cold floor. That, however, was not their situation, so they had daily to get up and to shlep around in the world and deal with its indifference, and it could be hard not to bring a hard day back to bed with them, into their tiny refuge.

"Mystery cult," Roger said.

"Yeah?" Mira had been a religious studies major. Whenever her expertise in this came up, it was entirely out of context and made her see once again how she had gone to a lot of trouble to make herself irrelevant.

"What were you saying about mystery cults?"

"I don't remember," she said. "How would that even . . .

I don't know."

"How do those work?"

"They're a mystery," she said. "You're not supposed to know unless you buy in. The Gnostics. Some of those weird Hollywood religions. You pay a certain amount of money, or join up, and eventually they give you your decoder ring."

"Well, say just a regular cult-cult," said Roger. "One that isn't a mystery. How do those work?"

"You don't really study that," she said. "Cults. Except somewhere along the line everybody in religious studies runs into the saying: Cult plus time equals religion—and that, that's about what I got out of all those semesters, you know, all that time and tuition and everything. I shudder when I think of it. Some people just want to surrender their will."

"Every morning," Roger said, "we spend thirty minutes in traffic to go to a place we don't want to be and do things we don't want to do with people we mostly don't like, so, you know—will? I mean—will? What's to surrender, really?"

"A little bit," Mira said. "I like to think there's a little bit left. A little choice, anyway. Coffee or tea. Good or evil."

"Yeah, but even when they don't have many choices to make," Roger said, "I think some people get sick of making choices. It's too much trouble, too much thinking. So, it's a service. Guru comes along and tells 'em what to do, what to think. That's a service." Roger warmed to it. "I mean, what does it take? What do you actually need to start a cult?"

"Charisma," said Mira.

"Charisma? Have you seen these guys? The Goohoo Resh Woebegone, or somebody like that? The buy-me-a-Rolls-for-God guys? Charisma?"

"It must be something," said Mira. "Some quality they have. Hairspray. You think we need to join a cult?"

"No," said Roger. "We could start one. That's why I'm asking."

"What? You think they offer a workshop in the Religious Studies department? —Religion 401, Build Your Own?"

"You could kind of reverse engineer one, couldn't you? With what you know?"

"Sure," said Mira. "First thing, you'd better quit shaving. Cut out all the carbs, go on the locusts and wild honey diet. Start listening for an angel, you know, some sweet nothings. Tablets might be good. Like stone tablets."

Roger was the flaw, he saw, in this and most of the other schemes that occurred to him. His personality, or lack of one—he lacked the force of personality even to ask for the raise he wanted at work. Mira, exhausted by his desperation was soon asleep beside him, there under the wonderful duvet they had splurged on, there in their shared warmth where they didn't need to be bold or be anything but themselves, and Roger was at once quite content and quite far from it, and when his own sleep came it came with some tricky dreams that he considered himself fortunate to forget almost the moment his alarm rang in the morning.

◊ ◊ ◊

Though Roger wore a name tag all day at work, no one but a particularly unpleasant supervisor ever called him by name; that was the job's chief benefit, how anonymous he could be in it if he wanted, how lost. He was spending the day way back in plumbing, among blue and white stands of PVC pipe, groves wherein he might hide on those days when he was in a funk. He had five reasonable explanations for why the two-way radio on his hip might malfunction. A small rebellion—he moped in the pipe forest with his personal phone out, researching the recently pressing question: Is this it?

For some months Roger had been entertaining the idea of obtaining a realtor's license, but over the last week or so that dream had come to seem implausible—Roger as a salesman of any kind? No. He lacked any useful capacity for self-deception or salesmanship; he'd just never been persuasive, so real estate, like every other improved destiny he'd ever imagined for himself, had dissolved upon further consideration. Disappointed as he was with the nasty world and his seemingly inescapable place in it, last night's mention of the metaphysical had made him curious, poked a nerve, made him suspect he must be missing something. Meaning. Or something.

He scrolled through information on the big-name gods and prophets, starting backward from Zoroaster and Zeus. Roger Max knew just enough churchy lingo to execute a search. He'd been raised a heathen, having spent the Sunday mornings of his youth upstairs with his ukelele and computer while his parents sat downstairs wreathed in cigarette smoke, sunk in crossword puzzles and beer and cursing at their television. He would describe his prior knowledge of theology as 'squat,' and he remembered his prior encounters with the religious, at school and in the navy, as embarrassing, remembered wondering if those people knew what they sounded like or how boring they were, how self-centered.

But Roger was overwhelmed by the lethargy that sometimes required him to be worthless to his employer, and while being worthless, he needed something to pass the time, so he spent the hours to acquaint himself with his wife's field of study, and, who knows, maybe some wisdom. Religion. Trinkets preserved in permafrost with the paleolithic dead; the march of civilizations with their discontents and their long parade of gods meddlesome and indifferent, and like any history, there was too much of it. Roger read until his shoulders were sore, his eyes a little crossed. He understood at once that he'd never make sense of all the details, keep the various stories straight, the endlessly subdividing and squabbling doctrines, but he read on, thinking there must be some overarching truth in it because people had been sorting themselves out this way for a long time. If funny beliefs were a mental technology for making it all bearable, maybe like any technology they would improve over time, and Roger read through ages of summarized dogma looking for trends, for useful bits he could take to heart, and it was good to see how the sacrifice of children, slaves, and goats had gone out of fashion, but nearly all the current faiths as he found them on his phone seemed to eventually want money, and those offering salvation or wealth or reincarnation were too clearly scams, and how ironic if being broke was going to limit his access even to some comforting creed.

But Roger did feel better for having goofed off so long. He knew he would second guess himself on the drive home, knew it must be some passive-aggressive bullshit to withhold his efforts this way, and normally he took pride in his diligence, but there were those days when he just had to prove to himself that neither God nor any corporate overseer was paying any attention to him, that he could be his own man, even if his own man was boring. But for the moment he felt good about having stolen seven hours from the company and being less than an hour from a weekend when he wasn't scheduled to work at all.

He turned his two-way on, and it spoke to him almost immediately. "Roger?"

"Check," he said.

"Where are you?"

"Plumbing," he said.

"We need you over in flooring."

"Check," he said. As a newly confirmed nihilist, this term really appealed to him.

Roger wheeled the big green cart he automatically took whenever he was summoned to flooring because almost everything in flooring was heavy and awkward. There were times when wearing his green apron and wheeling his green cart out into the store he felt every inch the useful man, and there were times he felt the hunchback peasant, and though he knew his self-consciousness was silly here, that he was invisible, he couldn't help it. He rolled out to the western wall where spools of carpet and linoleum stood tall. He was met there by a small woman not wearing the green apron but a green shirt of exactly the same hue with the corporate logo imprinted on it. He had never seen her before. Her name was Julia according to her tag; her unnaturally black hair and the fluorescence high above made her complexion seem sickly; she was wringing her hands as he came up to her, and she explained unnecessarily that she was a new hire.

"I'm so sorry," she said.

Roger cocked his head. "Sorry?" he said.

"I was afraid," she said, "I wasn't going to make one sale today. I mean it was getting. . . and I told these people. . . and they just had to have it today, why, I don't know, I mean it couldn't be installed, or even start to be installed, even if. . . so I told 'em we could deliver today. Sorry. I know it's right at the end of the day. For. . . I don't know."

"You called the loading dock?"

"The lady out front did. Mrs. Warnock."

"We should be good then. They'll hold a truck for it." Roger felt generous though he couldn't have said why. "Which one?" he said. At Julia's obvious confusion he added, "Did you sell?"

"Oh," said Julia, "that's the other problem." She had not ceased her theatrical hand wringing. She told him a story of beige carpet. In her inventory there were seven spools of beige carpeting standing side by side, and these differed from each other only slightly in tint and weave, but they were different, and one of these was the one she had just sold, but now she was somehow uncertain which of them. "It's one of these here in the middle. It was one of these."

"Didn't you get a tag number or something? On the receipt?"

"We got their address. Ran their credit card but. . . No tags. Person before me was fired—but—and, anyway, by the time we did all that, I got back here and realized I kind of forgot which one. Exactly which one they wanted. Which carpet."

"There has to be a code or something."

"All lost," she said. "That guy who was fired really. . . So, I'm not sure which one it is."

"Well," Roger told her, "your buyer probably wouldn't remember, either. Unless you were standing right here, looking at 'em side by side, how would you even know the difference?"

"I—I think they'd know," said Julia. "It was a hooty-tooty lady and a gay guy. And they really took a long time. And they weren't very nice. I didn't write the tag number on the invoice, if it even has a tag number, because every-thing was such a mess, but, really, this is my fault. Do you have to pay if you make a mistake? My first day."

"Pay? How do you mean?"

"I don't know," Julia said, which must have been especially terrifying. "They've already paid in full, is the thing. They have. The customers. They paid, so. . . I couldn't. I don't know."

"What if I just take the most expensive one?" Roger said. "They can't complain too much about that—if they get the most expensive one. They're getting what they paid for and maybe better."

"What about—Well, what if—I don't know."

"Accounting can always figure it out," Roger said. "Bookkeepers, that's what they do. Cover this kind of thing, if they have to. It'll be okay. Even if they don't like it, your buyers."

"They are so—I mean, they *are* practically identical, all these different ones. You must think I'm a real dunderhead."

He did. She was an angular little woman with quick eyes who seemed an old hand at anxiety, but Roger liked her quaint turn of phrase and met it with his own. "Heck," he said, "I'll just take this one. And don't worry too much. You don't want to be thinking this is an orderly operation. Sometimes it is and sometimes it isn't, and you'll make yourself crazy if you think it's always going to make sense. Lots of times it doesn't work the way it's supposed to."

Not everyone can singlehandedly maneuver a fifteen-foot roll of carpet through a crowded store, a project that made Roger proud and pissed him off by turns, and the boys on the loading dock were pissed off, too, to receive such a package and such directions for it so late in the day, but then it was no longer Roger's problem; all Roger's problems were lifting away, for he had achieved the sacred moment when he might return his cart and clock out.

The time clock was in the break room, a dismal place where Roger never went except to record his arrivals and departures from work. Julia was there. It seemed she'd been waiting there. Wringing her hands again. Her eyes fixed on him as he came in. Someone had abandoned a nibbled egg salad sandwich on the table; Roger made his way to the time clock, past the sandwich, past Julia—intent on his time card, his leaving.

"I wanted to thank you," Julia said from just behind him.

Roger did not wish to be thanked, and he thought this would seem humble. "Oh," he said. "No problem." The time clock slammed his time card, usually a satisfying thump. He needed to make just one more pass past Julia to get out. She wasn't giving him the room for it. She had managed with her small self to occupy almost all the space between the bench along a long table and the wall of the break room.

Was this a cold sweat?

"No, really," she said. "Thanks."

Was this a seduction? How, with absolutely no experience, could Roger be expected to know? He wanted so much to be headed home. She had placed herself so that he couldn't gracefully get back around her and get out of this room. This had to be deliberate. Very deliberate. Ugly, overheated, stinky little room. "Just doing my job," he said, and he almost said, 'ma'am'. She was intent on him, wanting something; Roger, a man of soft contours, was not accustomed to be the object of anyone's desire. He noted that she was too old for him and was ashamed for even making such a calculation. He believed himself completely faithful to Mira, but then he'd never been faced with any temptation to be otherwise. Large glasses in a lavender frame set upon a long, thin nose, and behind them her pleading eyes. Pleading? It seemed that way.

"So kind," she said.

"Just doing my job," he insisted. How nice to take refuge, for once, in the truth. What had he done?"

"Not everyone is," she said. "Kind."

"No," he said, an easy enough concession. She was in front of him. Blocking his way. "Everyone starts new," he said, "so. . ."

"That's what I mean," Julia said. "Understanding. You seem to understand."

"Oh," said Roger, who had no understanding of what was happening here or why the break room wasn't populated with people clocking in and out. Where were they? Vague as possible, he tried to reassure her, "We've all been there. After a while, though, I mean you come here day after day, and you can't help but learn the system. Can't help it. So, you know, you'll get there pretty soon."

"Oh," she said. "Work? I didn't mean that. About work, though that was nice, too. No. I mean really, really kind."

"Oh," Roger said, who wished he were at liberty to say unkind things. Julia still stood in his way, and she kept searching his face. "Well—good," he said. "Uh, thanks. Like, I say, you'll do fine."

Something about this stung her to tears. "Not work," she said. "I didn't mean about work. I mean when a person is, I mean when people are, or when I am—you know. Lonely."

He knew loneliness, of course, but couldn't know this Julia's particular brand of it; she shifted into full weeping, and now Roger was pleased that they were still alone in the break room. It was horrible having to meet her eyes, tears pooling on her cheeks, under her lenses, and her breath coming in gulps.

Roger did not know what to do; when he thought of it later, he realized he had done about the worst thing he could have done under the circumstances. He set his hand on Julia's shoulder and gave it a little squeeze. In the moment it seemed a sound move, the everything-will-be-okay squeeze that saved him from having to actually utter that lie, and his hand on her shoulder where he might use it to lever himself around her. But the gesture was met with more crying, though it was in a softer register, and Roger now understood the many ways this might go wrong. What if she thought this was an invitation? What if she tried to—what if she wanted more touching, other touching? Or what if she wanted no touching? Touching a woman at work, any woman, anywhere—consequences. The horrible realization that he needed this job. Only moments earlier Roger had been a step away from his weekend, now that state of affairs seemed far away; he felt moisture on his palms.

"Lonely," Julia said again, still more convincingly.

Roger was not the cure for this, and he considered telling her as much, and maybe even harshly. He only wanted to get around her, and it seemed so very little to want. Did she know she frightened him? Should he tell her that? She remained in his way. She had called him kind— maybe he should try that angle. "You're not alone," he said. "You know, you're never alone." He offered this proposition without thinking he might have to explain or defend it, but it stopped her crying. Hope invaded her leaking eyes, and she looked up at him so expectantly, and said,

"No?"

"Uh, no," he said. "Not really."

"If I could just believe. . ." She seemed prepared to cry again.

"You can't be," Roger said. "Lonely." Her hopeful,

expectant face returned. Roger was inching his way toward the door but was not yet in a position to make a clean break for it. What could he offer her? How odd that he had only just happened on several unsatisfactory explanations for why she might not be alone. It would be wrong to try and bring any heavenly fathers into it.

"You mean. . . ?"

"Well," Roger said. "Uh. . . Uhm. There's that little voice. You hear it all the time. It's in there. That's you, too, isn't it. So, that never goes away. So, you're never alone when you're with yourself."

Her mouth fell open. An appreciation. She was still in his way. His hand remained on her shoulder, more awkward and ambiguous all the time. "That's right," she said. "That is so right."

Roger nudged a little closer to the door.

"*Yes*," said Julia, triumphant.

Roger held her exactly at arm's length but knew his position could fall apart. What if someone, anyone should see them now. At least Julia had quit crying. Where was everyone?

"Oh," said Julia, enraptured, "that is *so* right."

There was still no route around her. Roger released her shoulder, reclaimed his hand. "Well," he said, "my wife will be expecting me." He didn't care if it was clumsy or even inappropriate to say so. Mira would be waiting for him. Sort of. She would be glad to see him, at least. Now he longed for it, and he ceased to be subtle about moving past her, but Julia moved in a way that suggested a basketball player playing defense on the perimeter. "Could I possibly ask for one more favor?"

"Right now?" he said.

"Oh, no," Julia said. "Not now. Later. It would have to be."

"Oh," Roger thought he shouldn't remind her so soon about his being married. It would practically amount to assault to squeeze by this little woman. "I don't. . ."

"Could you?"

Heat traveled all through him, and Roger thought he might be in the middle of something medical and further that he wouldn't mind a little emergency as a way out of this. "I'm usually, I usually, once I'm away from work I. . ."

"I hate to ask," said Julia.

Roger didn't think it bothered her very much to ask. What was she asking? "I. . ."

"My women's group," she said. "It's very small, not real formal. Just some friends, really."

"Oh," he said with as much reluctance as possible.

"My mother," she said. "My mother is part of it."

"Oh," Roger said again.

"We all have the same problem," said Julia. "Would you be good enough—I know you're so kind, and I hate to ask—but, would you be good enough to talk to us?"

It seemed his assent was the toll he must pay to get past her, so he said, "All right. But say what? Talk about what?"

"You'll know," said Julia. "You've already said it. You *are* it."

◊ ◊ ◊

Roger had failed to mention Julia or her women's group to his wife, and as the day approached when he was to meet with them, he grew more uncomfortable about not saying anything. He couldn't think how to explain the rendezvous and had even thought he might try to pass it off as a poker night, but then he thought he wouldn't be dressing or grooming as he would for a night with the boys, and how would he explain that? Better the truth, but how

100

to explain that? He didn't know what he was getting into. It happened, though, that Mira went out of town to visit her sister on the very day when Roger was to meet with the ladies, so no subterfuge was required of him. But guilt. Guilt? He'd done nothing wrong, yet he wore it as surely as he'd worn black slacks, loafers, and a collared shirt for the occasion. He had shaved carefully and the scent of his shaving cream was strong in the car. He constantly considered turning back and at one point did so, but it was only a four-block circle of indecision. He was curious.

The ladies. He had been thinking of them too much. Wary as he was of the unpredictable, his life had been at least uncomplicated and free of much wondering. Now, the ladies. Who would they be? What would they want? Roger's wife and his employer required little more of him than his presence, and so far as Roger knew he may not have much more than that to offer. Could this be something naughty? With women. Unspecified women. Something strange? That, at least, was certain. Talk to them? With the notable exception of Mira, Roger did not typically talk to people beyond bare exchanges of information. He had always suspected he might have more to say but had never formed a clear idea what that might be.

The restaurant he'd been directed to was part of a national chain with a familiar and somehow reassuring plastic sign above its parking lot; inside, he was met by a young hostess to whom Roger said he was expected, that he believed there was a party waiting for him. As Roger said this, he was struck that he'd never said such a thing before; he followed his prim hostess to a horseshoe booth in the restaurant's back room. There were women seated all around it, four of them, and at his approach they all looked up at once.

"All right," said the hostess, impressed with him. "Here

you are, sir."

"Hello," Roger said to them generally, and to Julia, "Hi." So far, at least, he hadn't fumbled. He'd been inflated to an unaccustomed tension by importance and anxiety.

Julia was a happier person under this light and in a shirt of her own choosing, a more flattering color. "Thank you, thank you, thank you," she said, and, as if on cue, the two women to her right slid out from the booth and with smiles indicated to Roger that he should take their place. Roger slid in, and now he occupied the booth's apex with the women packed in around him; it was good, he thought, that he smelled of the various grooming aids he'd used, and so far he hadn't said anything stupid.

Julia announced him. "Roger *Max*," she said, and she seemed to derive some importance of her own, just for knowing him. How did she know his last name? She introduced her mother.

Her mother, Dorthea, was as bird like as her girl; she wore a necklace of what Roger took to be large, deformed pearls and her daughter's beseeching eyes, and she repeated the name Julia had just called her. "I'm Dorthea," she said with a slight but sincere tremor. "The DePaul girls," she said. "We're so glad for you."

"Nice to meet you. I'm. . ."

"We *know* who you are," said Dorthea DePaul. "That's why we're here. Order anything you want."

A woman just to the other side of Mrs. DePaul said that she was Denise, and already Roger was becoming overwhelmed by names, D-names, but Denise was not at all like the DePaul women, probably a runner with her wide shoulders and high cheeks, obnoxiously healthy. The most striking woman who'd ever spoken directly to him, she posed a simple question he barely understood at first for his confusion.

"Lunch or dinner menu?" she said. "Or they serve breakfast all day. I think I speak for the ladies when I say we'd love it if you wanted something special. Lobster tail, anything—if they've got it, and you want it, crack on."

Roger wasn't hungry, but it seemed impolite to say so; his mouth was now too dry to let him say much at all. "Water," he said.

The women sighed collectively. The youngest of them, the one whose regard for him had seemed guarded, a bushy haired person under a houndstooth porkpie hat declared, "Okay. You're the real deal." She offered her hand, her arm completely straight behind it; it seemed he'd gained her absolute trust. "So, yeah," she said. "I'm Delphine. And I'm with these guys. We're all glad you're here."

Roger despaired of ever calling them, accurately, by name.

◊ ◊ ◊

Roger hoped that in the telling he could make some sense of what had happened, and he thought it would make the most sense if he told it as a joke. But Mira didn't laugh; she kept digging for details. Maybe she had become suspicious when there was paella waiting for her on her return from her sister's.

"So, it wasn't an actual club or anything? A what? What were they saying? A woman's group?"

"No, it was just, they were, they lived in the same apartment building. They ride the same bus. Except for Mrs. D. The old one. She's retired. Waiting for the bus, you know. Turns out they all had the same problem. They met each other at the bus stop. Then they started having coffee. Quite a story. They'd talk about their problem, but they weren't coming up with any solutions. Unless it was talking about their problem. I guess that got 'em together, at least. With each other."

"And they said they were lonely?"

"Yeah."

"Well. Isn't everyone?"

"Sure," said Roger. "But you can't just say, 'Get over it.' Can you?"

"You could," said Mira. "Maybe not in so many words. But. Yeah. Be realistic."

"I don't know. These ladies. Live in that apartment complex. Ride the bus. Realistic? See what I mean?"

"Lonely, huh? What, and you're supposed to fix this? Roger? Who are these ladies?"

"You should come and see."

"Come and? What? The lonely ladies? Oh, Roger."

"Mrs. D wants me to come and speak to her church. She actually belongs to a formal group. Of church ladies."

"What are you telling these people?"

"Not too much, really. Hardly anything."

"You must be saying something if they want you to come and say it again."

"That's the little bit scary part," Roger said. "I really *did*n't say much. There was a thing back at the store. You're never alone, or something like that. But I was just trying to. . . Now they've, they're really. I was just trying to say you're always with yourself, which, if you think of it, how does that make anything any better. I don't know. The ladies, they seem to think I said more. About loving yourself. Which is not a bad idea. But I didn't come up with it. I didn't even say it, but they think I did."

"That's probably what they want you to say now."

"Oh," said Roger. "Yeah. Maybe. It isn't the worst advice. I try not to say much. I haven't said much. You just sit there and nod, and then they say what they think you said. Sometimes you said some pretty good things, or they think you did. So—love yourself. Yeah, I could go with that."

"That seems awful to me," Mira said. "When you put it that way."

"No. It's nice. You'll see. Makes 'em feel better. You can just see it. And when do I? When have I ever? It's nice."

◊ ◊ ◊

In the first few weeks, when all his disciples were women, Mira could hardly help but be suspicious of Roger's little movement and the motivations that fueled it. Then the thing began to gather up men and children and rent its own space for meetings, and Mira's jealousy grew tentacles, and what had seemed at first a conventionally creepy situation got even worse. Roger kept having to change his phone number. He held his meetings on Saturdays, every Saturday for over a year, and it became a point of constant contention between them that Mira had not attended any of these. They both knew of her jealousy, though neither of them named it. One day he wounded her heart by saying, "I just thought you might be proud of me."

Mira owed him, she thought. She feared she wouldn't be proud or happy with whatever he'd got up to, even if it had brought him out of himself and given him purpose; there was something icky in it, but she felt she owed it to him to try and find out if she was wrong.

Things had come to them in the mail. Bulk things. A box of green aprons very like the green aprons that had from time to time passed through their wash, but hundreds of them and where his work aprons wore their corporate stamp this new batch bore a stitched assertion, You Are Never Alone. Beneath the inscription there was something that looked to Mira like a stunted capital 'H'. Roger took those first boxes to his next meeting and immediately several more boxes were on order; the aprons were very popular.

"Aprons?" Mira wondered, and Roger could only shrug and produce the rueful smile he now used so frequently. Disarmingly.

Next came the boxes of pamphlets, just five pages each but bound in brown leatherette stamped with fake gilt, a serious and heavy font, Club Happy. A book edited down to one declaration per page:

You Are Never Alone

Love Yourself at All Times

Then a line drawing of two people in profile, facing each other at arm's length, each of them with one hand on the other's opposite shoulder, their heads bowed; now that she saw it expanded, Mira understood this drawing as the source of the logo on the aprons, the stunted 'H'. There was a blank page of fake parchment at the beginning and at the end of it, and taken altogether it was the slimmest book Mira had ever seen. She had asked Roger very anxiously when those first boxes arrived if they had paid for them. He told her the Club had bought them. The Club was a phrase, an entity in his every conversation now. Later, when Mira learned how little those pamphlets cost and what they cost purchasers at point of sale, she wished the Maxes had bought into them.

The Club. Eventually, she just had to see for herself.

Meetings were being held in what had been a downtown movie theater, a building still equipped with a marquee. Club Happy. Mira had been driving past all week, and all week the same red letters were on the marquee; it seemed the title of a ghost movie, something Chinese—Club Happy. Mira felt she had reached the point of no return when she turned a corner and saw a woman in the ticket booth. Would this cost something? The woman wore her apron and barely contained bliss and a funny little hat, and she was serving an excited young couple as Mira approached. There was an exchange of pleasantries, of money, and the couple came away from the booth with aprons of their own. They unfolded, and admired, and donned the aprons while making their way into the lobby. Inside the glass doors they could be seen admiring each other.

"You must be happy."

Mira was not sure she had heard this correctly, but was certain she didn't understand it. The woman in the booth was of some indeterminate age and it seemed she'd gone through something especially tragic or hard to be here. With a cash box and a card reader by her side, she seemed to consider herself a real success.

"I'm. . . happy?" said Mira. "Am I happy?"

"You know you are," said the woman in the booth. "Or you will."

"I? Huh. Do you have to buy an apron?"

"Are you happy?" said the woman in a somewhat altered tone.

"I," said Mira. "Okay. Give me one." The apron was thirty-two dollars plus tax, enough to buy a dozen more at their wholesale price. All over America there were people in nasty jobs who couldn't wait to shed such aprons. Price of admission? Uniform? Mira thought she'd be damned if she'd wear hers, but then when everyone in the lobby was wearing theirs, she decided she must wear hers as well. Small children wore them with the skirts folded up so that they could walk. Mira didn't want to stand out in any way. She was trying to go incognito. Whatever Roger was doing here, he'd been doing it in her absence. She wanted him to think that was still the case.

A younger Mira had gone on dates in this theater, and even then it had been coasting on remembered elegance, showing pretentious movies. She climbed to the loge and moved all the way to the back to have a bird's eye view of the assembly. The audience gathering below was full of a polite murmuring reminiscent of the Presbyterian services her parents still attended. Roger had been trying to tell her about people being uplifted at these meetings, which she had doubted, but Mira was beginning to see, had reason to hope that it might be pleasant and benign after all. It was very hot, though, here at the top and the back of the balcony.

Everyone, absolutely all of them down there, and all those around her were wearing aprons. Everyone but Roger, Roger, there on a platform, in the middle of the dais, dressed as he'd been when he first met with Mira's parents and their mild enthusiasm for him. In any other place Roger, in his outfit, in his bearing and being, would not have been conspicuous. He was a black- slacks and brown-shoes customer of the high-volume hair cutters in the mall, and almost studiously undistinguished.

Yes. She had always liked that about him.

Her husband sat with his hands on his knees, being venerated. The crowd began to settle. He drew like a feature film, Roger. Someone gonged a gong and there was quiet. A man with dense white hair man rose from the dais and strode up to a lectern at the front of the platform. The people on the dais were diminished by the movie screen behind them, but the white-haired man had a voice good for crowds and almost overbore the microphone. "Are we all happy?" He wondered. "Happy here today?" he asked, asking not for assent but for true consideration. No one said anything. "He's here to help us remember." The white-haired man turned back to the main attraction, and with a deferential dip of his chin he said, "Roger, we're here asking you to help us out again, to remind us as only you can. Please speak to us, Mr. Max."

A momentary murmur and the audience fell back into its weird stillness; there was a quiet more profound than any church she'd ever been in, maybe even an empty one. Her husband came to the lectern silently. Crepe soles. Slip resistant. Lacking the imagination to generate much pretense, he did seem quite trustworthy.

Roger did not require a text or script. He set his naked hands on the lectern, folded them there. Because she knew him, Mira knew the look he cast over the audience to be one of puzzlement. After all these meetings he had yet to acquire any ease as a public speaker, and he leaned at the microphone as if he expected it to shock him. Even as amplified through the microphone his voice was very soft when he said, "You are never alone." He smiled in a way Mira had never seen him smile before, a smile full of gentle certainty. That quiet voice. Maybe that was why there was such a hush, so they could hear him. Just as quietly he then required them to, "Love yourself at all times."

Mira had never seen an audience so rapt as Roger's. Mira herself had never before given him such undivided attention. There was a stand by the lectern upon which stood a glass of water or something clear. Roger took up the glass, drank about a third of it off, and then offered them that weird, warm smile again. Mira felt a flight of doves fly up through her, certainly more than she had bargained for.

◊ ◊ ◊

Roger came home from the meetings ravenous, and food was central to the routines they used to reclaim their usual selves each Saturday evening. That evening Mira ordered in pad tai, an especially festive meal to be eaten in bed watching the latest installment of a period drama with a waif wanting to marry her way up in the world. Sunday was their day to wash bedding. Because she had always been able to reclaim her husband so quickly and efficiently this way, Mira had been pleased with their Saturday evenings. Here he was, hers again, once again himself, noodles slithering in through his lips with that sucking sound, little cardboard carton on his lap. Mira hadn't told him yet that she had been to the meeting; she was entertaining the hope that if she didn't tell him, if she were to pretend she had never been, and if she could damp the memory enough and never go again, then the portion of him that was hers would remain hers and return to her every Saturday night in just this way, and they would go on just as if he'd joined league bowling.

But if Mira had been curious before, she was more curious now. On the screen before them a coach on yellow wheels rolled through a heather countryside. Mira was abuzz with heavily sugared coffee. He was not the same, somehow, her husband, though as he lay beside her there was nothing noticeably different about him. No, he would never be the same again. They watched a long, long shot of that coach in the countryside, listened to an oboe and English horn, the score swelling.

At last Mira let it out of her. "Well, I. I bought an apron today."

"Bought?" There were hundreds of them in their closet.

"I went," she said. "To your meeting."

"Ooooh. Why didn't you? Where? Where were you?"

"Up in the makeout seats. Up in the top. The balcony. Full house, even up there. You really packed that place. I had no idea."

"Usually," said Roger, "I think I see everyone. Try to see everyone there. It's the least I can do."

"That's a lot," said Mira. "That is actually quite a bit. To do. To see."

"So?" said Roger. "Now you've been. So, you know. See what I mean? It's not bad, is it? Not bad at all if you ask me."

"Could I just recommend shirts of a natural fiber. You know, cotton. Those something-lon shirts you wear—Ewh. No."

"But what about the rest of it? You could see what it was doing for people, right?"

"Club Happy," she said.

"And now you're a member," said Roger. "Or actually, anyone is. Who wants to be. That's my favorite part. Inclusive, you know. Come one, come all."

Mira could only wonder how many smart people were in attendance. She wondered if one might be happy just by insisting on it, faking it until it was real. But they did seem that way in the theater; Roger had been understating his effect on his followers. Followers? Maybe momentary, but he did seem to produce some kind of stunned happiness in them. Club Happy. She'd felt a spasm of it herself.

"Is that how it goes every time? The meeting?"

"It's not always Mr. Quilty speaking," Roger said. "Usually, it is, but he's not always the speaker."

"Don't you speak?"

"Oh, yeah. Every time," he said.

"But. What do you say?"

"What I said today."

"Is that all?"

"Yeah," he said. "In fact, I try not to say *any*thing else. I think it's better to keep it simple."

"So, that's it?"

"Yeah. That, and I drink the water. That's an important part."

"It is?"

"It is now," he said. "I don't even remember how that got started, but they think it's important now. But, you know, the whole deal, the thing I do—really easy peasy. And they like it so much. Keep it real simple, that's my secret."

"Wow," said Mira.

"Yeah," said Roger.

A pale girl stepped out of the carriage, took down her pitiful valise, and stared resolutely at a moss clad manor house. The score swelled under her with strings.

"I'm real glad you went," he said. "So you can see. And maybe you'd like to. . . . You could sit right up there with me."

"If it's simple," she said, "why does that Quilty have to go on and on?"

"Oh, so people get their money's worth, I guess."

"Money?"

"Not money," he said. "But. You know."

"And what about that woman?"

"Denise? That's Denise. She's done a lot of this stuff. She came up with the logo. That thing Quilty calls the self/self. The little doohicky on the aprons."

"Not about money? Denise sure seems to think it is. Does she always do that?" Mira's knees had drawn up so that she couldn't see the drama on screen. "Roger," she said, "you're not? You're not?"

"Den*ise*?" he said. "Oh, honey. No. No, no, no, no. *No*. Denise scares me. She really gets things done. But, ooh. She scares me. They all do, a little bit. People are kind of weird. That's why it would be nice if you could come. To the meetings."

"Mmm," said Mira. "But she wants people's money so you can go on tour?"

"Just in the tri-state area," he said. "At least for now."

"And?"

"Spread the word," he said.

"You don't have that many to spread," she said.

"Maybe they just happen to be the right ones."

"Maybe," said Mira. "But what about your job? While you're on tour? Do you even have any vacation time coming? Do you have to deliver these words personally? What's the deal?"

"That's another reason," he said, "I'm glad you came today. Because. We'll, I'd been waiting until it seemed like it was going to happen. But now it really is happening. See, uh, the club might be my job. Could be my job. It would almost have to be."

"Roger. Your—job?"

"No. It's feasible, I think. It's coming together fast."

"So that's why there's all these aprons and pamphlets?"

"Way more in storage," he said, "and more on order. We're in seven cities. Already. This thing seems to work, so. . . Not money, honey. Remember when I was worrying so much about that? So, yeah. Now I'm taking my own advice, and it's way better. They were talking about other platforms, you know, but everyone thinks in-person is the only way to go. Me saying it. So. Yeah. This is way better."

"Wow," said Mira sincerely.

◊ ◊ ◊

This was the third time she had been deposed in the same windowless room, a room designed to induce claustrophobia. This was the third different lawyer to take her deposition, but they were all of a piece, dark, heavily bearded men, closely shaved and ponderous. This latest was at least apologetic, saying he just needed to nail down a few loose ends so his client could close the books. Then, for the benefit of the camera, he told her she was being recorded. She was put under oath. The lawyer read some preliminary hoo-haw and launched right into a very familiar line of questioning. He had promised to keep it short. Mira started by affirming that her full legal name was Mira Max.

"So, you retained your married name?"

"Yes," said Mira.

"Why did you choose to do that?"

"How is that any of your. . . I thought we'd probably get back together. It was Roger's idea, to, you know, because he'd started hating himself so much, and was not doing too well at the time. I hoped maybe he'd get himself turned around, or fixed or something, and we'd. . . I didn't want it to end. It wasn't my idea. But the thing is, Roger kind of ended. The Roger I knew." Mira was being filmed again, reprising her role in a calamity. They kept asking the same questions, and though she had nothing personally to lose, she didn't want to hurt, or implicate, or bother anyone else, even those who might deserve some hurt. She had been trying with some success to move on from this, but, no, here she was again, under oath.

Hair gel glistened in and on the attorney's scalp; he was off camera but preening anyway. "In your previous statements you have stated that you had no operational input in IN. Do you continue to maintain that position?"

"Yes," said Mira. Once, when she'd had an attorney of her own, her attorney had advised her to keep her answers brief in these things. How many interested parties there had been in the end. In IN. That erstwhile attorney had told her that IN was one of the biggest litigation breeders he had ever seen, a real windfall to the legal profession.

"Did you have any part in founding the movement?"

"No," said Mira.

"The Club?"

"No," she said.

"Did you have any benefit from the proceeds of the movement?"

Mira made the most disdainful face she knew—she wanted this on record—"No," she said.

"Did you at any time have access to the movement's or the club's financial records?"

"No," Mira said. "As I've said again and again. "We didn't even know there were records. Or not until—"

"You didn't know that IN had been incorporated?"

"We didn't know any of that until right near the end."

"Your husband was listed as director. Your former husband."

"As I've said before," Mira said, "and as you must have noticed if you've looked into this at all, my husband was no businessman. Even after he'd been burned a few times he kept signing things he hadn't read. He was flattered, you know. He thought they kind of worshipped him, and they'd never. . . My husband was trying to help people. He thought he had a gift, and maybe he did. Once he discovered that, that's all he wanted out of it. He was all in. All in for helping people."

"He didn't know who held the trademark for the IN insignia?"

"What?" Mira said. "What did my husband know about trademarks? Or me, for that matter. And I stayed completely out of it. Which I shouldn't have. But, what-do-they-call-it?—twenty-twenty hindsight. But—again—he was in the dark and I was in the dark. Maybe Denise, but I hear she's out of the country. Where she can't be extradited. Quilty. Quilty passed on. So."

"At what point did you become aware of IN's financial operations?"

"Late. Late. I didn't even know they were calling it IN until the thing was way out of control. Then one day Roger came home with his head in his hands. Whenever that was. And it just kept getting worse from there."

"Do you still maintain that neither of you received any benefit from IN, financial or otherwise?"

"Benefit? Well, Roger took some of that money, sure. When he found out he was a product and they broke his heart, sure. He went nuts. But you know he's paid all that back. Every penny of it. Paid people who'd been ripping him off. Roger has paid everything." Mira removed the small microphone clipped to her blouse, and she held it right to her mouth, and she remembered the camera again and looked straight into that, and said, "Everything, *you prick.*"

Though she had exited the interview, the lawyer continued making his record, stating for that record, a voice off-camera, "Ms. Max has previously indicated that she is bound by a confidentiality agreement arising from a prior litigation, and that agreement prohibits her from disclosing the whereabouts of Roger Max. That agreement is copied to the file."

She couldn't have helped them if she had wanted to; in truth, Mira Max had long since lost track of Roger in time and space. Mira knew only that he was long gone from her bed and that, wherever he was, the poor man had given up on that nonsense of trying to love himself.

To Ashes

Kevin Pooley descended a ramp toward the concourse and on seeing his sister there he lifted his arm and waved it like a stalk in the wind. The moment seemed to want some extra recognition. Lil saw him and duplicated the gesture, adding her killer smile. They were twins and his sister's beauty sometimes confused him, indicating as it did self-love. Unlike in sex and world view, they were otherwise very similar. That childhood. From that childhood they'd emerged at least with their flaring cheeks and high, knowing brows, even teeth, unthreatening eyes. Real beauties. Pooley was slightly ashamed of his belief that his sister might make better use of those looks. Lil reported, and she couldn't lie to her brother even when lying to herself, that she was happy, and in that happiness she was happy in a way that he was not. No strain or calculation in that smile. Pooley consulted his syncopated heart and reckoned the moment for the best part of this trip, a thing about to skid steeply downhill. They met in front of a pretzel vender and said at once, "Hey," and shook hands, just as they'd been raised to do.

"You look great," he said.

"You look kind of funny," she said, bending her neck to examine him from several angles. "This isn't the famous you, is it?"

Pooley had been on an extended break from work, to, as they liked to say out West, inventory himself, and he'd grown a guru's beard that he'd let run wild; his eyes were those of a deer peering over a thicket, his teeth like a beaver's within that beard. A longtime shill for a piratical and widely despised cellular service, his celebrity was shallow but pervasive, and if he should walk undisguised through the airport or any public place there would be a ripple behind him of puzzled looks, second takes, third takes, and sometimes even odd confrontations. Mr. ungroomed, however, enjoyed near invisibility.

"So," Pooley said. "Do you know where to get him?"

"I called the crematorium. We just have to go pick him up. It was all paid for. Sid had a policy to cover it. But we do have to pick up the ashes. They won't—so we have to get his ashes."

"We probably should anyway," Pooley said, "but I wonder what you're supposed to. . . do. Where you're supposed to put those. Sid wouldn't be down with this at all, would he? All this dust? This mess? We're on cleanup again, huh? Right back on cleanup."

"Now," Lil said, "don't get started. And don't get me started. Maybe he left some instructions. He probably did. He was pretty thorough."

"But was he expecting. . ."

"Oh, yeah," she said. "Sure, he was. I mean, as much as a person can ever expect something like that."

"You know," Pooley said, "this is the first time I've ever actually been in this airport. We weren't flying anywhere back in the day, were we? People we knew didn't fly anywhere."

"Because they didn't need to," Lil said. "Still don't. This airport is like every other airport. And this town. When we drove out a few years ago—to see him—which was. . . this town is now like every other town. Every. Other. Town. It's like you can't even go anywhere anymore that isn't the same strip mall. Except the country. The country is still different in different parts, because it hasn't been. . . Sorry. You knew I'd start right in preaching sustainability." Lil raised lavender and coriander and chickens whose eggs she sold, goats she sheared for her loom. This was at times a hard, hard idyl, and she sustained it with these pep talks she knew others found tiresome.

Her car contained an earthy odor sullen in its potency; Lil had been hauling sacks of potting soil just prior to this trip. Poorly sealed sacks. Pooley removed a doll's pudgy and one-legged torso from his seat where he sat in self-conscious fussiness with his bag in his lap, unwilling to lay that bag on any other surface in this car. Anything familiar in their home town as they passed through it now had more to do with what the place had become in their absence. Duplexes and triplexes had been built over most of what they'd known, and businesses that were exact duplicates of businesses in every other town. Franchises. Townhouses wrapped in beige plastic siding. Still, the unimaginative place was better than what they had known. It had been Old Town in name and in fact when they'd been here, and now, save one imperishable corner bar, there was hardly anything left of that rotting carcass.

"Red's," Pooley said, astonished. "Wow. Red's. You wonder if it's ever been painted. That's another place I never went. Never was tempted. It was pretty nasty even then."

"I remember walking wa-ay around it," Lil said. Then, two blocks later, "That's it. That must be it. Right next to the massage parlor? Really? Yeah, that's the address. See what I mean? Leave it to Cut-rate Sid. I wonder how he even knew about this place. They have these service contracts."

Their father was delivered to them with due solemnity in a cardboard box, but more securely they were assured in the sealed plastic sack within it. There were urns on display in the crematorium, pottery that Lil considered buying if only to rescue it from this dreadful location, but she managed to brush off the crematory's attempt to upsell them, and they drove through gentrifying Old Town with the box riding nakedly, expectantly in the back seat of the rental car. There wasn't much of him. There hadn't been all that much even before he'd been incinerated. Pooley and his sister had taken turns calling their father every other Sunday, and these were brief, dutiful conversations in which the old man never mentioned his health or inquired with any real interest after anyone else, and there was usually a word-for-word replay of one of the twenty or thirty episodes Sid chose constantly to retell, and then, in conclusion, 'Well, take it easy.' His grandchildren had been his grandchildren for more than a decade before he died, and still it had been necessary to sometimes remind him of their names, and worse, it wasn't senility but old habit that made him forgetful in this way.

A bag of ashes.

The house was already listed with a realtor who supplied them with keys to the place and some wonderful news concerning rezoning. Mrs. Maloney wore a boutonniere for some office function then in progress, and a bracing optimism, and she said revaluing their father's place was something they should talk about. That ground had become so valuable.

The place in question, which Pooley had last seen on the occasion of his eighteenth birthday, was, like Red's Bar, an anachronism, a sore thumb, about a thousand square feet of mustard colored shotgun shack surrounded by a fringe of gravel and weeds that were in turn contained by a chain link fence. To have gone anywhere at all was to have gone a long way from this. The yard. They had when very young called this 'the yard' and made mud pies of it. There was ironweed here that was probably as old as they were. Sid's cinderblock shop crouched now as an eyesore among newly erected eyesores, but industrially ugly with its hoist hanging over the door and its strong suggestion of a dark, greasy interior.

"You forget," said Lil.

Pooley parked. "You know, I haven't. Oddly enough, I haven't. But, then, what's to remember? Or how do you forget nothing?"

"I never thought of it that way," said Lil. "But I do see what you mean."

"I hadn't either," said Pooley. "Until just now. The nothing aspect. The nothingness."

"Well," she said. "Let's go in. It really isn't as bad as you'd think. Or at least it wasn't too bad when I was here before."

"Look," Pooley said. "I'm shaking. Interesting. Okay— let's go." He was an actor, or had once aspired to be, and his training that way had left him painfully alert to anything in his reactions that was not authentic. The shaking must be real, though. Too much. The gate did not creak on its hinge. Sid would have kept it oiled. The lock on the door hadn't been much used and now it needed a bit of manipulating.

Inside was empty. Not emptied, but empty as Sid had apparently lived in it. An overstuffed chair in the middle of the living room with it a side table for radio and tissues and water, and all around that the same old carpet, now in places nearly worn through—it seemed a lot of carpet with nothing on it, a lot of room with nothing in it; the walls were bare but for framed baby pictures of their children that Lil had hung when she had visited him. Pictures from before their babies were self- conscious. Their babies. Sid's grandchildren, should he ever glance that way. The windows were clean but gave onto a cinderblock prospect of the shop. Lil said, "You kind of wish he'd been a drunk or something. Or wish there'd been something really *wrong* with him. Know what I mean?"

"You don't think there was something wrong with

him?"

"Well," she said. "Well, I don't know. I mean he wasn't *hurt*ful or anything. And in this neighborhood that was pretty good. Just that was pretty darn good around here. Didn't drink. Or, or anything. Didn't. . . he just worked. I mean, he didn't *hurt* anybody. Did he?"

"Sheesh," said Pooley. "Look at this place. I wonder if someone snagged his television. His computer?"

"He didn't have those. Didn't want 'em," Lil said. "Which I thought was sort of admirable. I got him set up with this satellite service. Radio. It's ball games. Ball games all day every day. Sports channel. All sports. And what a person can get out of listening to a hockey game is beyond me."

"So that's what he did? You think that's all he did?" Their father had been a bachelor in this house these twenty years past, having lost his first wife to cancer, and then his children and then his second wife to an indifference which continued uninterrupted in their absence. "A real self-contained guy," said Pooley. "Hm." The radio service his sister mentioned was one of the few places in popular media where Pooley's mugging face would not from time to time appear, or his simpering voice be heard, so his father had not been entirely foolish or disingenuous when his stock question in their stock conversation was to inquire whether his son was working. "You working anywhere now?" Into his fifth contract with Gorizon Inc., Pooley worked ubiquitously, very profitably, and most of the civilized or semi civilized world knew his work, and he was heavily invested in the San Fernando Valley and as far as Bakersfield. Was he working?

He'd had a stock answer, too. To dispose of that question: "I've got some things going." Maybe Sid really didn't know. Maybe no one had told him. But he sure hadn't gone out of his way to find out. No interest in what his son had become, and he left no room for his son to brag about it.

Lil said, "I think he was out in the shop most of the time. Except for meals. Out there doing his thing until he couldn't see to do it anymore."

"Yeah? He never mentioned that to me. About his vision. Well," said Pooley, rocking the box under his arm. "I guess we should take it out there. Him, I mean. If we take him anywhere."

Their father was a fabricator; he owned two of most tools so that when he broke something in the middle of a project, he could grab its replacement and press on. The twins had not been paired up under the same principle, or any principle; the twins knew themselves somehow for a mistake, a mistake their parents had been decent enough not to repeat. They were an only child. Sid worked in wood and steel and even fabric here; there were heavy sewing machines crammed in one corner. He had so much in the way of tools and machinery in this one great room that if any one thing should go much amiss or astray it would suddenly all go to chaos, so nothing was let go astray, a condition that might only be maintained by constant fanaticism. He never sought business but had it through reputation, for he could make anything here, an end table of pallet wood, a cowling for a wrecked Cessna.

The man was indistinguishable, and probably in his own mind, too, from his tools. He could make anything. His shop lights banished almost every shadow. A gleaming cedar strip canoe hung suspended from the rafters.

"Well," said Pooley. "Here we are. Here he is. Was. Or—something. When I was little, you should have seen the way people talked to him. They were in awe. Look at this bolt cabinet. Wall full of clamps. Hand planes. Chisels. Perfect condition. Sharp. Oiled. You know."

"I saw that," Lil said, "a little bit. Later. What people seemed to. . . But by then I don't think it mattered much. To me."

"People would ask him for something," said Pooley, "and he could give it to them. That must have been very satisfying."

"Maybe," said Lil. "You wonder. How he felt about—anything. Is this stuff worth a lot, do you think?" She was abashed but wanted to know. "This is a lot of stuff. Isn't it?"

"Maybe an estate auction," Pooley said.

"Is that how you'd? I. You know, I hate to, oh like a—we are *so* broke right now. But I feel like a vulture, but we are *bad* broke, so. . ."

"It's all right," said Pooley. "We're doing okay, so obviously the proceeds would be yours. You and Phil. I haven't ever even—I *left*, so. It's obviously all yours. Sounds like the place could be worth something."

"We both left. Anyone would have, probably. But you. You never came back. That has been a little bit odd, Kevin. Not that I was real involved with him. But—*never*? That's been kind of odd, strange, don't you think? I mean, *why*? They weren't the greatest parents, I know, and this wasn't the. . . If you think of all the things some parents do to their children. Was there something I didn't know about? Was it because of Jeanie? I mean, she was awful, but she's been long gone."

"I didn't like her," Pooley said. "I doubt anyone ever liked Jeanie. It also kind of pissed me off that he married another heavy smoker. But, no, that wasn't it, either. I'm actually not sure what it was. Habit, after a while."

"But, Kevin, you *never* saw him. Never. That would be unusual, don't you think?"

"He didn't mind."

"No. But."

"He didn't mind, Lil. Didn't bother him even a little bit."

"Yes," said his sister. "But what about you?"

"Yeah, what about me? Turns out I'm strange the opposite way. I know I kind of overwhelm Felicity and the kids at times. Could be just as bad, the way I'm doing it."

"I know what you mean." said Lil. "I think I even overwhelm my girls, with the baby talk and everything else." Lil's girls would be her nannies, her little goats, both her children being sons. They were known, the Pooley twins, for doting upon their loved ones and their pets with heavy devotion.

"You can't give someone something you don't have to give." Pooley had known it always, recited it often, but knowing and saying this bare truth had never been any comfort; his father was an old hole in him now elaborately bandaged, but one that would never heal. The nothingness principle. Quite a machinist, though.

Pooley addressed one of his father's lathes. "You ever see him turn anything out here?"

"Turn?" said Lil.

"Wood lathe. Metal lathe. It was—well think of a potter's wheel, but horizontal. With chisels."

"I can't picture it," Lil said.

"It was like—sculpture. Give him his due. A sculptor out here. He was a wizard."

Pooley had condensed his father to several recurrent memories, memories reenacted in his mind much as scenes from an acting class, and who knows how authentic they'd be at this point, how accurate, but one of those scenes had to do with this very lathe, a set piece with Sid turning a table leg, a ribbon of wood curling beautifully away from his hands, but Sid croaking into every bit of magic he made, ruining it for the boy. 'Get that. Get that mess out of here. No, with the whisk, the *whisk* broom."

Pooley said, "What do you say we blow him out into the sawdust bin? Run him through the blower?"

"Kevin. Oh, you mean—you mean it?"

"Well, he wouldn't want to take up space on one of these shelves. He'd never stand for that."

"But," she said.

"Would you take him? Want to leave him here for the realty people or whoever buys the place? This is Sid. We shouldn't get oversentimental."

"This is kind of bad right now," said Lil. "I guess I knew it would be."

"It doesn't have to be," said Pooley. "Or at least no worse than it's always been. I didn't realize I still felt this . . ."

Resentment was the word Pooley didn't speak. All this trouble to confront it once more and to understand resentment as the baseline of his being, and now resentment and a big vacuum hose propelled his father into a bin recently filled with cedar sawdust where Sid's soul would continue, no doubt, in its customary contentment.

Tell All the Truth
But Tell It Slant

1

Mike Vinich had been told of a typhoon that had blown the roof off the Lower Court building a year or so before his arrival on island and of how the Feds had pledged millions to build a new one with all the modern bells, whistles, and bullet proof glass, but in the meantime, while construction was underway with its many delays, work stoppages, and island holidays, Judge Mandeville's court sat in a previously abandoned warehouse. Corrugated steel walls. The acoustics in this structure were atrocious, as was Judge Mandeville's hearing. The concrete floor had never been properly finished, so a fine dust lifted from it to find its way up the nose, and it was an unusually bad Monday for the thirty sweating, sneezing wretches who lined the wooden benches of the gallery, sunk in their fouled luck

Vinich rose from the counsel table, pressing his hand into the small of his client's back to indicate that he should do the same. The small man fairly leapt to his feet, and Vinich said of him, "Your Honor, Mr. Miramatsu would like to plead guilty to both charges and accept the court's disposition."

The judge puzzled long enough for Vinich to fear he'd not been heard, or not been understood, but finally Judge Mandeville marveled, "You've fully reviewed your client's case with him?"

The bus from the prison had arrived just fifteen minutes earlier with a dozen such clients, all of them wanting his exclusive attention, but having described such situations to Mandeville in the past, Vinich knew that the judge thought it a poor excuse for his lack of preparation. "There's a problem, Your Honor."

"Of course there is, counsel. What now?"

"Well—language." This court conducted the bulk of

its business bilingually in Samoan and English; translators were often on hand for Spanish speakers or the Tongan, the Fijian, but, "Mr. Miramatsu," said Vinich, "speaks Japanese. That's it, as near as I can tell. I can't honestly say he understands me. Or this. I think he gets the general idea, though."

"We're assuming, counsel?"

"Some," Vinich conceded. "As necessary, Your Honor."

"Japanese?" said Judge Mandeville. "Looks like he's off a Peruvian vessel. How do they communicate with him?"

"I don't know, Your Honor. Maybe it's just a Peruvian registry. Maybe he knows what he's doing, and they don't need to talk to him. If he came off a tuna boat maybe there's not that much to talk about."

Mandeville's eyes were sled-dog blue but less friendly; the judge shifted his disgusted gaze to the immigration officer at the back of the room, a man with a massive, shaved head, cowering a bit under the magistrate's attention. "Has immigration talked to Mr. Miramatsu?"

"Nobody told us," said the officer, "about any Japan type of people."

Judge Mandeville said, "Foreign nationals. You have a foreign national in custody. How many times do we go over this? Your procedures? What you are supposed to do. By law."

The immigration officer, who had about a molecule more authority than the prisoner, shifted foot to foot in his thick soled shoes, the kind of bureaucrat who can endure and survive much chastisement.

It was rumored that Judge Mandeville was Stanford Law, and this could be true, for he was viciously learned, and if he'd fallen so far as to preside over this steamy scene, then that might explain why he made such a purgatory of his court. Pleeeease, screamed Vinich silently, a sentiment, a prayer silently echoed across the way by the Assistant Attorney General and the Deputy to the Assistant Attorney General where they sat in sweat, boredom, and self-righteousness. The accused, massed there in the gallery to await their judgement, were more patient with the judge's meanderings—just so long as his eyes had not yet settled on them.

Mr. Mirimatsu had been charged with two counts of Disorderly Conduct in Pago Pago. *La Bailarina* was his listed address. Mr. Mirimatsu had with a few explosive bursts of his extra earnest language tried to explain himself, and Mr. Mirimatsu made graceful gestures with his hands; none of it had clarified anything for Vinich, but they all knew enough, just reading between the lines, to dispose of this case. The man came off a boat that may or may not be lying at anchor in the harbor now. He may or may not have an immediate ride off the island. Mr. Miramatsu had been arrested two days previous, and if he'd had any dollars on his arrival at the territorial prison, he wouldn't have them now—a fine would be pointless. Mr. Mirimatsu, poor, slim, East Asian man, had spent two nights in the prison and would by now be full of resolve never to reoffend here, never to set foot again on Tutuila or any other American soil. It was a given that the immigration officer would forget Mr. Mirimatsu the moment they left the room.

"I would ask that my client be sentenced to time served, Your Honor."

Mr. Mirimatsu's terror was obvious; he'd been thoroughly punished.

"How does the Territory feel about this?"

The Assistant Attorney General, his face flush as a raspberry, rose to address the Court. "A fifty-dollar fine is usual for these offenses, Your Honor. Per offense."

"Is it, Mr. Swanson?" said Judge Mandeville. "I see. For future reference, counsel, the Court already has some familiarity with its own usual practices. And the relevant statutes, the penalties. The Court was inquiring as to what the Territory thought might be appropriate here. You know the Territory *can* require quite a lot more punishment."

"Oh," said young Abraham Swanson, standing there on the brutal, brittle, brink of his career as a federal prosecutor. "Your, Honor, the Territory will recommend that Mr.—that the Defendant be sentenced to pay a fine of fifty dollars for each offense."

"Did you note where these offenses allegedly occurred, Mr. Swanson? Note the address? Do you know where that is?"

"Approximately, Your Honor," said the young prosecutor.

"Do you have any idea how out of hand someone would have to be to get arrested down there? For Disorderly Conduct? Twice? Maybe this goes well beyond the usual fine. Did you see one of these counts involved indecency?"

"We haven't got the police reports," said the prosecutor, knowing full well there were no police reports.

"When do you expect them?"

"It may be. . . Hard to say, Your Honor."

Vinich rose again. "Would the Court consider sentencing Mr. Miramatsu to time served and imposing a suspended fine contingent on his immediate departure from the territory?"

His client shuddered beside him, whispering from time to time as if he'd just been punched in the stomach.

Here they were again, Vinich and the other officers of the court, Palagis with their sunburned noses palavering over the fates of people who did not look, speak, act, or think like them, people they would never understand

and who in most cases didn't expect or need their understanding. Vinich often felt the colonialist here, but it was a two-bit falsity not too far removed from his experience of stateside courts.

Judge Mandeville's special Monday torture was this protracted pretense that he could by insistence, by long badgering and judicial fiat make the island work properly. The temperature and humidity were both well north of eighty, and not so much as a paddle fan to stir the air, and the judge would stare down anyone who dared bring water into his court room.

Vinich created a dumb show by pointing to Mr. Mirimatsu's citations then looking at him meaningfully; Mirimatsu's corresponding bursts of sincerity convinced the judge that he'd made admission enough, and Mandeville imposed the fines at last that had been requested by the Territory, along with further jail time that he suspended on conditions that Mr. Mirimatsu would never understand but would no doubt follow if he possibly could. By noon the unfortunate Mr. Mirimatsu would be adrift on the high seas or even more at sea somewhere on this island.

It had been a holiday weekend. There were many drunk drivers, most of whom admitted their guilt at their first opportunity to do so. All of these received the same sentence, and it was a long and detailed sentence concerning their fines and how they might arrange to pay them, and the schooling they were now required to take, and the loss of their driver's licenses and when and how they might be reobtained; it was a five-minute spiel Judge Mandeville delivered from memory but with great feeling every time, for each and every offender, and in most cases the whole thing was repeated in a mechanical rush of Samoan. Judge Mandeville meant to demonstrate how, even here, especially here, he would do his job down to the last little detail.

Every cleft of Vinich's flesh seeped sweat, thrilling rivulets sliding here and there. The last of the many misdemeanants he represented that morning was a man charged with criminal trespass for repeatedly passing out on the front yard crypt of his neighbor's grandmother, on a polished concrete slab that was, as Mr. Sione explained, so cool, and he meant the dead woman no, no, no disrespect. His apology was abject enough that he got off with Mandeville's admonition not to do it again.

The final people to be brought before the court that morning were those charged with felonies who would be bound over to the High Court but needed a bond hearing in the meantime. There came a fellow the clerk called up as Jesse Shard, but who breathed the name 'Bobo' into Vinich's ear when he arrived at his side. Shard, the kind of young man who'd obviously never been off island, was charged with possessing three joints at a street fair, of offering to share them with another. The charge was not only a felony, but carried a five-year sentence in the territory, and that sentence had in the past been imposed for amounts like this. If Mr. Shard were well connected, he had little to worry about. But if Mr. Shard were well connected, he probably never would have been arrested. If Mr. Shard were well connected, he probably wouldn't be wearing such a sensationally stained tee shirt. The young man's splayed and calloused feet had never been confined in any kind of enclosed shoes. The Assistant Attorney General claimed that the young man, because he was facing that five-year sentence, had a real temptation to run, so the Assistant Attorney General asked for a bond of twenty thousand dollars.

Vinich stood. "Your Honor. I think a hundred dollars

might be out of reach for my client."

Young Mr. Shard pulled at Vinich's sleeve, the gesture in all the world Vinich hated most. He leaned down to hear his client whisper, "I can't go back." Vinich arranged his face to express sympathy but not hope. Shard tugged detestably again at his sleeve, then indicated that Vinich should sit there beside him at the council table. Vinich sat down. With his back to the gallery, Shard told his attorney to look under the counsel table, and there Mr. Shard was sliding his lavalava up his interior thigh, higher and higher, spreading his legs. Bobo. Vinich could not look away until he saw what his client meant to reveal. "Ooooh," he said. "Oh. Okay. Your, Honor, may council approach the bench?"

"Is that necessary, Mr. Vinich? It all goes on the record." Judge Mandeville, expedient now, in a hurry.

"It could be—delicate."

"And pertaining to this man's bond? If so, let's just have it, counsel."

"Mr. Shard has a, an advanced case, I'd say, of elephanti. . . elephant. . . a condition."

"Elephantiasis?"

"Yes, your Honor."

"That's your medical opinion, Mr. Vinich?"

"The symptoms are severe, Your Honor."

Judge Mandeville stared at him, requiring specifics.

"Severe swelling," said Vinich.

Judge Mandeville stared at him.

"One of Mr. Shard's testicles, Your Honor—is about as big as a volleyball. How he even manages to walk, I. . . Out there at the prison, I don't think. . . Maybe I could arrange for him to be released to the custody of a relative or a matai. Maybe his pastor."

"A volleyball?" challenged the Assistant Attorney

General.

"A volleyball," said Vinich. "Take a look if you don't believe me."

There was laughter in the room, gaveling, laughter that only pitched higher for the initial attempts to suppress it, then a brisker gaveling. Once more in control, Judge Mandeville said the level of health care in the correctional facility would be a distinct step up from anything available in Mr. Shard's home village, then, pretending wisdom, he said, "I'll split the difference. Ten thousand. We'll make it ten thousand."

"Your, Honor. . ." said Vinich.

"*Ten* thousand," said Judge Mandeville. "With every one of the boilerplate conditions of release in the event he makes bond. Mr. Swanson, see that your office has that order on my desk by two-thirty this afternoon. No later. Not one minute later. And correctly drafted. I intend to be in some adequate air conditioning by two thirty."

There had been a buzz around the court that morning about a murder committed over the weekend. Vinich knew no details but knew he wouldn't be innocent of them for very long.

"Pule Ulu," called the clerk of court. The last matter on the court's calendar was the accused killer's initial appearance.

Mr. Ulu was a man of such height and mass that his standing up was a drama in several acts. His height was even greater for his high heels, made-to-order size twenty-ones, and by the hair he wore piled in a tilted top knot. Ulu's wrists were secured before him with the prison's pair of extra-large, island-made handcuffs, and he wore a dress, not a lavalava but one of those satin sheath dresses island women whip up for special occasions. For all the constraints on his movement, Mr. Ulu still managed to make his way toward counsel table with a sensuous, feminine grace, followed closely by two worried looking prison guards. Vinich had some trouble ordering his responses to this individual, so he simply shook his hand as he did with all his clients. Handcuffed as he was, Mr. Ulu could only conveniently offer his left hand; his grip, which might have been crushing, was feathery. Vinich's hand disappeared inside it.

"Are you Pule Ulu?" the Judge asked, a question the court translator began to repeat in Samoan.

"That won't be necessary, darling," said the defendant, "I am Pule Ulu." His seemed a costly dignity, his voice a thumping melody.

"Take a look at the citation Mr. Vinich has there. Is your name spelled correctly?"

"It is," said Mr. Ulu, loftily.

Anticipating the judge's next question, Vinich pointed to the portion of the citation setting forth Mr. Ulu's date of birth. When prompted, Mr. Ulu said that it was correct. He was thirty-six years old. Several hibiscus depended from his temple. He smelled of the flowers and some other pleasantness.

"Mr. Ulu," said the judge, "I am required to tell you that you are charged by citation with first degree homicide. I am further obligated to inform you that, upon conviction this offense is punishable by death in the Territory and carries a mandatory minimum sentence of forty years imprisonment. Do you understand the charge and the possible penalties?"

"Yes," said Mr. Ulu, "yes, sir, but if I could just say. . ."

Reflexively both the judge and Vinich raised their hands, palm out: Stop. "Whoa," said Vinich into Mr. Ulu's ear.

"You're not here to enter a plea," said the judge. "I'm

binding you over to the High Court. Bond is set at a million dollars, at least until your arraignment."

"Your, Honor," said Vinich, "once again I have no details, so I'm in not in any position to argue for. . ."

"Mr. Ulu is accused of bashing a man's head in," said the judge. "With a rock. Bond is a million, Mr. Vinich. I'm getting very tired of this kind of thing."

2

Vinich had spoken with his boss, the Public Defender, a total of five times, one of these when he'd interviewed by phone for this job a year and a half back. The Public Defender was a minor matai with a law degree out of some Alabama school and very little interest in the operation of his department apart from being certain it made a good showing at the annual government Christmas show; in his dealings with his Palagi employees, the Public Defender shortened the long ramble of his real name, a jumble of soft vowels and consonants, to 'Ahti.' Vinich had sensed Ahti was far too eager to hire him for his managing attorney, and since he'd been hired Vinich had come to understand that his managerial responsibilities would include doing himself anything he thought the department should be doing. It was almost touching to hear from Ahti now. To hear of his concern.

"Have you got too much on your plate?"

Vinich wanted to be succinct. "Yes." The boss was on a cell phone going in and out of service.

"Judge Mandeville called," said the Public Defender.

"Oh?"

"Where is Root? Is he gone for good?"

Jack Root was the young attorney who was supposed to be handling Lower Court. "Still in New Zealand with his girlfriend," said Vinich. "They're trying to get a visa together, he tells me. To get her back to the states."

"In New Zealand?"

"It's complicated," said Vinich. "He's in love, so. . . If you could hire someone. . . Have we had any bites on that ad?"

"I have some bad news for you," said Ahti. "This new murder—we're not subcontracting that out. So that will be something else you have to do."

Many months earlier there had been a case involving a Palagi drug dealer who had kicked a debtor to death and had his henchmen throw the deadbeat into the ocean, which didn't want him and cast him back onto the beach. The Public Defender, it was said at the time, lacked the resources to properly handle a capital case, and a crusader from California had been brought in to steer the thing very expensively to a plea bargain. Now that the office's resources were further diminished, it seemed it would be all right to assign Vinich this new murder along with his other duties.

"The judge tells me your translator wasn't there this morning."

"Elihu called in sick," said Vinich.

"Rugby weekend," the Public Defender surmised.

This was a condition that frequently waylaid Elihu the scrum half—self-inflicted, off field injuries. Vinich felt a loyalty toward his translator that Elihu had never earned, so Vinich changed the subject. "If you have any pull," he begged his boss, "with somebody in the building here. . . there's something dead up in the ceiling. Francis says the maintenance guys came this morning when I was at court, and they claimed they couldn't smell anything."

"Have you seen this dead thing?" Ahti asked him.

"No," said Vinich, "but the smell is unmistakable. Those guys from maintenance were—." The need to be culturally sensitive forced some tact on Vinich, so he only said, "You can smell it. It's unmistakable."

"In the ceiling?" Ahti said, as if it were somehow unlikely. "But you haven't seen it?"

"You hear them," said Vinich, rasping in exasperation. "They're heavy. You hear them. They skitter and thump around up there; it's a wonder they don't come right down through one of those ceiling panels, come crashing down on us."

"Hm," said Ahti. "I'll see what I can do. But, anyway, this homicide will be yours, and could be maybe more of a mess than usual. And keep that Root away from it, I don't even want him on second chair. I'm giving him a week to be back on island. If not, you better fire him the minute he shows up."

"But. . ." Vinich had meant to say something about the value of a warm body just now, even Root's, but the boss had drifted out of service and was back in his big silence.

Vinich knew that carcass rotting somewhere above him would continue to reek until it had rotted away entirely or he had sought it out and removed it himself. He had no ladder. His computer screen, a monitor he had cannibalized from another office only two weeks earlier, was now in its own death throes and flickered sickeningly.

"Frances," he informed the office manager as he fled, "I'm getting out of here. This is giving me a headache."

Frances Vainupo managed an office in which she was very often alone, one of several sinecures she held simultaneously with the government, and she may have been the best dressed woman in a building full of well dressed women; her hands were like fat, frolicsome puppies—at the end of these were fingernails where she had Korean women express themselves several times a week; Frances spent her days in the office, hour by hour, buffing that art with a lanolin rag and ignoring incoming phone calls, and Frances did not look up from this work to note Vinich's departure but did manage to say, "Okay." She sat in this stench all day, or at least until two-thirty.

"Guess I'll go out and have a chat with Mr. Ulu," said Vinich, wondering whatever possessed him to explain himself to this woman.

3

Vinich had bought and even driven a fun little Mazda about a hundred miles before its timing belt and water pump failed; while he waited for parts to come, as everything must come to this island, from halfway around the world and through several layers of incompetence, Vinich was back to riding the aiga buses where he was a curiosity. In his white shirt and tie and with his briefcase he must seem the superannuated Mormon kid on his mission. Vinich, however, wore sandals and a moustache; his fellow riders didn't know what to make of him. He sometimes enjoyed and was sometimes annoyed by being a specimen among them. The buses were a bad bet when he needed to get anywhere in a timely way, and often enough he was the anxious passenger fuming when his driver made an extended stop to chat with a roadside acquaintance. Today, though, there was no rush but a nice wailing of afro pop and Jimmy Clift on his bus and a gaggle of giggling, plaid skirted Catholic school girls gathered at the front near the driver, a Polynesian Errol Flynn. It was a right ride at first, but by the time Vinich stepped off at Nu'uuli he'd been a little overcome by the tassels swaying from the ceiling and the gas-rich fumes rising from the tail pipe just beneath him.

At a corner store he bought two tall bottles of water and drank one of them before he'd left the premises. During the day Vinich had soaked the shirt he was wearing three separate times with sweat, and he considered it a small blessing that he was unable to smell himself. It was now a short hike to his concrete cottage and that room with his bed and a fan aimed squarely at it where he might lie stripped to his shorts, watching his roommates the geckos parked on the ceiling considering their next move, and Vinich was halfway to that whirring quiet, that necessary meditation, halfway home when he necessarily passed the correctional facility, its gates wide open, a cricket match proceeding inside, the pitch under punishing sun with inmate devised wickets. Some tweaking of the rules and a delighted yelping made the game Samoan. Kilikiti.

Somewhere in there was Mr. Ulu. Vinich had said he was going to speak to Mr. Ulu, and though that had been an entirely unnecessary excuse to extricate himself from the office, and though it was likely Frances hadn't even heard him, Vinich had said it, and he was guided by a queer set of principles. Then too, if he was going to represent the man, it was probably best to get to him as soon as possible. Vinich was tired, and knew he wasn't on his best game, but he turned in through the prison gate and walked up to the guard house, slow and deliberate, holding his briefcase and umbrella well away from his body. The guard house was divided into two compartments, the first of these served as a sort of waiting room; the other, an air-conditioned compartment, contained a uniformed woman. Vinich approached the microphone that would allow him to speak with the woman, and she must have no peripheral vision at all not to notice him there on the other side of the plexiglass, so he said. "Excuse me?"

The corrections officer glanced toward him and away again. There was no obvious reason for her to be distracted, but it seemed she had already forgotten him.

"Excuse me?"

"Yes," she said.

"I'm from the Public Defender's. . ."

"I know who you are," said the officer. "I see you down at court when I have to go."

Vinich sensed disapproval, a near universal reaction to a public defender. "I need to see Mr. Ulu," he said. "Pule Ulu."

The corrections officer's lips were enlarged by lipstick, her eyebrows reduced to a thin, parabolic line. "Are you his lawyer?"

"I will be," said Vinich.

"I need to see an order or something," said the corrections officer whose duty cap rode precariously pinned atop her hair.

"He's entitled to see an attorney."

"I'd need to see something," she said. "In writing. He can't just talk to everybody."

"Writing?" Mike Vinich had always been a terrible, wilting kind of advocate for himself, so he did enjoy the yipping terrier he became when advocating for others. "There will be an order coming," he said. "In the meantime, if you want something to read, you might look at the United States Constitution, Sixth Amendment, or the Samoa rules of criminal procedure, there's plenty to read on the topic. The man has a right to a lawyer. At all stages of the prosecution. Which means right now. If he doesn't get one, then that's a violation of his rights. Which you wouldn't want to do in a case this serious. Would you, ma'am?"

"Ma'am?" said the officer. This form of address was, it seemed, beneath contempt, or it was when coming from this Palagi buttinski. "All right," she said, turning to another guard who'd been enjoying the cool guard shack. "Go get him," she said. The lesser guard paused long enough to register his injury and some uncertainty. "That big Ulu," she specified, and the lesser guard went reluctantly off, and the officer at the window, clearly loathing him, told Vinich, "You can wait out in the visitor's center. You don't need to be in here."

"You want me to leave my umbrella with you?" Vinich said. "Before I go out there?"

The woman sneered in reply.

In the sweltering anteroom of the guard shack was a man enduring his stolid middle age in a starched white shirt draped with puka beads and a chunky wooden cross; he sat in a plastic chair that must surely be sticking to him, waiting helplessly it seemed, a much-annotated bible lying on his lap, spread across his burgundy lavalava. Vinich nodded toward him, and the man smiled apologetically.

The visitor's center was an open-air pavilion, floor, tables, benches, and supporting columns all of cast concrete, a nearly typhoon-proof structure that could be pleasant when a breeze came at it from off the lagoon. Vinich settled in to wait. Anticipating a long wait, he tried to nurse his bottle of water. The prison housed everyone from the unruly tipsy to serial rapists in a cluster of barn-like barracks, men and women alike; there was little effort here to separate the various offenders by sex or by category or from the world lying just beyond that open gate. Vinich watched the bowler out on the pitch winding up and delivering a red ball to the batsman. What fun they were having, the inmates, a level of fun Vinich could scarcely recall; how easily they might come running over here and have their fun at his expense. Onto the pavilion came a young inmate with a pushbroom and the goatee of an eastern philosopher. He pushed the broom in a pattern that brought him gradually nearer to Vinich until he'd worked up the nerve to speak, and when he spoke, he seemed on the verge of tears. "You're the Public Defender, aren't you?"

"I'm with that office."

"But a lawyer? You do crimes, right?"

"Yeah," Vinich admitted.

"I need help," said the young man. His eyes had a bloodshot caste.

"Oh?" said Vinich.

"I've got to get out of here. I'm too young. Too young for this."

Vinich knew better than to express the least sympathy for the young man's situation; he made himself blank to hear the rest of the story.

"Seven years," said the young man, his lips atremble. "And I'm young. And that's no suspended time, no probation, no parole. Nothing. And I'm young."

"Yeah?" said Vinich. Knowing there would be more to this anyway, he asked for it. "What happened?"

"I was in here sitting out fines," said the young man.

"And?"

"And I was playing basketball. Just playing basketball." The young man gestured toward the prison's paved basketball court; it was presently unoccupied in favor of the ongoing cricket game.

"Okay. What else?"

"Oooh," said the young man, sighing and hiccupping with grief, "I killed a guy."

"Seems like a pretty hard foul," said Vinich.

"A great big guy," said the young man. "A great big guy. Even for in here. You know, he's just got to jump up and hang his fat ass on the rim. He's three hundred pounds. At *least*. And he bent it down. Way down. We couldn't get it back right, not even close to level again."

"Yeah?" said Vinich "And? Then?"

"I'm a shooter," said the young man. "In here I am definitely a perimeter player. I'd get killed going in the paint. I need my shot."

Vinich waited.

"So I did, I did get kind of mad. And I. You know. . . I did hit him. But if anybody was going to get killed, it should have been me. I mean this guy—Fiti—I mean he was so *huge*. But I caught him on the chin. Caught him just right, you know, real wahoo. He went down. Hit his head. Pretty soon he was dead. A lot of those guys thought he was just kidding us. But, no, he was dead. Right out here."

"Seems to be a lot of that going around," Vinich said.

"That's what everybody keeps saying. But why me? Why do I have to. . .? You know, I just need to get out of here. You know David? David kills Goliath and he gets to be king. But me? Not me. I get in here for it. I've got five years left, and I can't stand it."

"You have appeals going or anything? Did you get convicted?"

"I was in court," said the young man, "but it was just, you know, where you tell the judge what you did. They didn't call it murder any more after that. Manslaughter, okay. I told the judge what I just told you, and I was supposed to get two years, and I didn't even know if I could do that. But. . ." The young man had regained his composure but still wore his grief.

"That's a tough one," Vinich sighed. "Judge jumped the shark, huh?" What the lad needed to know, if anything, was that there was not one scrap of hope he might cling to. What he needed was resignation now.

The guard who had been sent to find Mr. Ulu never did return, but while Vinich was talking with the young inmate Mr. Ulu emerged from the ravine that contained much of the prison's small plantation. Shirtless under a pair of coveralls, Mr. Ulu hove into sight like the main attraction at a professional wrestling match, but with flowers in his hair. Vinich stood and called to him, waving his arm as a semaphore.

Puzzled for a moment, Mr. Ulu then called back, his reply rolling through the compound. "Oh. Hello." He executed his own big wave. His gait as he approached them was now unencumbered by handcuffs, silk, or impractical shoes, and even moving with all due deliberation he came on pretty quick.

"You got that big *fa'afafine*?" said the push broom lad, drifting away. "Good luck, I guess. He better hope you're better than my lawyer was."

Across the concrete picnic table Vinich reintroduced himself. "Mr. Ulu, I'm Mike Vinich. Call me Mike. As you know, I'm from the Public Defender's Office. It looks like I'm being assigned to represent you going forward." They shook hands again. Vinich sought signs of intelligence in his client's regard, and seeing it there said, "If you don't mind, I want to run through a few basics to get started. First—do not talk to anyone in here about your case. Never. That will bite you every time. Second—if your family can afford a private attorney, you should look into that. I'm as good as anybody else, but I'm dealing with about a hundred cases right now. It's like anything else, the more time you can give it, the better result, usually. If you can get somebody who can devote most of their time to your case, then maybe you should consider it." Vinich had concluded from Mr. Ulu's clean, white Converse All Stars that the man might come from money. "Third—" he said, "from now on, anything you tell me is confidential, whether you get another lawyer or not. It's between us. But if I represent you, and we go to trial, then you couldn't testify to something real different than what you'd told me. And, last but not least—don't talk to anybody else about your case. Not family, not anyone. No one has proven anything yet, so—and they do have to make a case; you never want to make that any easier for them." Having seen no charging document other than a citation so far, Vinich knew the Territory might file an Information jammed with facts and witnesses to support its claim, but "We should just wait and see right now," he told his client. "Wait and see what they've got before we get into any details. About what did or didn't happen."

"I see," said Mr. Ulu, pressing the palps of his fingers to his lips. His gestures and manner belonged to some indeterminate sex, an indeterminate time. Vinich, who had never attended a tea party, felt as if he were at one now. Vinich was accustomed to advising those who followed no one's advice, but he thought that might not be the problem here. Mr. Ulu was attentive, and the few phrases he had uttered thus far seemed modulated by thought. "Like a confessional?" he said in that voice coming up from a deep, cool well. "It would be like a confessional? When I speak to you?"

"I should also tell you," Vinich said. "I don't need to hear anything. You don't have to say anything to anybody. Including me. That's what I've been trying to tell you. We'll wait on that until we find out what the Territory has for evidence. Let's just see what they've got. But, yeah, as far as the secrecy part goes, it would be similar. I think. I'm not a Catholic or anything."

"I'm not either," said Mr. Ulu, poised at the edge of his first confidence. "You should know, sir, I'm an—I am an atheist."

"That shouldn't be a problem," said Vinich.

"Everyone in my village *knows* I'm an atheist," said Mr. Ulu, becoming solemn.

Almost any Samoan, upon learning your name, would then want to know your church affiliation, and in any village on this island Mr. Ulu would be an outlier from whom evil would almost be expected. Why had he proclaimed himself? "That shouldn't be a problem," Vinich said, though they both knew that if his village were in any way involved, Mr. Ulu's faithlessness could very well hurt him.

"It always has been," he said. "Quite a big problem where I come from."

"That's the kind of thing I'm supposed to prevent," said Vinich. "That shouldn't have anything to do with it."

"I think you'll be stuck with me," said Mr. Ulu. "I don't think my family will want to—And that's fine. I trust you, sir."

"Mike," said Vinich.

"Yes, sir," said Mr. Ulu.

4

Jack Root had returned from New Zealand to pass out on the stoop in front of Vinich's cottage. He lay under the sun, a mistake for a man of his complexion.

"Jack?"

Root opened his eyes and made a slow, disappointing inventory of his wellbeing; half his face inflamed by the sun, the other side pocked by the fine gravel on which he'd lain. He wiped something from his chin. "I got as drunk as I could," he said.

"I guess you did," said Vinich. "You should practice more, try and get the hang of it before you go all in like this."

"I do *not* feel better," said Jack Root.

"I wouldn't think so." Vinich wanted in his cottage. "Go get a shower," he said. "Puke, if you have to. But, you know, not here. Probably better hydrate."

"I can't go back there," said Jack Root, looking up through yet another pair of ruined eyes.

"What?" said Vinich. "New Zealand or—you mean your place?"

"Everything there reminds me of her. In my own house. That's why I—You know what she did?"

"I don't," said Vinich, "but. . ."

"She used me," said Root through his misused face, which was swollen.

"Oh," said Vinich. Root was the only one who'd misunderstood the nature of that relationship. Of course, she'd used him.

"She was just using me to get down to her *real* boyfriend. Her *real* boyfriend."

"Yeah?" said Vinich. "Well, let's get you under some shade before you melt." Most of Root's big bender had leached out into a noxious haze, his essence now, and Vinich, who had thought he was finished with the day's torrent of sad stories, had a guest. Root collapsed on the couch, a punishing piece of government-issue furniture, a stony futon just beginning to harbor mold. Vinich wet a bath towel and told Root to wrap his head with it, which he did, but leaving an opening for his mouth. Vinich brought him tap water.

Root struggled to keep this down. "She just wanted a way down to New Zealand," he said.

"Hm," said Vinich, unsurprised.

"She was so. . ."

Undulant, thought Vinich. She'd fallen right in with the bunch here at Lions Park where Palagis and other people drifting through some arm of the Samoan or Federal government were housed. She had wanted everyone to call her Kay, and she was fluent in English for a girl from Western Samoa. She walked like a camel, but her the gait carried very different implications, and poor Root, puffy, awkward, and perpetually confused Jack Root, never stood a chance. Vinich had watched this tragedy act by act without a word to the wise, because how to caution a grown man wholly governed by an unwieldy organ. Vinich had seen this or something worse coming, and Root, in losing the calculating miss Kay had dodged a lovely bullet, a slow acting poison. Vinich thought it best to change the subject.

"Well, I picked up a murder today. Looks like I'll be doing a murder."

Root revealed more of his face and some interest in the topic.

"So that means you need to step up, Jack. Pull yourself together and get back down to Lower Court, and. . ."

"Ooh, gaawd no," said Root. "I hadn't even been thinking about that. That. I don't think I can anymore. It's so awful. All those. . . And that *juuhdge*. It was awful even before, even when I was kind of happy."

"But that's what you signed up to do," Vinich said. "Contract. Contract. I hate to drag that into it, but—I don't think you want to pay your way back to the States, do you? Unless you've got something lined up back there. I guess I'm saying: You've got this job, and you probably better do it. I'll be needing more help in High Court, too. I think we better assume Ahti's gonna goof around and never hire anybody else. So, we're it. For the whole territory."

"But that Lower Court," Root despaired. "It's like, like when I was little, and we were in this funny church where they really liked to emphasize hell. It's quite a bit like I thought hell would be. But worse. Because it's real."

"Go home. Swing by Dr. Feelgood's if you need something to get you through the night. But tomorrow, bright and early, you'd better get back to being the champion of the downtrodden."

"When you put it that way," said Root, "it doesn't suck quite so bad. But I know five minutes after I get down there. . . I mean—you know. You've been down there. It's just hell."

"Go home," Vinich said. "Sleep it off," he said, though he knew the real hangover would be a long time healing.

"You just don't know, Mike."

"Work," said Vinich. "You'd be surprised what that can do for you. Go home."

Leaving, Jack Root declared, "I don't even know who I am. What I should. . ."

"Just do tomorrow," said Vinich. "And that's coming right up. Go home and go to bed."

◊ ◊ ◊

The cottage's exterior walls were louvered and let in much fresh air and very little light, so Vinich lived in a well-ventilated cave, an environment that sometimes soothed, sometimes depressed. As evening descended so had a numbness that did not equate to rest; Vinich thought of hiking to the noodle house where he sometimes went for sashimi, but his guts were still in an uproar from the wasabi paste he'd overenjoyed there the night before. Vinich required little dietary variety, so for his dinner he might warm one of the cans of beef stew he bought by the case, or he might have a beer, or both on a really special occasion, but lately Vinich had been developing a mystic's indifference to sustenance. He lay in his billowing boxers, toes to the ceiling, and he never did succeed in thinking of nothing, but his attempts to do so shattered any useful thoughts. So, he fell asleep maybe a little hungry and much earlier than was a good idea, and he felt lost in time when his phone rang. Morning? Had he missed something?

"Dad," said the caller.

"Oooh," said Vinich.

"You sound groggy," said his son.

"I was—" Vinich consulted his watch, "taking a nap."

"Sorry." Cyrus. His mother had been keen for ancient Persia around the time of his birth, so he was to this day Cyrus. "I know you probably need all the rest you can get," he said.

Vinich tried not to whine in their correspondence, but some mention of his workload was unavoidable as his workload often left him little else to say. Cyrus did not often resort to the telephone. Vinich said, "What's up?"

"Nothing bad. But I guess I'm done with engineering."

"Oh," said Vinich, "is that all? I saw that coming. Not for you, huh?"

"No." Cyrus shuddered audibly.

"Good to find out," Vinich said, "before you had too much time invested in it."

"A year was too much," said Cyrus. "Tooo much."

"Now what? Got anything in mind?"

"Oh, yeah. I do. Changing majors. Changing schools. I'll need a for-reals liberal arts school."

"Oh?" said Vinich.

"Not philosophy," said Cyrus. "I think I'm switching to Comparative Lit, which is, I know, just as bad."

"Oh."

"The thing is, Mom has been helping me here and there with expenses, been paying my tuition, but she says she won't do that anymore just so I can pursue a hobby degree."

"That's what she calls it?"

"As usual," said Cyrus, "she has a point. Anyway, I'm sure I can get work at the food service, but I might need a little help transitioning."

"How much?"

"Can I get back to you on that?" Cyrus said. "I want to keep it down to a bare minimum. I'll call you when I know what that looks like. I know you can't be making big money over there,"

"No," said Vinich. "But I have no expenses. Papayas knee deep out behind my house, noodles are cheap, and the bus is a quarter if that's all I want to pay. No time to recreate. I'm swimming in cash."

"It is kind of a hobby degree, you know. I probably wouldn't be able to repay you in under like twenty years."

"Nah," said Vinich, "I think it's a thing parents typically do. Pay for their kids' schooling."

"It's what interests me," Cyrus said.

"Okay," said Vinich.

Vinich did not expect to sleep again until an hour or two before it would be time to get up. He played the plastic recorder he kept on his nightstand—five minutes maybe, but a long time at that to play the one tune he knew, a child's tune he played for as long as he could stand it. Out in the dark the neighborhood's dogs, most of them unassigned to any human and scabbed with mange, snarled and barked, a swirling suite for many voices to accompany the memories near and far that came so predictably to carom around in him—and regrets, recriminations, contemporary doubt—and no resolution, no quiet in sight. Wary of such nights, Vinich had never learned to avoid them.

It's what interests me.

Here was a phrase the boy would have heard his father use to explain some of the decisions that had resulted in this lonely room. What interested Vinich had served him well when he'd strode plaid shirted through the crisp fall air on campus, putting himself through college by painting, remodeling, and trying with some success to get a handle on either Kant or Lao Tzu—who interested him— and into this prime moment came plaid shirted Cecily, young historian who adored him and his interests, and they married, graduated, sustained themselves on respectful and regularly passionate love and with the same work they'd done while they were in school, only more of it. Then Vinich lucked into a slipped disc and a severed index finger, a little incident on the loading dock behind the paint store during one of those rare times when he happened to be covered by Workers Comp. His settlement and the funds available for his retraining went to law school because it seemed interesting and was an interest he could pursue with his back so thoroughly tweaked. There was another lovely interlude with pure theory, but then Vinich was suddenly a lawyer needing a job, and the first work on offer had been court appointments here and there. They were as broke as they'd ever been, but at least Vinich had war stories to bring his wife, and for a while Cecelia would reconfigure these accounts as necessary to make her husband bright and shiny in them. And Cecelia had his son. And Cecelia was restless for a time before she felt she should also be a hero, and so Vinich, who could now bill about as many hours as he was willing to work, put her through law school and kept a nanny for Cyrus, and wondered all the while if he might be missing the point, and at some point as a law student Cecelia had decided that her husband had only been posturing as some kind of gallant when he was really just a shmuck who couldn't rouse himself to get out of the least lucrative area of the law, and Cecelia noticed she was tired of being poor, or nearly so, and those things Mike Vinich found interesting didn't interest her anymore; Cecelia as a lawyer in her own right hired on at a personal injury firm and fell in love with a junior partner there with the result that Vinich had gone down a long, bleak stretch of interstate to live apart from his son and his erstwhile wife and their persistent happiness. They'd been happy without him, and even after all this time he'd barely thought about it when he happened on a chance to slip even farther away.

What in life might be interesting if not the South Pacific?

5

Vinich had learned to come early to sessions of the High Court and occupy that portion of the lower veranda that would remain in the shade until the court room's doors were opened. The Navy had built it when Teddy Roosevelt cast his eyes on the vast Pacific for a new frontier, and the territory had been administered from this building during its first fifty years, and now, these many years farther on the thing still stood proud and shiplike with railings all around it, a wooden building improbably preserved against typhoon, tidal wave, and insidiously soggy air by applications of a paint so white it glowed as soon as the sun tilted over Rainmaker every sunny morning. This morning the other early arrivals to court were two groups in their best finery, happy people heavily bedecked in flowers, and when Vinich finally coaxed a final calendar from the clerk of court he noted the marriage and the adoption that were scheduled for the end of that calendar, and Vinich wondered how happy his happy companions on the veranda would be by the time the court had got around to opening its doors and wending its way through all its previous business—matters criminal, civil, and maritime and hard on a good mood.

Bored, Vinich checked his briefcase to be sure it contained a file for every case in which he was to appear, then waited with that briefcase between his sandaled feet; naked tootsies were never informal in Samoa, and Vinich liked the novelty and comfort of wearing open footwear to court. He came early to these sessions in part because he had a terrible time communicating with those of his clients who were not in custody. His clients were required by the rules of their release to stay in contact with him, but if they failed to do so Vinich could not ethically report this failure to the court. So, he waited here for clients who would not take or return his calls or who were never available when his translator was available, clients who believed Vinich was only an extension of the prosecution, the guy who seemed to be in charge of delivering the bad news. Frigate birds wheeled over the harbor, palm fronds clacked, and there was a lambent light on the water; Vinich found no ease in the scene.

His translator arrived. Elihu strolled up at last with a bright new shiner, a new crease in his forehead, and after greeting Vinich, the scrum half stood beside him offering not another word but his palpable indifference until he excused himself to go around to the back of the building and have a smoke. Then, all in a rush, the morning's business commenced with breathless Charlie Sapolu, the inveterate but inept thief who needed to be informed that he was about to serve time for his current beef, but also suspended time from several previous heists gone wrong. Elihu returned to help Vinich explain this. Sapolu seemed sad, but Vinich had never seen him otherwise. Then came an urgent wife, the great waddling wife of another client who wanted to recant her account of his assault on her before it was too late, and Vinich told her that it was already too late, her husband had signed something. And where was he? The woman said he hadn't come. He didn't think he had to if only she'd say he hadn't done anything. Her face wore a bright line of flesh from chin to cheek, a scar taut and proud from his attack on her; she'd been so seriously hurt as to vault this beating into High Court, so her story even if timely never would have been very convincing. Vinich told Elihu to drive as fast as possible to the woman's house and bring her husband back no matter what his condition. The woman named a village at a far tip of the island, and Vinich said, "Never mind. You'd never make it." He began assembling an excuse that might serve, something plausible with some flecks of truth in it to explain his wife beater's absence.

Vinich then spoke with Pete Iosefa, an embezzler who'd been standing by, cultivating an innocent air. Iosefa had meticulously recorded his own crime only to let those records fall into the hands of a man in his company whom he had recently cuckolded, and Iosefa was that practical kind of criminal who knows when his position is weak. He was relieved when Vinich told him, as he would later tell the Court, that the parties were still working on negotiating an outcome, and the Court would know this for code indicating they were looking for a way that Mr. Iosefa might be punished without impeding his ability to pay back what he'd stolen. Mr. Iosefa, at least, was pleased with the morning's news; he was in no hurry for the next accounting. Vinich advised him to deodorize his breath before things got started, told him the Chief Judge had thrown a man in jail just last week for coming to court smelling of alcohol. Alarmed, Iosefa hurried off, and Vinich hoped he hadn't scared him off entirely. Iosefa was wearing one of those clunky crosses that seemed all the rage right now.

The bus from the prison arrived with just two criminals for the High Court, both of them his clients, both of them here this morning to be arraigned. They were hustled out of the bus flanked by guards, and Vinich fell into the rear of this short procession to tell both his people at once, Mr. Shard and Mr. Ulu, "Nothing much happens today. I'll plead you not guilty, and if the judge asks you about that, I want you to say the same. 'Not guilty, Your Honor.' Okay? That's only if you have to say anything at all. It's always better if I do all the talking."

Mr. Ulu was in a white shirt and tie now, an ensemble he made heroic, the tails of his tie reached only to his sternum, his mane undone and lying on his shoulder. Bobo walked with the dual difficulty of being handcuffed and having that keg of flesh between his legs. The doors of the court room opened at last upon their approach, seemingly in honor of their arrival; Vinich and his clients had one small advantage before the court—their business always came first, and though there were good and practical reasons for this, Vinich believed that it was mostly a matter of decorum; nothing like a prisoner to muck up the atmosphere in a courtroom, so they were got into and out of it as soon as possible—right back out of sight. Mr. Ulu and young Bobo were guided by the guards to the front row of the gallery, prisoner's row. The guards stood to either side of them. Litigants, and a ship's captain came in and filled teak pews. Vinich, first on the calendar, went straight to the counsel table assigned to the defense, and he was standing at it when Swanson the young AG delivered him the Informations charging Pele Ulu and Jesse Shard, and Vinich saw at a glance that these documents were brief but he had no time to see whether they were or weren't convincing before the judges flowed in and occupied the bench, three abreast, the whole room bobbing up and down for the bailiff, that call and response, the ancient ceremony of deference—'All rise. Be seated.' For Vinich three judges was an odd number; the two old gents who sat berobed to either side of the Chief Judge served mostly as decoration, or recipients of paychecks, for the Chief Judge rarely consulted them, and never at any length.

Jesse Shard was the first to be arraigned, and he came forward wearing the same clothes in the same condition, or a little worse, that he'd worn to Lower Court twos days before. Though young he seemed well accustomed to misery, permanently bewildered. His name and birth-date were affirmed again, and there was another recitation of the crime alleged and the penalties it carried, and his rights were read to him once again, and finally Jesse Shard was asked if he wished to enter a plea.

Vinich said, "On behalf of my client, Your Honor, I will waive the reading of the Information and enter a plea of not guilty to the single charge it contains."

"Swell." The Chief Judge turned his weighty attention to Jesse Shard and asked him, "Is that how *you* wish to plead, Mr. Shard?"

"I. . ." Bobo could construct nothing more.

"Do you concur with your attorney?"

Bobo glanced wildly his way, and Vinich nodded as subtly as he could, but Bobo remained frozen.

"Are you guilty," the Chief Judge asked him, "or are you not guilty of this charge?"

The Defendant, no quick study it seemed, looked searchingly to his attorney and said, "Not?"

"Now that we have that on the record," said Vinich, "I would ask the Court to reconsider the bond that was imposed below. My client doesn't have the means to post the bond set, or any very substantial bond, and he also doesn't have the means to leave the island. He poses no flight risk whatever." Vinich, however, was a little at risk, because he was assuming all this, having never discussed the matter with Jesse Shard. The man's poverty was an easy proposition to sell. "Also, Your Honor, as Mr. Swanson can affirm, my client suffers from a very severe case of elephantiasis." Vinich had practiced the term while brushing his teeth that morning.

"How long has your client had this?" the Chief Judge asked.

"I'm not sure," said Vinich, "but, considering his visible symptoms, I would think quite a long while."

The Chief Judge once again cut out the middleman.

"How long?" he said. Then again, "How long, Mr. Shard?"

"Sir," said Jesse Shard, "I have always had it. My ancestors had it. It was in me before I was born."

The Chief Judge considered this. "So—you must be used to it by now."

"Your Honor," said Vinich, "ten thousand dollars, for a man of Mr. Shard's, for a man without *any* assets, that amounts to punitive pretrial detention, and I have to emphasize, he's in no condition to travel."

Abraham Swanson, buttoning his suit jacket, stood for the Territory to say that the other prong must be considered.

"What," said Vinich. "You mean you think he's a danger to the community? You think he's—*What*?"

"The Territory could have charged him with distribution," said Swanson. "Witnesses say he was trying to give marijuana away."

"Witnesses?" said Vinich, thumbing to page two of the Information to see the short list of them.

"The police," said Swanson, delighted with himself, "the police officers he was trying to give it to."

"Frieends," whispered Jesse Shard, "I wanted. I only."

Upon the entry of his plea he got a trial date six months hence. His bond remained unchanged and unattainable, and as he was led away from the council table young Bobo looked to Vinich for an explanation, a new strategy, anything.

The bailiff called the matter of the Territory of American Samoa versus Pule Ulu, and Mr. Ulu came forward in his massive way, with his massive problems.

6

Mr. Ulu's expression never changed as he was informed once again that the Territory might one day put him to death; his typical face was that of a sympathetic grandmother always endeavoring to understand, and as he was far more aware and articulate than Bobo; his arraignment went smoothly.

Then Mr. Sapolu was sentenced, and wept, and though his sentence was exactly what Vinich had told him to expect the first time they met, Mr. Sapolu was deeply disappointed that his tears and an apology full of muddy references to the gospels bought him no mercy.

Then Mr. Iosefa, awash in Lysol, came and stood beside him while Vinich told the Court that he had received discovery, that he had no pre-trial motions to make, and that the parties expected to reach agreement short of trial.

"In the meantime," said the Chief Judge, "it remains on my trial calendar. Along with four other cases that are set for trial on that same day. Do you know how a court is a like an assembly line, council?" Vinich knew. The Chief Judge was fond of this analogy. "The cases just keep coming," he said. "If we don't deal with them, they start stacking up—and they're stacked up, council. Already stacked up. You need to move these things."

Then, right on the heels of this pronouncement, Vinich had to tell the court that there had been confusion concerning the wife beater Taupau and his scheduled appearance that day. He was relieved when the Chief Judge, apparently too weary of attorney Vinich even to further rebuke him, made no further inquiries but only directed his clerk to schedule the thing for the next sitting of the High Court. Their fun with Mr. Taupau would be deferred until then.

After court Vinich could not bring himself to go straight back to the office, so he caught an aiga bus to Pago Pago where at a bayside café he ordered trifle and coffee and read the Information charging Pule Ulu with first degree homicide. It may have been the small jolts of adrenalin that had been his usual portion that morning in court, or it may have been the trifle and coffee coursing through him, but Vinich was beginning to hum a little.

The Information wasn't much, in fact Vinich could not agree with the magistrate who had reviewed it and found it contained probable cause. It alleged that on or about a certain date and time, in a certain village of the Territory of American Samoa, Pule Ulu did knowingly and with deliberation take the life of Talo Asenati. In support of this conclusion Assistant Attorney General Swanson meagerly offered on information and belief that the Defendant had been at a church bazaar, sitting with his aunts, weaving baskets, when the victim, Mr. Asenati, did approach him and tell him that he, the Defendant Mr. Ulu, wasn't welcome in that church. The men exchanged words; the Defendant left, followed by Mr. Asenati. A short time later three young men had been on their way to the bazaar when they found the Defendant and the victim along a trail a very short distance from the church. The young men knew at once that Mr. Asenati was deceased. Mr. Ulu was there looking down at the victim, and when the young men asked him what had happened, he said nothing. One of the young men described Mr. Ulu as calm. A bloody rock lay nearby. The young men had seen no one else in the immediate area when they came upon the scene.

The criminal docket was regulated in Samoa, as it had been in every outpost where Vinich had practiced, on the street where police were either called to or happened on enough crime that they had no time to go looking for more, and ordinarily they only wrote up such things as occurred in their presence. Then the Attorney General vetted them further, and if there were obvious problems with them no prosecution would follow, and after all that sifting there were still more than enough cases left to keep everyone busy. It was Vinich's usual work to process sad episodes that were largely done deals as they came to him. Mr. Ulu's, however, was a case with reasonable doubt written all over it, and Mr. Ulu himself had a rare aura of innocence about him. Vinich buzzed with wondering what the terms 'short time,' and 'very short distance' might mean, and he leapt astride his white horse to ride these and other mysteries down.

7

"Did those IT people come, Frances?"

Her look was bored, skeptical, dumbfounded.

"The computer guys," said Vinich.

She shook her head in the negative.

"Maintenance?"

The motion of her chin was continuous and remained so as Vinich asked her whether Jack Root had come in or if Elihu had returned after court. No, no, no, and no. His computer monitor lacked the last spark of life. His answering machine was functioning, though, and had recorded nine lengthy messages from Charlie Sapolu's wife who in each of them identified herself in English before ranting in Samoan. As near as he could tell, her thesis was that Mike Vinich must be a damn poor lawyer; Mrs. Sapolu would sometimes revert to English to ask him if he understood how much she needed her man. Once Vinich had the tenor of these calls, he was able to roll through and delete them pretty quickly, but it was not an uplifting exercise, and he boiled out of the offices of the Public Defender and across the building to the Attorney General's suite of offices where a horn-rimmed receptionist bade him wait and read Christian Life magazines until Abraham Swanson might become available.

He read a dubious story about a woman who had saved her daughter from anorexia by connecting her to the right church youth group; he read and tried to memorize a recipe for pineapple upside down cake though he lacked the kitchen ware or any reason to make such a thing. Vinich had better uses for his time; almost anyone drawing breath could use a moment more profitably than this. Still, he waited until Swanson came.

Little more than a decade out of high school, Swanson

was already cultivating the slick graciousness of the great man he intended to be, and each hair on his head had its assigned place. Humidity had no effect on them. The kid was paid twice what Vinich got for his work and had an office that might have functioned as an operating suite, and when they entered it together the young Assistant Attorney General began to look around, puzzled, alarmed. "What is that?"

Vinich explained the reek in his own office and offered his regrets that some of it seemed to have accompanied him to Swanson's. Vinich would have preferred not to be the disgusting party to this conversation but pressed on. "I came about discovery in the Ulu case," he said. "They gave that case to you, didn't they?"

"They did," said Swanson, a young gun with his first murder to work—excited about it. "I already made up your discovery packet. I did—not Bella."

"This should at least keep us out of Lower Court for a while," said Vinich, "But the thing is, I haven't filed my request."

"Well," said Swanson.

"And I *can't* file a request right now. My computer, there's probably a rat dead in that, too, and I can't get past the password on Root's computer to use it. So, I can't knock it out right now. But you know I will."

"We're kind of strict with the women in the office," said Swanson. "We do need something in the files before we release those materials. Motion and order. *Signed* order. The boss pays attention to these things—close attention."

"You *know*, I'll get you that to you. I have to." Vinich said. "Come on. I would dearly love to get something done today. For one thing, I think you've got the guy overcharged."

"Oh?" said Swanson, old and composed for his age.

"With deliberation?" This was the term of art, the particular accusation that put the thing into eye-for-an-eye territory—first degree homicide. "I can't see that at all. You just trying to scare the guy?"

"Well," said Swanson, "you can look at the discovery materials here in the office if you want. You did manage to get your notice of appearance filed, so you'd be the attorney of record. I guess you can look at it in the office. As long as none of it leaves the office." Swanson was the card player with a hand so good he just couldn't keep it to himself anymore. Vinich knew to work a prosecutorial tendency—they were prone, he knew, to revel in such evil as was theirs to address, their self-importance rising in proportion to its nastiness.

Vinich was taken to a back room containing files from various eras, and there Swanson placed the Ulu discovery packet on a counter and said, "Don't get this messed up, okay?"

"Messed up?" said Vinich.

"Out of order," said Swanson.

"It's my file," said Vinich.

"Not yet," said Swanson, leaving the room. "Keep it tidy," he said, and then, "*With* deliberation," in the tone of a man about to prove his point.

Vinich had in his career tried murders that had involved bankers boxes of evidence and filings. The Ulu file thus far, or his portion of it, was under an inch thick. There was an investigating officer's report with an account less grammatical and less organized but only slightly more detailed than the one he'd already read in the Information. The investigating officer wrote that the three boys from the church had been told to come in and give their recorded statements at the police station. There were pictures, and these would have been taken quite some time after an event of the late afternoon, for night had fallen when they were taken, and though the pictures were in color they had been shot under a light that washed everything to an eerily tinged black and white, and Talo Asenati lay very near, presumably, to where he had fallen, his face rolled up in a rictus by rigor on one side, and on the other his cheek bone was driven in so that his eye socket was widened and deepened. His face made concave. Both eyes remained open after so many hours, and they continued to express the corpse's surprise and disappointment. This shot was taken from several angles. There was another of Asenati lying at length along the trail, with Mr. Ulu still at the scene, staring down at him. Mr. Ulu in that outfit he'd worn that first morning to court. And a pearl necklace. His great hairy hand pressed to his silken chest. There was a picture of a rock coated with something that looked under that peculiar light very like chocolate syrup, Asenati's blood having congealed some.

And that was all. Vinich thumbed through the file to be sure of it. But that was all they thought he needed to know. Reassembling this was not nearly the task Swanson had led him to expect. Vinch brought it back to him, and briskly so as not to be intercepted before he reached the office, where with a discourteous knock he let himself in, and Swanson looked up, affronted, and Vinich lay the file on his desk in front of him.

"Recordings?" he said.

"A written statement is not really, you know—with these kids, a recording is the way to go."

"The next day? Come in the next day?"

"I didn't make that call," said Swanson.

"So now these recordings, they'll have to be translated, transcribed, and it'll be like getting at the Dead Sea Scrolls. You know this."

"Get an order," said Swanson. "If they don't get it done, get an order."

"And they'll say they can't, they'll say they don't have the funding or something. For the transcript. You remember that whoopdeedoo. We've been all through that go around before. Meanwhile, you've got poor old. . . And let's just say, let's go with all of the things you're assuming in that Information, let's say I granted you all that, let's say every one of your assumptions is correct, you still don't have anything like deliberation, and I still think you've got him overcharged. Way overcharged."

"Look, that thing with the cops, those statements, you think I like that any better than you do? But, that's almost how they have to do it. You don't get written. . ." Stern now, Swanson said, "Your guy picked up a rock. Read your case law on it. That's deliberation."

8

The church boys. Those interviews. Vinich thought to ask for the recordings, then he could have his own translation done, if translations were necessary; he knew he'd be typing the transcriptions himself, and he was not sure that Elihu would be any more accurate or sympathetic than any other government translator might be, but Vinich wanted the news, the devilish details as soon as he could have them. Upon opening the door of the Public Defender's offices, though, he recalled that he presently had no way to draft that formal request, and he caught a dense whiff of the environment within and turned on his heel to go home; along the way he passed once more by the prison, and Vinich thought of having another chat with Mr. Ulu, but then thought better of it.

Mr. Ulu's silence was something a magistrate could properly consider damning in finding probable cause, but that silence should never be used in a final determination of guilt. Technically.

Mr. Ulu had been there with that body such a long while without offering what he might know about how it had become a body, so the man must have some of the right instincts, and Vinich thought to leave well enough alone until he had some facts in hand. How often it had happened that the most destructive evidence in a case came from a client's own wayward or penitent mouth.

Vinich went to his cottage by way of Jack Root's where he knocked on the door much as he'd knocked on Swanson's earlier that day, the rap, rap of a cop serving a warrant, necessary here because of the explosions and automatic weapons being fired inside. Root came at once to the door, his mouth ajar. The room behind him was dark save for a screen occupying much of one wall upon which a creature like a cubist painting lurched and snarled through a heavily bombed future. Root's friend Clayton Knapp sat crosslegged on the floor and held the control, apparently, that could make the thing stop.

"Goddamnit," said Vinich. He didn't need to elaborate, but he did. "Jack, you need to get your ass back to work. This better be your last day off."

"I," said Root.

"No," said Vinich. "You've run through all the vacation time you've got on this contract, this year and next year both. And you've got no way home. Do you? And I'll just bet you're broke. As I told you before, we're it. We. Are. It. And don't be turning your phone off anymore."

Root's mouth got more agape; now everyone was being mean to him.

"Gee, Mike" said Clayton Knapp. "Have a cold one. We got this delightful *Dutch* beer." Knapp was an air traffic controller on his first assignment in the tower at Pago Pago International where many a long shift might pass without a single flight coming in or leaving. Knapp's mission was to not die of boredom here and this required a languid attitude he wanted to urge on everyone. "Wind down, man. Relax a little."

Vinich could not understand these young guys' affection for their blaring, beeping games, and noticed he'd become a curmudgeon—his rare fun to berate the kid. Relax? Vinich made a face, and as he was walking away heard their noise resume behind him.

Soon enough he was in his own cottage where the very quiet he'd been wanting became its own sort of problem and where he happened to reflect that he had never liked card games or board games either, that he found strange most events designed to bring people together. His work had made him tired of people, or a good plurality of them, and it was by dint of will alone that Vinich did somehow continue to love humanity a little, but this was in the collective, in the abstract. He opened a can of stew and peppered it gray when it began to burble on the hotplate.

The Territory had offered to pay for shipping his stateside car to Tutuila, but Vinich, suffering maybe from delusions of strolls between palm thatched huts, and not wanting to expose his good old Taurus to quite so much salt sea air, had declined that benefit but had instead shipped himself boxes of books, some sixty pounds of leather bound wisdom concerning cultures east to west, epochs and eras, the great ideas. This was a mistake Vinich had made with a book club decades earlier, and he had imagined finally correcting it in his leisure, consuming evening after evening under the tropical moon with this monkish distraction. Could there be a more a harmless pastime? A more feckless soul?

Vinich sat in the screened enclosure at the back of his cottage, listening to fruit fall and feral dogs misbehave, and eating stew that was an antidote to and a source of boredom, and he turned once more to Kant's categorical imperative which would be more of the same. This sort of thing had seemed so immediate to him as a young man. Did the maxim of Mike Vinich's actions conform to all he might wish nature to be? He'd negotiated under two impenetrable pages of Kant before his thoughts veered back to Mr. Ulu, and these thoughts had a quality he knew too well. There had been those cases that for months on end gave him no peace, invaded and occupied his every random, waking thought. Years had gone to some of these cases. Years of his life. His marriage. Cases. He'd been too small to manage it all. Cases—and the most devastating of these had involved some truly sympathetic character such as Pule Ulu seemed to be. Vinich was uneasy.

The maxim of his actions? Vinich subscribed to a simpler ethic now, the one governing the defense bar and the Oakland Raiders: Just win, baby.

9

Vinich was at the office building in Utulei that morning when the people arrived to ratchet up its steel doors; he did not go in but loitered around the food trucks outside, smelling the coffee in its five-gallon urns, pacing near knots of food truck workers with their incomprehensible gossip, complaints, and jokes. Vinich crossed the highway to the beach club where outrigger racing canoes were drawn up on the scant beach, sleek hulls sculpted in fiberglass. Vinich smelled the bay, paced the beach, crossed back over the highway and continued waiting near the parking lot until nine when Jack Root pulled up, right on time and more than a little startled to find his lately bossy supervisor waiting for him. Root said "Hey?" as he emerged from his car.

"I was waiting to go in," said Vinich. "Thought I might as well wait until I could do something up there."

"Oh?" said Root.

"You'll see."

The office still reeked that morning.

"*Man*," said Root, the game face he'd worn to work that morning already falling away.

"Goddamnit," said Vinich. "Okay. Get into your computer, Jack. I'll see if I can. . .Whooh. Get into your computer. Then see if you can find me some garbage bags."

Vinich made two stacks of Pacific Reporters on his desk, each six volumes deep, and he climbed onto his desk, then onto the reporters, a foot on either stack, and he stood up through the ceiling, lifting a panel of acoustical tile, and then he was up in a great space of ductwork, of which he could see only a few square feet. That stink was certainly coming from somewhere up here, but just where would be very hard to say. Vinich lingered to let his eyes adjust to the lack of light, but even with pupils fully dilated he couldn't penetrate much of the darkness. That stink with some new component—the dust he'd raised lifting the ceiling panel. Dust. Guano? Fruit bats? Hanta virus? Plague? Vinich lowered the ceiling panel back onto its rails and climbed down from his desk.

"There's definitely something up there," he reported to Root. "Good luck finding it, though, without a searchlight, or you'd have to go panel to panel, poking around."

"Something?" said Root. "Find it? It must be a whale up there."

Vinich chose not to divulge the worst part yet, that the smell in question might well cling to them even after hours. He said, "Pull up your discovery requests, would you? One for High Court, if you've got one. My machine finally passed away."

Vinich hijacked Root's computer to cut and paste discovery requests in his two new felonies; Root stood by for a time, ashen faced, then bolted. He returned to say that the smell had cost him his breakfast, that he was still a little hung over, two days after the fact. And he said, "You know what, you don't look that great, either, Mike."

"Didn't sleep," said Vinich. "It happens sometimes."

He printed requests and orders with Root standing by, mooning out the window at the rain forest that reared not far beyond it, looking like he may bolt again, but this time to go far, far away. Vinich then assailed Frances as soon as she came to work with renewed requests that she somehow convince building maintenance and the IT people to do something because, "This is impossible."

"Nothing," Frances said, "is impossible with Jesus."

"All right," said Vinich, "then call him."

Frances glared at him. "You better pray," she said.

Vinich then called Elihu's cell to ask, "Where are you?"

"LBJ," said Elihu.

"Why?"

"It's my foot," said Elihu. "Sprained, maybe broke. I got to get x-rays. It's my kicking foot."

"Well," said Vinich, "how long?"

"X-rays?" said Elihu. "LBJ—I don't think I'm gonna make it in today, Mike. It's LBJ. They probably gonna amputate."

Elihu, when he wanted, was almost impervious to injury. He didn't want that today. Elihu was Vinich's translator sporadically, and his investigator, nominally, one so incurious that he had never to Vinich's knowledge investigated anything.

"I need you for something," Vinich said.

"Okay," said Elihu, meaning exactly nothing by it.

"We need to find some people and talk to them. I don't know the village at all."

"Okay," said Elihu again.

Vinich understood he'd be getting no commitment from the man today. He said, "All right. Get it wrapped up. Get one of those boots on it. I need you. Soon as you can. . ."

"Mmhm," said Elihu, having drifted out of the conversation.

It had been curiosity concerning those three church boys that had prevented Vinich from sleeping. Had those interviews taken place? If not, would the cops be honest about it? If so, when could he expect to know what was said? Among the few specifics provided in that Information were the names of those church boys and the name of the village where they lived. Rather than wait around for interviews, transcriptions, and probably some unanticipated folderol, Vinich would go straight to the source, and once he'd hit on the plan, he could hardly wait to do it. The village was as remote as a village could be on such a small island, so the need for a translator might be greater there, but the church boys were "young", which made it more likely they'd be fluent in English. Maybe he could talk directly to them. Vinich had been surprised to discover how English was for many Samoans a very secondary language though this island had been immersed in it for a long time and it was the lingua franca of most trade and scholarship and popular culture here. There seemed a willfulness about this lack of fluency, and Vinich had resented it because it so complicated his work, but eventually he remembered that his own grandmother, born and raised in the states, had never been especially happy in English, either. So, maybe these folks were just tropical bohunks, people resistant to change that has already long since happened. Samoans. Vinich needed more than language translated here, for there was much he did not understand about their *fa'asamoa*, a tribal culture that probably hadn't been entirely pretty even before the missionaries infested it. The people seemed to love it, though, while Vinich wasn't sure he could so much as identify a culture he might call his own. He was in no position to judge, but there were times when he just couldn't help himself—some things were so clearly fucked up. He was somewhat accustomed to the view from the outside looking in.

"Frances," he said, "where's that sign out sheet for the publicdefendermobile?"

10

There is no place on the island that is more than two miles from the sea, but the village, enclosed by rain forest as it was, seemed far inland and was steamy. There were no views of the ocean from here, nor any breeze from it. The church Vinich wanted stood in a small clearing at the mouth of a ravine, a thing of ornately cast concrete, architectural scallops and balustrades in luminous white and trimmed in a cool blue all out of keeping with its jungle setting. Another house of worship. Vinich was the great grandson of a Wobbly and the religious gene was generations extinct in him; he found the many churches here confusing, gaudy, beautiful, and to all appearances full of an optimism that was something else he'd never understand. He returned to the jeep for the long, stout stick that was kept handy for excursions into unknown neighborhoods, the tool to be carried against the possibility of dogs.

Now and only now did he think he might need a plan. Had he expected to walk up to this place and find the church boys, as he'd come to think of the three witnesses, sprawled out front, wearing name tags and waiting for him? As Vinich went up the steps, and as he went inside there was no evidence of anyone at all. 'Sanctuary,' he thought—a cool interior, that mass of concrete, the windows arrayed high above, and his every footfall a series of echoes. He liked an empty church well enough. The architecture of faith. But this wasn't getting him anywhere. Vinich went out and wandered to the back of the church where there was a squat a man working a taro patch with a machete. "Hello," said Vinich.

The man, who'd been bent at the waist to work, remained bent with his forearms on his knees as he examined the newcomer. There were white streaks in his hair, something like a skunk's markings. Vinich was without his tie and brief case today, and he'd left his umbrella behind, but he'd still never give anyone the impression he belonged. "*Talofa lava*," he said. The man's position and expression had not changed. Both that expression and the machete hanging from his right hand became more ambiguous the longer the man remained silent. "Hi," Vinich tried, hoping an informal tone might help.

"What?"

"Hello," Vinich said again, sounding silly to himself, keeping it light, "I'm Mike Vinich, and I'm with the Public Defender."

"A lawyer?" said the man, surprised anyone would admit to such a thing.

"I am," said Vinich. "I'm here looking for some people."

The man resumed his impenetrable expression.

"They go to this church," said Vinich. "I think." This prompted nothing from the man, but then Vinich realized he hadn't given him a specific question. "And this is—this is your church?"

The man stood erect at last, his chest and face were uncommonly broad; he seemed a direct descendant of Genghis Khan.

Vinich went on. "There was an incident not too long ago. A man died here, and I'm looking for some boys who may know something about it."

"Died?" said the man. "Talo?"

"Yes," said Vinich. "Mr. Asenati."

"Died?" said the man. "Talo got killed."

"That's what I'm looking into," Vinich said. He also said the three boys' names as best he could pronounce them, and he asked the man, "Do they live here in the village?"

The machete man bent at the waist again, looking

sternly toward something at his feet.

"I'd really appreciate it if you could help me find them," said Vinich. "I just need to find out what happened, or as much as I can."

The taro farmer swung the machete at a wrist-sized root, and it passed through at a swipe despite his instrument being dull this late in the day.

The ravine narrowed behind the church and the village commenced, a pair of ragged streets with residences scattered upslope. A piggery announced itself, though Vinich couldn't see it. He walked in. How they loved their concrete here, a substance at last that wouldn't rot or be blown away, and nearly every home was built of it, as were the tombs occupying many front yards. Vinich wondered just how many generations this practice could go on. A pickup truck came toward him, three big women in the back, and they looked at him and laughed, passing, and Vinich looked back, wondering idly if these might be Mr. Ulu's aunties.

Uncertain of the language or the etiquette of the place, still he needed to speak with someone. Vinich went into a little enterprise that would subsist on its sales of cigarettes and beer; there was a Korean woman, probably, at the register with that massive disdain for the customer that must be taught at all Korean schools of commerce. "Hello," said Vinich, and once again this failed in its desired effect.

"Buy something," she said.

"All right." Vinich selected a bottle of water from the store's cooler. The woman scowled at him. He determined that he would on no account buy any of the chips they carried in these places, things that tasted of squid juice. Just be polite, he thought. "Maybe you could help me," he told the woman.

Her look told him it was unlikely.

"Noah Satele?" said Vinich. "Manuita Salave'a? Filemoni Leava? Would you know any of these boys? Or maybe they're young men? How. . . Their families? Where they live, or. . ." The woman was blank in a way that told him he'd bought no answers here; Vinich noticed at last a bone structure suggesting she'd once been pretty, or as pretty as such an attitude could ever be. "All right, then. Thanks, anyway."

Back in the street, Vinich was met with two of the expected dogs and as he continued into the ravine they followed him at a strategic distance, looking to nip at his heels. He regretted his sandals. Vinich walked on glancing backward and yelling, "*Halooh*." When this produced only canine grins he jabbed at them with the butt of his stave, catching the boldest, the one with weeping sores, square on its blunt head, and this sent the pair of them running, a triumph Vinich savored momentarily before he was ashamed. Dogs. Their neighborhood, not his. There had to be a better way of doing this. He stood in the street drinking his water, wishing he'd bought another bottle, thinking he'd become a filtration system here for converting sweet water into sweat. A loud, bright whine came to life, then another, then another, and when this chorus was in full cry he headed toward it, back in the direction of the church grounds. Along the way Vinich examined the trails leading out from the village into the all-consuming vegetation, wondering which of them had been the scene of Talo Asenati's death.

Talo Asenati. A name. A name with a life recently attached to it, a life still fully resonant here, a life the man had no doubt taken for granted until the moment it ended. Nothing about any of these trails seemed familiar from the crime scene photographs, just as that disfigured face Vinich knew for Talo Asenati would not be familiar to anyone who had known him. Loved him. Vinich knew he'd better go carefully. But what would that look like? How would that work? He'd have to just keep poking and hope he didn't hit a hornet's nest.

The machete man was gone from the taro patch behind the church. Now the grounds around it were being groomed by three young men with their keening weed eaters. Vinich, struck by their age and number, wondered if he hadn't somehow hit the jackpot. It wasn't too unreasonable to think these were the very three he'd been seeking. Two of them wore lavalavas, the third, wearing pants and a pair of boots more suited to the work, was the oldest and the slightest of the group, and this was the one Vinich approached. The booted fellow wore his machine on a harness, heavy with an extra-large gas tank; he wore goggles and earmuffs and, for an absurd amount of time he did not look up at Vinich hovering there in front of him. Another swinging blade. Vinich waited until the man could no longer pretend he was invisible and let off his trigger at last.

"Hello," said Vinich, his doofus introduction, his voice nearly inaudible in his own ringing ears. "Hello," he said again, maybe too loud.

The man nodded, removing neither his goggles nor his earmuffs.

"I'm here looking into the death of Talo Asenati," Vinich bellowed, and it occurred to him he'd better say why. "I'm with the Public Defenders Office. I'm representing Mr. Ulu."

The young man nodded again, but without any obvious comprehension. One of the younger, bigger lads approached, his googles up on his forehead. He wore no ear protection. Vinich explained himself again. The groundskeepers looked one to the other, then back at him.

The younger of the pair, a Buddha-looking boy, shook his head in the negative. Their mouths were set.

"Noah Satele?" said Vinich. "Manuita Salave'a? Filemoni Leava?" He had learned these names like a song lyric. When he spoke the last of them, he saw the chubby one's eyes cut. But the pair said nothing.

"I'm Mike Vinich," he said, extending his hand. Both young men shook it, limply, dutifully, but neither offered anything else. "And I'm just trying to find out what happened. Talk to some people who might know something about it."

And who would deny a truth seeker?

The younger one began to turn away; the man in pants had not yet shown the first trace of understanding. The language barrier, whether real or not, looked to be insurmountable today. "Wait," said Vinich. "What about the Ulu family? Can you tell me where they live?"

The younger one turned back to him. "Ulus?" he said. "No."

"Well, do you. . ."

The booted man triggered his machine back to full snarl.

11

He had met this immensity flying over it in a jet, hour after hour looking down at a deep, deep indifference. Vinich drove a section of highway running close by and parallel to a sea wall, and now he had a look at it from ground level, the surf washing a reef, the featureless ocean beyond, and it was a view that sponsored a better humility, a lighter heart. It was a source of much fresh air. Not wanting to return the jeep just yet to the government parking lot in Utulei, he found a pullout along the coastal highway where he sat regarding the great blue.

These island people, or their forbearers, had got here in open boats, negotiated a truly trackless expanse of this earth without so much as a compass to guide them. No one here, and probably no one living would have that knack now. The decline of instinct. Vinich considered his own instincts, such as they were, and knew them to be nearly useless in Samoa. Pule Ulu, for instance: Having spent an hour in the man's presence, Vinich had somehow concluded that this was the mildest human being he'd ever met, someone incapable of committing even a discourtesy; it was hard to imagine the big guy hurting anyone, but was Vinich seeing what he wanted to see, needed to see from time to time? Was it actual innocence or a redeeming mirage? A man's head had been caved in. Somehow. And Pule Ulu, way up some trail in his high heeled shoes.

There had been, as Vinich understood it, four genders traditionally recognized among Samoans, the usual two and two admixtures, feminized men and masculine women. Though there were now only womanly women here so far as he'd observed, *fa'afafines* were still to be seen at any sizable social gathering, often glorious. Queens, as they might be called in the states. Here they enjoyed some of that acceptance of old and were sometimes even celebrated, but now the old ways had got infused with evangelical Christianity with all its notions of what men and women were and weren't, and other forms of foreign prejudice had found their way onto the islands, and Vinich, working in the criminal courts, had seen how frequently modern *fa'afafines* were assaulted. The ground under their feet must be so uncertain.

He had yet to think of Pule Ulu as anything other than a victim.

If the prosecutor couldn't fill in the blanks in that Information, then Vinich in all competence should see his man walk, but Swanson would be hard after his facts, wanting to prove himself by proving his case, and Vinich was almost certain the three church boys would eventually be heard from. But what would they say? When and how competently would they be interviewed? Vinich wanted those transcripts. He had probably already poisoned the well in that village, and he didn't think that investigator Elihu would do any better there, even if he could be induced to try. That was a closed village. Even before his hitch in the law, Vinich had bounced off many such environments, the closed neighborhood, the ominous neighborhood bar, an unusually ugly household, those cauldrons of secret that had produced so many of his clients, so many of his friends. The lives led in these locations could be unknowable even to the people living them.

His career in high-volume, low-resource criminal defense had trained Vinich to quickly dissect a case as it came to him, to separate what he knew from what he might reasonably expect to find out and compare these pieces to what the prosecution should be able to prove. It was an analysis he'd performed thousands of times, but this one had more than its share of variables and unknowns. This was a murder investigated initially by the newest lieutenant of the Territorial Police, and his shoddy work might prove Mr. Ulu's saving grace, but for right now it was crazy making.

A man was dead. Yes. Blunt force trauma. Definitely. What else? His client nearby, not really dressed for the bush, nor for a church bazaar; Pule Ule had been turned out that day as if for a *fa'afafine* pageant. Pearls? Was there blood on that dress? Vinich hadn't seen any when Mr. Ulu had come that first morning to Lower Court. Mr. Ulu had been wearing it still two days after Talo Asenati went down, an especially strange look for an inmate, and at that point the dress or his improbable shoes had not yet been seized, so maybe they never would be. Were they or were they not going to be in evidence? Would it matter? And the rock. Good luck lifting prints off something so porous as volcanic rock. But it was a nasty artifact to find its way into evidence—the region's favored weapon, a brown crust on it by now. Proof of intent. Because he'd picked it up.

Or had he? No one had claimed so far to see Mr. Ulu do anything worse than stand dumfounded over a corpse, so any proof of murder would necessarily be circumstantial, but those church boys may have stories to tell containing observations, a timeline, and maybe there would be altogether too many circumstances to overcome, to leave even a reasonable doubt. It was fruitless to keep circling back around to the church boys; they were a black hole for now.

Mr. Ulu's aunties should have something to say, though. They would have been present for the 'words' their nephew had exchanged with Mr. Asenati, and they might be able to explain why Mr. Ulu had been kicked out of the church, to clarify when and how the two men had left the premises. Mr. Ulu's aunties would also probably be happy to confirm that, no, Mr. Ulu was not a bellicose guy. Basket weaving. How on earth had that turned nasty? The fat boy had said there were no Ulus in his village, and this meant it might still be possible to talk to the aunties. They'd be family and anxious to share their side of the story. Maybe. But where were they? Who were they? Again, that shoddy investigation. No Ulus. It then occurred to Vinich that maybe the village kid thought the stranger had been looking for breadfruit, and that's why he'd said, 'No'. Ulu, that's why the name seemed familiar—people selling breadfruit in the farmer's market. Ulu. Fresh ulu. What endless potential for tropical confusion.

Vinich would talk to the aunties if he could, and he counseled himself to try and approach those conversations subtly enough that they had some hope of happening. How to find them? How to approach them? He needed to talk to his client again.

So far Pule Ulu had neither confessed nor lied to him, and that was the one piece of the status quo Vinich didn't want to disturb.

12

"It's so good of you," he said, "to come see me again."

Vinich could not remember if this phrase had ever previously been directed at him, and he was certain he'd never heard it from a client. "I," he said. "Well—yeah, we've got a few things to cover. We'll probably be talking a lot as things play out." Play out? That probably wouldn't sound too encouraging.

"Mm," said Mr. Ulu who seemed to anticipate a series of pleasant, informative conversations. His beard was coming in wiry, and he was wearing those coveralls someone had brought him for his prison wardrobe; his hands lay folded on the concrete picnic table, veins thick as pencils snaking up his corded wrists. Much about Pule Ulu ran contrary to Vinich's initial impression of him, but that impression hadn't changed. Mr. Ulu's eyes were of such a sympathetic cast, and his voice was comforting in the way of safely distant thunder. The guy was an immense Madonna.

Vinich had as always waived the reading of the Information at the arraignment; now he produced the document from his briefcase with a bit of fumble and a bit of flourish and read it to his client in a more private setting, an otherwise empty visitor's pavilion. He paused a beat and said, "And so far, that's about all they've got. That we know about. Some pictures. Picture of you at the scene. They've got a rock. The pictures aren't too pretty, either, but all they really show is the guy was dead. And you happened to be there. Now, they may come up with more, or they may not. So, I guess what I'm saying—for right now it's best to tread lightly. You haven't been talking with anyone? About the—you know."

"No, sir," said Mr. Ulu. "On your orders."

"You've got to quit this 'sir' stuff," said Vinich. "I. That's... I don't give orders, I give advice. Which I do strongly advise you to follow, but it is advice. And it's Mike, okay? Please."

"Yes, s. . . Mike. Whatever you prefer."

Vinich tried to remember anyone other than a waiter or salesperson calling him 'sir' and wondered why it made him so uneasy to be addressed that way. "That dress you were wearing when they brought you in," he said, "what happened to that?"

"My mother took it home when she was bringing me these things."

"Your shoes? Those high heels—what about those?"

"She'll have those wrapped in velveteen. Those were *so* expensive. I shudder to think of the cost. One of a kind, and I love wearing them if I don't have to wear them too long." Mr. Ulu nodded meaningfully toward the Converse he now wore. Immaculate, impossibly white, he must wash them every night. Every piece of his clothing would be expensive unless he were to wear the one-size-fits-all lavalava, a unisex wraparound garment understandably popular here among people of his outsized dimensions. "A guard got my pearls," he said without much resentment. "Those were real, so I think someone's girlfriend should be very happy."

"You doing all right in here?"

"This garden is the best," said Mr. Ulu. "Someone makes *palusami* almost every night."

It would need a huge caloric intake just to keep a man like this breathing, and food would necessarily be his first thought when he thought of his wellbeing. Vinich had never known him when he was not in custody, but Mr. Ulu was so oddly at ease with his grave situation, and Mr. Ulu went so far as to claim, "It can be somewhat festive. I've met some of the dearest people."

"In here?" Vinich had always suspected this prison to be a party facility. Still—a party with no way out was not his idea of a good time. "Do you have any priors? I haven't got your record yet from the AG. Have you been here before?"

"We used to visit. Everyone has a cousin here. Every family."

"But you—any kind of, oh, trouble?"

Mr. Ulu upon reflection and with a dreamy smile said, "Crimes of omission. I'm constantly in the wrong, or so I'm told, but never illegal. So far."

"Oh," said Vinich. "I see," he said, though he did not. His client sounded a little like a lawyer. Vinich was about to give up on ever understanding this person—to understand the man exceeded his brief; Vinich was only obliged to defend him—but the one thing would very likely involve the other, and so he was confusing himself again, and Vinich thought he'd better dive after raw information; he got from Mr. Ulu his home village, and it was not the village where the killing had occurred. Mr. Ulu named his own village and those members of his family whom Vinich wanted to interview.

"What would be the best way to approach them, do you think? I mean," said Vinich, "I don't want to scare anybody off. Sometimes I'm a bull-in-a-china-shop."

"You should go through my father. They'd all defer to him. If he tells them to talk to you, they'll talk to you. If not, they won't. My father is the mucky-mucky, you might say." Mr. Ulu's odd turns of phrase and his whole suite of gestures placed him in some civilization at some remove from this island.

"And those ladies at the church, those were your aunts? Did they get that right?"

"Yes. *Oh*, yes."

"Would they be able to. . . How's their English?" Vinich hadn't heard anything like Mr. Ulu's version of the language since the regal Mrs. Foy had guided him through civics in junior high.

The big man was proud of his aunties, even defensive. "That won't be any problem for you. Carol was in the Air Force. She was in Alaska quite a while, so she's—but they're all, you know, conversant. Inina is a nurse, and Fiame was. Fluent. Thank *good*ness. The girls are very fluent."

"They were there when Mr. Asenati spoke with you?"

"In the church. Yes."

"They would have heard that conversation?"

"Most of it," said Mr. Ulu. "We were just, they were just. . ."

"Whoa," said Vinich. "For right now, don't volunteer anything, all right? Real specific questions with real specific answers for right now. That's what I mean by treading lightly. So—you were there that day—to weave baskets?"

"Theoretically," said Mr. Ulu. "I do go through the motions, but. . ." He unclasped his hands and opened them out as if to demonstrate how far an impulse would have to travel to reach his fingertips. "I'm not too deft, but they are, the girls. They can really turn them out. Congregationalists. Samoan craft fairs—it's quite a thing with them, they rotate through the churches. Which is nice. Usually. Sometimes—lately—I tag along and keep them company. Ask me about the dress."

"Well," said Vinich.

"Appropriate?"

"Personally," said Vinich, "I usually don't concern myself with appropriate. The appropriate fashion, anyway."

"But for a church function?" said Mr. Ulu. "Outrageous, wasn't it?"

"Seemed a little unusual," said Vinich. "But I'm no

authority on dress codes."

"Fabulous, though," said Mr. Ulu. "Wasn't it?"

"Stunning," said Vinich.

"I don't attend services, and I don't frequent bars, so there was really nowhere else I could wear it. I'd spend a whole morning on my hair just to go to one of those silly things. I'd be *glist*ening with coconut oil."

"I see," said Vinich, though once again he did not.

"Also," said Mr. Ulu, "I had an ulterior motive."

"Wait. . ." said Vinich.

"It's all right," said Mr. Ulu. "I don't think it's too bad— when I wore that dress, I didn't have to sit on the floor with them. In the traditional way. I couldn't. Physically impossible in that dress. But really—where else was I going to wear it? One wants to look terrific. Sometimes."

This was an impulse that had little disturbed Vinich. "Was that the problem at the church? This Asenati had a problem with your dress?"

"No," said Mr. Ulu. "Or, I. I would say that poor man had so many problems."

"All right, then," said Vinich. "We'll leave it at that for right now."

13

To land on such a recently erupted speck as Tutuila, so far from everything, should be a quick and permanent shot of humility, but it had worked no better that way for him than life on spinning little earth; Vinich—you keep turning down the rabbit hole of self, and you can't help it, you keep mistaking yourself for the big picture. This case, at least, was becoming a great excuse to go driving in the department's jeep, to lose himself in someone else's more pressing problems, these field trips into worlds apart. There were probably family farms back home about as big as this island, but Tutuila, for no bigger than it was, was ground on the Greek or the Appalachian plan, land tortured into discrete pockets sponsoring pools of people who lived in near self-sufficiency and deep suspicion of their neighbors from the next ravine—micro civilizations. Mr. Ulu's village lay along the north shore, and Vinich had never been to the north shore before, though it was so near; Massacre Bay was also supposed to lay somewhere along this side of the island, the site of Samoa's first and most successful encounter with Europeans. He'd have to visit, see if there was a plaque.

It was almost the idyl he'd had in mind when he signed up for Samoa, a village facing out to sea with its plantations terraced up the slopes all around it, and at its center a church in primary colors like a superhero's costume. A new building was being raised on the grounds. Two cement mixers were manned by two competitive teams who with shovels and buckets fed their machines sand and broken volcanic rock and water and Portland cement, and churned it, and fed the mix into five-gallon buckets they lifted to crew who stood on scaffolding to pour it into forms. This, in the heat of the day.

Vinich didn't see any rebar going into these walls. An artist had built the forms, so another fantastic structure was emerging one bucket of mud at a time.

This time Vinich had a number. This time Vinich had called ahead. He'd spoken with a woman he believed to be Mr. Ulu's mother, though she was a little coy about saying so, and she in turn spoke to someone there with her, and then she'd said. "Okay."

"Okay? You mean—?"

"Now," she said.

"Now? All right. But where do I. . ."

"The church," she said. "You couldn't miss it."

"I'll need to. . ." he said, but the conversation had ended at the other end, so he'd got here as soon as he could, and it was true, though hardly unusual, the church was unmistakable. Walking up to it, Vinich passed by the construction crew, and the younger ones, the boys on the ground, yipped in that peculiar way, and the men on the scaffold regarded him gravely. The thing about Samoa—Vinich had never previousy been anywhere where he felt frail, and he found he didn't like it. And that yipping, though it was probably some kind of joy, did get on his nerves. He went in under a bas relief of a little lamb, its legs folded under it; was he to genuflect or what? It was cool, or cooler inside, and again the resonance of a big, empty room, the sound he made walking. He knew to look for the pastor's sanctuary. Reportedly, Mr. Ulu's father was the pastor here, and Mr. Ulu's father was a high chief hereabouts, and Mr. Ulu's father was a representative to the Fono; Vinich could not recall that he'd ever met anyone so nearly approximating a god in his local authority. He noticed himself almost mincing back behind the alter. He knocked at a door. Timidly, he thought.

"Yes." A soft boom from within.

The elder Mr. Ulu wore a drill instructor's haircut and a crisp red shirt with the tattoos of his rank snaking out from under its sleeves. His belted lavalava encircled a torso like a standup freezer chest. He was glad, or so he said, and so he initially seemed, to see Vinich.

"Sir," said Vinich," thanks for seeing me so soon. Your son told me you were the first one I should speak with." The chief nodded and sat behind his desk. Vinich remained standing in a posture something like parade rest, his hands behind his back, and he pretended to be unaware of the chair just behind him. "As you know," he said, "some accusations have been made. I think they're very likely false."

The chief mumbled in his trim van dyke as if he had to be careful lest something he said be taken for an order.

"I'm trying to get to the bottom of things," said Vinich.

The chief said nothing. His big face was fixed.

Vinich wondered why he so often had this effect, how he managed to close people up this way. Was his curiosity so raw? "I'd like to talk to some of your. . . Some of your family members. I think the police may be coming out to talk to them, too. If they haven't already. But I'd like to hear what they have to say. Personally, if I could. Straight from the. . . These would be your sisters, or maybe your wives' sisters?" Or maybe the term 'aunty' had a wider meaning here. But Vinich had names. Once he had permission, he had only to name names.

The chief was locked, his eyes turned up in some remote consideration. Or he'd lost interest. Vinich, a certain kind of snob, noticed there were no books in this room—not a hymnal, not a concordance, not even a Bible. What was the guy's source for his sermons? Or did they do those here? The walls were hung with photographs of the chief shaking hands with other wreathed worthies, one of whom Vinich recognized as a prominent stateside senator. Mucky mucks. The chief revealed nothing, sitting there. "If you have no objection," said Vinich. "Sir."

The chief's gaze moved back to him, but Vinich felt it pass right on through. Nothing for it but to keep talking. "I'm just trying to represent your son in the best way I know how. And that includes not being surprised by any information. If I can help it. Your wife told you, sir? I'm sorry, She? It was your wife? I assumed. . . Well, let me start over. I'm Mike Vinich with the Public Defender, and I've been assigned your son's case." Vinich extended his hand. The chief looked at it, then in that way of his, through it.

"Even if I happen to get into things that don't look good for him, it's better if I know that first." Vinich was about to say, 'before the government', before he happened to think that this guy *was* the government. Then Vinich happened to think that *he* was government, or was paid by them. Poor Pule Ulu should probably consider himself screwed. "Before the prosecutor gets it," he said. "And, as I'm sure you know, your people would have to speak with cops or the AG's investigator. They'd have no choice. I just want to get there first. Make sure what they have to say doesn't get distorted."

And who could deny a truth seeker? Everyone, so far.

"So—" said Vinich. "Sir. If it's all right with you, and I understand I need your permission, I would like to speak with the women who were there at the church with your son that day."

The chief was in a meditative state, or bored.

Then Vinich considered how the man had said under

five words since they had met, and maybe the bulk of this conversation was passing right by him. But, no, the chief was a boss through and through, and his silence would have significance. Wouldn't it? This could be a little trial of some kind. There stood Vinich, his hands still clasped behind his back. He thought to try their names. "Carol Ulu," he said. "Inina Falaniko, and Fiame—I won't even attempt her last name. I've mangled that every time I've tried it. But. Those three ladies."

Vinich waited. No books in this room, no art but the many framed pictures of the chief gladhanding strangers and one of a fautasi long boat, fifty hefty rowers in mid-stroke, driving a red hull into a bow wave. The man's desk looked to be polished frequently; it was entirely unclut-tered, as was his expression.

Vinich felt he must now wait for an answer. And he waited. The chief was responsible for everything, after all, so he would have to weigh his every move. Was the chief weighing now? Hard to say. Vinich had never been so thoroughly ignored. Eventually he removed the note pad from his hip pocket and paged through it until he reached a dry page. He began writing. "I left my number with your wife, sir, or—she was your wife? I. Anyway, I've never had any cards made up, but just to be sure, here's my number, my e-mail. That's my direct line, which is what you want. The office number is usually no-go." Vinich lay the infor-mation on the chief's desk, a tattered edge where it had been torn from the notebook. No doubt impressive. "I know this is hard on a family," he said. "Thing like this. Thing like this can blow up and—who knows? It's hard. But I am trying to help your son." If Vinich could not quit waiting, he hoped he could at least quit talking. He'd now reached that point where nothing he said sounded other than foolish to his own ears.

The Chief nodded at last in the manner of a man who has at long last made a hard decision. He brought Vinich into focus, standing there before him, and he asked him, "You want to know?"

"Yes," said Vinich. "If possible. As much as I can, anyway." Shut up, he told himself.

"You want to know my shame?" said the Chief.

14

The chief never did explicitly grant or deny him permission to speak to the aunties. Vinich reckoned that he was no member of the man's clan, nor of any clan, really, and he shouldn't be constrained too much by the local rules. But Vinich didn't press the issue. He should have got an answer from the man. Shadows led into darker shadows on this sunny rock. The best way he could think to ease his frustrations was go home and take a shot of the cheap vodka he kept in his freezer as antiseptic against days like this, maybe read some really blistering Nietzsche. He was out of moves for the moment.

But when Vinich reached the office, a crisis was in progress. Frances informed him the moment he came in that the Lower Court had been calling and calling, asking for a lawyer. "What about Jack?"

"Sick, he says."

"No," said Vinich, and he called Root's cell.

The thing rang, but then went on ringing for a long time. Vinich waited.

"Hehloh," Root said.

"What are you doing?"

"Oooh," said Root.

"Well—?" said Vinich.

"I gaht rhoohlled, bMike."

"What?"

"Tahk to, hehr, talk to. . ."

Vinich heard the phone change hands. "Hey, Mike. It's Clayton. Jack's on a lot of pain pills; his mouth is pretty screwed up."

Now in the background, Jack Root said, "Ih'm be a bvfucking haihrlibp, bMike."

"Yeah," said Clayton. "His lip got split. Real deep.

207

Stitches, LBJ style. Not too pretty."

"He got rolled?" said Vinich. "Is that what he said? Jumped?"

"We both did," said Knapp. "But I ran. I used to run track. . . so. They got poor Jack, though. He tried to reason with them."

"They? Who were they?"

"Some guys. We went to that club in Nu'uuli, and we actually picked up a couple girls. They seemed very nice. But then their, I guess it was their cousins or brothers or something got involved, maybe just some jealous guys. But all of a sudden I'm running and Jack's getting hit. I mean, they only hit him once, I think, which is kind of a blessing. They kicked him, too, and he can't sit down. Sore butt."

"Wasn't he supposed to be heartbroken?"

"I think his lip is bothering him more right now," Knapp said.

"Give the phone back to Jack," Vinich said.

"bMike," Root began when he got on.

"Shut up," said Vinich. "Just shut up, Jack. You're coming in to work tomorrow. That's it. And every day."

"Bhudt, I can'd ebvehn tahk. Ihd hurts."

"Better brush up on your fucking sign language, then."

"bMike, I. . . "

"Shut up, Jack. I've got to get down to Lower Court. This one last time."

It was a juvenile matter in Judge Mandeville's court, a boy of twelve that the Territory was calling ungovernable and seeking to detain in juvenile custody. Judge Mandeville, two Territorial policemen, one Territorial social worker, the juvenile Rex Maufau, and his mother Mrs. Maufau had all been waiting two hours and fifteen minutes when Vinich arrived. The judge ascended the bench that had been built for him in this warehouse, and before Vinich had been given a chance to read the affidavit supporting the lad's detention, before he'd had a chance to talk to young Rex, he was required to account for his delay, account for that into the court record, a clunky tape machine. And Vinich said that he'd been out of the office and that Mr. Root was having some serious health problems. Vinich apologized for any inconvenience.

"I'm taking this up with the Chief Judge," said Mandeville. "I'm going to ask him to take it up with the Governor. That office is supposed to be staffed with four attorneys, including the Public Defender. Two full time interpreters." Mandeville was that sort of tiresome know-it-all who does in fact know everything, or at least everything he might need to use against you. Vinich hadn't known about this staffing mandate, though as office manager he certainly should have. "So, what do you have?" said Mandeville. "One. Effectively. One attorney. It's worth a referral to the American Bar Association."

Refer away, thought Vinich. The disorder of his office was hardly news to him, but there was nothing he could do about it, and there were times when he even felt embattled, ennobled by the situation. Those times were rare, and this was not one of them.

"Talk to your client, counselor. I'll give you ten minutes. You can ask for more if you need it."

Conferences with his juvenile clients were anything but private. Mom and the two guards must be present, and though the social worker wasn't necessary, she came along as well. Come one, come all. As they walked down the hall to the room where they were to meet, Vinich read the affidavit and several short, handwritten statements. The kid had hit not one but several of his teachers in incidents several weeks apart. A reedy boy, Rex, and as their meeting commenced Vinich felt he'd got enlisted into a pack attacking something wounded. He explained, "This hearing is just about whether they can keep you down at the juvenile detention center until you get another hearing on these juvenile charges. They're claiming you're dangerous."

Rex was not about to deny it.

"You hit some people?"

Rex moved his head to the right and down but continued looking Vinich right in the eye.

"You answer him," said his mother.

"Four," said Rex. "I hit four people. I might hit more. If they come up too close. If they breathe on me. I will hit them."

"We're trying to line up a psych eval," said the social worker, a woman supporting her momentous bosom partly with the aid of the clipboard she held under it. "But—that would have to be somebody from off-island, so. . ."

Vinich told his young client, "You're not doing yourself any favors right now by talking that way. Why do you think you have to hit people?"

"They stink," said Rex. There was a slick of fur on his lip. The boy was immature from the neck down but had a face full of well-traveled expressions.

Vinich, to his dismay, understood exactly what his client meant. "Yeah," he said, "but you can't hit 'em. It tends to make things a lot worse. As you can see."

"We discipline," said Mrs. Maufau. "He gets discipline. He gets his discipline again and again. Can't get the evil out." Her arms were thick as her son's body.

The social worker approached young Maufau and said, "Just relax, Rex. You relax a minute. I want to show your lawyer something. You don't hit me, okay?" She lifted the back of his shirt. The two policemen stepped in in case there was any reaction; they stepped back when the boy's crosshatched back was revealed. Welts old and new. There were two semicircular marks, one arcing just under his shoulder blades, another facing up at it from his waist. Vinich said, "What's all this?"

"From brush," said the mother. "From in the brush."

"The brush," said Vinich so that Mother Maufau would know she was known for a liar. He pointed more particularly to the two arcs on the boy's back.

"Old," said Mrs. Maufau. "That is from a long time back. When he was so bad."

"Rice cooker," said Rex. "You kneel down, he puts it on you."

"Shit," said Vinich.

The lad was dangerous just as claimed, and even if he should go before the judge and deny it now, his eyes would certainly give him away. It would be useless to claim Rex Maufau was not dangerous, just as it was hopeless to think he might ever be anything else. Defense counsel was here for window dressing; Vinich would now urge that help be found for the kid, knowing no meaningful help was coming, and that young Rex would be detained for a time then released back to what had made him. But, really, was there anywhere a fix for what they'd already made of him or for how he'd been born? Rex looked to be a nasty long-term loop of a puzzle, or a young casualty, and what of the lavish explanation for what he'd become. No matter how he'd got here, he was a problem now. Mercy was become almost beside the point. He would be detained, sent home with a list of rules he wouldn't follow, and grow up mean if he grew up at all.

The bailiff poked his head in the room where the group had been conferring. "The judge is ready," he said.

"I can ask him to send you home," said Vinich, his tone drooping in the futility of it. "There would probably be quite a few conditions."

"*Many* conditions," said Mrs. Maufau.

"Don't bother," said Rex, more than realistic, looking forward to it. A trip to juvey could only enhance any standing he cared about.

It is every lawyer's secret hope, even the most cynical of them, that justice will someday, somehow be achieved through their efforts. Out in the field, though, justice can be hard to identify much less achieve. Vinich tried to content himself with thinking that his presence at least prevented a prevalence of grave injustices where he practiced. But those injustices that were done to his people didn't ordinarily consist of their being falsely accused, or even of being mistreated by the authorities. His people, so many of them were like young Rex, victims of something long past, things from the womb, and they came to him fairly accused of paying their injury forward. They came to him when nothing much could be done for them.

Vinich was in the mood for a clear win for a change. He wanted one.

15

Jack Root came into work with about a third of his face buried in a gauze bandage he slowly saturated with pink drool. He retired into his office, doing something there that took him back and forth to the copy machine out near Frances. Did he know he was whimpering? Did he know Frances laughed at him when he went back into his office? Now that Vinich didn't particularly need them, the gang was all here, even Elihu was in his office, listening to Radio New Zealand. He followed the All Blacks very closely, the world's greatest side. But cricket, too, and American football, and Australian Rules football. The endless sporting news. Vinich suspected Elihu of running a sports book.

Death with a sweet chemical bouquet—the maintenance team had sprayed something to combat the smell from the ceiling, but the odors had only conjoined. Vinich, however, had a new monitor, a fully functioning computer for once. He'd been upgraded. And Vinich had at last found the discovery file for the Ulu case that morning in his inbox, and it was his to consider at his leisure now. The thing had expanded some over the version he'd seen in the AG's office. Now there were autopsy photos. There was a transcript of a conversation between Noah Satele and the young lieutenant who'd been sent out to bungle the initial investigation; at the police station they'd been recorded on a digital camera as well, but the sound had got muffled so much that he almost had to take the transcription on faith. He couldn't make out what they were saying, though the scraps he did understand, and their rhythms made it clear they were speaking English. They looked so out of place these Samoan boys, both cop and witness, surrounded by filing cabinets, the importance of the moment. They spoke so quietly, sure in keeping with the seriousness of everything, but a numbing nuisance when you're trying to hear, and the microphone is all but turned off. Vinich read the transcript. In it the young Lieutenant, Samuel Samia, identified himself and the time and place and date of the interview. He got from Noah Satele his name and date of birth; it was evident on the video that the young lieutenant made frequent recourse to a manual, or a script, that he was wearing bulging body armor for the occasion, and that he had no facility in the art of the interview.

Q: You are not under arrest.
A: Oh.

Noah Satele, was twenty-nine years old; he wore a Lakers jersey and the air of patiently allowing experience to melt over him. He was not one of the maintenance people Vinich had encountered in the village.

Q: This is because you were a witness. Why you are here.
A: No.
Q: You will be a witness.
A: Why?
Q: You saw.
A: I didn't know anybody.
Q: When? You mean when that guy got killed? That day? You didn't know them?
A: Out there on the trail. I didn't know those guys. The big one. The dead one.
Q: Wasn't that victim from your village? That Asenati?
A: I saw him around before, yeah.
Q: You didn't know him? You had to.
A: We're Mormons. My family. We stay on our side.

Q: What about the boys who were with you?
A: With me?
Q: When you came on the scene.
A: They weren't with me. I got there after they did. We just all—inaudible—that little trail through there, everybody using that now.
Q: How long?
A: Long? What—inaudible.
Q: How long after? Those guys? How long they been there?
A: I don't know.
Q: You didn't ask?
A: No.
Q: You didn't ask those guys what they knew?
A: No.
Q: Did you know those guys? Ones on the path.
A: I know them.
Q: But you didn't even ask?
A: What would I ask? You were there. You came. What could we say? There he was. What do you say about that?
Q: Inaudible.
A: Inaudible. Called the police.

In the video the men sat in steel folding chairs, legs splayed, palms down on their knees, leaning toward each other; despite these frank postures there was no sense that anything was being revealed by their exchange. Or concealed.

Q: What about the suspect? What did he say?
A: You mean the big guy. He didn't say nothing. Not one word.
Q: You asked him?

A: No.

Q: You told me you asked him.

A: That was Filemoni. He told you. He ask him. Big guy wouldn't say. He acted like he couldn't say nothing. You saw.

Q: Inaudible. Filemoni?

A: Army got him—inaudible—displayed in cutter now.

Q: He wasn't supposed to go.

A: He had orders. Already had orders. Had to go.

Q: You better tell me everything you know about this.

A: I did. I already did. Swear on that.

Lieutenant Samia stood, loomed at the camera lens, and it went dark.

Noah Satele was a fine example of that universal type who stand off to the side, cracking wise and contriving in all circumstances to be useless. Noah Satele was a cypher, and he wasn't going to lay one brick in the prosecution's wall, not even if he were to be questioned competently.

What about the other two? Vinich called Swanson to ask him just that, and he waited on hold listening to a whimsical version of Winchester Cathedral and looking through the packet of autopsy photos, glossy eight by tens shot in the operating suite at LBJ, full of detail as only a man lying dead on a stainless-steel tray can be. The law prescribes an autopsy in every unexplained death, but this one was especially unnecessary. The first of the pictures was a complete explanation of Mr. Asenati's death and of mortality generally. The odd, deep indentation in his head, his cheek and temple pushed concave. That blow had done too much displacement for anyone to survive, still the Medical Examiner had thought it necessary to cut a hole in the skull, just to be sure, and the pictures that followed showed that, sure enough, his brain had swollen, erupted right through the new window. The actual seat of Talo Asenati's soul looked like macaroni and cheese forgotten for a year or two at the back of a refrigerator. The violence, once started, just kept coming. Even as late as the autopsy, no one had thought to close the man's eyes, thus every shot of him was marked by that stark surprise. The trouble with pictures like these—if they fell into the hands of a jury, that jury may be inclined to think that *some*one should certainly pay, just to allay the ugliness of it.

"Vinich?" Swanson finally answered.

"What about those other two guys on the trail? When do I get those statements?"

"Well, we're. . ."

"Filemoni?" said Vinich. "I get the idea that guy is gone."

"We can get him back if we have to."

"But what about in the meantime? What did he have to say? Did you get a statement?"

Swanson sighed elaborately, precocious asshole. "We can get him back if we need him."

Another hole in their case. "All right, then," said Vinich. "What about Salave'a? This Manuita kid?"

"He's disabled," Swanson said.

"Disabled?"

"Mentally," said Swanson.

"How?"

"He's. . . retarded. Okay?"

"How bad?" said Vinich.

"He's also," said Swanson, "he's also kind of freaked out. See, Filemoni was his buddy. Filemoni used to take him around places. Then they got involved with this thing, and the kid thinks that's why Filemoni had to go away. So, he completely freaked out. Had a melt down, the Lieutenant tells me. So. You can talk to him if you want. You've got his name. I guess he's real hard to understand."

"You know," said Vinich, "your people out on the trail, they featured pretty prominently in that Information. Now they're a puff of smoke. You want to talk about this a little bit? Reconsider where we're at?"

"No," said Swanson. "Oh—I'd take the death penalty off the table."

"Big deal," said Vinich. "We both know the Territory is not going to build a gallows at this late date. So, that's nothing. That's less than nothing."

"You have an obligation, don't you? Ethical obligation to present that offer to your client. He might want it."

"Yeah?" There would be no more previews of the ways he intended to tear up Mr. Swanson's case. "Thanks for the advice," said Vinich. "I always treasure your professional guidance."

16

Perpetually and permanently pissed off, he knew his for a less than handsome state of mind, but Vinich could tolerate himself so long as he lived alone. Whenever he'd tried to keep company with some well-adjusted person there had been irritation both ways. He was crusty. So be it. But Vinich tried not to get too angry, or too specifically angry, or too personally invested during the course of a case. It was his job, he thought, to cast a clinical eye on a client's circumstance. Clinical, cynical—these categories had over time begun to merge, and Vinich thought he might do well to unwind. He rode an aiga bus that evening, straight from work to the noodle house, borne on hymns pumping through a loudspeaker with several cannery girls just off shift and singing along, soaring above the fish smell they bore so strongly. He welcomed this calming trip among the decent. A younger Vinich had taken his occasional shot of adrenalin from skiing a ridegeline or the like, but by now he was mainlining the stuff nearly all the time just by going to work, and he felt he'd been in a weeklong fistfight, and he was feeling that way much too early in this case.

The noodle house greeted him with dragons wrought in wood and glowing paper lanterns and swanlike women gliding around with menus and teapots. Vinich took a seat at the bar. "Seltzer and lime," he said, thinking he'd better approach his milder mind gradually. "Can I dine here at the bar?"

Of course, he could. Wongs. Chinese, or so he assumed, and here the customer was always right, they had never lost sight of that principle, and here he would have a mound of Kung pao chicken, tender tummy be damned, and it would come to him with effortless, courteous efficiency, steaming, and whatever bullshit these good folks were entertaining in their hearts of hearts they would have the good sense to keep to themselves. Would it be wrong of him to think of them as inscrutable if he saw nothing wrong with inscrutability? Vinich wallowed and sank in that barely audible sigh, some stringed instrument that sawed hypnotically in company with a plucked, stroked harp, and at times a Cantonese soprano warbling up as if from underwater. Vinich meant to linger here in their ideal air conditioning until he was tired, maybe a little drunk. Willows and waterfalls, brush paintings on bamboo. Wongs. Vinich meant to dwell in sensation for a while and get out of his head.

But, no. He should have known better. The Ulu case was looking more and more like one he should win, and those were the most frightening. Was Swanson sitting on something he hadn't shown? That alone might cost him the case. Was the prosecutor confident or stupid? He was ambitious. He was probably smart, but he was new to this and burdened with some bad police work. Swanson was ambitious more than anything, and he wouldn't want to go to trial to lose, and maybe he hadn't been to trial enough to know what a crapshoot that always was, how often the jury when debriefed afterward would mention something not one of the attorneys litigating the case had ever considered as the moment, the piece that would decide the thing, and, win or lose, those litigating attorneys felt the whoosh of months of meticulous preparation made irrelevant by a whim, the will of the people.

Vinich thought he might move for a bench trial, try and take that joker out of the deck. Not the defense attorney's usual move for sure. Would that call Swanson's bluff? Was it a bluff? Vinich felt that if they should try the case on facts alone, with such facts as he presently knew, then he would have no business losing, but maybe those Ulu aunties had something to say after all, something to tie their nephew to the death. Vinich thought that he would drive right back out there tomorrow morning, with Elihu, and he'd confront the elder Ulu again and get his permission, or go around it if necessary, and talk to the aunties.

But tomorrow was a court day.

And he wouldn't be confronting elder Ulu again. He'd been intimidated. Vinich didn't know what to do in the face of such unaccustomed presence. But Vinich must somehow get to those aunties. He should have never asked for permission in the first place. That was his first mistake. Try calling again? See if he could manage to ask it over the phone? And what if the chief said, 'no', then what? And hadn't Vinich long since learned that anyone in a position to say 'no' was almost certain to say exactly that? Permission? Shit.

"Could I also have a gin and tonic. Please."

He had several of these, but because he nursed them, and drank water as well and ate successive courses of dinner, he never got so much as a tipsy. Which seemed a shame. This was a rare indulgence for him, especially the drinks. He had only succeeded in not going home. It was as if he'd thrown himself a party and hadn't come, a waste of resources that hurt the cheapskate in him, but he'd likely be dogged by hard sobriety so long as his mind's eye kept recycling that high resolution photograph of Talo Asenati taken just before the Medical Examiner sawed him open—of all the things Vinich had seen—those eyes flung wide in eternal surprise or imploring it to be otherwise. Not good. It might be unprofessional just now to feel much sympathy for the man, but it would certainly be inhuman not to. Vinich was stuck with something more like resentment for Mr. Asenati. The man had set such an awful example.

The restaurant staff fell to pushing a number of tables together and redraping them with tablecloths to make one long banquet table, then with much bustle place settings were restored and pitchers of water placed at intervals, and this had only just been accomplished when a large group, at least three and possibly four generations of a prosperous family came pushing in all at once, a happy, confused swirl of family. They took possession of the long table. Vinich, maybe a little touched with drink after all, warped sentimental and caught himself being nostalgic for a situation he'd never personally known, a big, shambling, boisterous family. Women scolding children, menfolk floating serenely behind the mix.

But in truth, in bitter truth, he was only missing his own little family, a very real risk he ran with alcohol, to start actively missing again that family he'd made for a while, and missed now, had missed continuously for so much longer than he'd managed to keep them together. Vinich did not wish to be the drunk at the bar. He was preparing to leave when a member of the newly arrived party bought him a drink. This worthy saluted Vinich as his drink was delivered; it was Henry Faiive, a young attorney from the AG's office with whom he was only slightly acquainted. As Vinich understood it, Henry Faiive, had gone to the University of Colorado on a football scholarship, gone straight to law school on graduating, and was now biding his time with the Attorney General until he could be assigned to the Fono and ascend eventually through the ranks of Territorial government. Young Faiive had explained all this to him while they were waiting one day for a hearing, offered it by way of explaining why he was so rarely to be seen in court. Why offend anyone? It was not consistent with his career objectives.

Vinich, despite himself, had found the young princeling charming, and he'd seen him out and about before with a beautiful wife, driving a beautiful car, and he seemed to wear his good fortune well. But their whole acquaintanceship had happened during that wait in the hallway and a few lesser negotiations, and Vinich didn't know what to think of the man's gesture. He was, after all, of the enemy camp. Wasn't he? Vinich, had never given much thought about fraternizing with the enemy, because it hadn't really come up before, because he rarely fraternized with anyone, and, thinking he should really try to get out more and socialize with the non-criminal element, and grinning stupidly, he tipped his glass at his benefactor. They were a generous people.

Vinich, troubled by envy and dyspepsia, thought he should drink up and leave, but he lingered with that long table in the corner of his vision. There were several ravishing women in the group, and almost all of them, even the grandmothers among them were handsome. Little eruptions of laughter. Genuine laughter. How did they do this? Or what was so funny? Henry Faiive sat near the head of the table and seemed to be looking at him still. Vinich wondered if some further acknowledgment was needed, if he should go over to be introduced to the group. Henry Faiive was looking at him, leaning into a man at his side who was also looking at him; they were speaking to each other but never ceased to look, very intently Mike Vinich thought, at Mike Vinich; Henry Faiive and the man there beside him, beside whom a Neanderthal might seem a debutante, a man with the thickest set of features Vinich had ever seen, the eyes deep set in them but so unmistakably aimed his way. They seemed to be assessing him, so Vinich, somehow certain he'd be found wanting, and still grinning thinly, almost apologetically, got right out of Wong's.

17

He had only one matter before the High Court that morning, but Vinich, despite many efforts to do so, had not managed to speak with his wayward wife beater and urge him to come in and take his medicine. He waited on the veranda for Hiram Taupau who was finally dropped curbside by some shy ally who immediately drove off. From the veranda Vinich hailed his client "Hey, come on. Come on, come on, come *oohnn*." There had been no chance to discuss with the man the importance of being in court before the judges that morning. Mr. Taupau had avoided him from the outset, but at the outset of all this Mr. Taupau had not avoided the officer who'd been called to the village to investigate the damage he'd done his wife—he'd been widely heard hurting her—and this investigator was an old hand who'd got all he needed by way of confession in ten minutes with Mr. Taupau. There was a written statement in the investigator's hand with Mr. Taupau's signature underneath.

Initially Hiram Taupau was charged with felony assault for having left such a nasty mark on his wife. Just how Mr. Taupau had done this was never made clear because he and his wife claimed immediately after the fact to have forgotten the details of the incident. But Mr. Taupau had, in that first fatal interview at least, generally admitted to assaulting her, and Mrs. Taupau had generally confirmed it while still bleeding. And, of course, that fresh scar. When the prosecutor had offered a reduction to misdemeanor assault with a thirty-day jail sentence and the mandatory fine imposed for crimes considered domestic abuse, Vinich thought it at least as good an outcome as he as the man's advocate might have suggested, and a far better one than Hiram Taupau deserved; his one brief conversation with Mr. Tapau had consisted of Vinich calling it a good deal and recommending that he take it, and Mr. Taupau had balked, and still refused any responsibility having now built a new truth he liked better. Maybe Mr. Taupau suspected an offer that had come to him too easily. An angular man in his early middle age, he gave the impression of slithering up the courthouse steps; equipped for a picnic it seemed, he carried a reed basket draped with a cloth.

"Are you ready to do this?"

Hiram Tapau's was a narrow face upon which resentment, hatred, and wonder were written all at once.

"Are you ready to plead out today?" Vinich said. "Man, you left it 'til the very last second, didn't you? Come *on.*"

"I didn't do anything," said Taupau. He had convinced himself of it.

"All right," said Vinich. "Then I'll tell the judge to set it for trial. And he'll throw you in jail for contempt, for not showing up last time when you were supposed to, and you'll sit out at the prison, probably, until it goes to trial. Trial on the felony, catch a couple years if you got convicted. And even if you were acquitted, that would be a lot more than thirty days from now. Before we could get you a trial date. So, if that's what you want, that's how we'll do it. Or—I can walk you through a plea. Either way, come *on.* You can't take that thing into court. You'll have to leave that by the door."

Clearly, and accurately this Taupau had got the idea that his lawyer despised him. By his manner he also meant to suggest that his lawyer had sold him out, which was not true. In no event would it be in Taupau's best interest to see his wife and her bright, fresh mark in the witness box. She could not be compelled to testify against her husband, but a canny prosecutor would know that she could at least be compelled to come in and reveal that face, and anything the poor woman had said while she was bleeding would now be admissible hearsay.

"We're first on the calendar," Vinich said, leading his client right to counsel table, and only just in time for the judges to come in. All rise. Vinich and his client hadn't even got sat down yet. Their case was called. The chief judge asked Vinich if his client intended to enter his plea. Vinich removed the written agreement from his briefcase and said, "Your Honor, we have here an agreement to be executed in the presence of the court." He heard a certain lift in his voice that made of this a question as much as a statement, and Vinich glanced sidelong at Taupau, and the sonofabitch still would not signal his intentions one way or the other.

"Is that correct, sir? You intend to enter a guilty plea today?"

Taupau seemed somehow to view this as his moment in the sun, and he milked it for drama for several long beats before he looked up at the judge and soulfully said, "I will do what I'm told."

"Who told you?" the chief judge asked him.

Taupau pointed laterally toward Vinich.

"Have you read this agreement you're about to sign?"

"Your, Honor," Vinich volunteered, Mr. Taupau has been unable to. . ."

"He hasn't read it?"

"No, Your Honor."

"Counsel," said the chief judge.

Swanson rose for the Territory, buttoning his jacket, and as this boilerplate agreement had originated with his office, and as the defendant hadn't read it, Swanson was going to have to read all six pages of the thing into the record, and no one was happy. Swanson droned; Vinich followed along with his finger, provision by provision down each page, and Mr. Taupau and all the judges were soon adrift in unrelated thoughts. Then it was over at last and Vinich's forefinger had come to rest on the signature line provided for his client. With his other hand he produced his pen and said, "Let the record reflect, that Mr. Taupau is now signing the agreement in the presence of the court." Taupau, once again looked indecisive, coerced. Vinich lay the pen before him. Taupau looked here and there, and sighed, and signed it. Vinich added his own signature and walked the document over to Swanson, who also signed it, and rose again, and buttoned his jacket again, and moved the court, consistent with terms of the plea agreement, to amend the charge to assault in the third degree.

"That's your charging decision," said the Judge. "That will be on your office, counsel. Motion granted. Before we get to the rest of it, though, we should probably hear Mr. Taupau's allocution."

"Yes, your Honor," said Vinich "I'd be pleased to assist Mr. Taupau with that." Two signed admissions were not enough; good and nearly universal practice called for the person making a plea to describe aloud and in sufficient detail their crime. This was precisely where these things often hit a snag. Mr. Taupau was of the clan of the weasel—across every culture, age group, and sex that Vinich had encountered in his work this subspecies was becoming always more prevalent, people without foresight or any capacity for remorse who refused ever to be held to account for anything they'd done or failed to do. As a strategy it seemed to work pretty well—until it didn't—the allocution, for instance, where he might be required at last to say his sins. Mr. Taupau was presented with a bible, and he took the oath, and Vinich suspected he would take that oath seriously; Mr. Taupau probably wouldn't overtly lie now, not with a bible involved, but that wouldn't prevent him from clamming up. The weasel must squirm and squirm away. It remained the nature of the beast even as it became a bad strategy.

"Mr. Taupau," said Vinich, "I'm referring now to a night about two months ago, September sixth. Do you remember talking to a Sergeant Shine?"

"There was a man with a badge. That could be his name."

"A man with a badge came to your house?"

"Yes."

"The neighbors called the police?"

"I don't know," said Mr. Taupau. "Must have."

"And a policeman came to your house?"

"No uniform."

"But the man had a badge. He showed you his badge."

"Yes," said Mr. Taupau.

"He asked you some questions and wrote down your answers."

"Yes," Mr. Taupau reluctantly affirmed.

"And you signed that and said it was accurate?"

"I signed it," said Mr. Taupau.

"Were you being honest with Sergeant Shine?"

"I," said Taupau, "I don't know what happened."

"You told Detective Shine you were upset.

"Yes."

"You'd been upset," Vinich said. "You said you thought you hurt your wife."

"I said that then," said Taupau.

"Were you being honest with Sergeant Shine?"

"At the time," said Taupau.

"And Mrs. Taupau had an injury."

"Yes."

"And there's really no other explanation for her

injury?"

"Well," said Taupau, "—no."

"So, Mr. Taupau, you've chosen to take responsibility."

Mr. Taupau was silent for another of those long tense moments, no doubt he'd be trying to devise some way to scotch this plea and shoot himself in the foot, But Vinich had cinched him in, and eventually he said, "Yes."

18

His was a job always noble in principle, often ignoble in practice. Vinich felt he'd done a full day's work with his hour in court that morning, the whole moral whipsaw thing, and the drinks from the previous evening were finally announcing themselves as today's malaise. Gin leaking back through his pores, Vinich thought he needed to go home and spend the remainder of his day in the shower—another necessary and futile routine in Samoa. He could find no sympathy or excuse for the abusers he represented so ably, those nasties, men usually, who kept their households always hostage with their always imminent rage. These turds were in bad shape whenever they hit a situation they couldn't with their lies or their threats manipulate, and it became Vinich's job to protect them from themselves. Why? What value did that advance? It was almost fortunate that the law was so tolerant of this type; Vinich for the most part didn't need to advocate too strongly in their behalf. But how tiring just to be in such a presence.

It was not always and not necessarily his to defend the innocent, but to always and always defend the possibility of innocence, or of redemption, and it can be hard after a while to dwell so much in the theoretical, to find satisfaction in one's strange duty. Vinich decided he at least owed himself a lunch of several hours at that café where with any luck there would be a breeze across the patio and a certain willowy waitress would also be circulating and improving the scenery, and it was only a bus ride away, and it came to pass much as he'd hoped; he got the very table he wanted, and after two servings of trifle and five cups of coffee he did feel much restored, certainly recharged, but Vinich had little improved his mood because he was once again replaying those autopsy pictures through his thoughts, and if these images of the mangled Mr. Asenati were now to be his permanent companions he was in trouble. There were a lot of other things he might be thinking of—'do not obsess' Vinich told himself. 'Relax.'

His cell phone quivered in his hip pocket, a rare enough occurrence that he flinched. It was Frances calling from the office, something still rarer, almost alarming. "Yeah, Mike," she said, "you got somebody here to see you."

"An appointment? I had no appointments." Appointments were another rarity in his routine.

"It's somebody important," said Frances.

"I'm down here in Pago," Vinich said, "and I don't have the jeep today."

Frances spoke indistinctly with someone there with her in the office, got an answer, and reported back to Vinich, "He's waiting. He says he's gonna wait for you."

"Who. . .?" Frances was gone.

Trying not to hurry back, Vinich hurried anyway, or hurried as best he might by aiga bus to Utulei. Was he at someone's beck and call? Who might that be? Who did Frances consider important? Not a client. No, it wouldn't be a client. Was he in trouble somehow? Vinich felt comfortable, at least, with respect to job security, because who else would want this job? And if he should for some reason lose this job, man, that might be the kindest cut of all. Someone important? He came into Public Defenders suite wondering whether he should have his back up or be wary. From her desk Frances motioned with her head toward his office, and Elihu of all people was loitering outside that door, brandishing a notebook and all but prancing in unprecedented glee. It was not a good look for Elihu. "Got his autograph," he said. There was a flourish of signature and, more legibly, 'Best wishes brah.' Elihu was transformed.

Confused, Vinich knocked at his own door before entering it; the visitor had been looking out the office's tinted picture window, something Vinich himself never did as the window overlooked a parking lot. The man wore a shirt of a slightly glossy fabric, white, that draped nicely across the escarpment of his back, and when he turned to greet Vinich, Vinich saw that it was the man from Wong's, the one with a battering ram for a face who had been eyeing him there last night, and who eyed him now as he offered his hand, taking his measure. Vinich just knew that one of these days, one of these guys was going to crush his hand in a handshake, but it wouldn't be this one. "I'm Doak," said the man familiarly. He lacked the look of the salesman he was, but he possessed a gliding voice that erased this disadvantage at once. Doak seemed to think that Vinich should know him or know about him. Vinich didn't—even so, this Doak made of himself an instant ally. "I'm Pule Ulu's nephew," he explained. "I flew in when I heard what was happening with him."

"Oh," said Vinich. "I'm sure he'll appreciate the support. His nephew, you say?"

"He's only three years older than me. That's a pretty common sort of thing around here. Thing is, Pule was my hero. My idol, you could say."

"Oh?" said Vinich.

This Doak was a celebrity in some sphere. "I wanted to see," he said, "if there was anything I could do." He was ugly but handsomely dressed, Doak, with a pleasant way about him. "I wanted to talk to him, of course, but he says he can't say much about the. . ."

"I've asked him not to," Vinich said. "I'm glad I made my point. He really shouldn't be talking to anyone right now about the. . . charges. Anything to do with that."

"Do you think he's guilty? Is that why?"

"It's not a matter of what I think," said Vinich. "Or of what anybody *thinks*, right now. It's all about what they can prove. And right now, the way things stand, I don't think that's very much. That could change, but for right now your uncle's position is reasonably strong."

"Except he's in prison. Could I put up his bail?"

"A million?"

"No," said Doak.

"Yep," said Vinich. "On an island. For a guy with no priors. A million."

"Well, that's ridiculous."

"It is," said Vinich, feeling impotent about it. "You know, if you wanted to help, and you have the means, you might want to consider hiring private counsel for him. I brought this up with your uncle. If you have the means, you might want to consider someone with more resources, more time."

"He trusts you," said Doak. "He wants you to be his guy."

"That's flattering," said Vinich. "But from the cases I've tried here before—maybe a little dicey. I'm not exactly working with home field advantage."

"A trial?"

"It's a real possibility. The way I deal with these—until it doesn't happen, I assume it will. You start preparing for trial right away. The trouble is—the thing I can't prepare for —I don't know the—the people here. I wouldn't know how to read them at all. That's probably true of the other guy, the prosecutor too, but. Also, there may be firms on the island, private guys who can pull strings, call in favors. All I can do is work the law for what it's worth."

"Pule thinks you're his guy. He trusts you. He says you get him."

"Well, he's a likable person, decent I think, and that

goes a long way with me. I wouldn't claim to understand him, though," Vinich said. "Most days I don't understand anyone. If it sounds like there's a lot I don't understand, I guess that's what I'm trying to say here."

Doak was another man of his family notable not only for bulk but density; that face, though—it wouldn't take much shift in such a brute brow to raise alarms. "I have to admit," he said. "I was thinking on the plane about hiring somebody. But I know some of them and—I agree with Pule. You're his best bet."

"Okay, then," Vinich said. "You flew in, huh?"

"From Sacramento," Doak said. "Oh." He withdrew his wallet and from that a sheaf of business cards, two of which he handed to Vinich. He was Doak Falaniko 'The Man in the Middle'.

"Are you a—a body guard?"

"Oh," said Falaniko. "No. That's just a play on—I used to be an interior lineman—I'm a developer now. I thought it was clever. Maybe not. It never occurred to me someone would take it that way."

"Sorry," Vinich said. "I didn't know about the football. So that's why you're. . .?"

"I was in the league. Could be still, I think, and making great money. I went two ways, nose guard and long snapper, so I was valuable. I did get paid, me and my agent and my accountant. Always dinged up, though. They were all so pissed around here when I quit. They go nuts when an island boy makes the league. But no one is stepping on their fingers when they go to work."

"Sacramento," said Vinich.

"Yep," said Falaniko. "Got out with my health—I think—and I'm doing commercial and residential, just hand over—what is it?—fist? Anyway, doing well. Lovely wife, lovely kids. And I do not tithe. Nope. But I wanted to see if there was anything I could do for Pule. I think that bond is—I couldn't make that for him. Anything else, though."

"There might be," Vinich said. "Falaniko?" He paged through his documents to the mention of, "—Inina? Are you related to Inina Falaniko?"

"That's my mother."

"Hm. This is getting us somewhere. See your mother and a couple of other ladies were with your uncle before this man was killed. I should really know what they have to say about that. That's the big question in the case right now, as far as I'm concerned, and I tried to go out and talk with them, and your uncle. . ."

"You should call him 'Pule.'"

"Anyway, he told me to go through his father. To get permission. So I went out and talked with the—the chief?—the pastor, matai, and I asked him about it, but he wouldn't give me an answer one way or the other. I don't know if I'm supposed to be waiting for him to make up his mind, or—I'm not sure how things stand. Kind of left with my tail between my legs. That guy is something else. I wasn't about to push it."

"Trog, huh?"

"Is that his name? I never actually got his name," said Vinich. "Pastor Ulu, or something, but—I really didn't know what to call him."

"Noo," said Falaniko. "No, no. You wouldn't want to call him that. That's my name for him."

"Trog?" said Vinich.

"He is *sooh* dumb," said Falaniko.

"I thought he was such a powerful guy."

"He is. *High* chief—all of it. He does call the shots around there. But he is dumb. Let me guess—when you saw him, he didn't say much, did he? See, that was the one good idea he ever had. When he decided to shut up."

"Seems to work for him," said Vinich. "He had me buffaloed."

"Oh, yeah. People think he's thinking," said Falaniko. "Which is about as far from true as anything could possibly be. You get him at a family gathering, or somewhere where it's safe to open his mouth—and you would not believe it. The guy is just ultra dumb."

"Hm," said Vinich. "That's something else I didn't get right. But maybe, if I went through you, I could talk to your mother? Maybe those other ladies?"

"You should just go and talk to them," said Falaniko. "They'd be happy to talk to you. They love Pule. They'd say anything for him."

"Well, I don't want them to. . . Well, no," said Vinich, "I got off to a kind of bad start. Maybe I muffed it when I tried to talk to the pastor. I had no idea what was on his mind."

"Nothing," said Falaniko. "Really close to nothing."

"Would you let them know I need to talk? Kind of smooth the way? Let 'em know whose side I'm on?"

"I don't think you want me—I'm not real popular out there. There's some who are mad at me for leaving the league before I had to, some mad at me because I didn't move back here after football. My kids have never seen this island. I run into a lot of static out there. As I say, I don't tithe. Not to their church, not to my church in Sacramento, so that really pisses those guys off. No, I don't carry any real weight out there, but I can tell you how things are. The aunties love Pule. I love Pule. Anyone with any sense loves Pule, but for me he was the big inspiration."

"I see," said Vinich, a sort of lie he kept repeating.

"You know genetics?" Doak Falaniko asked. "Traits are supposed to get passed down. You know, father to son.

But Pastor Ulu, who is just bone-dumb, has a son who's the smartest guy I ever knew."

"Pule?" Vinich had sensed a sort of moral intelligence radiating from the man, noted his ornamented speech. This was a claim he could believe.

"Oh yeah," said Falaniko. "Far and away the smartest guy I ever knew, and he's like wise-smart, you know."

Vinich hadn't really known but gave himself some credit for guessing something good was going on there.

"Also," said Falaniko, "Uncle Pule is the strongest guy I ever met. Physically. I've been in a lot of weight rooms, and I've never seen anyone who could touch Uncle Pule. And he doesn't train. Not at all. Doesn't like to get his hands dirty or break his nails. Most people, even right around the village there, most people have no idea how strong he is. He's the quiet one. Quiet. I owe him everything. You know why? He's his own man. He showed me how to do that."

Vinich feared tears might at any moment leak onto the grateful nephew's stony cheeks and chin, and that would be another image he'd be a long time losing.

19

Morbid as any ten-year-old boy, he thought, Vinich got out the pictures again. These were to be all the physical evidence except for a rock now in a baggie at the police station. How curiously hurt he'd been, Talo Asenati, the wound that had killed him was a neat concavity in his head such as a cartoon character might suffer. No blood there. The wound itself was a dry crater, all the blood had issued from the other side of his face, blown out his nose and coated the half of his mouth drawn up into a sneer that was so completely inconsistent with the look in its eyes. Again—poor Talo Asenati. But that dry wound. Vinich examined the photograph of the rock, a surprisingly detailed photograph of a grapefruit-sized chunk of porous, volcanic rock; if this abrasive thing had made that ditch, he thought, it would have scoured it too, fleshed it to the face bones. The new stone age. How odd, Vinich thought, to have got this expertise in rock wounds.

How to play this? Young Swanson seemed to consider the rock his evidence of requisite malice. When a man arms himself—But what if there was no rock? What if the rock wasn't used?

The rock hadn't been used. How to play this? When to play this? If Swanson or one of his cops didn't wise up, they might get as far as trial still offering the rock as a murder weapon with no fingerprints and with every forensic indication that it hadn't made the fatal wound. That's all the reasonable doubt Vinich thought he'd need, and someone in the jury box would surely know the result produced by even incidental contact of flesh with that kind of pumice. The autopsy report was cursory, a technical description of the utterly obvious. A wound described, and the secondary wound inside the skull, but no mention or speculation as to the source of those injuries. Blunt force trauma. No doubt. But no rock.

What if he were to call Mr. Swanson now with this new observation, maybe use it to see if the charge might be walked back, the bond amount reconsidered? No rock. How would that play? No rock, maybe, but still that crater pushed deep into a man's head, a crushing that had to signal a certain amount of intention. A big blow from somewhere. From somebody, probably. And prosecutor Swanson was an obtuse piece of ambition and righteousness—he wasn't going anywhere softer. He'd consider it his duty to yield nothing.

There wasn't much to see in *post mortem* Talo Asenai, to suggest what and how the man might have been in life or if there was anything about him that seemed to contribute to his death. He was a slight man by any measure, but particularly here. His face as rearranged in death was damnation in a nutshell and so extremely human, but not in any usual way. On the trail he'd been wearing a tie. He'd lain along the trail in his tie and a pair of black oxfords, here in that rare place on earth where such shoes were exotic—and staring up in his eternal horror at Pule Ulu, who equally incongruous in his dress and pearls, and almost equally horrified, stared back at him.

A mystery—an ugly one, and Vinich didn't necessarily want to see it completely untangled, but a still a mystery, or a number of mysteries joined at the top by the keystone of a spectacularly nasty moment, and Vinich thought himself a nasty man, because it interested him, particularly the ugliness—and all this scheming with a man's life in the balance. It was too interesting if anything.

20

"Mrs. Falaniko?"

"Yes," she said, another soft-spoken member of her family.

"My name is Mike Vinich. I'm representing your nephew—his lawyer. I believe he'd be your nephew. Mr.— or Pule Ulu."

"Yes," she said.

"I'd like to talk to you if I could. I'd like to know what you can tell me about what happened that day in the church." Vinich waited while Mrs. Falaniko made it clear there would be no response to this. "I got your number from your son," he eventually said.

"Doak?" she said, as if Vinich had become his stand-in.

"Yes."

"He called you?"

"He told me," Vinich said.

"Told you?"

"Yes," said Vinich, hoping now to limit his honesty.

"You mean he came here? He came where you are? He was on-island?"

"Yes," said Vinich.

"He came and saw you? And he was talking to you?"

"Yes," said Vinich.

"And he was on-island, and he didn't come see me?"

This was probably accurate, given her tone, but since he didn't know it to be true, Vinich felt he was spared having to agree with her. "Ma'am, I would really like to speak with you. Speak with those other ladies who were at the church with you. It's—it's quite important."

"You want me to say something?" said Mrs. Falaniko.

"I'm just trying to find out what happened." This was and was not true. "I don't know if anyone else has. . . As

I told Pastor Ulu—I expect the police or someone will be speaking with you. I don't want to be surprised."

"Surprised?" said Mrs. Falaniko, still annoyed with him. "I can't talk here."

"Oh?" said Vinich. He didn't want this explained.

"You know the beach club?"

"There's one right across the road from me. That one?"

"I have a shift tonight. I'll come in early. I'll be the big woman in scrubs. About three. Three, all right? I drive a Toyota. You could tell I wasn't there to do any sailing."

"This is great," Vinich said, no overstatement.

"And he came and saw *you*. . ." said Mrs. Falaniko.

◊ ◊ ◊

She wheeled into the little parking lot at the beach club almost exactly at three, a punctuality not necessarily *fa'asamoa*. Big woman in a little red car. Vinich walked across the sandy lot and risked another adventurous handshake; this was the first he could recall being made to feel a stripling by a woman. This family was built on a different scale, dipped out of a booming gene pool.

"It's great to meet you," Vinich said.

"Sure," she said. "So. . .?"

Vinich recounted in brief the allegations of the Information, he described the interview he'd seen, told her of the pictures that had been taken, that one of them included Pule Ulu. Pule Ulu, out there on the trail with the body. But no one had seen or heard Pule Ulu do anything to that body. This seemed very thin to Vinich, an increasingly weak case to support anything like first degree homicide. "So," he said, "I have to wonder if there isn't something more. And that's why I'm very interested to talk to you. I want to make sure I'm not missing anything."

"Pule didn't do anything bad," said Mrs. Falaniko. She

was a nurse, she had that authority. There were clouds adrift on her uniform, her scrubs. A rainbow on her shoulder.

"I've had that impression, too."

"He'd be the last guy," said Mrs. Falaniko.

"Seems everyone but the prosecutor feels that way."

"Can you get him off?"

"It's unethical to make guarantees—*and* stupid. But that's what I'm working toward. That's why I wanted to talk to you about that afternoon. It was afternoon, wasn't it?"

"The church?" said Mrs. Falaniko. "I thought we got there in the morning. We did go in the morning. And you go, and you sit around, and every village makes its own circle. You sit and weave baskets, mats, and they judge who made the nicest ones. We almost never win, but we have so much fun when Pule comes with us. That's how we got in trouble."

"*You're* in trouble? Who is?"

"We are," said Mrs. Falaniko. "The girls. Worse than usual this time."

"Why are you in trouble?"

"For laughing," said Mrs. Falaniko. "Lauging in their church."

"You can't laugh in church?"

"It was too much," said Mrs. Falaniko. "They said it was too much, too loud. And that's how everything got started, from us laughing. Pule really got us going, and we made them mad in there."

"Was everyone mad with you?"

"I thought it was mostly that one guy. Lot of people were laughing with us, so they didn't mind. They were having fun."

"The guy with the tie? He was the one with a problem?"

"Yeah, and he thought it made him official, too. Acted like. . . He was the problem. He gave us the stink eye for a while, and then he came over and he's blah, blah, blah about we're disrespecting his church. And we piped down, but poor Pule, he felt bad. He doesn't like to hurt anybody's feelings. And he went outside."

"Did the guy in the tie tell him to go outside?"

"Did he? I—I don't think so. I don't think he said anything just to Pule. You know, directly to him." Mrs. Falaniko was no longer stern or guarded, only immersed in memory.

"Did Pule say anything to him?"

"No. He, just looked sad and went outside."

"Was he mad?"

"No. He doesn't get mad. He wouldn't about something like that. He just goes off. I mean away. And that's what he did. Just went outside. Meanwhile, the girls, we're thinking about leaving now, but we came in my sister's pickup, and her little poophead Douglas has the truck, and he's with his poophead girlfriend, and we can't get him, so we were kind of stuck there. Then that moron kid comes running in and says somebody got murdered. After that everything has been real downhill, I would say."

"This is what you told the officer when he came?"

Mrs. Falaniko paused either to be sure of her truth or to construct a good substitute. "I know this much—I told him Pule didn't do anything wrong, and I will tell that to anybody at any time."

"Good," said Vinich. "Did you happen to notice when Talo Asenati, the guy in the tie, left the church?"

"I did," said Mrs. Falaniko. "I noticed, because I was thinking maybe he wasn't such a bad guy after all, and he maybe he was going to check on Pule because he hurt his feelings."

"Did he follow him right out?"

"Oh, no," said Mrs. Falaniko. "We'd been there a long

time before he went out. We made a lot of phone calls. Couldn't seem to get a ride out of there, and after a while we even quit trying. Just went on weaving. But it wasn't very nice anymore."

"Were you worried?"

"About us? Oh, no. About Pule? No. He does that. Goes off. He's off by himself most of the time—he'll find some hidey hole. I don't remember if he brought a book. But he'd been out there quite a while when that guy comes running in."

"By 'quite a while' what do you mean? How much time passed, would you say, between when Pule went out of the church and Talo Asenati left? The guy in the tie?"

"Quite a while," said Mrs. Falaniko. "I was bored, so—forty- forty-five minutes?"

"And how long after that did the kid come and say there'd been a murder?"

"Maybe another, oh, forty minutes. Hour? I was real bored by then. You're weaving baskets, just weaving baskets and you don't feel like you can laugh any more. That weaving, you know it's cultural and everything, but for me it gets dull after a while, just doing that. It really was quite a shock when that boob came running in, even when I didn't believe him, and I had no idea who he was even talking about. Then he took me out there, and ooh gee, my word, I mean, I see it at work, but usually not like that. I didn't even bother to feel for a pulse."

There was a small flotilla out in the bay of privileged children learning to sail in dinghies. There were purposeful sailors and other boats swirling aimlessly around them. Collision seemed likely. The lawn Vinich stood on with Mrs. Falaniko had somehow got dried out; a curious thing in this climate. Maybe the salt air.

"Do you remember out on the trail if anyone was

saying anything while you were there?"

"Who?"

"Anyone," said Vinich.

"Oh, that babbly guy said a few things when he took me out there, but they didn't make any sense."

"How did he know to take you out there?"

"He didn't. It sounded like someone might be hurt—so. I'm a nurse. I had him show me. I didn't even know who he was talking about until I got there. That kid was quite dumb, and he couldn't seem to pick his language, so then it was me, and him, and the guy who called the cops, and that other guy who just stood there, And Pule. And we all just stood there then. I think we were all so surprised."

"What about Pule? Do recall him saying anything?"

"Nothing," said Mrs. Falaniko. "I treated him for shock, and he never said a word. He was so—I don't think he could say anything. He's a sensitive person. It took me a while to get him to lay down. Get his feet elevated. We couldn't get him to leave, either. He stayed right there until he was arrested, and that was quite a while. Like he was trying to protect that guy. But he didn't say anything. He hasn't said anything yet to me. Can't. That cop who took him away told us we couldn't have contact with him. We have to send him things through our kids. Out to the prison. He likes to look nice. We send him his clothes. Clean clothes. Can't say anything, though, and I feel so bad for him. We all do. Now of all times we'd want to be able to say we love him."

"I'll mention it next time I see him," Vinich said, realizing he was a little jealous of Pule Ulu and the admiration he seemed to cause.

"I like you," said Mrs. Falaniko. "You seem like you try for him. You're gonna try, right?"

"I try for everybody."

"You're not one of these silly guys they bring in, I hope. Instant expert on the island ways?"

"No, I'm not that. Definitely not that. But I do try. When I've got something to work with, I probably try a little bit harder. This case, I have to say, it's almost too good. For the defense that is, for once. To me it looks like the prosecutor expects people to make some assumptions, and it shouldn't take very many assumptions to completely gut a murder charge."

Vinich kept warning himself against optimism, and worse, expressions of optimism, but this looked more and more like a high, slow softball of a case, and he couldn't help but wind up a bit. Shift gears, he thought. Dig. There must be bad facts lurking somewhere. "You may be contacted. I'm surprised they haven't yet. The cop never came back after that evening?"

"He got our names and everything, but I haven't heard from him. They never do come back, the cops, once they've been around to your village. They write on their pad and load somebody up, and that's the last you see of the cop, sometimes the last you see of the person. A lot of people get deported out of our village, we've got families back and forth to Apia. But if it isn't just hauling people away, if you want to find things out, that kind of cop work, you will probably have to find out yourself—find out yourself, I mean it—don't ever think those people will do their jobs." She was emphatic. She was right. Vinich was coming to like Mrs. Falaniko and to regret the sad estrangement from her boy, Doak. He was coming to like this family very much, all of them so immense and, with the apparent exception of the Chief, thoughtful people.

"You couldn't see anything," she said. "On the trail. I mean, you had to be right there to see that. Real deep in the trees there. Whatever happened there. . . Well, nobody.

You had to be right there to see anything."

"How far was this from the church, approximately."

"Between three hundred and four hundred meters." Mrs. Falaniko explained her explanation, its precision. "You can tell I never was a runner, but I got through college throwing the shot. I spent a lot of time at track meets, still do, so I know my distances pretty well."

"So," said Vinich, "I'll be talking to. . . the other ladies, sorry their names escape me at the moment. Just to follow up. But you say they never were out on the trail, never saw Mr. Asenati after he'd been—So, they stayed in the church?"

"I made sure," said Mrs. Falaniko. "After I saw, I made sure they didn't go out there and see it. So. . . they didn't even see that. And I'm not so sure they will talk to you. You can go out there and try."

"What?" said Vinich. "Problem with the Chief?"

"In a way," said Mrs. Falaniko. "We are in so much trouble. Ever since this happened the people in our church, the people in our village, they don't want to talk to us, won't even look at us. Too ashamed to look at us. It was supposed to be nice. It was supposed to be, what do you call it—wholesome. And it was nice. Traditional crafts. And there's always a lot of cake. Cake all day. Nice. Now this, and it's going to be something my children's children will hear about, I'm not sure how long we're supposed to hang our heads."

"All because. . ."

"The laughing," said Mrs. Falaniko. "And the judgment we got from it. I hope this is the last time I ever have to say anything about that day. How we went and laughed in that church. Somebody's church."

21

It was a sun favored village, most all of it lying within the sound of the surf, and there was building going on—prosperity. This must be as unlike winter in Riverton, Wyoming as any circumstance could possibly be, and Vinich was grateful for it, his work environment of the moment. But now that he'd been talking with the inhabitants and former inhabitants of this place he was aware of a dark vein through it as well, something old and ugly that ran unseen through these tended groves, among their bright houses—blue was a favored shade, a blue to repeat the ocean as it repeats the sky, and a certain yellow was also popular, a tint reminiscent of sunrise, and Vinich could only wonder how he managed to feel anything ominous in such a place. Maybe he'd come to expect that any place his kind of curiosity led was likely to have something wrong with it.

He had from Mrs. Falaniko a simple set of directions to the home of Carol Ulu. Vinich was told to take a certain turning and follow that to its endpoint. Though Carol Ulu was without a telephone, Fiame Tagataese did have one, and through that connection he had arranged to meet with the remaining 'girls.' The house he wanted was a long way from anything resembling pavement, and the track leading to it looked less and less used as it went along until, where it disappeared altogether there sat a squat cinderblock hut, unpainted and surrounded by free range chickens, free range hogs. There was a boar, in fact, fully tusked, that gave Vinich pause before he got out of the jeep, caused him to consider bringing the public defender stave, just in case.

He passed an herb garden, a kitchen garden on the way in, strongly fenced against the pigs, and that fence was by far the stoutest thing about a residence that wore a corrugated tin roof that seemed designed to be frequently replaced. Vinich knocked at the door, but as it stood propped open and the women inside could see him, his knock was unnecessary. They beckoned him in.

The approach to Carol Ulu's house was extra rustic for Vinich's purposes, but the interior of that house was cozy in a hippy way, all draped in fine mats and with scented candles burning and Maxfield Parish posters curling in the humidity and some brass knickknacks, vaguely Indian, scattered around. The women sat at a low table trimming marijuana over a large screen. "I'm Carol," said a woman draped in a teal sarong. "I'd shake your hand, but we just got this thing set up the way we like it, and I don't want to stand up. And my hands are *real* sticky. There's a pipe over there, pipe and a lighter if you want to smoke."

"Not while I'm working."

The other woman spoke. "I'm Fiame," she said.

"Hello. You sound very different over the phone."

"I had to be quiet over the phone," said Fiame.

"Yeah," said Carol Ulu. "Fuck that. Hey, have a seat, just throw that shit off the couch. Obsidian eyes high on her high cheeks. "Inina seems to think you're okay."

"Pleased to hear that," said Vinich. "You wouldn't want to be on her bad side, would you?"

"She's like all those big ones," said Carol Ulu, who seemed given to pronouncements. "Gentle. Basically gentle. I think they have to be."

The 'girls' as they sat there were the first of this extended family that Vinich had met who would not qualify as big ones. Carol Ulu was of ordinary stature and girth, and Fiame Tagataese did not appear to be very tall at all; her fine boned hands fluttered in their work like hummingbirds. The girls were quite a various batch of sisters, physically and otherwise as unlike as any three women might be, but for all that they did seem deeply bound to their sisterhood.

"She was mad about Doak," said Carol Ulu. "But that wasn't your fault."

"No," said Vinich who wanted always to be spared, if possible, any detours through a family dynamic, any unnecessary trips through a funhouse full of wobbly mirrors. "She was able to help me quite a bit." He had been lulled somehow so that he only gradually gave much thought to the crime he'd got into here, a crime taken most seriously on this island. "She was really helpful," he said, "so there are only a couple things to kind of fill in, follow up on. Shouldn't take long."

"We've got orders to fill," said Carol Ulu. "Got to get a certain amount of this stuff trimmed up, but give us about twenty minutes and we'll break for lunch. You'll eat. We'll talk."

This was an invitation, Vinich knew, not to be declined without giving grave offense.

"You like shake?" said Carol Ulu. "Send you home with a sack full of shake. Free, if you want it."

"I better not," said Vinich. "But thank you."

They worked for about an hour then, and while they worked, he learned quite a lot about them, but nothing touching on those things they knew he'd come to discuss. Carol Ulu, upon closer and longer examination never for a moment ceased to be delicious; she didn't seem to find her own beauty too interesting. She said she didn't like trimming because she was a cultivator, she was a breeder. She described getting out of the service, and she'd gotten out the instant she was eligible for any retirement, and she'd brought a strain home with her from Alaska, but what had worked in Alaska couldn't stand its good fortune in the South Pacific, and so she'd had to develop a whole new strain, it had taken her years, a good deal of trial and error, but at last she was into her version of the kind, and her customers were getting what they deserved, harvest after harvest, cutting after cutting.

"Smells nice," Vinich observed. You do have quite the pitchy smell going, but—and I do hate to be a lawyer about it—you do know that they don't make much legal distinction here between marijuana and say—heroin. They really, really bust heavy on marijuana here."

"No one will bother me," said Carol Ulu. She did not seem naïve in this, but momentarily cynical, so Vinich took some comfort in her confidence "And Fiame," she said, "is a midwife. What can they do to a midwife?" They treated him to some of that laughter that had got them in trouble. Little Fiame's laugh, he would learn, was varied, a collection of musical phrases to describe the different ways she was amused and that she used for the most part in lieu of speech. Vinich wanted to direct them back to their encounter in the church with Mr. Asenati, but the conversation between 'the girls veered into other matters. Vinich learned, for instance, that Carol Ulu was unmarried, never married, and that she was the chief's sister, his very much younger sister, that they were all his sisters, and he'd always thought himself cursed by his sisters, and she summarized her own attitude toward her brother the chief as, "And fuck that dumb matai and the horse he rode in on. What a nimrod." Inina and Fiame had husbands who were in her estimation, "Also tools. All these guys." She blew through slightly compressed lips. "Crap. It's a wonder the boys turned out so nice. Doak and Pule. It's an absolute miracle they're so nice. And I feel for Inina, you know, when Doak doesn't even want to set foot back here. But she has to understand."

She herself had been on a plane off-island the day after

she left high school. Carol Ulu had become a radar technician, a supervisor of radar technicians, and during her twenty years of service she hadn't come back much either. She had waited those twenty years until she could return on her own terms, with the independence of her own small retirement. "Live right," she said. "Live free."

Though entirely distracted, Vinich clung to work, to doing what he had come to do. "So, I should ask you about the church," he said. "What you remember about that day at the bazaar."

"Ah, nooh," said Carol Ulu. "Let's have some lunch. Now, don't look that way. I'm not going to feed you any *pisupo*, okay? And I swear I haven't dragged anything off the beach lately. We'll eat, then we'll talk." She rose then moved efficiently, there was still much of the noncommissioned officer about her as she prepared their meal. Fiame's hands fluttered over the dope screen, and Fiame served as her sister's well practiced audience.

"Mango?" said Carol Ulu "You like mango?"

"I think everyone likes mango," said Vinich.

"Papaya?" she said. "Little squirt of lemon juice?"

"Sure," said Vinich, and she was doing a fine job of selling this lunch; he was imagining a novel explosion in his mouth

"You know what else you're going to like?"

"No," said Vinich whose lawyer ears thought they may have just heard the most leading of all leading questions. No? She was too gorgeous, and he probably shouldn't expect himself to be saying anything clever.

"Bacon," she said. "My bacon."

"Oh," said Vinich. "I'm a bacon guy from way back."

"A bacon guy?" said Carol Ulu.

"Well—" said Vinich. "Which is to say—you know—I like it. Bacon."

"A *real* bacon guy?" Carol Ulu asked him.

"So to speak," said Vinich. "I do like it."

"I smoke my own," she said.

"Oh," said Vinich.

"You don't need a smokehouse," she said. "You can do it in a drum."

"Oh," said Vinich again, aware now that the other sister had gone into a sonata of constant giggling at his expense.

"I clean it out," said Carol Ulu. "You have to get all the oil out. Obviously. Before you even cut it open. The drum."

"You would, yes," said Vinich. Yes. No. He'd got mired in a limited range of expression.

"I slaughter, and butcher, and smoke 'em," said Carol Ulu. "Did you say you were married?"

Fiame giggled in a different key.

"I didn't," said Vinich. "I mean—I'm not. Married. But I have been."

"Recently?"

"No," said Vinich. This was a theme he might elaborate on—such a long time, and the woman asking all this of him was so striking, so proud, so entirely off limits while she could still be a witness in this case. "Work," he said, the word he now used to explain himself.

22

It occurred to Vinich after the fact that the sisters might have avoided speaking of their encounter with poor, dead Mr. Asenati only because there was so little to say about it. They might have kept him only a matter of minutes with their brief accounts, and ordinarily Vinich would be outraged to be jerked around that way, held up, but today he'd been charmed or well beyond charmed. How novel and how nice to be anywhere where his company was wanted.

When they remembered it to him at last, they remembered it much as Mrs. Falaniko had. Carol Ulu differed in one possibly significant way. "He didn't want to kick Pule out," she said. "He just wanted Pule to quit making us laugh, that tie-guy; but he was trying to kick *me* out, and good luck with that. I think I called him something I learned back in boot camp."

The sisters were also agreed in their unspoken lack of sympathy for the victim, however he'd been undone, and the sisters had all been quite vocal, even Fiame, in their insistence that Pule had done nothing wrong, that he simply couldn't. As Vinich said goodbye to them Fiame pressed a fat book on him and said, "Would you give this to him the next time you see him? I can get my boys to take him clothes and food and things; they'd take him a bible if he wanted one, but they wouldn't be caught dead with this out at the prison." It was the complete poems of Emily Dickinson, with annotations and commentary. "It's his favorite," she said. "It's just about his favorite thing. He should have it with him."

Vinich lived by a rule he regularly broke. To remain objective and sane and not depleted he should never be wound into the emotional lives of his clients; his clients, however, were often emotional people and even the staid among them came to him in some trying situation. He tried not to like or to dislike them very much for fear that it could cloud his judgment, color his effort. He served his duty, whatever that might be, and it shouldn't matter what shape that duty came in, for if he were of service to only those who didn't lie to him, or snivel, or misdirect, or try to evaporate, if he were to serve only those clients he found pleasing, then his would be small clientele and his workdays might often end at nine. They were humanity as he knew it, but even in the company Vinich kept there were those occasional jewel personalities. He needed them.

What he had sensed at once in Pule Ulu, a judgment he therefore mistrusted, was a gentleness embedded in decency; now people who'd known the man always were confirming it, raising these traits to mythical dimensions in their boy. Vinich suspected that Pule Ulu's social circle had consisted primarily of the girls, that he and his aunties had been a sort of cell, a tiny clique in the village, in their family. They seemed a bunch of misfits, and that would be why Vinich had been so taken with them. The girls were all in for Pule Ulu; they might never lie for him, even if it were necessary, but they would never say anything to hurt him—he was one of them. Did the prosecutor know yet how little use these witnesses would be to his case? If a motive for this supposed killing might be established, the girls would be the witnesses to do it, and the girls weren't going to do it. Any prosecutor is quick to say as necessary that motive is not an element that must be proven, no, a crime need only consist of an act with a dollop of intention. In this case, though, where the other proofs were so slim, the lack of any apparent motive should hurt. As Vinich saw it right now, the prosecutor couldn't establish motive, had no physical evidence that wasn't going to do him more harm than good, and no one to bear witness to what had happened to Talo Asenati. The prosecutor meant to pursue a capital case on the strength of a suspicious aftermath and some ugly pictures.

Vinich had in his career argued several lost causes in which he faced much eyewitness evidence, and former philosophy dweeb that he was he'd built a little thought experiment by way of explaining to jurors how eyewitness testimony should probably be completely discounted. Finally, his three credits of epistemology were to be of some actual use. He asked them to imagine themselves at a high school basketball game. A foul is called. There is reaction in the stands, on one side agreement, on the other complaint and disagreement. And the janitor at the end of the gym, leaning on his broom and with no stake in the outcome, but seeing it from another angle, sees yet another version of that event. And they're all eyewitnesses to the same thing at the same time and place, and each of them would describe it differently. This explanation pleased Vinich very much, though he was nearly certain he'd never been too convincing with it. Juries might not buy the proposition, but with their odd decisions and their odd reasons for even their ordinary decisions, they certainly did demonstrate it: People see what they want to see, and as they remember what they've seen, they tend to like it even better.

Vinch knew there was some danger in having a client he liked so well.

23

He was, in theory, resting, unwinding, but out of his mind's eye and the white noise of his fan came swimming thoughts of Carol Ulu, and these were not restful. He remembered and savored even the most inconsequential things she'd said, a voice that might have been cured in a charred cask. Rather than die of self-pity, Vinich had convinced himself that he had outgrown loneliness, or gotten used to it, and this delusion had sustained him pretty well but could not be maintained in the memory of Carol Ulu flowing around in that sarong, speaking her piece. Even as he lay there trying to determine if it was a good thing or a bad thing that he had come to know of her existence, she called him.

"It's me," she said. "Carol Ulu."

"Oo-oh," he said, elated, terrified, fourteen again. He sat up and swung his feet off the bed to plant them on the floor.

"Fiame let me use her phone to call you."

"Oh," he said, treading water until he could reach some articulate shore.

"I had another question for you," she said. "I never got around to asking while you were here: You have a girlfriend?"

"No," said Vinich. "No."

"You gay?"

"No," he said.

"So, you're not gay. No wife, no girlfriend. How's that? I mean, how is that?"

"Not great," said Vinich. "It's—peaceful, I guess."

"Hm," said Carol Ulu, dubiously, and then she seemed to think better of that reaction. "I know what you're saying, though. I do know what you're saying."

Vinich sought for a thought, an observation, something. "Quite peaceful," he said. He feared she would hear how unreliably his voice was connected to his lungs, and it was just as well, he thought, that she wasn't present to see his tongue hanging out.

"Well, I liked you," said Carol Ulu. "You seem all right."

Vinich said, "I. . ."

"And now you know where to find me," she said. "You wouldn't have to call. Well, you couldn't. But if you ever felt like dropping by."

Vinich could not imagine a moment when he wouldn't feel like dropping by Carol Ulu's location. This was a nightmare without fear and without sleep for its explanation. "I. ." he said. He was wide awake.

"You wouldn't *have* to," she said. "It was just an idea I had."

"It's a great idea," he said. "A *great* idea. I—" His mind pinballed—Where was his water pump? Where was his timing belt? Container ship. He imagined again the contents of Carol Ulu's sarong, absent the sarong. He tried to remember when his luck had ever taken such a turn. Maybe once before. Maybe never. Carol Ulu. "I—" he said. "But I can't."

"As I say," said she said. "It was just an idea."

"It is," said Vinich, "it is a *great* one. But I can't. You're a witness."

"I am?"

"You could be," said Vinich. "If we go to trial in Pule's case. In fact, I'd probably subpoena you myself."

"Subpoena me?" she said erotically. "Wow. You don't think you'll have to have a trial, do you? I thought you had this figured out."

"I have to assume we'll try it. I have to assume that's where we're going."

"I thought you said something before about assuming, and how that was bad."

Vinich thought he should attempt something Shakespearean here, an expression of his adoration, instant but profound. The last thing he wanted to do was try and explain why he would choose an obscure ethical consideration over her. He said, "It is and it isn't. Bad. Depending."

"You're not one of those guys, are you?"

"I'm. . ."?

"Is-and-isn't guys? You one of those?"

It was questions like this that really destroyed him. And of course, that face. "I try not to be," said Vinich.

"Well, all right," she said. "But you know where I am if you change your mind."

"The minute this is. . ." Vinich thought better of saying 'over'. "As soon as I. . . I."

"Well, all right," said Carol Ulu. "It was just a thought." And she left him with it.

She had already torn the scab off his loneliness, and now, with this invitation Mike Vinich had begun to throb with it; he lay there wondering how long he'd be quite this overwrought, watching brother gecko on high alert, traversing a wall; Vinich foresaw a long night of listening to the dogs. His social graces, his work habits, his paltry income, an attitude in general that was rarely warm—there was much to explain why he might be alone so much, that it was to be expected, really, tolerated. Love in any form was not commonly one of his profession's risks. His profession? His life. Vinich lay there where he'd meant to rest, calculating that for a long time he had been taking all the wrong risks.

He had tried with some success to keep the phone he kept in his pocket isolated for personal uses; it didn't ring much. When it rang now he thought that here was his second chance to reach some—any—accommodation with Carol Ulu, and Vinich felt one or more of his organs calcify, a pleasant shock.

"Dad."

"Oh," said Vinich. "Cyrus." He hadn't kept the disappointment out of his voice.

"Are you okay?"

"Sure," said Vinich.

"You sound kind of funny. You're all right?"

"You could say," said Vinich, "I've been hip deep in local culture. Sure, I'm fine. How about you? How you doing?"

"That's what I called to tell you," Cyrus said. "You're off the hook."

"I'm—?"

"I was going back to school," Cyrus said. "But an opportunity came up. I got a job with a paving company. It's its own company, but also part of a big-ass construction deal—and they've got contracts 'til the end of time. *And*—I get to run the paver."

"Oh," said Vinich.

"It's an apprenticeship at first, but I'll be getting paid. So—I won't be needing any help. I'll have some serious money of my own for once. Mom was happy to help out with the union dues. I had to join the union."

"Oh," said Vinich, another variety of disappointment creeping in. He knew it was wrong, but he could not evade a dreadful image, his son in the cab of a smoking, steaming machine, his son's currently flat belly flowing out onto his lap year by year, his son's now searching mind numbing all the while with the various vibrations of his machine. Vinich came of working folk and had few illusions concerning these industrious, useful existences. "Well, that sounds good," he said.

"Now," Cyrus said, "maybe you can take a vacation."

"What do you mean?"

"You said you had some money set aside. Now maybe you could use it to take a vacation."

"I won't be doing that any time soon. Things are kind of wild right now."

"When has it ever been any other way?" Cyrus, having made his big, deliberate move, seemed to think he was now in command of practical wisdom. "You have to take care of yourself."

"I do," said Vinich, "take care of myself." He justified a half-truth with the thought that everyone has their own requirements.

"And you're feeling all right? I mean, in a good place?"

"Oh, yeah," said Vinich who didn't ordinarily attend much to his feelings, a practicing stoic he liked to think, and who when he was too plagued by emotion, as now, was certainly not about to report it to anyone.

"The back?"

"Fine," Vinich said, returning to an unvarnished truth at last.

"Sometimes I can hear it in your voice," Cyrus said. "You wear yourself out. I don't want—I want you to be healthy."

"I'm in the pink," said Vinich, which was also, oddly, true. Except for insomnia he felt fine so long as he didn't challenge his digestion too much. "How's Gloria?" he digressed. "What does she think about all this?"

"We split up," said Cyrus.

"You did? I never even met the girl, and now you've split up. That's been, what? Three years you were together?"

"About that," said Cyrus.

"You okay?"

"Oh, yeah," said Cyrus. "It's been a while back. And it

was coming on a while before that. We were incompatible."

"It's possible," said Vinich, "that compatibility is overrated. I don't know."

"Yeah," said his son. "But you kind of want a pal, don't you? In your significant other?"

"That does sound good," said Vinich. "But it might be a little easier said than done. Might be asking too much."

"Well, what would you look for? In a—mate."

"I've given it very little thought lately," he said, while thinking, 'Carol Ulu.' His every train of thought pulled into the same station; Vinich was in a bad way.

24

The woman with the high arcing eyebrows was behind the plexiglass again. "Is that a law book?" she said. That hat of hers had to ride at least three inches above her skull on a black crown of wound hair.

"No," said Vinich.

"Is it dirty?"

"It's poetry," said Vinich.

"That isn't what I asked you. Is it nasty?"

"No," said Vinich. The woman's hatred of him had reached an alarming pitch in nearly no time. He had to wonder if his race was the problem, his point of origin, his profession, the way he had once called her 'ma'am.' The guard gestured toward him with a backsweep of her hand as if to shoo away an unwanted animal, and Vinich took this as his permission to head out to the visitor's pavilion.

While awaiting his client there, Vinich watched a basketball game then in progress on the prison court; the goateed shooting guard of his recent acquaintance was deeply engaged in it; his voice, which wasn't deep, rode above the others, "Why you even try? You can't. Guard. Me." A twitchy kid, he had a crossover, could make his own shot, and that shot was a sweet one, elbow to wrist to release and to rim, and the kid's mouth, Vinich thought, was likely to get him killed in here before he could finish his time.

The young corrections officer who had been sent to find Pule Ulu was young enough that he seemed to take his mission seriously, and so it wasn't very long before the pair of them were coming across the campus, looking something like a father and his little boy out for a stroll, the boy sharing some observation or secret with the big being beside him. Pule Ulu was never going to be hard to identify or locate. Vinich was pleased to see his client clean shaven again, it suited him better. Those white tennis shoes remained immaculate—All Stars—Ulu's top knot had been oiled and was draped with tiny shells and a small blue blossom. He gave the guard a benevolent smile as the man returned to the guard shack; he then turned this on Vinich in the pavilion. When he saw what Vinich had brought him, Pule Ule's mouth—he'd contrived to outline his lips with something dark—and through them passed, a rapturous intake of air, then, "Oooh. I am. Oh, the happiness. Thank you so much."

"Fiame sent it." Vinich said. Pule Ulu had located a prison vendor of rouge, or he had learned to manufacture it inside. Vinich, who was unused to having opinions about makeup and its use, found himself thinking that Pule Ule's complexion didn't need nearly so much improving. Vinich had learned quite a lot about this man since they'd last spoken, had learned there was far more to him than that gentle aura, but Pule Ule's comfortable and even comforting presence still seemed what was most important about him. "I've met most of. . ." Vinich was about to say 'most of your family' but then considered how large the Samoan notion of family might be. "I've met a lot of people who care about you," he said. "Doak came by to see me."

"He seems so happy, don't you think?"

"I. . ." Vinich had given Doak Falaniko's happiness less than a moment's consideration. "He didn't seem *un*happy. But he is concerned. He'd have to be. He's a big fan of yours. They all were."

"I knew you would have to love them. Inina? Carol?"

"Them, too. And your father. I met him, too. Met him first."

At the mention of his father a hood of sorts slid momentarily down Pule Ulu's features. "Family," he said in the full ambiguity of that word. One of his many smiles crept back.

"They're great people," said Vinich. "I thought."

"Judgment," said Pule Ulu. "Good judgment—I must have seen it in you. That is why you are trusted." He held Ms. Dickinson's poems in his hand where the volume looked like a pocket bible, and he accorded it at least that much reverence. "Thank you *so* much."

"I took the liberty of glancing through those," Vinich said. "I always thought I was a Whitman man—'Leaves of Grass'—but she really won me over. Kind of a tough little thing, wasn't she? And sweet? Everything all at once. Quite something."

"From her bedroom window she saw to the end of the world," said Pule Ulu. "That's from one of my own. Poems."

Vinich knew he'd be wearing the wary look one wears in an encounter with a confessed poet.

"I burned them," Pule Ulu assured him. "About a year ago."

"You shouldn't do that," Vinich said. "It says she left instructions for these poems to be burned—Emily. And what if they had been?"

"The difference, I think, is that my poems were bad," said Pule Ulu. "Awful. Dull. No bliss or terror in them. They are no loss. A brief catharsis."

Poetry. Cosmetics. Catharses. Vinich had come to talk to a man about a murder charge. "I thought I'd try and tell you where we're at," he said. "As best I can."

He began by recounting the interview of Noah Satele, what little there was to say of it. Vinich said that the other two boys from the trail would offer the prosecution even less, nothing, in fact. Vinich described the various ways that things that had been claimed in the Information were contradicted by what he had learned from witnesses and his examination of the physical evidence. He admitted to his client that there were so many of these problems that he thought he should somehow be able to use them to get this thing gone without the necessity of a trial. Vinich admitted he hadn't thought of a procedural way to do that yet without the risk of giving away his trial strategy, and they were still headed to trial. The Assistant Attorney General was bound to be an ass, so it looked like they should be prepared to go. Vinich said they should win on the evidence, or its absence, and that he would, if Pule Ulu wished, try to get an expedited trial date. "From what I can see," he said, "they'll be able to show a man died, but they won't be able to prove that you or anybody else killed him, so everything I told you before still applies. About staying quiet. You've done yourself a real favor so far. We're in fair shape because of it."

Pule Ulu followed him with the studious look of an attendee at a tax law seminar, nodding a little here and there until he said at last. "You do keep telling me to keep quiet, though. That must mean you think I'm guilty."

"No," said Vinich.

"But you think I *could* be."

"Far as I'm concerned," said Vinich, "anyone *could* be guilty of anything at any time. I have come around to that unfortunate point of view. People are always surprising themselves with the things they're capable of doing. If we locked people up for what they're capable of doing, then the whole world would have to be on constant lockdown."

"Which it already is," said Pule Ulu.

"The point is," Vinich said, "I don't have to defend people for what they *might* do."

"And what about something they *did* do?"

"That is not for me to decide. What my people did or didn't do. You leave that up to the trier of fact. The jury.

A judge. It's my job to give 'em the evidence in a way that makes 'em decide the way we want."

"I never did understand how that worked before," said Pule. "I don't think I understand it now."

"It's Anglo-American law. Adversarial—goes back to good old Celtic trials by combat."

"You like that?"

Vinich had never been asked this question, hadn't asked it of himself for as long as he could remember. He did like it when he won, and not always even then, so he said, "No. But I like it better than seeing people railroaded or poor people being jerked around any more than they already are."

There was the first trace of slyness in Pule Ulu's mutable smile, but then he drifted off to stare at the end of the world, he stared off, hand long and soft along his throat; he stared off, the belle of Territorial Prison.

25

Returning to the moment, Pule Ule turned to his lawyer apologetically. "This right to remain silent that everyone keeps talking about—if there was a trial, I wouldn't have to testify, would I?"

"No, you wouldn't. Have to. And that's entirely up to you—whether you did or didn't testify at trial. Or, as far as that goes, it's up to you whether you go to trial at all."

"Can we do the other thing, whatever that is? No trial? How would that work?"

"That's how it usually works," said Vinich. "Usually you cut a deal."

"A deal," said Pule Ulu, grimly amused.

"A plea bargain," said Vinich.

"I've heard of them. They sound unsavory."

"They've been called worse, much worse," said Vinich. "And they are bad sometimes. People don't know it, but if every criminal thing that passes through these courts went to trial, anyone who's eligible for jury duty would have to figure on doing that about half of every year—making twenty-five bucks a day. What my client has to offer the deal, usually, is he can save the state—the territory—the expense and trouble of reaching a foregone conclusion. Spare 'em the slim chance they'll be embarrassed and not get a conviction."

"What is the territory's part in the bargain?"

"Depends," said Vinich. These discussions made him feel as if he were the tour guide at the sausage factory of juris prudence. "They can reduce the charge, have you plead to a lesser charge. Or you plead out to the original charge, and they recommend a lenient sentence. Or maybe something else you want. But that's what I mean about our prosecutor. The little ass, he's not offering any of that. Right now. He may come around. When he looks at this case a little closer, he may come around, but even if he does, he's still sitting on a case he can't prove. I really don't see what he could offer us. Short of a dismissal, which seems kind of unlikely with this guy."

"I admire your confidence."

Vinich was too smart ever to be entirely confident.

"If there was a trial," said Pule Ulu, "and I didn't testify—wouldn't people expect me to *say* I hadn't—you know?"

Vinich could never accurately know juror's expectations, especially here. Here he'd have to make his case to people who harbored even stranger and more startling beliefs than he was accustomed to encountering in a jury box. "I imagine it's better," he said, "it would usually be better if you could take the stand and testify in your own behalf. If you can testify credibly, which I believe you could. If you chose to, that is."

"And honestly?"

"Yes," said Vinich.

"I would have to put my hand on a bible? Is that actually done?"

"It's a formality," said Vinich. "I don't think it means much to most people."

"It does here," said Pule Ulu. "It would here."

"So I've heard," said Vinich. He'd been advised early on by an old hand in the Samoan courts that while Samoans were as given to fabrication as any other lying crowd, once they'd taken the oath they considered themselves truly bound, and this sometimes resulted in their stories veering wildly at the last minute when you would least want them to.

"It doesn't matter," said Pule Ulu. "I don't want to testify." This sounded final.

"Good," said Vinich. "I might recommend that anyway. You wouldn't need to. If they don't have anything, why would you expose yourself to. . ."

"I *couldn't* testify," said Pule Ulu. "Honestly. Not without. . ."

"Well, then you won't," Vinich said. "That's your privilege." To have a client too concerned with honesty was not the problem he typically met.

"I am so tired of this silence," said Pule Ulu. "It has always been my one luxury, you know—the luxury of not being silent. Where I live, the things I say often sound like code, or raving, or blasphemy. I know they do, but since I'm misunderstood anyway, I can say them."

Vinich was familiar with this existence, this problem; he'd never heard such a clear description of it. And here again it was evident that he'd never met a man like Pule Ulu. Mike Vinich was charged with too much responsibility, the rest of this man's life, and dully he said something so dull it might serve to soothe. "You're in a tough spot."

"I would like to tell you some things."

"You're absolutely sure you won't be testifying?" Vinich said.

"Yes, s. . . Yes, Mike. Quite sure."

"All right, then," said Vinich. "Tell away." On those occasions when he wore the confessor's cap, Vinich sometimes found the voyeur in himself happy for this little peak into some dark moment or other, but how he hoped Pule Ulu wouldn't mar his precious self too much with whatever he was about to say. "Get it off your chest," said Vinich, "if you have to."

Pule Ulu's chest, riding just behind the bib of his overalls, hove powerfully. His sighs, and he couldn't help it, were amplified. He was dainty without a dainty voice. "Can you bear with me, please, Mike? It could be tedious, but I think I should start at the beginning. I have been thinking of this so much. There seems to be a beginning and a middle to it. Not an end, so far, but. I should start at the beginning."

"All right," said Vinich, flinging out all the rope his client might need to hang himself.

"I think it all starts with this," said Pule Ulu, "I've been in a marriage, a spiritual marriage, with Emily Dickinson."

"Oh, no," said Vinich.

"Don't be alarmed," said Pule Ulu. "I'm only an autodidact." His grin returned. "When Doak went to college he started sending me his textbooks after he finished with them. That is how I met her. Sorry. How I first read her. She was in an anthology. Three poems and a paragraph about her life, and I thought, 'This, dear, dear person.' I thought she would be worth knowing, and I was right. Since then, I've dipped my toe in Auden and T.S. Eliot, South Americans and Spaniards, some of those suicidal American ladies, and, please don't misunderstand, they've all been wonderful in their way. But Emily. Emily has been the beginning and the end. Maybe it was her life. That she was able to live it. I've read everything. I know as much about her household as I do of my own. Maybe I thought her bravery would rub off on me. Maybe it did. We puzzled our families, the people of our village, but she did it so bravely."

Vinich settled in for a long telling, and he wished the visitor's pavilion offered better furniture than his concrete bench. It was cool, at least, in the shade. This promised to be in some way sad.

"Maybe it's silly to call that the start. It started when I was born such an outlandish thing. But then poetry. I met people who were so true, so determined to get to their clarity. It was thrilling. You're being patient, Mike, but I've been thinking about this so much, there just seems so much involved in it. How I got here. But, anyway, I read poetry. Then I started trying to write it. Have you ever wanted to be wonderful?"

Vinich gave this some thought. "Wonderful? Mm—no."

"Transcendent?"

"No," said Vinich, "that would be far too far beyond me."

"I'm sorry to lose focus. But that might have been the problem. Those poems of mine were, I could not bring them into focus—and, of course, that is exactly what you want from a poem. That superb focus. I didn't have that. My poems were just no good, and they weren't getting any better."

"Did you show anybody?" Vinich had never been called upon to comfort a failed poet. It looked futile.

"When my people are lyrical, it's in Samoan. My things were English. Would you go to your people with a poem you had written?"

"It's never come up," Vinich said. "I know my limitations."

"I don't know why I thought I might have talent," said Pule Ulu. "I wanted it so much. My great blooming. It never happened. When I knew it wasn't going to happen— well, disappointed is such an inadequate word.'

"The world needs its readers, too. There aren't that many great readers."

"Why, Mike. What a beautiful thing to say. How lucky I am we met." Pule Ulu's face arranged itself in another of its saintly expressions. "But I was, I was wallowing in self-pity. You know how dangerous that can be."

"I have some idea," said Vinich, and, of course, he did. Is this where the killing came in?

"It is a hard tragedy to explain. 'Oh, boo hoo, I'm no Pablo Neruda.' I wasn't doing well. When you burn your poems that, I think, amounts to ceremonial suicide. Then all that is left is this big gross fellow I've always been, and I was for a time in quite a fugue state, a funk. Mercy, what a mess, and I had even stopped cooking which is how I usually justify my existence." Pule Ulu recited with his eyes cast mostly upward, searching his empty heavens. He smiled again. Reflectively. "Then," he said, "I found my little gift. Don't we all want more from our circuits round the sun than to eat and defecate, eat, and defecate?"

Vinich took this for a rhetorical question and didn't answer. His man was nearing the meat of the matter.

"I was a comedian," said Pule Ulu.

26

Pule Ulu claimed that a person like himself must possess either a developed sense of humor or deep, deep stupidity—it was no fun to be such an anomaly. He had always been funny. Given a certain situation, a certain audience he could be uproariously funny, and the chance to do that was what had brought him to those church functions. "I told you about the dress before," he said. "How I couldn't sit on the floor with it. A practical consideration—but, with me on my chair and the girls sitting around me on the floor I had a stage. A stage. After I had been to a few of those things, I started writing material, saving it for the bazaars. Bizarre bazaar. Isn't it silly how little it takes to serve one's vanity? My tiny audience. How I loved being anyone's guilty pleasure. I had them laughing."

Vinich realized that Pule Ulu probably couldn't know how much the girls' laughter was costing them now, that they were being ostracized for having laughed. "I had a whole set," he said, "a whole routine around my father and their husbands, the menfolk you might say, and maybe I was a little unkind toward them, but the girls weren't the only ones laughing. I think most of those churches were very pleased to have us there. The people, the people were happy. They were having fun."

The sad part loomed now.

"Is it so wrong," Pule Ulu said, "to be a little vain? To make people laugh? I enjoyed that. I enjoyed being enjoyed. The last thing I wanted was to hurt anyone. What else did I have to contribute? Darling, I must be the worst weaver in the history of Polynesia."

Pule Ulu looked down at his huge hands, regretting them. They were, even in prison, obviously manicured, his nails trimmed square. "Then," he said, "that little man came to us. I know his name now. Talo Asenati. Talo Asenati. It rattles between my ears. But then, when he came to us, he was only a little man in a tie, a little guy from the straight and narrow, you know. He wanted me to stop, wanted the girls to stop laughing. Carol gave him an earful. Carol—well, you've met her. She chased him off, but not before he had made me feel terrible."

Pule Ulu said he had been a free thinker from the first such thought he could remember. He had found the Bible in its entirety implausible, and all the tribal myths, and the myths promoted by every other religion he had investigated. He was a skeptic without so much as the solace of science, much of which also seemed unlikely to him. But he had lived, he said, among a very religious people, and he saw and respected the comfort their religion gave them, and however often they used their creed as a license to hypocrisy he never disrespected those beliefs. Not aloud. He was in his village a minority of perhaps one, and often, far from disrespecting the truly faithful, he envied them. This was the history swirling around in him that day in church. He hadn't come to offend anyone. He had not intended to offend anyone. He had left that church rather than weep in front of them. Where would he perform now? He had only hoped to entertain, to let his doubts be of some value, too. To make jokes. He left that church thinking that all that had been taken from him.

"I went outside to compose myself. Then, when I did, and it was back to the usual—how do most people live, do you think? But I got back to the usual—resignation I would call it—and then I was too embarrassed to go back inside. Too self-conscious. My routines, you know, were kind of an armor. So, I was lurking around out in the—jungle, I'd call it, what a horrible village—and feeling self-conscious about that, too, because I knew the girls would be wondering what had become of me. I knew they might be worried. So, when the little. . . When Mr. Asenati came along, I was touched. He actually started by saying he was sorry. You know, 'Everyone is welcome in our assembly.' That kind of thing. He seemed, in fact he *was* very sincere at first. I was quite touched. But still, I didn't want to go back. I felt I would be on display if I went back. Now, Mike, I know you may think that would be my preference. You have every reason, I know, to consider me flamboyant. But I am shy. And, uh, that is what I told Mr. Asenati. And I thanked him, oh, I thanked him. I thought he was trying to be kind. I still think he might have been trying to be kind. At first."

Plunging on, Pule Ulu said, "Thank you. Thank you for listening. I am trying not to excuse myself, and I am sorry to burden you with this. I'm sure no one really wants to hear something like this—that poor man. I saw something awful in his eyes, and then they were looking up and down the trail, making sure we were alone. He was terrified. Not of me. Of himself. Have you ever seen that, Mike? Seen someone just—maybe you're seeing it now. But he was so frightened of himself, and then he grabbed at my crotch, or where he thought my crotch must be, it wasn't too well defined in that particular dress. That dress," he said, remembering the one fond piece of this memory.

Talo Asenati had said ugly things out there on the trail, things Pule Ulu didn't wish to specify or repeat now. His cursing and ugly talk was something he didn't seem too familiar with, and he had sounded like a young boy trying to be naughty, and his voice wasn't much deeper than a boy's, and he had a boy's furry moustache, and he was cursing at Pule Ule, saying his ugly things, and reaching out from time to time to try and locate the penis under that dress.

"It was so odd," said Pule Ulu. "I mean, I think we were babes in the woods. And he kept looking up and down the trail. He was hating himself, but it was a flirtation, too. Clumsy. He had no experience. And. And I know I must seem flamboyant, but I am shy. I may seem worldly, but I am not. I have my armor; I wear my armor, but in stark, stark fact I am a virgin, or I was then, and not because I prized my virginity. No. I didn't know what he hoped to accomplish, poor Mr. Asenati, but I could see that something had gone wrong in him, and he had lost control of himself. Here is the shameful thing—I was somewhat flattered. I am not often—desired, I had been living such a sheltered life. Bookish in the islands. I am, you know, the strange man living at the back of the matai's house. I had been exposed to very little outside the literary life, and I did not understand what was happening. He did not understand what was happening. Yes, babes in the woods, and I wish I could say that I had no sense that it might be turning ugly, but he was being ugly, saying his clumsy, ugly things, and I could see he was terribly confused, looking up and down the trail. His skinny little black tie. I was naïve. I thought those kinds of things only happen in the dark of night."

Vinich decided that nothing could come of this story that was going to alter his opinion of Pule Ule, except perhaps favorably.

"He was being frisky," said Pule Ulu. "I think he was attempting to be frisky. Touching me. Cursing. We were both confused. I'm not sure about Mr. Asenati, but it was something I had never. . . I could tell that he was hating himself. And I. Strange as it was, and ugly as it was—I do have to admit his attention wasn't completely unwelcome. Isn't that awful? To me that is the awful part. Some of it. I didn't know exactly what he wanted, but I saw that I was wanted. In some way wanted. You have no idea how overwhelming that can be for a person like me."

Here at last, Vinich thought, was something he did fully understand.

"He wasn't in any way attractive," said Pule Ulu. "And yet—And then he slapped me."

He hadn't been hurt but startled by that first slap. The second slap didn't hurt. Maybe they weren't meant to hurt. Pule Ulu could not tell. Was this the little man's way of playing? Some dance of doubt or disrespect? Was he seeing how far he might go? Pule Ulu had slapped back.

"I know I'm strong," he said. "I do know that. I helped a friend with his car one day, and for a while after that I was on call as a human car jack around the village, a novelty act. I had to put a stop to that. I am strong, but to no particular purpose. I have never gone in for roughhousing of any kind. Even when the other boys were. . . I had never in my life hit anyone. Never tried to. Never thought about it as other men seem to do. All that is repugnant to me, darling. But."

What worried Pule Ulu now was all the reasons he'd had to strike that man and knowing that all of those reasons were accumulated in the back pressure that launched the blow.

Was he afraid? Yes. The little man was losing his mind or locating a fetish or something dangerous. Was he offended? Yes. Talo Asenati and his skinny black tie was the living embodiment of a bald two facedness Pule Ule did not like, hated in fact as an attitude that circumscribed his whole existence. Was Pule Ule himself a little overcharged with desire? Yes. Did he think he was being invited to frolic, to play? Yes, though in retrospect it seemed such a faint hope. Pule Ule knew he had been trying to play, setting a limit, a warning. Yes, it was all of that, his slap.

"But I missed," he said. "No experience. And I hit him with my wrist. And I felt it go in. I felt his skull yielding, imagine that. And I knew. Too strong. Way too strong. I knew at once. I knew I had killed him. Imagine that."

They sat for a moment, lawyer and client, pondering death and happenstance. "You expect," said Pule Ulu, "if something like this happened to a decent person, they would wipe it from their memory. But I—when his head gave way like that, and I felt it. Everything. Everything. Every moment of it. He didn't fall, Mike. I drove him down, slammed him down, and his nose, his nose was a geyser. He landed on his back. No one touched him. I certainly didn't. And he lay just like that for—until the policeman came. Frozen there. And his eyes. So much had been in them, so much fear, and lust, and confusion. But now it was just the one thing. Just like that, the one thing. Or nothing. He was so surprised. He didn't expect that."

"Maybe he was lucky," said Vinich. "Those who do expect it, it's probably because they've been suffering."

"It is an awful thing to see. An awful thing to feel. Maybe I shouldn't complain, but it seems to me that for containing what it's supposed to contain the skull is not a very sturdy vessel." Pule Ulu looked down at his hands again and noticed that in one of them his precious volume of poetry was bent double. He relaxed his grip. "So," said Pule Ulu. "I am sorry to say you have a problem. You have a guilty client."

"No," said Vinich.

"I wanted to tell them that day," said Pule Ulu. "If I could have, I would have. It was hours and hours before I could say anything at all. And I know it can't look good. That I wouldn't tell them anything. I wanted to. I think. It was too much. And I'm sure I was afraid."

"You did well, Pule."

"Where does this leave us? Should I tell them now?"

"No," said Vinich, so vehement as to startle himself. "I mean—no."

"Would you tell them? I mean, could you tell them for me?"

"I wouldn't," said Vinich. "I couldn't ethically confess anything in your behalf. And if I could, I wouldn't."

Vinich set out the situation for his client's benefit, and for his own. "They've got you charged with first degree homicide. If you're sentenced on that charge, no matter how you got there and how sorry you said you were, those judges on their nicest day can't hand you less than forty years in here."

Pule Ulu remained attentive now that he had unburdened himself, but his interest seemed more academic, an effort to be polite. They had been in talk long enough that word had got around the prison that a defense attorney was on the premises, and other inmates had come to the pavilion to hover at the edge of their conversation, awaiting a word with Mike Vinich.

"I trust to you, Mike," said Pule Ulu. "Whatever you think is appropriate."

27

"I cahn'd. I jus cahn'd do eh." Jack Root had got infected, the split in his lip a jagged yellow line with red, pink, and violet radiating around that. Something was now wrong with his tongue as well. He taped the bandage back over his face, and through it and through his pained mouth he offered the news that he'd be departing the island next Tuesday; he was getting a loan from his mother to buy the ticket. The tropics. Hard as it was for him to say so much, Jack Root said he was never coming back and would never again go south of a certain latitude. From now on, Nebraska was southerly enough. He was going to work for his cousin, after all, selling insurance. When his face healed. He said he was very sorry.

The man had been sorry for himself since he'd stepped off the plane at Pago Pago International, and Vinich had guessed upon meeting him that Jack Root wasn't going to be good help. Sorry was a term that just rolled off his lips. "I'mb sahb, bMike."

"All right," said Vinich. "I need a letter of resignation. This morning. One sentence is plenty, but get it done so I can get one to Ahti. Pack up your shit. Get that Bob Marley poster out of there. That thing has always been an eyesore."

There was another muffled expression of regret from behind Jack Root's bandage, something to do with never having met the Public Defender in the whole time he'd been on island. Bitter. Heartfelt.

"All right," said Vinich. "Anything else? I've got to—." What? Do something. He needed to do almost everything, so Vinich, wondering why he had ever bothered to be scrupulous about the office vehicle and the gas card, took the public defender jeep without even bothering to sign it out, and vaulting entirely over the proper protocols he drove it to Tisa's Barefoot Bar, which was, fortunately, hours from opening upon his arrival. Vinich lay out on the little beach there and watched the tide come surging in through the brain coral. It smelled, as small inlets will, intensely of sea rack and salt. He found he was once again in no condition to absorb such pleasures, and it was well that the bar was closed and the moon was nowhere in sight to be howled at.

Vinich hadn't heard a whisper concerning the new attorney Ahti was supposedly recruiting, and he hadn't recently given it any thought himself. Until now. Now it had fallen to him to manage every serious criminal indiscretion committed on the islands or in the territorial waters of American Samoa while simultaneously being the sole defense attorney at work in a murder case. Vinich had learned since his arrival here that the pool of applicants for work in his office was very select, consisting of those few demonstrated incompetents who would consider working for the offered wage. It was possible that no one had applied. It was possible that no help was coming, certain that none would be coming soon. He knew nothing would induce the Public Defender to lend a hand, and the one brief he'd seen from the man was not the work of a lawyer you might want on your side.

Vinich saw himself soldiering on. It would not be pretty. He would not be especially effective, couldn't be under these circumstances. His careering career, the weight of it. He would have been in better shape to receive the morning's news, he thought, if the night that preceded it hadn't been another sleepless one. Though Pule Ulu's revelations were not very surprising, now that the man had made them his case was become an even thornier thicket of moral and practical problems.

After they talked, Vinich had gone straight home to a tepid bowl of stew and a lawyerly combing through that part of the Samoan criminal code describing the various crimes that result in the death of a human being. Crime by crime, element by element he walked back through Pule Ulu's story, which he took for the full and unvarnished truth, and fitted its sad details to the sad statutes regarding killings. Last night and now again this morning Vinich followed the same analysis to the same conclusion.

Taken at his word, he had not described first degree murder. This crime required a level and duration of intent entirely lacking in his act. The statute was odd in that it specified not only what the crime was, but what it was not: ". . . not the instant effort of impulse." Prosecutor Swanson, relying on some obscure case he'd found with a rock and a sudden feud, and relying on his serious misreading of the evidence, had set a trap for himself if he thought to prove deliberation at trial by means of that crusty rock. Vinich had been tempted to gently or not so gently set him straight on the real implications of the rock by way of getting him to at least reduce the charge. Vinich had decided, though, that the man was never going to move that way, and if his pet theory was blown up at trial then he'd look silly and over-reaching and all his other assertions and conclusions would come into question.

Vinich would keep the rock in his pocket until needed.

Pule Ulu was not guilty of first degree murder. But Pule Ulu had not yet been acquitted of that charge, a fact that hovered over every other consideration.

Second degree murder required merely an intent to cause death or serious injury or at least a recklessness amounting to extreme indifference to human life. This intent, presumably, was sufficiently bad if formed in the moment. Pule Ulu had not been guilty of this, either, not by his telling of it, but here the physical evidence did not support him. The concavity in Talo Asenati seemed to require more than a little intent; any normal man would have to wind up all day to make such a dent in a healthy skull. Pule Ulu's story might take him to second degree murder if he told it to unsympathetic ears, and that would leave him facing ten to thirty years.

Manslaughter? Probably. Recklessness, it must certainly seem that way. If the kid juking and jiving out there on the basketball court had got the max seven years for his little run-in, then Pule Ulu, who was after all the goliath in his scenario, couldn't expect less.

Negligent homicide? No. But in the way Vinich had come to understand this thing, actual negligence might have been more blameworthy than what Pule Ulu had done.

Vinich had come to understand his client as the person least in need of reform or punishment among all the people he'd ever met, and that was it, the additional urgency to this one, an almost palpable need to get the man out of harm's way if he could. Just deserts? Pule Ulu came in peace. He deserved peace. Vinich reminded himself that it was not his part in this to determine or secure justice but to serve his client and expect justice would be the byproduct. Vinich reminded himself, too feebly, to remain objective.

But as he saw it the territory lacked the evidence to prove beyond a reasonable doubt that Pule Ulu had committed even the least of these crimes. On a level playing field, the Territory really shouldn't win this one.

What about self defense? No. A problem of proportionality. The defense must be no more than necessary to the threat. Those ugly pictures. Talo Asenati rendered unthreatening on the trail, the steel tray of his last hurrah. No. Self-defense is an affirmative defense to be asserted and proven by the defendant. By the defendant's testimony, so—no.

Their defense would be general denial, putting the Territory to its proof.

<h1 style="text-align:center">28</h1>

His brain and the dogs of Lions Park had been unusually active of late, and the heat had been those few degrees hotter, night and day, that made it intolerable; sleep had abandoned him, and Vinich had been experiencing woozy bouts that promised to descend at the wrong moment and cause him to make some awful mistake. He rushed into High Court that morning with the pennant of the harried flying behind him, his shirt tail. Wiping at his dripping face with his sleeves he came into a room that seemed to have been silent for some time; a pregnant waiting had been awaiting him with the judges, and the bailiff, and the court reporter, and the clerk of court, his clients, the prison guards, the Attorney General's knot of lawyers, all of them with eyes only for him as he made his way to counsel table and Pule Ule's side.

"You are very lucky," said the Chief Judge who with his head shaved slick and his thick neck sloping only slightly as it descended into his robes formed a perfect mound. "Very lucky, counsel, that they called over from Judge Mandeville's court and told us where you were."

"Yes, Your Honor."

"You were causing some trouble over there?"

"Trouble?" said Vinich. "It was a detention hearing. A contested detention hearing. My client didn't want to be detained. Further detained."

"Your office had no one else they could send?"

"No, Your Honor. The Juvenile Officer was up against his hearing deadline. The hearing had to happen immediately. I had to go."

"No one else? I will be reporting this to the Governor's Office."

"Yes, Your Honor." Please do, Vinich thought.

"Are you prepared to go forward with these omnibus hearings, Mr. Vinich?"

"Yes, Your Honor." Hazy. Vinich, so long as he could proceed by rote this way, would probably do no damage.

The Clerk of Court called the case, an omnibus hearing in The Territory of American Samoa versus Pule Ule, and the Chief Judge began to march down through a checklist, inquiring of the attorneys where they were at in the matter. Had the Territory provided full discovery?

"I have one witness statement," Vinich said. "From all the witnesses mentioned in the police report, I have a recorded statement from one of them. If that is all the Territory has to disclose, then, yes, I've gotten full discovery."

"Any problems about potential exhibits, counsel? You've had access to all that."

"I have," said Vinich.

"Mr. Swanson," said the Chief Judge, "what about your witnesses? Will there be some kind of statements made available before we reach trial, or are you afraid of ruining the surprise?"

Young Swanson was admirably composed, rising, buttoning that jacket. "Mr. Vinich," he said, "has the investigating officer's report, the medical examiner's report, and he has had access to every item taken in evidence. He has the transcript and a video recording of a statement from one of the other two witnesses we would expect to call. The witnesses are listed in *our* hearing memo."

"One of?" said the judge.

"Our other witness is in Qatar, as Mr. Vinich very well knows."

"Qatar?" said the Chief Judge.

"Right across the gulf from Iran," said Swanson, attaching much significance to this fact. "He's in the army."

"If the man is in Qatar how do you propose to have his testimony, counsel? I'm telling you right now I would never allow any kind of tele-something or other, nothing on a satellite, nothing like that to take testimony in a case of this seriousness."

"His family tells us this is his last posting, Your Honor," said Swanson as if to announce the end of a long heroism. "It's the end of his enlistment; he's standing guard out there. He'll be home in four and a half months, possibly sooner, and there shouldn't be any speedy trial issues."

"Maybe not from your perspective," said Vinich. "You're not in jail."

"The defense has had complete access to everything else, everything we can presently provide."

Vinich wondered if young Swanson's way of speaking—as if from a bottomless well of rectitude, as if to patiently explain what should be obvious—was as annoying to everyone else as it was to him. "Four and a half months," said Vinich, "waiting for the mystery guest."

"I take it from your tone," said the Chief Judge, "that the parties do not expect to settle this short of trial." He stared at each counsel table, heard from each of them, that, no, negotiations were not going forward, then the Chief Judge, whose disgust for the Palagi attorneys practicing in his court was only more or less obvious at any given proceeding, spent a moment more to stare at each of the counsel tables significantly before setting a jury trial date five months hence and droning out a schedule of deadlines for pretrial motions.

Vinich said, "As set forth in my hearing memo, Your Honor, we do not seek to present affirmative defenses. We anticipate only one pre-trial motion and that would be a motion to proceed with an expedited bench trial, accompanied by my client's waiver of a jury. The Territory doesn't have that many witnesses, and none of those would have that much to say."

"What about the soldier?" Asked the Chief Judge.

"Full faith and credit, Your Honor," said Vinich. "If the man is in the United States Army, all the Territory has to do is issue a subpoena to the Judge Advocate General of his command. They'd surely cut him orders to see that he complied."

"And fly him three quarters of the way around the world at the Territory's expense?" Swanson had been taken by surprise.

So tired now as to be giddy, Vinich shrugged. He was having too much fun, wondering as he sometimes did, where his lawyering came from, these things that occurred to him on the fly, most of which he didn't come to regret.

The Chief Judge said that when and if the motion was filed and a proper waiver of jury trial was received the Court would attend to the matter of possible rescheduling. In the meantime, he was ordering them as a matter of record—and not requesting—that they grow up and talk to each other about this thing like adults. Again," said the Chief Judge. "To be clear. That is an order."

Fuzzy. Sleep deprived. Vinich, however, had spent a good deal of time calculating the moves he had just made and didn't think he was careening. Pule Ulu there beside him had dressed soberly as he did for court and he had come entirely unadorned, no cosmetics. Massive. Still, his bearing alone expressed his nature. The Defendant had visibly relaxed as he began to understand that this day's business wouldn't require him to say anything. Those long hands of his, folded into each other. Vinich thought to complain of his handcuffs, but knew it for a waste of time. Look at him. They brought an extra deputy from the jail on days he was brought to court.

Look at him. Vinich momentarily caught a frightening glimpse through the fog, an understanding—not everyone shared his personal response to Pule Ulu. Look at him.

Pule Ulu was in Vinich's estimation the most innocent man he had ever met, and he needed to do right by him, he needed, at least, not to be inept or headlong in his behalf. But he wasn't sure. He was woozy, and on his best day when he found himself in the middle of such messes, Vinich wasn't sure. Kant's moral imperative—act so as to secure the world you want to live in; tall order. Now some additional vagueness settled on him—dehydration now?—and Vinich had for Pule Ulu that brief, sidelong smile by which an attorney signals his client 'We're done.'

An omnibus hearing was had in the case of Jesse Shard, the witless Bobo, he of the huge testicle with confusion written permanently on his face. The Defendant seemed to be moving better now than he had at his arraignment and his clothes were cleaner. Vinich acknowledged that the Defendant had received the evidence in his case which consisted of a handwritten paragraph from each of the police officers the young man had approached with joints; he'd seen the joints themselves, skinny little things; some test results, homegrown weed, apparently, containing just enough THC to damn the boy. The Court did not inquire about plea negotiations. The Territory could offer no lesser included offense, and a mandatory minimum sentence was prescribed by law, five years in the territorial prison, a $5,000 fine. Nothing to negotiate. The thing was set for a trial Vinich knew Jesse Shard couldn't win.

Bobo. Here was another client innocent in spirit if not before the law, but there was nothing it seemed Vinich could do for him but hope the Territory somehow screwed up its prosecution, a hard thing to do in such a simple case. To his shame, Vinich hadn't spoken to Jesse Shard except for their quick, hushed exchanges in court, so he had only briefly explained just how bad his situation was, and having said these things left the man out at the prison to stew in them, for Vinich lacked the emotional stamina to face the incomprehension he met in faces like Jesse Shard's, and Vinich lacked the time to offer such people his sympathies for some ruinous outrage he couldn't find a way to prevent, though many of them might have profited more from his sympathy than whatever legal wrangling he might do on their behalf. Out of all the people he might approach to burn one with him, Bobo had lucked into two plainclothes cops. Vinich thought that Jesse Shard's judgment of character must quickly improve now that he was imprisoned; he would need to be a lot more discerning inside.

29

Frances handed him a piece of paper with a stateside phone number and told him that Ahti had instructed him to interview the guy.

"Interview him?" said Vinich. "Interview the guy? What else? Grease the jeep? Wind the clock?"

Frances did not understand these references and would not bother to be confused by them. Frances was at all times draped in dense equanimity. "He *said*," she said again, "you're sup*posed* to call."

Vinich had dosed himself with caffeine and sugar to get through an afternoon's work, and as he considered his office telephone he thought that it would after all be a very short interview. There was only the one applicant, so far as he knew. Are you breathing? A member in good standing of any state bar? How soon can you be here? Three questions should do. It would be a short interview, provided no questions were asked of the interviewer. Suddenly his stimulants stopped working in him and Vinich thought he would rest his eyes for a moment.

At some point during this rest his cheek, having grown greasy with sweat and drool, slid off his forearm and onto his desktop blotter which served also as a day calendar, and as Vinich slept the written reminders of several important occasions came off that surface and were reprinted on his face. Unaware, he didn't mind. Now that sleep had found him again, at last, it didn't need comfort to carry on. And the dreaming, he drifted as far back as basketball in a dirt driveway, as far forward as the arms of Carol Ulu. In color. People long departed or detached from him returned in this realm to say the sweetest, most unlikely things. This was a nap long enough to contain different eras; sometimes Vinich could hear his own distant snoring, sometimes it subsided. A ringing phone entered into this and then, by degrees, brought him up out of it.

"Vinich," he sounded, even to his own ears, a little impaired.

"It's Swanson."

"Oh," said Vinich, his wits draining back into him. "All right."

"Following orders," said Swanson. "You serious about this bench trial?"

"I am," said Vinich. "I see no reason to have my guy sit out there while the Court carves a big hole in its calendar and the circus comes to town. I think if we try this in front of somebody with some legal training, maybe some passing understanding of logic and proofs—I think we're good. Three, four witnesses. It's a day's work."

"You think I won't get the soldier back here?"

"You know I can't be concerned with your problems," said Vinich.

"My problems? I will get the guy. Thanks for the tip, by the way. Got the subpoena ready except for a date, and we know where to send it. If your guy loses, by the way, they can assess the costs of prosecution, the cost of that flight to him."

"Then, I guess we'll try not to lose," said Vinich. "Do you even know what he would say, this Leava?"

"I know what he saw," said Swanson.

"Didn't he see what the other guy saw? That doofus you got on tape? That Satele kid? Or the super doofus you didn't even bother to interview? Have you talked to, or has anybody talked to those women in the church? They sure got mentioned in your Information. Now they're not interesting?"

"They're the Defendant's family," said Swanson. "Why bother?"

"What do you mean?" said Vinich.

"You know what I mean."

"No," said Vinich. "What do you mean?"

"They're family. Family here—they'd lie for him. You don't think they'd lie? I hear maybe you would know. I hear you've been sniffing around those people."

"*That* you know about," said Vinich. "Sniffing around? You know what we call that in the legal profession? Due diligence. And everybody lies. Everywhere I've ever been. I think that's the understanding sometimes known as adulthood. But if you knew this place, and I'm sure your investigators do, it is really easy to get around that here—if anyone is lying. And they wouldn't, by the way. Not his family. They wouldn't lie, but they wouldn't tell you what you want to hear. You're just not interested. You don't want to hear what they have to say."

"I have what I need. If you like what they have to say so much, then you can call them to testify."

"So, I'm wondering," said Vinich, still resenting the disturbance, "Why you're calling me."

"The Chief Judge ordered me to," said Swanson. "He didn't tell me what to talk about though. He can't."

"No offer, then?"

"I made my offer," said Swanson.

"Really? That death penalty thing?"

"I think you said that was 'nothing' before," Swanson said, apparently offended. "Did you ever talk to your client about that?"

"No," said Vinich. "We have serious conversations. About real things."

"Real?"

"All right," said Vinich. "The Territory has no death row, no execution chamber, nobody on your staff to handle appeal after appeal in a capital case. Much as it might like to, the Territory can't really afford to kill anyone. Also, there's a whole list of factors you'd have to prove to get to a death warrant, and you can't prove any of those. You can't even prove the underlying crime. And, and this is the best part—you've missed some filing deadlines if you wanted to pursue the death penalty. So, if at any point you want to get serious and return to reality, then we'll talk."

"I'm very serious," said Swanson.

"You never even started to look for a reasonable way through this," said Vinich. "Did you?"

"If I've got the right charge on him," said Swanson, "there's not much I can offer."

"You don't know what happened out there. You're not gonna know any more about it when you get Sergeant Leava back here. Your Filemoni, if he had anything real good for you, don't you think he would have mentioned it when your investigator showed up? I mean, Sergeant Leava? He'd have said something if there was something to say. Don't you think?"

"Who knows?" said Swanson.

"I think you're supposed to," said Vinich. "Know. When you accuse somebody of murder."

"There's been so much of this going on," said Swanson. "I've heard you say so yourself. People knocking each other in the head. Fatally. Seems like it's been a trend."

"Maybe. But that doesn't mean my client should be the whipping boy for the whole deal. You picked the wrong guy for that."

"They're such violent people here," said Swanson.

"Maybe," said Vinich. "But you can't fix that all in one case. Especially the wrong case. There's thugs and assholes everywhere; folks I've met here are mostly kind, even the majority of my clients."

"This Ulu, I know he did it," said Swanson. "If not,

how does the Asenati get that way, all bashed in?"

"That's your theory of this case?" Vinich said. "You don't know what happened, so it must be murder? Because you don't know how else to explain it, and from there you jump again to Pule Ulu must have done it." Though speaking on the phone, Vinich shook his head dismissively; even so, he could not dismiss how the same logic had led him early to the same conclusion—that there was a strong likelihood, at least, that Pule Ulu was a killer.

"I go after him," said the young prosecutor, "because I know he did it. That guy, your Mr. Ulu, he makes my skin crawl. All those guys like that. They make my skin crawl." Swanson's was a dry voice, monotone even in the grip of strong emotion.

30

"You like it so much here," she said into her microphone, "you should just murder somebody yourself, then you could stay all the time." The woman behind the plexiglass had now done something even bolder with the shape and brightness of her red lips to match the high-flown drama of her eyebrows; she had a lot of time to kill here and must more than occasionally notice that time was killing her. Sure, she'd be a little snippy. Vinich had the impression she was always at work, nearly as imprisoned as the inmates she oversaw. She waved Vinich through to the visitor's pavilion and sent her unhappy subordinate off to find Pule Ulu. Vinich made his way from the guard shack out to the pavilion, clasping his briefcase to his chest—once again the guard had not asked to look into it—how trusting, how haphazard—and Vinich jogged humped over the thing to keep it from the rain. An umbrella in such rain was of no use, his raincoat was also overwhelmed, and Vinich congratulated himself on keeping the briefcase and the paperwork it contained dry while he himself was soaked from head to squishing feet. The rain lashed, a constantly peeling thunder on the long metal rooves of the prison and on the roof of the pavilion above him.

Vinich was from the arid parts of trackless America and monsoon was for him the biggest peculiarity of a peculiar island. Ten minutes of this was equal to a year's moisture in many places he had been out west, and now he had drifted as far west as it is possible to go, to within a few meters of the jiggered International Dateline where the far west and the far east and one day and another all collide along a jagged border. What unimaginable rain, a rain so hard it bounced off grass, so hard it menaced. He paced the pavilion, tracking a stream on the concrete floor. The rain drove a haze out of the ground.

He had come to recommend a strategy to Pule Ulu; Vinich could only hope the young guard who had gone to find him hadn't got lost or distracted somewhere in the prison. They'd be gathered up in their barracks now, prisoners unseen, huddled in their confinement like trays of hatchling chicks, massed in there, breathing nearly airless air and each other's bad ideas. Hard time all around. Vinich did not need or want this time to rethink his understanding of the case, to rehearse how he would explain it to his client. Vinich had been over this in his mind too often if anything. The deluge was tiring; the wait seemed long.

When he came Pule Ulu had no cover but to shield his eyes with his hand, and he cut across the prison's empty playing fields toward the pavilion under full power; a fast and purposeful runner as necessary, and once under the roof of the pavilion he stood draining for a moment, washed clean, his shirt clinging to a musculature scarcely human, his overalls wet through. Vinich was glad the man had always shown the good taste or discretion to wear loose clothes to court; his body was the mark of the beast.

"My goodness," said Pule Ule. "You have to wonder if all this is really necessary." He smiled helplessly up toward the sky.

Vinich's scuffed briefcase lay on the concrete table between them; both men stood well back so as not to drip on it. It contained only a pen with blue ink and a waiver of jury trial which Vinich set about explaining, yelling his explanation here and there to be heard over the surging weather, explaining against the storm why he thought Pule Ulu should rush to judgment.

And Pule Ulu listened from out of his quiet patience, attentive, interested in an academic way, and so unlike the quibbling, amplifying, sniveling client with whom Vinich usually held such discussions. His sympathy. The man's face was an animate cliff where decency and constant sympathy were writ too large. So vulnerable. The man's listening face somehow broke Vinich's heart even as Vinich had come to tell him in not so many words that he was being hounded by a madman. Swanson wanted him here for forty years, and Swanson's motives were improper, but there would be no proving that, and Swanson's judgment was unsound, but it looked like they would have to prove that at trial. Vinich, yelling all this, yelling over the rain to clarify that what they didn't have to prove was his innocence, and everything hinged on that.

With the rain driving Vinich was not inclined to show his work entirely, his thinking. To date Vinich had tried three cases to Samoan juries and found them especially inscrutable, suspected his translator's brief translations couldn't possibly reflect what he was saying. Language wasn't the only problem. Those who did understand his words didn't understand what he meant by them. But that was his problem. Always had been. A defense attorney usually prefers the odds with a jury, where you have only to convince one of twelve not to convict, and even in the face of good evidence you might find one ringy holdout for acquittal. With a jury trial there was a much greater chance of the Court making some reversable error, too, so even if they should lose, he and Mr. Ulu might have a second bite at the apple.

But here, Vinich thought, a jury room was almost certain to be dominated by some asshole pastor, or some other authoritative cretin whose opinion would be adopted as a matter of course. Here, Vinich thought, a jury might not be the best device.

A judge, Vinich had been thinking, would be obliged to support his verdict with written findings of fact. The

Territory couldn't show the judge that anyone had seen or heard the crime alleged. Vinich should be able to demonstrate that the weapon alleged had not been a weapon. He could call the aunties to testify to how the Territory's Information had misrepresented what had happened in the church; Pule Ule had never been kicked out. Vinich further calculated the Chief Judge's dislike and distrust of the Palagi lawyers who practiced before him, and how the Chief Judge seemed to feel this most intensely for Assistant Attorney General Swanson in his insufferable youth, and there was a very good chance that the Chief Judge would enjoy to publicly spank the prosecutor for bringing him such an ill-conceived, ill-prepared case.

What the judge could not mention in his findings would be the implication of Pule Ulu's silence, an implication he would instruct a jury to ignore and couldn't therefore seize on himself. Truth be known, it would have to haunt the judge a bit with wondering, because anyone would wonder why a man wrongly accused of such a crime wouldn't be quick to say so. But it wasn't supposed to matter.

The Territory had pictures of the big dent in Talo Asenati's head and no explanation for how it had got there. That shouldn't be enough. The Chief Judge prided himself in being a serious, New Zealand-trained jurist. It shouldn't be enough.

But Vinich did not tell his client how he suspected that the judge might, even on such thin evidence, reach a finding on the lesser included offense of manslaughter, just to seem like he was placating everyone. Seven years was better than forty, but—Vinich did not like to mention the role that personality played in these things, how his client's future might hang on the personal quirks of strangers. The prosecutor's prejudice was driving him to some poor decisions. This was not something he would share with Pule Ule, and still less would Vinich share his concern that his own prejudice might be clouding his understanding of this. He simply told Pule Ulu that they would get to trial much sooner before a judge, such a trial being so much easier to arrange. He told him that the Territory could not prove its case.

Vinich didn't tell his client that he didn't want some spasm of enthusiasm or competence or happenstance to improve the Territory's story, their ability to tell it. He only said that he didn't think the territory could prove its case, and they had to proceed with that understanding because the Territory had given them no choice. Vinich said that, in his estimation, the sooner the better. "And we can get this thing set for trial. But, it's up to you."

31

At some point the rain had stopped, and suddenly, but there was still a lot of noise with water running in sheets off everything and newly formed creeks coursing through the prison's dirt road and its footpaths. Vinich had got used to shouting. He shouted, or nearly shouted all he had to say; then, when he'd said it, he noticed how unbearably hot it had got again and that he was chilled in spite of it. What next? Malaria?

Pule Ule, understanding it was now his turn, began with a long, foghorn sigh, a fond appraisal, "Oh, Mike. I am so moved." His gaze went out past the gate to the lagoon beyond it and to the ocean beyond that. How the ocean must beckon to those no longer free to touch it. There was a peace on him. "Do you know what it is to have someone so completely on your side? I see it, and it is so precious to me."

Vinich was afraid now that he might have oversold his optimism and made the trusting Mr. Ulu think he was already as good as acquitted, and before Vinich could begin to backpedal, to qualify, Pule Ulu continued his praise. "How you juggle these facts and rules. It's something to see. To me, that would be like playing a piano, trying to make my hands do two different things at once. I have enjoyed your, uh—you're like those dreadful men who talk about the football games my father watches on television, but interesting—your analysis. It's so nice of you to share this. It's like visiting the fortune teller."

He enjoyed it? What a strange and wonderful fellow, this poet; they were on an island in the middle of an emptiness and Pule Ulu was an island in the middle of that. Vinich felt humility and fever whelming.

"I hope I haven't wasted too much of your time," said

Pule Ulu. "But the other thing you mentioned. I think I'd prefer to do that. Plead, I believe you said?"

Vinich thought he had explained the implications. "No," he said. "You'd gain nothing by doing that. Besides, the thing they've got you charged with, you didn't do."

"Since we talked before, I've felt so much better. To let me unburden myself that way, that was so kind of you. We go to court, and I see all the things they have you doing—it makes me feel guilty, Mike. This must be taking up a lot of your time."

"No," said Vinich, and by 'no' he meant that it was the very best use of his time to ride for once in a purely, clearly righteous crusade, headlong and lance lowered at a pending injustice. He was tired, sure, but he could take it. Vinich said, "I do my job," a claim prideful enough coming from the son of a hard rock miner. "I'm supposed to try and keep you out of—what?—out of their vengance if I can, and that ain't the way to do it, Pule. I'm fine. Now *I'm* touched. Nah, I am fine. We are good to go." He hoped there was a go-team tone to this. Except for the fever, or maybe because of it, he felt himself boiling toward a fight. Righteous. Damn right. Beginning to ache a little, a weight, a pressure behind the eyes.

The big man said, "I felt so much better when I told you; and we are sort of stuck with the fact that I did kill that—man—little man. Ex-*ting*uished him, Mike. Oooh. Rammed his soul right out of him, felt it going." Air escaped Pule Ulu, a sigh as powerful as a weather event.

"Yeah," said Vinich. "I'm not calling that a technicality, but what they want to do about it, do to you—nothing that happens now is going to result in that guy being un-killed. He read you, Pule. He didn't think he was taking any risks. Surprise-surprise, he was wrong. Personally, I don't see why you're supposed to pay for that."

"I already am. Paying. I have been. I will be for. . . Talo Asenati—it's even worse since I know his name. I don't know why that makes it so difficult," he said. "His name. I just know that I want to go away from it all, and—no trial. I couldn't testify, and I don't want a trial. Not any kind of trial. Those were my decisions, right?"

"Yes," said Vinich.

"I hope you're not too angry with me."

"Angry?" said Vinich. "That wouldn't be the word." What would the word be? He didn't know it. The word— bird. Careful. Tired or sick. Track. Get tracking. Yes. Yes was the word. These were Pule Ulu's decisions to make, and Vinich had given him the information he needed to make informed decisions, and now Vinich feared he had undersold his optimism, or that his own fear and misgivings had been obvious through all his yelling in the rain. "No," he said. "But—yes. I mean, yes. I have to honor whatever you decide, but if you decide that way you'll be acting against advice of counsel. Maybe you'd like to talk to someone else. Some—I don't know. I'm sure I could get a burner phone in here if you wanted to talk this over with your cousin."

"Doak?" said Pule Ulu. "I already know what Doak would say. He would agree with you. Cousin Doak is the soul of practicality, bless him. So many interests, too. At least half my little library must have come from him. Over the years. I wind up throwing the self-help books away— the church won't take them. Sacrilegious, they say. And. . . I know he would want me to do the smartest thing. He is a very practical man. But, no I won't need to talk to Doak. I know what he would say. 'Get low', he likes to yell that, apparently it's motivational, something some coach used to yell at him. 'Get low.' Anyway, he is always so busy with his business. Quite a force, Doak, as all those football people would tell you, and I hope he doesn't blow his heart up with all that striving. If I had any courage maybe I would have been the one to. . . It's not that I don't trust you, Mike, please know that. I do trust you so much."

"Man," said Vinich. He had failed.

"I could not stand a trial," said Pule Ulu. "I couldn't stand it. That kind of upheaval I do not care for."

"It can be a little ugly," said Vinich. "But—man. You know we could be talking about years? Years of your life depending how this thing goes."

"I feel responsible," said Pule Ulu. "I *am* responsible. There's nothing you can do about that. That's more in my father's line, and I don't believe in absolution or whatever he's selling down there at his church. So, I am stuck trying to do the right thing. It's a shame, too. I'm sure you would have been magnificent. But—is it funny to say?—all that disruption just seems too distasteful. I did dream of blossoming one day, you know, in performance, live performance as they say, but I certainly wouldn't want to be at the center of something like *that*. I think they maintain a very poor atmosphere, don't you? In that court? They keep the woodwork shiny, at least, like father's church, and I don't mind a certain amount of formality, that can be charming. But the court, it seems a little mean, don't you think? Small. Or mean spirited. What is the term I'm looking for?"

"Nasty," said Vinich. "That's what it is; it's bound to be kind of grim in there when the criminal code in this territory is such a nightmare." His mind was running like a calculator. The ache was general in him and if the chill went any deeper, he might start to shiver—the tropical shakes. What else? "All right," he said. "I get it. You want to fess up. Come clean. All right. All right. If. But. If. Okay. But what we need to do is figure out how to get something for it.

Your honesty. You know, don't you, that's probably going to be kind of lost on these assholes?"

Having sold himself on the inevitability of trial, Vinich had prepared for nothing else, given no thought to this contingency, an unlawyerly oversight that might have come of being too invested. He was not at all confident that he would get a proper return for Pule Ulu's offer of the truth. "I do worry something like that will be beyond these assholes' ability to comprehend. We can't be real sure they'll get it. I'm not even sure I do. You know what defense lawyers say, Pule? 'Stand-up guys do hard time.'"

Something in Pule Ulu's life had required great patience of him. He used this now to wait his lawyer out.

"All right," said Vinich. "All right." He began to think aloud, hatching the next plan. "We've got to do some engineering, because it really isn't the usual thing." He described the usual thing, the plea bargain, as a contract, and that was just part of the problem—he didn't know how to negotiate a contract when the other party would offer no consideration at all. Often the state—the Territory—would reduce the number of crimes charged, or reduce the severity of a serious charge, and this was really the best consideration, because the judge had little choice but to accept such reductions or amendments. They were money in the bank for the defense, and often a meagre fund, but something. The Territory was offering no reductions to Pule Ulu, though, none at all, and the prosecution couldn't even recommend much leniency in sentencing while riding a charge that carried a mandatory forty years' confinement upon conviction. The usual trade-off wasn't going to happen. So, the usual song and dance wasn't going to happen.

Vinich described the ceremony by which the court conducted most of its business. "Usually," he said, "you'll have an agreement drawn up, and when you come into court you start by pleading guilty, then the judge asks for something called an allocution—you have to tell him *why* you're guilty. What you did. That won't work for us, though. That would be the cart before the horse in your situation. What we want is to have you tell the judge what you did, and tell him just the way you told me, then he can decide what you're guilty of. There's no regular routine for doing that. We could maybe do an offer of proof, but that would probably be a written statement, and I think what you need to say works a lot better if you can *say* it to him. Maybe an open pleading, but that doesn't quite fit the bill either. Man, if you just had to be honest, Pule, you should have stuck to poetry. It's a lot better suited to it."

"*Nolo contendere,*" said Pule Ule. "Didn't I hear the judge say that? I thought that was a lovely phrase."

"No," said Vinich. "That's just throwing in the towel. No contest. Hardly ever a good idea, and *real* bad in your situation. We're already giving up too much."

"But if a person does that, then they don't have to describe their crime, do they? They don't have to specify what they did? Or what happened?"

"Well, no," said Vinich, "which is what makes it the worst of all possible options for you. If you're going to come clean, you'd better come all the way clean, hope they'll see it for what it was."

"What was it, Mike?"

"Oh," said Vinich. "Manslaughter, probably. They'd call it that, at least. I think I could argue for that. Manslaughter with a lot of mitigation. You're already setting yourself up for seven years, but it gets a lot worse for you if you don't explain it."

"Do you think they would believe me, my version of events?"

"I know I do," said Vinich. "For what that's worth."

"Should I even believe myself?"

"Yeah, I would say so," said Vinich. "And that's not advice I would give just anybody."

"When I told you what I told you, that was private, wasn't it? Strictly private?"

"It was," said Vinich, sensing already that he would regret being bound to this.

"Good," said Pule Ulu. "Because I don't want to tell that story ever again. I had to tell someone, and I'm sorry it had to be you. But I'm done telling that story. I needed to tell it, and I'm glad I did, and I am so grateful to you for hearing it. But never again. Too awful. Stir the pit of your—substance. Saying that. Once was more than enough, but what I can't say enough, is thank you, Mike. Thank you. You have been so very kind."

"Oh, wait." Vinich did not shake, but he was obliged to sit on the concrete bench and there he did begin to sway a bit. It must be a steamy eighty in this pavilion, and no particle of him could possibly be cold, yet his body wanted to be curled near a woodstove, wrapped in an Afghan blanket.

"Are you all right?"

"I'm okay," said Vinich. "But you're driving me crazy. You are in the middle of some ugliness, and you kind of have to wallow through."

"This is the part I didn't—I didn't tell you," said Pule Ule. "I couldn't do that to him. You know, I have killed him, after all, and now if I dragged his name through the mud just to make it easier on myself. What kind of thing would that be? When the tortured thing can't even defend himself? I know what that is, and I won't do it to someone else. Not someone I'd killed, anyway. You can see how that would be too much."

"If that guy was a creep," said Vinich. "You don't owe him anything. You didn't mean to hurt him."

"See?" said Pule Ulu. "Is that how you heard it? My story? Because maybe I did. Not that much, but. I wanted it to sting, at least, and how could the poor guy know he was the living, breathing symbol of all my frustrations. He wouldn't know to expect that any more than I would."

"Well, he wandered into it," said Vinich. "Life is dangerous. And it *should* be more dangerous for assholes. You don't owe him anything. You can be pretty sure he'd been an asshole before that afternoon."

"No, for *me*, Mike. I don't want to stoop to. . . I still *hate* Mr. Asenati. Which is probably the most shameful part of it." Washed clean now, no makeup, no adornment at all, Pule Ulu was all Madonna, a thing of impossible integrity. He said, "But he made me feel bad about telling a few jokes, and they were harmless, harmless jokes, Mike. And then he pur*sues* me, to make me even more confused, and then—the feeling—I felt it—*yielding*. His head. Oh, that. Feeling. I used to think Emily was a little too absorbed with death, but then in a moment, you know, you understand—yes—or, no—but you understand. That soft head of. I couldn't make jokes in church, and then, since I hit him I have not had one funny thought. I don't have that anymore, so I can't stop hating him. But he is. . . Are you all right, Mike?"

"I'm fine," said Vinich.

32

Forty years. A hard forty. Vinich told his client that if did what he was talking about doing he would be arranging to spend any life he had worth living in the Territorial prison. Did he want that? Pule Ulu said he didn't want that. Vinich said that if he were to let a client do that to himself when there was no earthly reason for it, no legal, moral, reasonable reason for it, "I should be disbarred. I would disbar myself if I tried to punk out like that." He reintroduced the idea of a trial, and said it recommended itself because it was the one way through this where Pule Ulu wouldn't have to say anything at all, no oath taking, no testimony; at trial he would sit on his hands just as planned and watch the Territory fail to prove anything against him. He wouldn't be obliged to tarnish Talo Asenati in any way, and that was exactly what Vinich had been recommending, and, yes, it would be ugly theater, but not too long, Vinich promised, not too many acts. The Territory had little to present by way of a case, and it shouldn't take him long to destroy that case, either. They were headed toward one ugliness or another, and Vinich was still convinced a quick trial should be the least of them. "Sign that waiver," he said, "and I can get it set for trial. We can always back out later, if you want, or if I think of something else, some other way to go, or maybe the Territory will wise up somehow. But in the meantime, let me get it set it for trial. Force their hand. You know, a secret can be a secret for several different reasons."

"Are you sure you're all right, Mike?"

"Not completely," Vinich said.

It is a lawyer's lot to build beautiful, airtight arguments and have them ignored and see the matter decided on some other basis entirely. Vinich did not convince Pule

Ulu to his plan by sound logic or fearsome prospect; when Pule Ulu signed the waiver it was mostly because Vinich, swaying and rambling some, was visibly failing, and the visitor's pavilion was not a good place for it. Vinich did have just enough health to make his way back to High Court, file his papers, bring the jeep back to Utulei, make his way home by aiga bus and a short but convincing death march through the rain.

He was sick for a week during which he happened to realize there was no one he might call for help or sympathy. Sick alone with something undiagnosed, Vinich told himself he should try and make some friends in this world. One vague morning he managed to wave down a neighborhood kid and give him fifty bucks to return with wrapped racks of bottled water. He was not too surprised when the lad returned in the back of someone's pickup and bore him armloads of water. Vinich in his sickness had been sweating more than usual, more than he'd dreamed possible, and if he survived this—alone his imagination ran to its own fevered devices—but if he survived this, wouldn't he be clean? Cleansed from the inside out? If he didn't, would they be good enough to bury him at sea? Would he even be found before he was putrid?

In time he felt better, and not noticeably cleansed but noticeably weakened, he went back to work, and Vinich was very briefly flattered to see how the criminal docket in American Samoa's lower and higher courts had got completely stalled in his brief absence. Then he was overwhelmed with work, old work left undone, new cases all the time. Work, and more work, until just as before there was no room or time for any other good intention. And he would think, fleetingly, that maybe he got mired this way by design. Vinich made no progress toward making new friends.

One day he was in the High Court's law library; he remained more proficient with paper and ink, with case reporters and venerable smelling digests than with the balky digital research tool the Public Defender had bought them; also, this room enjoyed the most sophisticated air conditioning on the island. Vinich was giving himself a quiet afternoon in a quiet place to poke around and see if he could find some remedy for Jesse Shard and the disaster of pressing homegrown joints on cops at a street fair. Was Bobo the same vague boy he'd been going in? Had the family jewels ever receded? Vinich hadn't seen the kid since his arraignment; there was nothing new to tell him, certainly no reassurances to be offered, and the old news, the bad news, was still current. Vinich could pretty easily imagine Jesse Shard dreading what he had every reason to dread, the next five years, and Vinich was equally sure the lad felt abandoned by his lawyer, but Vinich did not need to see Bobo's puppy face.

The law. The kind of dumb shit that gets written on stone tablets, in stone hearts, and can take forever to undo when it's wrong. Whoever had drafted the Samoan Criminal Code made regular use of the phrase, ". . . with no possibility of probation or parole."

Vinich thought immediately of the eighth amendment and thought he could certainly demonstrate the cruelty of this particular law by cataloguing vast instances of easier sentences handed out for far worse offenses. As provided by law. But that was an appeals issue, and even if it went in Bobo's favor he would have sat the whole sentence, probably, before it was decided. Vinich landed on a stool between two stacks, the Territorial Code opened to the law in question, and beside that on the floor at his feet a leading treatise on statutory interpretation. He needed to attack it up front, find some chink in the wording, but this law was in no way ambiguous and provided no way back from or around an absurd result. When Vinich rose to shelve the treatise he found that the feeling was gone from his legs from his hams to his knees while his feet were electric, and found the Chief Judge there on the other side of the stack; they were mutually startled.

"Afternoon, your Honor. Hope you don't mind if I use your library."

"Not *my* library, counsel. It is open to anyone, not that many are interested." The Chief Judge had a diction part island-boy, part upper-crust Kiwi, and he disdained anyone who was not him, particularly anyone trained in a stateside law school. He gave the impression of having been born a judge, a man who'd got his start by inflicting that agony on his mother. "We received notice today," he reported, "that the subpoena was served on Sergeant Leava. They're giving him an early discharge because of it."

The Judge seemed to think Vinich should regret all the trouble he had caused. Meanwhile Vinich was telling himself, again, that Filemoni Leava was very unlikely to add anything to the prosecution's case. If the witness had anything very telling to say, the Territory should know it by now, and Vinich should know it. Shouldn't they? Wouldn't the Attorney General's people have taken the trouble to find that out? The Territory was approaching this matter like a clumsy fat man in a fight, and Vinich worried about taking their competence for granted. Their approach to this could produce surprises all around.

Wanting to breathe nothing of that case at the moment, Vinich said, "May I ask you a question, Your Honor? I don't think it would be in the nature of an *ex parte* communication. It's theoretical. More to do with tradition, Samoan tradition." Vinich making a poor attempt to flatter and toady. "I was looking through the sentencing provisions and I came across the section that mentions the *ifoga*—I'd heard it mentioned before, down in Judge Mandeville's court. It's a public apology? How is that performed? Is there a. . ."

Silence was in the Chief Judge's arsenal of mannerisms for always having the upper hand. He seemed to have forgotten Vinich was there until, roused by sudden impatience, he said, "I don't use it much. How is it supposed to be done? Ask any three *matais* to tell you and you'll have three answers to choose from. I am fine with tradition—but I want my law written out. There are good reasons for that. As you may have noticed, counsel, I'm a black letter man. I take it you have someone who wants to apologize."

"Actually, Your Honor, I'm looking for a way to provide the Court with some sentencing options in possession cases with real minor offenders. No one can think some of these sentences are proportionate."

"The Fono has left us very explicitly with*out* sentencing options," said the judge.

"Every piece of legislation has to be field-tested, your Honor. That's more or less why we're here, isn't it?"

The Chief Judge made a face when Vinich used the pronoun, 'we'. "What about the *ifoga*?" he said.

"Defendant makes his apology," said Vinich, "and the court is authorized—in black letter law—to bump the offense down one full category."

The Chief Judge for the first time Vinich could recall attempted a smile, not a pleasing expression, and it was just as well that he was nearly always somber. "Well," he said, "that is circuitous. And to whom would this offender apologize?"

"Everyone," said Vinich. "A public apology to everyone."

"And for what?" the Chief Judge wondered.

"Oh—" said Vinich. "Offending the peace and dignity of American Samoa? I think you're making my point, Your Honor. For a victimless crime—they want to take a kid who's never seen a hundred bucks in his life, throw him jail for five years, then expect him to pay a five thousand dollar fine when he gets out. It's ruinous."

The judge was silent again, long enough to indicate he found this outburst distasteful. "The law is the law," he eventually said, just to ground the conversation. "This one will change when some rotten child of an influential family bungles his way into it. The next sitting of the Fono after that—the law will change. But for now, it is the law, and the law is the law. I will say, Mr. Vinich, that you among all these mutts do at least choose to work. I might go so far as to commend your diligence," he said. "But you never want to get fancy in my court, counsel. That won't serve you well. The law, you might say, is my rod and my staff, and I don't like people messing with it."

33

Evil belly laughs and techno pop were drifting around the compound at Lions Park. Vinich heard the party. When he'd been sick, he had at least been able to sleep; his body had demanded it of him. Now, with restored health his usual wakefulness resumed, those long, long, barking nights when Vinich did his best and worst thinking. He might almost choose to be sick again if it meant a few more nights of dreamless, twitchless sleep. He had aimed at a judge trial in the Ulu case, and now a judge trial was roaring right up with Vinich wondering night after night what the Chief Judge might mean by 'getting fancy', what he was being warned away from. The law is the law. Indeed. The powerful everywhere are fond of their idiot tautologies and roll them out as their idea of wisdom, and Vinich could never rest easy when he had placed Pule Ulu's life in the hands of just such an ass. No matter how often he reviewed it, though, he could think of no better option. But he continued to review it, continued to try the case in the claustrophobic courtroom of his mind.

They didn't always win these trials.

Meanwhile there were the many lesser trials that were his work. He had been presented with a sheaf of spread sheets as the entire body of evidence against one of his clients, documents that meant little to Vinich and even less to his investigator; no forensic accountant, Vinich, and he didn't even know where he might find such a creature. A rash of juvenile cases came in combination with a vogue among certain youngsters for sniffing glue. The new hire had arrived on island—Tod, who had described himself as, 'really eager to try this.' Having come with a surfboard in his baggage, Tod was about to be disappointed by Tutuila, an island whose surf was underlain everywhere by coral which would wait no longer than a surfer's first fall to shred said surfer and surfboard. Tod was blond. There was some difficulty getting him admitted to the Samoan bar though he was a member in good standing in Arizona. The Arizona surfer? Vinich did not expect Tod to adjust to his first job in criminal law or the disappointments lying like abrasive coral just under a tropical paradise, but then Tod, not merely blond, but curly blond and blue eyed, had acquired a girlfriend. No ticket to practice yet, but a girl-friend already—so maybe Tod was adaptable after all, if not noticeably bright. Meantime, down in the Lower Court, drunk drivers were being processed by the dozen as were various instances of love and friendship gone sideways, street beefs, and Vinich distracted in the middle, trying to mediate. He had asked for and got an expedited trial for Pule Ulu; it was roaring right up now. Sneaking up.

Not at night, though. At night the trial came lumbering slow and menacing, and the thing couldn't come soon enough. Maybe afterward there would be some sleep. These nights. During one of them his phone rang, and because it was his private phone, and because of the hour, Vinich assumed it must be Cyrus calling, and with that assumption came a spurt of paternal apprehension. What's wrong?

But it wasn't Cyrus calling. "Fiame let me have her phone again," she said. "We've been drinking wine, and that is another thing I should never do. I am a pothead. This stuff makes me foolish. My head will hurt tomorrow. Red wine."

Carol Ulu was one of the last people Vinich would consider foolish, or one of the least foolish, or too welcome a voice in the night.

"So, I have Fiame's phone," she said, "and I am calling you. We got those things from the court. "Subpoenas," she said, having her way with that word. "We're coming in to testify. It's on, isn't it? We're so excited. He's innocent, and we know. . ."

"We can't talk about that," said Vinich. "We probably shouldn't talk about anything right now."

"You don't want to talk to me?"

"I didn't say that," Vinich said. "I mean—yes, I do want to talk to you."

"Good," said Carol Ulu. "I know you must get lonely. I know I do. How are you? We get the paper. You're in it every time."

"Don't believe anything I'm quoted as saying in there," Vinich said. "Their reporter is very creative."

"I've got a girlfriend who works for one of the judges. She tells me you're looking terrible."

"Nice of her," said Vinich. "I was ill for a bit. It's over now."

"They think you're funny, the court people."

"Funny?" said Vinich. "Man, we've seen how that can work out."

"No," said Carol Ulu, "if you're a Palagi, funny is the best thing you can be. You say things they wish they did—to the judges—so they like you. And—you're sure you're okay?"

"Good," said Vinich, seizing on the moment to say it true, "I had a nice little win today." He described how he had thought to have Jesse Shard's three sad joints independently tested, and he made a motion to that effect, which was granted, and, voila, it happened that those very joints were gone from the evidence locker. Bobo would be a free man as soon as the Attorney General's people could figure out how to dump the case without too much embarrassment to the Territorial Police.

"You have a way to test for THC?" she asked him.

"No," said Vinich. "I was bluffing. That's what makes it special. I was bluffing, and I win. Or he wins. Tomorrow morning, I get to go over to the prison and deliver some good news for once."

"You ever need a tester," she said, "I can test. With my nose. I can tell you about the terpenes in it, everything. Of course, I might have to smoke a little to really give you the scoop. You need to get some rest, Mike. I think I know how you feel—When I was in Alaska, up there waiting for the end of the world, we were supposed to be expecting it all the time. That tires a person out."

"I didn't mean to give you false confidence," Vinich said. "There have been a couple of those cases, pot cases, that I didn't win, and those guys are sitting their five. So be—careful. Okay?"

"I didn't call for legal advice."

"No," said Vinich. "No. I mean, I'm glad you called. Very glad, but until this thing is over, we probably shouldn't give the appearance of, or do anything to suggest—"

"What?" she said.

"You seem so nice," said Vinich. "Believe me, I am *glad* you called."

34

Jesse Shard broke into tears on learning that he was soon to go home. Vinich thought he would deliver the news with Tod in tow and familiarize him with the Territorial prison, show him that their side did occasionally win. Jesse Shard, spoke of himself in the third person as Bobo, proclaiming through his tears that at least Bobo's mother loved him. She would be so happy. He said he'd be coming home better than new—they had been giving him a drug, and his ball was shrinking, and he felt light. He said in prison no one wanted to touch him, which saved him having to fight and—do other things—he was all crammed in with these people, but lonely as hell. His mother loved him, he said. Jesse Shard lacked much English and sought to express his gratitude with embraces; he had one for Vinich, and he had one for Tod who when embraced, and not knowing what made Bobo so untouchable, could not prevent himself from recoiling, grimacing.

"It's okay," Vinich said. "What he got, he got from a mosquito."

Jesse Shard seemed especially grateful to Tod, and his tears and his lavish embrace continued. Tod had a knack for making friends.

Vinich was enjoying the moment when his phone vibrated in his pocket, his private phone, a thing that always startled him. "Damn. Everybody's got this number now. This is probably the only prison in the world where you can just walk right in with your telephone."

It was Assistant Attorney General Abraham Swanson, and before Vinich could ask him how he of all people had gotten this number, Swanson asked him, "Can you get out to the airport?"

"What is it?"

"Can you meet me out at the airport?"

Swanson's voice was more than usually grave—and that was part of the young man's problem, wasn't it, too much gravitas for his age, not enough joy, there was something dark in him. Somewhere very near the Assistant Attorney General, there at the other end of this transmission, a woman was weeping. What an excess of emotion this morning. A monsoon of tears.

"What is it?" Vinich said.

"I want to tell you face to face," Swanson said. "Not on the phone." His voice so level now as to be spooky.

Vinich could think of no interest he and Swanson might share at the airport except the arrival of Sergeant Leava, and that wouldn't usually result in their forming a welcoming committee. "All right. I'll be there. Give me about fifteen minutes." He might have got there much sooner, but Vinich told Tod, "Go ahead and take the defendermobile back to the office. Think I'll stroll down to the airport. Take the air." So, he went out of the prison at a tropical pace, and past the next neighborhood, Lion's Park where his own government shack sat cheek by jowl with his clients' gated community, and the airport was not far past that—all these facilities along a half-mile stretch of road, and it occurred to Vinich as he walked along that escape from them should really be far more common. An inshore breeze raised chop on the lagoon, a field of flexing golden scales under that hour's sun. It occurred to Vinich there really should be more freedom in general. Freedom to, for, from what? Freedom. The mountains here were abrupt and primeval green, the ocean endless, and between them those fringes of habitable ground, that little strip round the island describing the exact limits of freedom here. Vinich walked just fast enough so that it wouldn't look like he was drunk along the highway. It was hard to think that Swanson would summon him to something he was going to like. Maybe this Leava had seen something, heard something. There had always been that risk. Maybe Swanson had called to gloat about it. But from the airport? And he hadn't sounded like he was enjoying himself.

Until this trial was over, Vinich could expect to fret about nearly everything. And probably afterward.

He had been to the terminal before only for his own arrival and to greet Root and then Tod when they had flown in. This was the first time Vinich had seen the place so nearly empty. By day it offered a nice view past the runway and out to sea. Arrivals and departures here involved ramming heaps of extraordinary luggage through slow-motion and extremely curious customs agents. And a crowd. Today there was only Swanson, pacing, and his wife and the two older Samoan women flanking her, trying most diligently and ineffectually to comfort her. There was a pyramid of luggage, some of it roughly packed. The next scheduled flight out was one to Honolulu nine hours hence. As Vinich approached this group, Mrs. Swanson's lament rose in pitch and volume, and she pressed the back of her fist to her lips to keep from making it more specific, but Vinich could see that he had something to do with her anguish. Now he came walking very slowly.

"Janelle," Swanson said to his wife, scolding, pleading, "Now. Please?" He tilted his head to indicate to Vinich that they should step out onto the tarmac. Leava? Evidence? Contraband? What? And what in the hell were those women doing there but staring holes through Mike Vinich?

Swanson was dressed like a vacationer, but for as long as he had been here, he had never acquired a tan and looked silly and pale and small in a lime sport shirt. Once they were out of earshot of the women, and out of the building, and around a corner and out of sight, Swanson turned and said, "She's upset. We were thinking about getting pregnant here, if you can imagine that; she thought the humidity would be good for a baby's skin, but she hates the humidity in Oklahoma. So. She thinks it's all your fault. You win, by the way."

Swanson had almost scoured the Okie from his accent, but now that he mentioned it Vinich thought he'd always heard it there. Something dustbowl, a hardness, a twang.

"Oklahoma?"

"Underton," said Swanson, as if to explain something.

Vinich, for his part, made an uncomprehending face and they regarded each other for a moment. Heat waves lifted off the tarmac.

"In Underton, Oklahoma," Swanson said, "right there on Main Street you've got Swanson Drugs. My father's store, my grandfather's store. The second floor has never been used, except for storage. I'm opening up a practice. A solo practice. An ethical practice."

"Congratulations?" said Vinich. "What, uh? I think I must have missed a few things."

"We thought there were upright people here. And there are. The people in our church, that congregation has been just fabulous to us. But. I have to be ethical. I *will* be ethical."

"I'm sure you will," Vinich said, and to his surprise he meant it. "But. . ."

"But the other thing," said Swanson. He was a small man, further reduced right now. In that idiot shirt, but his hair was not at all misplaced, nor the certainties that drove him. "Underton; I worked so hard to get out of there."

Vinich knew he must look puzzled, but it seemed Swanson wasn't seeing his confusion, "I think you're thinking I know some things I don't know."

"You didn't get my motion in your box this morning?"

"I didn't look in my box this morning," Vinich said. He ritually ignored that box in the morning.

"It's a motion to dismiss. *With* prejudice. I'm sure you wouldn't oppose. It's over."

"What?" Vinich said. "What is?"

"Your Mr. Ulu. He's out of there. Scott free."

A combination of this news and tropical sun sat Vinich down on a baggage cart.

"You know," said Swanson, "the shopping in Underton, the restaurants—even worse than here."

"Back up," Vinich said. "I'm still missing a few pieces of this."

"I moved to dismiss," said Swanson, so florid under the sun and in his ripe despair.

"You said that," said Vinich. "But why? You seemed, uh, fixated or something. Pretty set on it, I thought."

"So, you didn't? I know I'm. . . a little scattered. This has been such a. . . Janelle really hates Underton, I mean she *really* hates Underton, and she was just getting adjusted here. Talking about that baby. . ."

"But, wait," Vinich said. "Could you back up a little? "

"Okay," said Swanson. "I know, I. . ." He was not entirely himself, not entirely a bad thing, that lockstep mind having briefly slipped some cogs. Vinich remained opponent enough to note what pressure did to this guy's composure; Vinich thought that if he had lost this trial to this lawyer he would have been devastated.

"Okay. Here's what happened: I was in with the Attorney General, in his office. I was actually there to talk about a contract extension. The baby thing, you know." About to describe an outrage, Swanson rolled his eyes upward. While Swanson had been in his office the Attorney General had taken a call from someone obviously his pal, and they'd jabbered away in Samoan, tricky in their own lingo.

"Like lawyers?" said Vinich.

"I'm not that kind of lawyer," said Swanson, and he wasn't: diligent, deeply prejudiced, and well groomed, but he was not, for better or worse, tricky. He had been in his boss's office, in the middle of something he thought he needed to finish, talking about an extension with a raise, some better housing for he and Janelle and their maybe baby, and the boss took a call and talked and talked with somebody, and it was awkward sitting there, but the Attorney General had given no indication he should leave, and though Swanson had understood no more than one in twenty of the terms the boss was using he thought the conversation had something to do with sports; it was jovial. Pal talk. Then at the end the Attorney General said, "Okay, sure," still smiling, "we can do that." And he hung up and told Swanson to dump the Ulu case.

Swanson had protested. "A murder?"

And the Attorney General had said, "It's too weak." Vinich didn't think he should remind Swanson just now that he'd been saying the same thing.

Swanson had stood by principle, thrown professional caution to the winds, and challenged the Attorney General. Had he looked at those pictures, had he even looked at those crime scene photographs? Did he know their victim was a lay pastor? And all the Attorney General would say—"Dump it. Like I told you."

Swanson had refused that order, and as he recalled himself making this stand, he regained a measure of calm. He had refused. Then, when he'd refused, he'd been given a choice; it happened he had stepped in it worse than he'd imagined, for the Attorney General told his young charge that he could now move to dismiss the Ulu case, *with* prejudice, and submit his letter of resignation with an immediate effective date—or he would be dismissed for insubordination and moved immediately out of government housing. The point the Attorney General said he wished to make was that he should *never* be crossed.

"So I took door number one," said Swanson. "The lesser. . . evil, evil, evil. This is such a de*vout* place. We thought. . . I don't know what we thought now."

"You better sit down," Vinich said. Swanson had become mottled in alarming ways; he'd be a candidate for heat stroke the way his luck was running.

Swanson sat, his shoulders initially drooping, but almost at once he thought to draw himself up. He looked out to sea. He was taking the long view. A young man taking the long view, and Vinich was a little sorry for him because he still wasn't seeing all that was out there ahead of him, and there was probably a good deal of that he wouldn't like. "I wanted to talk to you," he said. "Try and catch you before we left. A couple things—One, I don't hold you responsible. I wanted to tell you that. You were doing your job and I know that. You played by the rules, as far as I know."

Considering the circumstances more than the source, Vinich did feel complimented.

"It was an easy decision," Swanson said, "but I have to admit, the way that man barked at me made it a lot easier. You don't like to think you're easy to intimidate."

Vinich thought this might be an opportune time to ask this young man just how it felt to be powerless, but he didn't ask it. Instead, Swanson asked him, "And the other thing I wanted to know: How does it feel? I mean, how do you feel when you help these people get away with things? I'm not accusing, I'm really not. I'd just like to know."

Vinich might have told Swanson that he had no

category so broad as "these people," that he had in doing his work sometimes helped bad people avoid consequences they probably deserved, but that it was not for him to determine what kind of people got what kind of representation, they must get the best he could give, all of them; he could not choose whom to champion. Vinich might have taken this rare opening to explain himself, but instead he said. "How does it feel? Feels good."

35

Vinich disabled his telephone and established a new personal record, sleeping continuously for twenty-one hours, after which his bladder was angry with him, and he did not feel as if he had been sleeping so much as suffering a subtle but continuous beating to body and soul. Once awake he ate three cans of beef stew, food that became uninteresting early in the banquet. He wasn't sure what had become of his sap but knew he would be wanting it back, so he ate to refuel, but then when he'd regained the capacity to ponder, he did wonder—to what end? His was a curious talent, and his victories, most of them, were ambiguous, outcomes he often stumbled into more than won and were likely to gain only slight and temporary relief for his people whose problems were layered and legion. His people. And that was part of the problem. The way he came to think of them. His people, his principles; Vinich knew he should be happier right now, happier at almost any given point.

He'd had time to reflect on the triumph of Jesse Shard who was returned to his loving mother—but would he also return to the condition in which she had loved him, greasy and horribly hobbled? Had his crippling innocence been in any way rectified? Bobo was going home.

And Pule Ulu. Pule Ulu was going home.

Vinich could not recall a more successful week in his practice of the law and his successes had only somehow punctured his sense of purpose; he turned his phone back on to call the office and tell Frances he would be taking at least ten days of accumulated vacation, starting now—Tod was just going to have to figure out how to cover—and he called to book a seat on a fairly imminent flight to Ofu; he turned his phone off again and lazed around napping and reading Julius Caesar's brag about his big adventure in

Gaul until just forty minutes before the scheduled departure when he hiked down to the airport with a gym bag to carry on to a little tube of an airplane He flew to Ofu because he'd heard somewhere it was pristine.

He'd made no plans about bed or board for this vacation, wasn't even sure such accommodations would be available in an allegedly uncluttered place, but a Samoan man and his Teutonic looking wife were running a bed and breakfast at the airstrip with adjacent cabins, one of which they rented to Vinich. Several doors down there was a Dutch anthropologist, a lovely man, remote as he could make himself in cabin eight. Bacon and eggs in the morning in the large cabana that was their drawing and dining room. Clean white sand leading to a shallows patterned by coral into figures like a backlit Persian carpet, but living, and when Vinich went in amniotic water, he frolicked in it, the clumsy otter, and, charged, he hiked down to the bridge connecting Ofu to Olesega where a group of six kids, brothers and cousins by their similarity, were jumping from it midspan. Vinich joined them. A drop. A necessary whoopdeedoo. Vinich jumped twice, falling through the boys' derisive and admiring laughter; one of them said the Palagi fell like Jesus on the cross. Back at his cabin and a source of fresh water to rinse the salt off, Vinich discovered that the tops of his feet were sunburned. He was not a practiced tourist. That scorching sun. That scorching, scouring sun, hadn't it felt so redeeming?

Ill prepared for the trip, he hadn't brought a thing to read. Or maybe he'd meant that, to get away from everything, but Vinich was pleased to find a lending library in the dining room, and in that good old Nordhoff and Hall. *Mutiny on the Bounty.* He consumed that lovely mess in a hammock strung between palms constantly nodding their approval. Vinich read and slept. That soft surf, that cradling hammock, that inshore breeze, someone else's already irrelevant problems. This was the Samoa he had sort of imagined, but more paradise than he could stand; before his ten days were done, and as soon as his feet had ceased to be tender, Vinich was learning to his horror that he was not accustomed to peace, that he had in the course of his campaigns succeeded, if nothing else, in making peace boring. In his restlessness he flew back to Tutuila, where he didn't find anything more engaging to do, and he paced around in his shack, thinking about quitting. He had reason enough to be tired, but couldn't understand why he was so unconvinced, so unmoored. If he had any sense at all, just that of self-preservation, he should by all rights go somewhere and do something else, anything a man lacking a forefinger and charm might do, anything that might get him used to peace again.

"Go away," he said, "I'm busy." The knock was soft but insistent, and Vinich was overagitated about having to put on his pants just to insist, face to face, that he be left alone. This would be someone from work or some of the roving evangelists that occasionally plagued him. "Go away," he said again, but it would not suffice. Vinich meant to be crude and perhaps even rude in the encounter but was glad he'd pulled his pants on at least when he finally did open his door; shirtless men are anything but rare in Samoa, still he felt naked standing there shirtless before two of the aunties, the biggest and the smallest of the sisters, Inina Falaniko and Fiame Tagataese standing side by side in identically cut, lavender sheath dresses. They were between them a botanical garden. Little Fiame tittered something like a meadowlark's song, and Mrs. Falaniko was a little stern with him about not calling them, about leaving his phone off so they couldn't call him; she broke into a knowing smile to tell him that they had come to take him to a party. The party seemed to be commencing about ten a.m. A big party Mrs. Falaniko said suggestively. Her voice when she was having fun had all the better qualities of a trombone.

"How did you know where to. . .?"

"It's Samoa," said Mrs. Tagataese. Fiame, the sprite, quickly drew a lei over his head, a thing made of orchids for all Vinich knew.

He looked down, thinking he was so weak in botany and horticulture, and that the flowers looked incongruous on his fuzzy white belly. "Well, okay," he said. He almost never received such invitations and never did accept them, for parties filled him with a small but intolerable dread. The aunties meant to take him with them, their smiles wide and warm. They were offering friendship. Vinich was skittish about this, but wasn't this the very oddness he'd been meaning to overcome in himself? He pulled on a jersey falsely suggesting he was a Miami Dolphins fan, but it was clean and an improvement over his naked flesh, and they loaded into Inina Falaniko's red car. They had got as far as Pago Pago before Vinich learned that Carol Ulu's house was to be the scene of the party, the mention of her name, though it was hardly unexpected, shot through him and left a residue of terrible anticipation. In Pago Pago he had Mrs. Falaniko stop at a liquor store and, after consulting with the sisters bought a box of white wine with its own pull-out spigot. When he returned to them with it Fiame asked if he were a wine drinker, and he said he wasn't drinking anything these days, that he stayed away from drink when he had the blues. "You get a bohunk drunk—and sad—man, that is no kind of celebration."

"We will fix that for you," said Inina Falaniko. "You are gonna *eat.*" Her confidence did not flag even when making their final approach to Carol Ulu's house, up a gulch, up a road that was not regularly a road, riding on well compressed springs. "Wait til you try some of Pule's *umu,*" she said.

Fiame trilled and said, "Then you had the best."

A rough palapa had been raised in Carol Ulu's yard, and under that Pule Ulu was piling stones on a fire burned down to hot coals. He wore a red lavalava, a sheen of sweat, a headband of plaited leaves, and the smooth efficiency of man in a state of nature. He stood as Vinich walked up to him, and he said, "Of course, I'm grotesque. But I *am* cooking, so I think you'll forgive me."

Vinich would not be deterred. His childhood had not involved men hugging men, and the craze had never caught on with him; Vinich in fact found very few embraces comfortable, but to hell with that, he walked up and hugged Pule Ulu. Vinich felt his back being patted and felt more the child than he had probably ever felt as a child.

Carol Ulu had come to her door wearing the same lavender dress as her sisters, they would have sewn them for this occasion. She smiled and lifted her chin, and lifted her brow, the co-conspirator. She said, "We do *umu* way up here. That way none of these village shits have to come. We don't have to share anything with those people, and we definitely don't need them bringing us down with their village-shit shit."

Repurposed car seats were arranged around the fire pit and the aunties arranged themselves on these like something out of a couturier's folk tale, so elegantly the big, the little, and the just-right. Pule Ule cooked. Requiring no help, permitting no interference, he quickly mounded his select stones, and despite what he had said of himself he was a wizard with his jungle's broad leaves which he conditioned to form into cookware, pouches containing shark, and pork, taro, coconut milk, other ingredients Vinich didn't recognize at all. Pule Ulu overlay all this with more leaves, layers of them to make his oven. There were songs for each stage of the cooking, and the sisters, drinking a Polynesian sangria and the box wine and smoking, sang them where they reclined, and when Pule Ulu sang at the bottom of these harmonies Vinich felt the evil spirits float out of him and the hair stand up on the back of his neck. He was otherwise sober, though he took some ribbing from the aunties about it. Pule Ulu was also sober, as this was his habit when cooking.

When the oven was built and contained, even more leaves were distributed among the aunties, and weaving commenced. The time it would take to weave these baskets was the time to cook the *umu*. They turned the green materials in their hands, even Pule Ulu who was nowhere near as clumsy with it as he claimed, and they sang and gossiped and laughed. Vinich, grinning generally, looked out of the palapa and down the cleft in Carol Ulu's ravine that gave onto a prospect of the sea.

He did not cease to grin as he sat there learning that the call that concluded the Pule Ulu case had come from Pule Ulu's father, who might have quashed the thing at any time but waited until subpoenas arrived in the village. Pastor Ulu had waited to make one of his points and to further express his shame. His shame? Vinich inquired after this and was told that Pastor Ulu was not much concerned that a man had been killed, that he may in fact have been a little proud of it; one of Pastor Ulu's chief complaints with his boy was that such a monster as his son didn't want to be a warrior, a terrible waste. Inina Falaniko said they were never satisfied, that even when a boy like her Doak went out and beat people around, then they wanted to fall all over him and treat him like a bear with a collar on its neck. They were never satisfied. The real crime, and the real shame they had all committed was going to those people's church, people of the exact same faith, and being so disrespectful there with the laughing. That was the crime as Pastor Ulu saw it. And they were all considered guilty, and none of them felt at all guilty despite the village's effort to force them that way—except for Pule Ulu with his too tender conscience.

This little group apparently didn't quite fit, had set themselves aside, and Vinich thought that would be why he felt he fit among them.

With a light delivery Pule Ulu intoned several of Emily Dickinson's poems, things none of them understood; unsettled glances flew around the palapa, and soon Pule Ulu grew sheepish and stopped reciting, and soon enough they resumed laughing. When the baskets were made, big green baskets having even handles woven in, they ate. There was food enough for thirty, but they did their best and ate with reverence, without pause or utensils until they had all drifted off to sleep on their car seats, stunned by food and heat and fun.

Vinich was the first to wake and he used the opportunity to stare in perfect frankness at Carol Ulu there across the fire pit, and Vinich knew this pleasure must be temporary, and it was, because Carol Ulu was the next to waken, and it happened she was returning his stare the moment she opened her eyes; Vinich didn't know what to make of this. It wasn't nothing. It wasn't coincidence. It lasted a while, a sort of stand-off.

Carol Ulu flowed up from her car seat and went into her shanty. Vinich did not rise, but waited in some limbo that seemed his whole life. She had gone in to change into shorts and a tee-shirt, and when she came out she beckoned him up a trail. A pea hen flew up before her. Vinich saw that her shoulders were wider, her legs longer than his. Her hair, undone, fell to the small of her back, and he followed her up the trail, and because he was behind her she would not see his head turning side to side in its slow spasm of disbelief.

They came to a a patch of tall bushes growing where a small cistern had been built of rock. Pails, gardening tools. "It's all growing season in Samoa," said Carol Ulu. "I rotate, grow year around. That's got its own dangers, but. . ." she reached toward the patch and her finger traced the heights of the plants, higher to lower, older to younger. "I've always got something," she said, "or just about always got something budding out." The tall end of the patch smelled like a pine forest. "So," she said, "do I take it, you don't like to smoke? You don't approve?"

"I don't here," said Vinich, who was that rare instance of someone actually discouraged by a law. He had a near superstitious dread of anything prohibited on this island. "Back in the day," he said, "I loved a good smoke."

"Back in the day?" she said. "What are you, old?"

"I feel that way at times. Like I've seen too much to be, you know, real optimistic. Too much of the wrong kind of thing."

"I think I asked before," she said. "But are you lonely?"

"I didn't think I was," said Mike Vinich, drawn right up to the nub of the thing and breathing less than instinctively. He sucked in a big draught of the pitchy air at the tall end of the garden. Desire squeezed his head, a band round the temples, and he breathed. "I do not," he said. "I could not. Disapprove. Of anything you. You wouldn't think I? No, I wouldn't."

"I didn't think so," she said. "You didn't seem like that kind of weasel. In fact, you seemed pretty decent, I thought. Kind of, oh, promising."

It was very hard to imagine the woman as the sergeant she had been. She would know the effect she had on him. He was becoming dangerously enthusiastic. Old? He almost wished he felt appropriately old right now, it might keep him from the wrong move; he'd had so little practice in this kind of thing, and that so long ago. "Well," he said, "my parts have come in. My water pump and timing belt."

Even as she failed to grasp the significance of this, Carol Ulu was extravagantly beautiful, but kindly too, watching him writhe.

"I can fix my car," Vinich said. "Maybe drive up some time. Times. We could. . . And see you."

This made her thoughtful. Hadn't the idea, the hope, been hers in the first place? Yes. He hadn't misunderstood her. But time had passed, and he could only suppose that as a beautiful woman her opportunities must be constant. Other opportunities. Jealousy flared, unsupported by any information or any right to it. Change the subject. "I don't object," he said. "Like I said, to anything you might—no, but I do worry, about—They are so crazy about that here. I've seen some terrible things happen."

"I'm all right up here," said Carol Ulu.

"It is a good location," said Vinich, "but. . ."

"No," she said. "I'm all right. Between my brother and some of my customers, I'm all right."

"Oh," said Vinich.

"The pastor takes his cut," she said.

"Oh?"

"Of everything," she said. "So, I'm good. Or—not exactly good. I wanted to talk to you. Tell you. See—my thing was to be free. I had this plan to be free, and now I am up here, and I like it, it is a lot of what I wanted. You can see I like it here?"

Vinich could see that, had even momentarily thought how he might like it here himself. The end of the trail.

"I wanted to be free, and I don't have your standard Samoan husband standing over me, but—I am not free." Her limit was her brother, the matai who in some kind of feudal arrangement had to approve her tenancy here, and it wouldn't be at all unlike him to withdraw that approval if they ran afoul. In fact he had threatened it. Pastor Ulu had during their brief conference developed a fierce dislike of Mike Vinich, so much so that he had forbidden his sister to become involved.

"How could even know that we were, that it was, that it ever came up? That it was any kind of possibility?"

"Samoa," she said.

"And he can do that? He can dictate?"

From out of a woman's deep and practiced resignation

Carol Ulu said, "He can. He has. I know it's not right. I don't like it. He likes people who are the same kind of creep he is. And you're not, so he doesn't like you."

"But what he feels is. . ." said Vinich. "What *you* feel is. . ."

"Let's not get into that," she said. "We can't. It wouldn't do any good. Maybe the best way for you to think about this is you won."

"I won?"

"Your case with Pule," she said.

"I didn't win anything," he said. "That wasn't me. For all I knew I was driving the guy off a cliff."

"If it wasn't for you," she said, "the pastor would have screwed around and got poor Pule locked up forever. Between the two of them they are a real mess. It was a *good* thing you were there."

"But now—" said Mike Vinich. They had climbed to a height from which he could see exposed a wider crescent of deep blue sea. Vinich felt his heart, though very dense, floating out on it. "Usually," he said, "usually when you get a view like this, see far out on the ocean, a person should be grateful for that. For the view."